UNDER A DIFFERENT STAR

MICHAEL METZGER

Published by:

Streamline Publishing
13/50 Scotland Ave
GREENSBOROUGH 3088.

Edited by Cathy Oliver
Cover artwork: Lynne Muir © 2021
Cover images: iStockphoto.com.au
Typesetting: Lynne Muir, www.artscribe.com.au
Printing: IngramSpark Pty Ltd

ISBN: 978-0-646-84307-0 p/b
         978-0-646-84308-7 HB
         978-0-646-84469-5 Ebook

A catalogue record for this book is available from the National Library of Australia

DEDICATION

For my Mother and Father
in whose love all things have been possible.

*"...in dir ist schon begonnen,
was die Sonnen übersteht."*

*"...In you has already begun
What endures beyond the stars."*

Rainer Maria Rilke
Buddha in der Glorie
(from Neuen Gedichte anderer Teil, Leipzig 1918)

ACKNOWLEDGEMENTS

My greatest thanks go to my parents, Franz-Theo and Anita Helene, whose history and whose love form the basis of this narrative and provide the foundations on which my own life and that of my sister Vivien Anne have grown. It is no coincidence that her name should echo her mother's. Her contributions to this work have been in the recollections of stories shared out of a relationship as closely devoted as Anita's was with her own mother.

Thanks also to my loving wife and clear-eyed critic whose understanding and patience, as I withdrew from the world to immerse myself in a very different time and place, has been both inspiration and comfort.

Likewise, for his insistence that I write this account of his aunt's life, I thank Dr. Eberhard (Pino) Müller who would be well able to add many other related chapters where his family's engagement was inextricably linked to this story.

For her invaluable support in recognising the significance of this work, for her enthusiasm to publish it and ensure its narrative dynamic, my deep gratitude to Catherine Oliver. Her skill, time and generosity have made possible a project that has burned long for the telling.

To Beverley Lello, Marian Robinson, and a host of interested friends, my gratitude for your contributions, guidance and enthusiasm in shaping the way the humanity of this story is revealed.

PREFACE

Where you go, I will go; where you lodge, I will lodge;
your people shall be my people,
and your God shall be my God.
Where you die, I will die –
and there shall I be buried.

(Ruth 1: 16–17)

This is a work of fiction, but a true story. The main characters are real people whose lives were impacted by the extensively documented historical events of the Second World War. In some cases, the names of secondary characters have been changed to protect their families' privacy. Minor characters who contextualise the time, place and events of those years have been imagined. Conversations, of course, are conceived out of the stories told by Franz-Theo (Frank) and Anita and their shared recollections with family. Documents, letters, photographs and recorded conversations form the evidentiary basis for this account.

Apologies are made in advance for any historical inaccuracies relating to the war or to particular places and the writer invites correction as appropriate.

What can never be in dispute is the love and courage shared by two remarkable people whose lives spanned two hemispheres and some of the greatest upheavals the world has known.

GERMANY

PRELUDE

THE DOGS OF WAR

The morning is torn open. A commotion rises from the cramped street below. A cataract of voices, shouts and tramping boots. Iron shod hooves clatter and ring on the stone of the road; the iron bound wooden wheels of heavy gun carriages spark the cobbles.

A girl, just seven years old, her eyes wide, stares in alarm from the upper window of the Goldenen Engel. Her mother and older sister have climbed the narrow stairs to join her. They look onto Adolfstraße in Bad Schwalbach in the Rhineland. Today there are French troops cutting a swathe between the buildings, pushing back the villagers who shout and wave their clenched fists at the invaders, or stand with a hand over their mouth in disbelief. Children cry.

They do not know whether it is the Eighth or Tenth Armée under the command of Général Charles Mangin, 'The Butcher' who has come into their town. There are African soldiers among the troops. The horses are restless, heads tossing, the jangle and glint of harness threatening control. The machinery of war is fearsome.

At the corner, on the other side of the street where it sweeps further downhill, is Onkel Willy's and Tante Lena's jewellery shop. Its windows are bright with trinkets and porcelain – Meissen and Limoges; harlequin crystal goblets; silver and gold. Among the trades and merchants, it sits a rare and quiet jewel unto its glittering self. To the right, people spill into the road from the Marktplatz as the cavalcade swirls ever nearer.

A rider pushes into the crowd. It surges and swells and there are bodies on the ground. The horseman rears and, beside him, two pairs of horses shy, swinging the limber to one side. Behind it, the gun carriage skitters across the stones. Suddenly, there is a blistering crash as one and a half tonnes of wood and metal smash against the astragal windows, shards of glass spraying across the roadway. Inside, shelves collapse on one another, spilling the finely wrought work of human hands in a cascade of shattered dreams.

Anna Gallo cannot look and turns her girls away from the window. Erna, who is fourteen, had thought the war was over and this makes no sense. Anita's face is streaked with tears.

On the fifteenth of December, 1918, Général Lecomte, Commander of the 33rd French Corps, will claim the French occupation of Wiesbaden just 17 kilometres to the east.

∽

Twelve years pass. On the stage of the Staatstheater in Wiesbaden, the orchestrated tragedy of an opera is being played out. Anita sits with her family in the second row on the first level, next to the Kaiser's box. It is her place of privilege among the social elite. As the drama unfolds and the voices rise, she is carried with the orchestra in a tale of loss and suffering. But she knows, even now, that war and death are not an abstraction and the mirage below serves only as a reminder of a deeper memory, a deeper apprehension.

When it is over, she will descend the sweeping marble staircase into the soaring baroque beauty of the foyer with its domed and painted ceiling, its courtly scenes illuminated by the glittering chandelier. She will be joined by her father, Carl Gallo, immaculate in his black tuxedo and tie, as well as her mother Anna in a long gown, gloves and fur stole. She will step with her sister Erna, elegant damsels in dresses of flowing line, a hint of ankle and high heels, long strands of jewellery swaying as they sashay into the milling throng animated by the artistry they have just witnessed. They make a pretty sight. Storm and yearning are eased aside, together with the disquieting politics of the re-emerging Nationalsozialistische Deutsche Arbeiterpartei, the NSDAP, the National Socialist German Workers Party. Nazi Germany still has a little way to come.

∽

A
LOVE
DISCOVERED

CHAPTER ONE

Ordinary People

The Soldier with the Pale Blue Eyes

Each day, a large portrait of Hitler greeted Anita as she entered the offices of Veltrup-Werke. She looked down, refusing to acknowledge the red armband with its swastika or the iron cross on the pocket. She was focused solely on the task of managing the company's correspondence. She resented the commanded loyalty of the Führer. If not freely given, neither loyalty nor love meant anything.

Besides, she was already caught in such a complex web she struggled to know if she would escape or be devoured. Working for the war effort was very different from being an English language interpreter and working abroad. Meeting half Jewish Franz-Theo had put her dangerously at odds with her father, marking her the black sheep of the family rather than the "good child" so loved by her mother. The man in the brown uniform with his hand on his hip had created division and conflict.

Bizarrely, the same man also believed that a woman's natural role was to be the kind and gentle mother and homemaker rather than a woman in paid employment. Why else the Nationalsozialtisische Frauenschaft, the Nazi Women's League, and the praise of Kindersegen, those women blessed with children, as national heroines to be awarded the Cross of Honour of the German Mother? So why was she here, in a factory, where other women wore work boots or overalls, robbed of their femininity? Her whole world seemed at odds with itself. It seemed better to keep to herself and remain silent.

Today, she had been called to her supervisor's office. Standing outside his door was a tall, uniformed soldier. He looked directly at her with pale blue eyes. Anita's heart banged in her chest, sensing danger. She stopped. Why was he here? What did he want? She must remain calm. She must reveal nothing.

"Good morning," he said, with a slight bow.

"Good morning," she replied, politely but coolly. "Excuse me," and she passed between him and the door before knocking. On the signal, she entered and carefully pulled the door closed behind her. In the conversation that followed, only one thing gripped her mind: the fear of discovery; some event of which she was unaware. Her manager's voice came from far away, as if under water, instructions she would barely remember. She answered automatically, accepted the sheets of paper handed to her and was dismissed.

Outside, the soldier approached her.

"May I ask your name?"

She looked at him, saw the pale eyes, the blonde hair, the face of a man from a good family and high position. Why did he want to know? What did he know already? She could not afford to play games.

"Fraulein Gallo," she replied.

"So, you are not married," he asked, feigning surprise.

"No." She looked at him, waiting.

"You know, you should look at the Führer when you come in to work. I'm sure he would like that very much."

Her mind raced. What had he noticed? What was he suggesting? Was this a trick to question her allegiance? There was no answer to his suggestion. She stood a moment and then, with a tilt of her head and small shrug of her shoulders, walked away. She listened for his footstep. Nothing.

Back in her office, she let herself breathe again.

Over the next few days, the soldier with the pale blue eyes appeared at her office and tried to engage her in conversation. She maintained her air of unapproachability but sensed there was something deeper. Perhaps he simply liked her, though nothing she had said or done could warrant or justify that idea. She learned he was married, but without children; that he was an engineer who had served with the Einsatzgruppen but was now on leave. He was polite, even deferential and had made no further enquiries about her background. Knowing that she could not afford to avoid him, Anita listened, locked within herself.

"I have been transferred here to the factory. I found the experience in Poland quite difficult."

"Poland?" asked Anita. "Where? Why?"

"Bircza, near Przemisyl, not far from the Ukraine border."

Anita remembered what Franz-Theo had told her. His father had come from there, a small, mostly Jewish community that dated back to the sixteenth century. Strange how suddenly, and unexpectedly, the past had become the present, how separate lives could overlap. She was curious but hesitant.

"What did you have to do there?"

"I shouldn't tell you. There are things that are best left unknown. That said, some things should never be forgotten – indeed, cannot be unremembered."

He hesitated, obviously troubled.

"I think I have made up my mind and I sense you are a strong woman who knows more than she says. You will know, better than I, what to do with the burden I carry. I apologise if what I am going to say offends or upsets you. In the end, I suspect the world will know and will be ashamed."

Anita waited, apprehensive about what he might say.

"I am a soldier. As a soldier, my duty is to fight and, if necessary, to kill. In the heat of the moment, when one's life is threatened, one shoots. That is not so hard. When one is not threatened, that is much harder.

As a soldier, I am expected to obey orders and to obey without question. Mostly, that is not difficult. Besides, division between soldiers and their commanding officers can be deadly and therefore not tolerated. For me to disobey would mean being shot."

Anita feared where this was going but kept silent.

"We were sent to Bircza to round up Jews. They were to be executed. We came into the town and were joined by some of the local Polish farmers who were told to bring their guns. We went into every house and drove them into the street. They were mostly silent – shocked and afraid. They were then herded to a field where a trench had been prepared. I still do not understand why there was so little resistance. Perhaps they already knew any struggle would be futile. Perhaps they had already accepted they would die. Those who were old, lame or slow were pushed, prodded or hit with the butt of a rifle to hurry them along. We had been told how to shoot."

He paused as he remembered the instructions: 'Stand well back so that you are not sprayed with blood or bits of flesh. Aim for the head if you can, but the heart if you are not sure. You will get better with practice. After a while, it is not so hard.'

"So, we lined them up along the ditch and then one of the officers fired a shot and the rest followed. Mostly the Jews fell backwards into the hole. Those who didn't were dragged or kicked into it."

The soldier fell silent, remembering. The crack of the rifle, the thump of the bullet hitting flesh; the fracture of the skull split open. Saw again the spray of blood; heard the blow of the body hitting the earth. The cry of a voice as blood gargled from the lungs.

"I fired my gun but did not hit any one of those terrified and defenceless people. Others seemed not to care and paused to smoke a cigarette, or urinate into a bush. Some joked among themselves about how grotesquely a person had died.

When it was all over, more than fifty on that first day, my commanding officer took me aside. 'I saw what happened with you today. You will learn to do your job, to do your duty. We have no room for weakness or sentimentality. They are Jews and they will all be exterminated.'"

Anita sat immobile, numb. What could she say? She was confronted by a man with a gun; a man conflicted and traumatised by what he had seen. He was unpredictable and yet he was telling her a story of unspeakable horror. Her thoughts swung to the hapless souls stumbling to a violent and brutal end; their families, their children, the homes they had left behind. Saw them startled out of their every day to their last day.

After a long silence, the soldier collected himself and continued.

"We had a report of a farmer hiding Jews in his barn. It was a Sunday and while he was at church, one of the parishioners informed us. So we went there, searched the place and found three of them hiding under the straw and dragged them outside. When the farmer returned, we found shovels and set him to work with them to dig a grave. My Commandant then ordered the wife to be brought out. She had a baby on her hip.

When the hole was big enough, he casually shot the three Jews in the head, in front of the farmer and his wife. Then, in front of her husband, he turned and shot the wife. As she collapsed, she dropped the baby."

He paused again. He was shaking. He swallowed hard; his breath came thick. He saw again things he could not say; could not repeat. Could not describe how his officer picked up the crying child by the heels and bashed its brains out against the corner of the building before flinging it into the pit.

Anita had her hands over her ears. Unable to help herself, her voice shaking, she could only cry, "No! Please, no! I don't want to hear. You mustn't tell me. No more!"

Pulling himself together, the soldier continued.

"So, we buried them there and marched the farmer to the town square where he was hanged for all to see. To show what happens if you dare to undermine the authority of the Führer.

The whole traumatic day was meant to be a shock for me; to teach me a lesson. I was supposed to adopt the same detachment as I had witnessed. Not that everybody could be like that. For many soldiers who struggled, there were increased alcohol rations to dull the reality of what we were doing. For me, it didn't help.

Our next assignment was to execute another group of Jews, this time by a river. Knowing that it would be difficult, if not impossible for me, I reported sick. I was told that if I did not present myself as required, I would be shot.

Fearing for my life and having no idea of how I would be able to cope, I dragged myself to the place. The poor souls had been gathered, mostly standing, some kneeling and, as before, the shooting commenced. Next to me stood the commander, with his pistol aimed at my head. 'Now shoot,' he ordered. I had no choice and fired blindly. The bullet struck a woman in the shoulder, flinging her backwards into the water. As she floundered, her arm useless, she shouted, 'You swine, you can't even shoot straight!' The current was dragging her away when my officer stepped forward and shot her in the head. As she sank slowly, the stain of her blood rose and drifted on the river.

Around me rifles cracked, bodies fell. There was the stench of gunpowder on the air and, to this day, I have no idea why I am not dead."

The purging was over – a confession without absolution.

"So there it is," he said. "I have witnessed things I can never forget; have seen things I cannot un-see. I have done things that cannot be undone. And when I think of my loving wife, I am glad we did not have children because they would never have had a father. For as much as we love each other, I am no man for her; cannot lie by her side without starting in the night and recoiling from the nightmares that inhabit my sleep.

In telling you this, I am also telling you that my career is finished; that I intend to go to the front where the fighting is heaviest and I do not expect to return."

The storm was over. They both sat in silence, locked in their respective worlds. At last, Anita quietly said, "You poor, poor man. I am sorry for what you have said, for what you have done and for what it has done to you. I do not know how to help you."

"There is nothing you can do. But I tell you this – when you tell my story to your Jewish friend, tell him to be careful. Both of you must be careful, because Germany has no patience for friendships such as yours. You already know the consequences."

He stood and turned towards her. "Forgive me."

"So you know. You know who I am?"

Without looking back, he turned and left, closing the door quietly behind him.

⌇

Rejection

The train from Köln pulled into the station. It brought with it a cloud of black smoke, the harsh protest of brakes on iron wheels, a perfunctory snort of steam and the heavy clank of compacting couplings. For a moment it seemed to hold its breath before the doors opened, spilling threads of passengers towards the platform gate where they briefly knotted before unravelling into the adjoining streets and trailing into the evening mist.

The cut of her woollen coat was stylish, its lines clean, although a little crushed from the long journey. The hat was chic, the smart handbag and shoes an elegant statement of self-assurance. She was alone and walked deliberately along the platform, beneath the sign that read "AACHEN", turned through the narrow gate and into the street.

After the shock and claustrophobia of the day, the fresh air was welcome. She stopped, raised her head and drew a long breath. But the dusk settling over the city that day brought little refreshment and none of the usual birdsong, only the desultory cawing of crows and the languid flap of black wings into the darkening sky. Gathering herself, she took Bahnhofstrasse, then left towards Theaterplatz and turned into Kapuzinergraben. The Hauptpost and home above it on the first floor loomed comfortingly.

She stopped at the front door, took her key from the back pocket of her handbag and let herself in. A flight of stairs led to the apartment where her parents would be waiting, anxious for the day's news. She took a deep breath, composing herself. It would not do to cry.

"Anita?" A pause. "Anita? Is it you?" Anna Gallo emerged from the salon to greet her daughter. As she asked the question, she already knew the answer. "How did it go?"

"Not well, Mutti, not well." Eyes lowered, she shook her head, searching for words, overwhelmed by the news she was carrying. "After all the hope and the planning …" She broke off, tears stinging her eyes. Then she stepped into the pool of compassion and hugged her mother, holding her close before saying, "I'll just change out of these clothes and then we can talk."

When she returned, her father had joined the table where a hot mug of cocoa waited for her. "What did they say?"
"Basically, that there was work enough for me here in Germany. They didn't have money to send students overseas."

There was silence as she again digested the amputation of her hopes. Presently her mother asked, "You told them about Leipzig?"

"Yes, I explained that when we were in Koblenz I had gone for three months to Leipzig to learn English at the Bachs Fremdsprachler-Fachschule. With outstanding results. For what? They had no interest whatever."

"You loved it."

"It was wonderful. Immersed in the language; lots of different teachers. English, shorthand, interpreting – everything I wanted to do. I explained that I had made all the arrangements to go to England. 'No,' they said, 'Germany needs you here.'"

Tears welled in her eyes.

Carl Gallo frowned. "But you had already made arrangements; met the parents of the girl who had been a paying guest of a family in London. You obtained the address from her, so you had people you could go to."

"Yes, and they knew my English was good enough to express myself properly. I explained how I wanted to be a foreign correspondent, a secretary or interpreter, and they said it was all right for me to come."

"They were very generous to her," Anna remembered the stories; how the host family had taken her out to the theatre and the opera and what a great impact it had made. She had been there long enough to absorb an 'English' way of living and gave entertaining accounts of the stodgy food, the music, the pomp and ceremony, evenings in the smoky interior of a pub with warm conversation and even warmer beer.

"Yes, but she was a paying guest. The government only provides, or I should say provided, foreign exchange currency and a permit. She had her own connections and resources to go so that she could improve her qualifications. I explained all that in Köln, but their response was they were calling back their overseas students because they no longer had money for programs like that. Germany under Hitler had other priorities – I could stay here and work. That was it."

A wave of giddying darkness engulfed her and Anita saw again, as if from a great distance, the faces so resolutely hardened against her one desire. Their voices, harsh and remote, were fogged by her heart dinning in her ears. She struggled to surface, afraid to breathe, desperate for air. Slowly, her vision cleared and the room seeped back.

"You poor darling," Anna put her hand on Anita's. "Such hard words. What did you do?"

"I left and walked along Tunisstrasse and cried my heart out. I was so angry, frustrated and miserable – I felt terrible. At twenty-nine, just when I felt I was really beginning to get somewhere, it's all over. Everything I ever wanted to do, just crushed, just snuffed out like a candle."

Carl Gallo, conscious of his position as Oberpostrat, Director General of Posts in Aachen, and aware of the attitudes of the Reich, was silent. He had contacts in the government and the SS but was a cautious man. He knew there was unrest in the East and that it may in time have repercussions that could impact on Germany's security, his position and the welfare of his family. Now was not the time to intervene in these affairs.

Instead, his words were kind, optimistic. "Anita, this may all be for the best. We don't know how things will turn out and perhaps you will have an opportunity in the future. Don't let this decision change your life."

Anna patted her daughter's hand. "Perhaps your father is right – we never know what the future may hold."

Given that the date was July 1940, their sentiments were more prophetic than ever they could have imagined.

⌣

In the weeks that followed, Anita had plenty of time to reflect on the direction her life had taken. The days of privilege growing up in Wiesbaden, keeping her mother company, wandering together through the Kurpark, sharing coffee and cake at Café Blum on Wilhelmstrasse, nights at the Staatstheater in elegant gowns to be paraded later down the sweeping staircase to the opulence of the baroque foyer, all that had been dissipated by the two years that followed in Koblenz. From the elegant social circle at the height of her youthful bloom, she had been unceremoniously uprooted when the family relocated as a consequence of her father's transfer in his position as 'Postdirektor'.

It wasn't the first time there had been upheaval. When her father had returned from the war, having served in the west at Ypres, Rheims and the Somme where 'the earth was drenched with blood and the elite of German youth perished in the terrible waste', he was assigned Oberpostpraktikant at the post office in Rhinestraße in Wiesbaden, having to travel by bimmelzug from Bad Schwalbach to Wiesbaden and back. With the authority of having earned the Verdienstkreutz, the Iron Cross of Merit, as well as the Karl-Truppenkreutz and the Fortitudini Bravery Medal, he wrote to the authorities declaring that Germany had promised people would be looked after when the war ended. The reply came back icily declaring, "Der Ton Ihrer Korrespondenz gefällt uns nicht", that the tone of the letter was inappropriate. However, shortly after, the family was offered the house in Westerwaldstraße 2. Anita smiled as she remembered - the corner block, the three big timber balconies, the small one from the dining room where the family went out to light fireworks for Christmas Eve. The kitchen balcony with a hand-operated lift at the side to bring provisions up from the cellar. Life had been serene, comfortable, with a maid and even a dressmaker who would sit at her worktable and sewing machine while Anita did her schoolwork at the big oak secretaire.

She paused in the gallery of her recollections. Then Koblenz. Without friends, and in an unfamiliar city, there was little to stimulate the mind of a young lady curious about the world, inspired by the music of Beethoven, Brahms and Chopin and the literature of Schiller, Goethe and Rilke.

A brief interlude of four months boarding in Leipzig was partial consolation. She arrived in the spring, finding the city poignantly beautiful at that time of year. She graced the Thomaskirch and listened to Bach on its famous organ, attended the language classes that gave her the English she so desperately wanted and found friends again with whom she could share her artistic and cultural interests. For all that, there were equally disturbing moments. The Nazis were already well established in the city and making their presence felt implementing new and unsettling policy. Among Germany's rehabilitation programs was the 'Pfundspende', itself generally regarded as a fine and upright idea. Once every month, everybody was obliged to donate a pound of whatever goods they had, to be collected by the Hitler Youth and distributed among the needy.

Returning from classes one day, Anita saw a crowd gathering in the street. Curious, she approached and slipped between the onlookers to discover the cause. A cart had been brought and several officers were bundling a man into it, tying him there with coarse ropes, some shouting, others laughing. The victim was no common vagabond, but appeared well dressed, prosperous, dignified.

"What's happening?" Anita asked of the people around her.

"He's a Jew, a millionaire. Look at him, the miserable cur – he deserves to be humiliated. He has so much and he gave so little."

Then Anita noticed that a crudely scrawled sign had been hung around his neck. It read, for all the world to see, "I gave one pound of barley for the Pfundspende". Suddenly the tragedy was clear – it was not that he had failed in his duty, but that he had succeeded as a Jew and given so little. Troubled, she turned away. If such things could happen, where would it lead? In all her life, such differences of race or religion mattered nought. People of all nationalities, of any faith, faced the same struggle to make something out of the life given them. Kindness could come equally from a Protestant or a Jew. The fear in this man's eyes was a human fear, not a Jewish one. Was it alarm for himself, his family, his children? And what would they do to him now?

Despite the spring sunshine, she shivered and quickened her step, struggling to push aside the brutality of the authorities, the antagonism of the mob and the suffering of the man.

⌒

While it had long been Carl Gallo's belief that his youngest daughter should be an adornment on his arm and company for her mother, Anita's ambition was to find meaningful work doing what she loved with language or music. It was a wonderful indulgence to attend the opera, sit in the sunshine in the Wiesbaden Kurpark or shop in the stylish boutiques along Wilhelmstraße after taking coffee in Café Blum, but such a life of privileged leisure suited neither her temperament nor the changing times.

Leipzig had confirmed her talent for language and secretarial work and, encouraged by her older sister's insistence that she find something useful to do with her life, Anita returned to the city of her birth, Düsseldorf. There, on the basis of her glowing reference from six months working at a fabric finishing company in Aachen, she found work with the large shipping firm, DDG "Hansa", sending weaving machines to Italy.

The office was busy and even busier for someone whose work was multilingual, competent and error-free. As the days became shorter with the onset of winter, her walk home through the dark became longer. She remembered with dread the events of Kristallnacht that had so shaken her and her good friend Téa with whom she shared the apartment on the Königsallee. Who knew what horror, what madness, might erupt around her? What she had witnessed in Leipzig was unsettling; what had happened in Düsseldorf – indeed across Germany – meant waking to each new day with a sense of dreadful foreboding.

Additional responsibilities in the office took her mind off the anxieties that troubled her sleep. Apart from Téa's assurances that the unrest would dissipate and the world return to normal, she doubted such optimism and kept largely to herself. She missed her family, her mother's warmth, Erna and her two little boys; the illusion that the world was generous, safe and ordered.

Christmas came and went with a rising feeling of unease. She was further entrusted with the company's wider operations and cartography department, areas which only served to emphasise how much larger a world existed beyond the confining troubles of the present. Her resolve to leave Germany, to travel, to work abroad, became more obvious. Just how much clearer manifested itself out of an incident in March 1939.

Arriving outside Schadowstraße 14, Anita saw Liesel Moller, obviously distressed, standing outside the door. As one of her colleagues, Anita had always seen her bright and talkative, her grey eyes bright above her smile, smartly dressed, her hair neatly held with a comb. Yet here she was, dishevelled, her face stained with tears and too distraught to enter the building. Anita's heart went out to her.

"What is it? Dear Liesel, what's the matter?"

"It's terrible. Terrible. I don't know what to say. I still can't believe what happened."

"Come Liesel. Let's walk and find somewhere you can sit. Then you can tell me."

So saying, she took her arm and they walked slowly in silence; the morning air clearing her sobs. Finding a seat, Anita waited before turning to gently ask, "What happened?"

Liesel looked at her, trying not to cry before composing herself. She took a deep breath.

"You know I'm living with a family, a Jewish family, in a boarding house. Lovely people, kind and generous – husband and wife with their two little children. The grandfather, her father I think, lives with them too. Somehow, we were all safe on Kristallnacht, but it was so utterly nerve-wracking they were making plans to leave Germany. I was already starting to look for new accommodation."

"That was an horrific night that will stay with me forever too. Unbelievable what they did."

"This was worse. In the middle of the night, there was a pounding on the door and shouts to open. We got such a shock; we didn't know who it was. We looked out of the window and there was a truck parked in the street with police standing there. Then more banging on the door. The children woke up and started crying. Herr Solomon was in his pyjamas trying to put on his dressing gown when they broke down the door. Then boots on the stairs. I didn't dare come out of my room, but the next minute the door was open and the Staatspolizei were standing there. They looked at me for a moment and must have decided they didn't want me. Maybe my blonde hair, maybe I looked more German than Jewish."

"You must have been terrified."

"I was. They had no respect for anyone or anything. They ordered the parents to collect their things, bring any money and valuables and go out to the street. When they resisted, the SS turned over furniture, pulled books from the shelves, smashed vases and a mirror and shouted even louder. They asked whether anyone else lived there, to which Frau Solomon quickly said 'no'. They obviously didn't believe her because they headed upstairs to the next floor, the fourth one, under the attic.

We could hear voices, an argument, and then..." Liesel stopped, shaking her head, her eyes filled with tears, "... and then they threw him out of the window. From the fourth floor. They killed him, just like that, in cold blood."

"No, no. Surely not!"

"From the fourth floor. They just threw him out. Onto the street. Such a lovely, kind old man. His head smashed open. Dead, on the footpath."

Anita put her hand over her mouth, giddy with the image of what had happened.

"Poor Frau Solomon. She had to walk past the body of her father, seeing him mangled and his head in a pool of blood. She wasn't even allowed to go to him as the soldiers pulled her away and pushed her towards the truck. It was horrible, just horrible."

She sat there, unable to make sense of what she had described; still numb with shock.

"Then they shoved the family in the truck and drove off."

They sat there in silence as the day broke over them. Eventually, Anita said, "I can't believe the brutality of the police. How can anybody do such things?"

"You know, when they're not wearing their uniform, they're probably just ordinary people. They'll go home to their wives, tuck their children into bed and read them a story. It's when they pull on their boots to go outside that they turn into monsters."

Anita tried to digest the idea, so seemingly impossible. There was another long silence, interrupted only by people passing and the odd, curious glance.

"When you're ready, we should probably go in."

"Thank you for listening. I'll try to work today because staying behind in the house will be too hard. I don't even know if I can ever go back."

Throughout the day it was difficult for the two women to focus. Liesel may have been spared the interest of the Gestapo but was now homeless while she re-lived the brutality she had witnessed. Anita's bewilderment as she imagined what would happen to Jewish families was compounded by her mounting anxiety about where Germany was heading. After the heady days of society balls and elegant gowns, she had become more introspective, reserved, more comfortable in her own company than the fripperies of polite conversation. Having been so many times uprooted from one end of the country to the other, it seemed her life was fragmenting just as Germany was.

The turmoil of the last few months had brought on a series of increasingly debilitating migraines. She became more anxious and, in the end, requested some time off for sick leave. The company, regretfully, relinquished her service altogether.

It was time to return to Aachen. Increasingly she had missed her family, although she little knew what was to come. She carried with her a new and troubling truth: ordinary people can do monstrous things.

$$\backsim$$

CHAPTER TWO

The Language of the Heart

Language Classes

Professor Baumann, in less troubling times, had enjoyed the opportunity to visit England to study the language of Shakespeare at Cambridge. On his return to Germany he brought with him a slightly effete manner and the caricature of wearing a tweed jacket, though with rather more impeccably pressed trousers than his English counterparts. He was a slight man with greying hair and wore gold-rimmed spectacles precariously at the end of an unremarkable nose. He supplemented his income, and his reputation, by conducting English classes around the dining table of his first-floor apartment overlooking the park on Hartmannstraße in Aachen.

Anita, devastated by the government rejection of her application to study in England, had heard of the good teacher from one of her girlfriends, thereafter making the necessary arrangements to become part of the small coterie sharing her interest and enthusiasm. And while her mother warmly supported her daughter, understanding her hopes and her disappointment, her father was quietly sceptical and kept his own counsel. Other matters were, to him, more troubling. Besides, his eye occasionally continued to give him trouble after the escapades some summers past while on holiday at St. Anton in the Voralberg high in the Tyrol on the Swiss-German border. Since Erna had recently completed her Praktikum and become employed as a pharmacist, she had remained at home with Anna, leaving Carl and Anita to go alone. In the village, situated some 1400 metres above sea level, they found an informal local hotel from which they made their sorties, enjoying long country walks, hiking in the foothills and about the lower peaks. Long summer days, the distractions of other people and the countryside provided respite from the pressures of responsibility and the scrutiny of government bureaucracy. For Anita, there was plenty of time to lose herself in the beauty of the landscape, the delight of the birds and animals she encountered, and to escape the drowning disillusion of life in Koblenz after the delightful days of her girlhood in Wiesbaden.

Abruptly, with little warning, these days of clear skies and unburdened hearts came to an unexpected end. In an afternoon of alpine meadows, rocky rises and winding paths, scudding clouds gathered, the wind sprang up flailing the grass and trees, and the light changed to that surreal luminescence created by brilliant sunshine against a leaden backdrop. As the first drops of rain began to fall, the mountains darkened, the air became chill and then such a torrent was unleashed as would soak them to the skin.

Overhead, lightning crackled, followed by the reverberant crash of thunder resounding through the steep valleys. With one hand holding coats over their heads and the other holding each other for support, Carl and Anita scurried across the rocky path, through the splashing puddles and the clamour of rain and wind, lashed by the fury of the storm. Heads bowed from the blast, desperately seeking a footing, they were driven relentlessly down the mountain. How could it have been so far?

Approaching a turn on a steep part of the track made even more perilous by the water running across it, Carl slipped and fell heavily backwards. His head hit the soft earth of the embankment, leaving him stunned and exposed. Desperate, Anita knelt beside him, checking that he was breathing, that there was no blood. His feet lay crooked on the path, trousers soaked with rain.

"Papa, Papa! Are you all right? Can you move?"

He stirred and blinking dazedly, tried to sit up.

"My head. My head is ..." He raised his hands, felt the back of his skull and then inspected his fingers. "No blood?"

He gathered his legs and struggled to stand up in the buffeting wind. Anita noticed with relief that he appeared to experience no further pain and that his feet had somehow righted themselves. Straining against his weight and the elements, she hauled him upright. After a moment of reorientation, they gingerly resumed their teetering way down the path, hesitatingly picking those patches that seemed secure, to catch their breath before descending once more.

At last they came to the outskirts of the village, the streets disappearing under a watery mirage pocked by rain and swirled by wind. Each flash of lightning brought stark outlines and even deeper shadows till, against the din and breathless haste, they reached the inn and sanctuary.

Such a drenching did not come alone. Despite the hot tea and the rum, dry and warm beds, both of them contracted crippling colds. Anita developed a raging fever. In her delirium, an opaque world swam ever larger behind her closed eyes and then receded in phantasmagorial shapes, the sound of the storm heard as if under water. Incessantly, with countless variations, the flight down the mountain replayed itself in her fevered brain, bursting her skull and gripping her throat, saturating her sheets until, after five days, the world finally recomposed itself and she slept.

Meanwhile, Carl had fared little better. Each time he coughed it seemed his skull split and the pain in his right eye became more intense. Then, after a series of flashing lights in the perimeter of his vision, there remained only blackness. With his hand over his closed left eye, he strained against the darkness with his right, opening and closing it. Nothing. Absolutely nothing.

The doctor who arrived, peered with his torch, administered drops and peered again. Only fear allowed a man such as Carl to acquiesce to this investigation and his fear was confirmed by the diagnosis.

"I regret to inform you Herr Gallo, that the retina in your right eye appears to have become detached. Such an eventuality is possibly caused by a combination of events – the severe infection you have sustained, the altitude at which you have been exercising, the severity of your fall and the ructions of your coughing. I am sorry."

"So, what will happen now?"

"Unfortunately, we do not have the means to rectify such a problem. Neither surgery nor drugs are available and, unless by some miracle, the tissue were to reattach itself – and that is most unlikely – you will have to safeguard your remaining eye as best you can."

With that, he departed and Carl Gallo was left to digest the implications of this prognosis alone.

Anita was, of course, devastated by this news and, as dictated by the natural kindness of her heart, was infinitely solicitous of her father's wellbeing. Ever stoic and finding it difficult to respond to emotion, he acknowledged her attentions with an embarrassed brusqueness and even less complaint. So studiously did he avoid the issue that later, while walking with Anita in Wiesbaden, he bumped into another gentleman in the street and continued as if nothing had happened. The collision raised the ire of the passer-by and it was only Anita's apologetic acknowledgement that her father was blind on that side, that calm was restored.

In the years that had elapsed, all that had changed was the adjustment to perform his duties as Director of Posts and Telegraphs ... and a narrowed perspective of the world.

⤶

Like a disoriented hiker in the forest as the fog descends before nightfall, Anita was experiencing a growing sense of frustration with the turns her life was taking. Erna, as the responsible, independent and accomplished older sister, had already asked why Anita should be indulged, living at home without the obligation to find gainful employment or make her own way in the world. Her mother had gently explained that such efforts as Anita had made had been frustrated by the authorities and that events would find her in their own good time. Her father had added, surprisingly generously, that Anita's role in life need only to be company for her mother and his comforter in old age. Such fond wishes were hardly likely to be fulfilled - tell your dreams aloud and you will hear the gods laugh.

Nevertheless, determined to keep her hopes alive, Anita settled for Professor Baumann's language course for interpreters. On a late summer evening, elegant in embroidered blouse and skirt, a light coat over her arm, she made her way to the rooms. The outward poise and assured determination belied a deep introspection and reserve that isolated her from the others.

A small but eclectic cross-section of Aachen's citizens was represented at Hartmannstraße that evening – a retired couple looking to travel abroad, several teachers, a young photographer and a sprinkling of company secretaries. They arranged themselves in tentative groups around the table, proceeded with shy introductions and thus began a process in which each imagined he or she would find new feathers in freedom's wings.

Anita's previous experience in Leipzig, together with her natural inquisitiveness and quickness of mind, renewed her confidence a little. They worked through vocabulary lists, revised the grammar notes and practised elementary core phrases. Translation passages set as homework would form the basis of the next session. Thus the classes progressed, each week lending a focus to Anita's days. She learned quickly and looked forward to the conversation sessions that often brought much laughter with the struggle for words and syntax.

It was during one such tutorial that she heard, more distinctly than before, the softly modulated and careful tones of the seemingly foppish photographer. He spoke with such a resonant intensity that she turned her head the better to listen to what he was saying. His face was obscured by the people sitting next to her, but she noticed his outstretched hand, perfectly manicured long fingers declaiming his words. So young she thought, but so serious and, usually, so reserved. He paused and others resumed the conversation, leaving Anita in their wake as she idly wondered at the contradictions that had momentarily arrested her.

The language class continued, coalescing into informal groups as people discovered shared experiences, mutual acquaintances and similar interests. The work of communication was accelerated by familiarity, despite the obstacles of a foreign tongue. Nonetheless, Anita remained largely outside these clusters, her disposition less amenable to frivolity or idle chatter, preoccupied with the task ahead and the uncertainty of her aspirations.

At the end of the fifth week as people prepared to leave, Anita was in the hallway retrieving her coat when the photographer, Herr Metzger appeared beside her. With a crookedly concealed smile and in slightly clipped and formal English he asked, "May I help you, Fraulein Gallo?" offering his hand.

"Thank you. That is very kind, sir," she replied, likewise in English.

He continued, in German, "Given the lateness of the hour and the darkness of the street, it would be remiss of me not to offer you safe escort to your home. Might I have the pleasure?"

Slightly taken aback, but not ungrateful for the attention, Anita acquiesced. The young man helped her into her coat, reached forward to open the door and let her pass onto the landing. Together they descended the steps. When they reached the street, he turned and offered his arm.

"You seem to know where I live," she remarked, curious.

"I have often sighted you crossing Theaterplatz with your family to attend the Opera or coming home from an outing. I have a small atelier in the attic overlooking the square."

"You live there by yourself?"

"No. But I came alone to Aachen and found temporary lodging with my Aunt and Uncle in the Großkölnstraße nearby. The studio I use for my photographic work."

"Are you not lonely?"

"Indeed." He paused, weighing his thought. "Despite the great kindness of my aunt and her husband, there is no-one else."

"But your family. Where is your family?"

"This is not a time to explore such matters. Suffice it to say I am fortunate to have a roof over my head, some employment to sustain me - and the intrigue of your company. You appear to have a fine grasp of English, and a pensiveness that quite separates you from the others, if what I observe is true."

"I enjoy the language classes – they are, after all, what I had hoped would lead to real opportunities. The German authorities however, had different ideas and so my plans have had to change." So saying, she related her story until, rather sooner than she expected, they arrived at the main door of the Postamt. There, she disengaged his arm, a little surprised by her own frankness as well as her escort's gallant but impeccable manners. Politely she bade him goodnight, found her key and turned to the door.

"Goodnight, Fraulein Gallo. Thank you for your company, thank you." With a slight bow he turned and Anita watched the night swallow his retreat before closing the door and climbing the stairs to her room.

Autumn came quickly, lighting the foliage through prisms of fire against the deepening cloud. As the days grew shorter, the mists of evening extinguished the leaves, endowing softness to the bare branches and the chill portent of days to come.

Anita paused before the mirror in her room, pinned the stray hairs that had slipped from her chignon, adjusted the collar of her coat and, satisfied that she was composed, opened the door. She made her way to the sitting room, said good-bye to her parents and headed downstairs and into the street. As she walked, she noticed her heart was beating faster than usual. There was still plenty of time before the class was to start, but she sensed an odd mixture of apprehension and exhilaration. She relaxed her step, making time to consider the confusion of her feelings, remembering last week's lesson, mentally checking the notes in her bag, seeing the faces she would shortly meet again.

The true cause of her agitation appeared rather sooner than she imagined. Turning into Hartmannstraße, she recognized the young Herr Metzger who had so graciously helped her with her coat and escorted her home last time. He was a little distance away, facing the sky and lost in some reverie of his own, solitary, somehow vulnerable despite the outward self-assurance. She was glad he hadn't seen her start or heard the thud of her heart or the sudden dinning in her ears. She took a deep breath and walked up to him.

"Good evening."

Startled, he turned. In the instant before he spoke, she knew he had been waiting for her, the deep brown eyes exploring her face before, with a slight bow and the beginning of a smile, he replied, "Good evening Fraulein Gallo. It is a real pleasure to see you again. I must confess I have been looking forward to it."

"Thank you, Herr Metzger. I too anticipated that you might be here today, but I did not expect you quite so early."

"Then, since we still have half an hour before we go up, perhaps we might take a short stroll in the park?" So saying, he offered his arm and, matching step, they set off to a polite conversation that began by reviewing their respective activities during the past week. Arriving at a bench, Franz Theo motioned Anita to sit and, side-by-side in silence, they watched the evening descend. Presently, Franz Theo, looking directly ahead, recited,

"Der Abend wechselt langsam die Gewänder ..."[1] to which Anita replied, "die ihm ein Rand von alten Bäumen hält; ...".[2]

He turned to her smiling. "You know it?"

"I do." She continued:

---

[1] "Slowly, the evening changes its robes..." from "Abend" (Evening) by Rainer Maria Rilke, Autumn 1904

[2] "held for it by a fringe of old trees..."

„... du schaust: und von dir scheiden sich die Länder,
    ein himmelfahrendes und eins, das fällt;"

Together, they spoke the remaining lines in unison:
    „...und lassen dich, zu keinem ganz gehörend,
    nicht ganz so dunkel wie das Haus, das schweigt,
    nicht ganz so sicher Ewiges beschwörend
    wie das, was Stern wird jede Nacht und steigt -

    und lassen dir (unsäglich zu entwirrn)
    dein Leben bang und riesenhaft und reifend,
    so dass es, bald begrenzt und bald begreifend,
    abwechselnd Stein in dir wird und Gestirn."[3]

They looked at one another and smiled, suddenly self-conscious at what had taken place so unexpectedly, at the verse that seemed so mysteriously appropriate.

"But that's amazing. I had no idea you would read Rilke. And you remember it."

"I love his work, it's beautiful, it's musical. And it's sad, while at the same time it suggests something beyond ourselves."

---

[3]**Evening**

    Slowly, the evening changes its robes
    Held for it by a fringe of old trees.
    Before your eyes, worlds part,
    One ascending heavenwards, one that sinks.

    And leaves you not at home in either one,
    Not quite as lightless as the silent house
    Nor calling you unswerving to eternity
    As what turns into stars each night and mounts –

    And leaves you (quite hopeless to unravel)
    Your life, uneasy, vast, to ripeness tending
    So that it, now confined, now comprehending,
    Turns now to stone within you, now to star.

"You're right. Great literature, great art enlarges our awareness of ourselves, and our self in the world." He paused, guessing he might have sounded a little formal, slightly pompous. "You know, Rilke and Rodin were great friends. He lived in a cottage in Rodin's garden for some six months, as his private secretary."

"I had no idea."

"Rodin had collected statues of the Buddha. I suspect they were the inspiration for Rilke's three poems on the subject - and his ideas about spirituality."

For a moment there was silence as they reflected separately on a situation that had surprisingly enclosed them both. Then the words tumbled out as they found more and more common ground in the landscape of language and ideas that had led them to this moment. Abruptly, they realized the class they had come for would be starting and in haste and confusion, relinquished one reality for another.

⌣

From then on, the dialogue between them grew, each week a tide of anticipation and delight in the discussion of religion and philosophy, the politics of the day, the moral underpinnings of a world temporarily removed from the breakers of a reality that would soon wash over them.

Then, on the twenty-fifth of August 1940, British planes attacked Berlin.

When Franz-Theo and Anita met the next day, she was concerned to see how he tried to suppress his agitation.

"Is something the matter?" she asked.

"You have heard the news?"

"Of course, though it is not something my father is keen to hear. The war is progressing more dangerously all the time. And now we are under attack."

"I am sure these are reprisals for Hitler's attacks on London and certainly it will get worse. Already in March, Mussolini and Italy joined the war; in April German troops invaded Denmark and Norway. Now we have this."

He stopped, unwilling to persist with a conversation that presented more questions than answers. Compounding events threatened more lives and, increasingly, their own. Anita must have understood his momentary rumination as she added, "What started as unrest in the east is gradually spreading towards us, but now from the west. We don't know how long we will be safe."

"The invasion of Poland represents the start of a far bigger agenda. One has only to remember Hitler's speech to the Reichstag three weeks after my mother's death – he would once and for all settle the Jewish problem. War in Europe would lead to the annihilation of the Jewish people...Auswanderung oder Evakuierung, migration or evacuation. And for those sentiments he received thunderous applause."

Anita looked bewildered.

"Your mother is dead?"

Franz-Theo suddenly realised he had said more than perhaps he ought. He had already resisted answering Anita's question about his loneliness; now, reference to the Jewish problem would necessitate further explanation. Giving away his family situation would lead to further questions. Was he prepared to expose the underbelly of his sensitivities, the traumas of loss? Even harder, how could his father's situation, and therefore his own, be understood in the light of Anita's family background and her father's dangerously heated threats? Franz-Theo understood perfectly well the reasons behind Herr Gallo's fear; irrespective of his political leanings, his loyalties needed to be seen to lie with the Führer if his family were to remain safe.

He looked again at the woman before him, her face a picture of concern and, suddenly disarmed, allowed himself a moment of trust. He took a deep breath and, with a quiet resolve, answered, uncertain where it might lead.

"Yes, on the ninth of January last year - and much has happened since then. Poland has proved closer to me than Berlin."

"Oh, I'm sorry to hear about your mother. That's terrible." Anita paused, unsure what to say. The thought of losing her own mother was incomprehensible. How hard must it have been for the man before her, someone who, she guessed, had already found himself on the wrong pages of history. Now was not the time to question that. She returned to the story.

"But why Poland? Didn't Polish soldiers attack a German radio station?"

"I'm convinced that whatever excuse needed to be staged would have been. It is widely suggested that SS troops wearing Polish uniforms executed the attack at Gliewitz. Hitler has always resented the fact that the Treaty of Versailles gave Poland West Prussia, Poznan and Upper Silesia. He wants those provinces back."

"But he signed a non-aggression pact with Poland years ago – in January 1934, I think."

"He did it only to avoid the possibility of the French and the Poles forming an alliance while he re-armed Germany. His agenda is far more dangerous, more cynical and ruthless than just Poland. You have heard his speeches, seen the direction of newspaper editorials. You must have witnessed events that are more than disturbing?"

"Yes, but what do you mean?"

Franz-Theo paused, considering his situation, weighing the wisdom of his intended words. "I think perhaps it is time that I told you my story, even though I fear where it may lead. You see, my father was born in Bircza, in Poland."

He waited as the implications of this caused Anita to swallow, her grey-green eyes searching his face.

"Bircza is in the district of Dobromil near Przemysl in Galicia. The area had been taken over in 1772 by Austria and, after the war in 1918, was returned to Poland. While my links with Poland are tenuous, there are other matters that threaten even greater peril."

Franz-Theo understood only too well that his choices now were more critical than ever. The revelations of one's origins, one's affiliations and allegiances were dangerous. Governments topple, regimes change. What was once heroic becomes heretical. Political nationalism and anti-Semitism had created a beast whose maw would devour untold lives. He was already on the run, evading an enemy he didn't even know he had, together with a past that could not, nor should ever, be undone. He had already lost more than he could have imagined and now, here, with this extraordinary woman who had captured his imagination, he was about to risk more again. If his story should provoke rejection, he would find himself lost beyond recognition. Yet to not lay himself bare would only complicate matters further. Besides, what would obfuscation say about his belief in the integrity and clear-sightedness of this daughter who had already compromised the bonds of her family for his sake?

With that, over the next few days either at a café or going for long walks, he unburdened himself of the history that had reached up from the past and overtaken him.

"My parents became engaged in Dortmund in February 1918 while my father – also Franz - was on leave during the War. He served in the mountain artillery unit of the Austrian army in the Dolomites. Shortly after, he was taken prisoner and was sent to Borgotaro in Italy from where he wasn't released until September the following year. While he was still a prisoner-of-war, my mother, Maria – whose maiden name was Kopp - visited him when he was ill and transferred to Sopron, and later in Vienna where he was discharged from his regiment. They were married there a month later in the church of St. Josef.

They returned to Dortmund and settled where, on the third of September 1921, I was brought into the light of this world, not without great difficulty for my dear mother."

He paused, caught on the memory of the woman who had given him life and had lost her own while still comparatively young. Too painful to dwell on the recent past and too much to tell of childhood and a son's love for his mother. He centred himself again and continued.

"I was baptised in the Catholic Kreutzkirche." It was an important point he let rest for a moment.

"At that time, my parents lived in a middle-class apartment in a middle-class area – Neuer Graben 59. My father was a tailor, an expert cutter and a designer of ladies' fashions for which he had outstanding talent and ability. My parents decided to start a business on their own, my father providing the technical expertise and my mother handling the business side. They prospered and became so busy that they had to hire a housekeeper and a nurse, the two girls looking after me till I was about six or seven years old. Both of them were lovely, especially my nurse Erna, and they were treated as part of the family. In fact, I think Erna was chosen because at the time she appeared the one most in need of the position. Her father and brothers were miners and had come to Germany to work in the Ruhr where thousands of Polish miners were already employed. I visited Erna's family in a crowded attic in another part of the town and it was wonderful to listen to the men playing their mandolins while guinea pigs scampered about the room. Poverty had not diminished their zest for life."

Anita listened, spellbound. The soft timbre of his voice that had so captivated her during language classes was now imbued with sadness and a longing for a world that was slipping away. Family had brought security. She heard about his aunt Jenny, her husband Toni and their menagerie, and how she died of complications from diabetes. She learned of Tante Tina and Onkel Willy, living nearby in Aachen no less, and their children. For a moment, she sensed happiness in the heart of the reserved and thoughtful man who had chosen her company.

"My parents' business grew. The clientele became more exclusive and we moved three times to ever more spacious and elegant homes better suited for the staging of fashion parades and to accommodate an atelier employing about a dozen people. My father's reputation attracted business from neighbouring towns and he received public recognition from the trade authorities. To keep up with the latest fashion trends, my parents often travelled to major centres like Berlin.

All seemed well and secure and yet, by the time I went to the Gymnasium for my Abitur, I developed an uneasy feeling that the apparent security and stability might be but a veneer. I could not help observing that my parents sometimes seemed concerned over financial difficulties or liquidity problems. Perhaps it was too expensive to keep up a glamorous front or, far more likely, the socialite customers were not too prompt in their payment of bills."

He shook his head and let slip a huff of disdain. When he spoke next, his tone had changed as he carefully assembled the fractured past.

"What disquieted me more was a matter I did not understand too well. I was born in Germany, but when forms or questionnaires were to be filled out at school, I had to describe my nationality as 'Austrian', which tended to make me a foreigner and an outsider. As it was, my contact with the other boys was only superficial because I preferred books to their company. I knew that my father had been born in Bircza, then in the Austro-Hungarian Empire, and that his brother had been killed in the war, but that was all I knew. As we lived in Germany where my father had lived most of his life, I could not understand why he had not become a German citizen. He never mentioned his family background, and whenever I asked, he became irritable or angry. I became suspicious that all was not as it seemed and sensed there were matters my father wished to keep to himself, which made him a lonely man."

He stopped and smiled ruefully.

"I have, in recent times, learned to understand that loneliness a little better. Anyway, in November 1938 my father was in hospital for a kidney operation. On my way to school on Thursday the ninth, I noticed destruction and fires in the streets everywhere. Windows had been broken, furniture thrown out of them and set ablaze. I had no idea what was happening or why. Returning home, I found my poor mother in a state of great agitation. She explained that Jewish homes had been broken into, their inhabitants beaten or arrested and that the synagogues were burning throughout the country, all as the result of a 'spontaneous' action by the followers of the Führer."

Franz-Theo paused again as he re-lived a situation so summarily described yet portending so much. Anita waited before putting her hand on his arm, gently acknowledging the wellspring of his hurt. Presently, she added softly:

"You know, I witnessed that too. I can understand why your poor mother was so upset. And you too; how could you understand what was happening? Worried about your father in hospital and you innocently on your way home. It was horrible, terrifying and horrible."

She shuddered at the recollection before continuing.

"You might wonder how I happened to see some of what went on. I had worked in a cloth manufacturing facility in Aachen as a secretary writing letters in English. They had a lot of machinery weaving material for India and needed someone with shorthand who could manage the correspondence. Everything was fine until the Nazis were boycotted because of Jewish persecution and the contracts to India dried up. With nothing for me to do there anymore, I applied for work at another shipping company in Düsseldorf.

At that time, my Dutch friend Téa, who worked for Helena Rubinstein, was also there, so we shared an apartment. I was terribly upset by what I had been seeing and hearing about the unrest and hatred and the way Jews were being treated. I ended up sick and in bed with a migraine. Then there was a knock at the door and Téa, dreadfully agitated, told me I had to get up because something terrible was happening.

I went to the window and next door to our place there lived a Jewish doctor. Hooligans had smashed their way in and threw every one of his possessions out of the window while the crowd below shouted with delight as each piece smashed to bits on the pavement. An umbrella was thrown out and didn't break, so someone picked it up and bashed it against a suitcase until it too was ruined. I had no idea why it was all happening, but later heard it was because a German ambassador in Paris had been shot by a Jew. Whether that was true or not, I don't know.

Anyway, I got dressed and we went down the Königsallee and saw buildings set alight, windows smashed and looting from homes and shops. The next day, the owner of a shoe shop that had been robbed told me that the thief who had stolen two right shoes had come back demanding the left one. Unbelievable!

And you know, on the opposite side of the street was the Christian church, with its doors closed – and its eyes unseeing – and nobody did anything." She shook her head. "Who knows how it will all end?"

Franz-Theo listened in silence, recalling his own bewilderment and watching the expression on her face as she spoke, re-living the agitation that had upset her years before.

"My dear Anita," he continued, "I do not know where it will end, but I know it will not end well. Kristallnacht was only the beginning in an evolving story of madness and death. You will understand that an event like this, while my father was recovering in hospital, did not help my mother who was ill. The doctor had been treating her for some stomach trouble that often caused her to throw herself, writhing in pain, on a couch. The treatments seemed of little help. Eventually she was taken to hospital for an operation. There was no improvement. Tante Tina came from Aachen to visit and be of whatever help she could be and on January the ninth, father and I were called in. Mother was in unendurable pain and agony. I prayed that someone would come to end it, but nobody did. She died at about 10 o'clock in the morning.

I was seventeen. I hated all the people who came to our home to eat and drink and talk noisily before and after the funeral. I wanted only to be alone.

Without my mother, my father was a broken man. I could be of no help to him, nor could I persuade him to get any sleep. He kept working all through the day and much of the night. There was no-one to share his grief nor his loneliness.

Three months after my mother's death I spent the Easter school vacation with friends of my family in Gantenberg. One morning the telephone rang with the message that my father had been arrested by the Gestapo on the grounds of being Jewish by race and Polish by nationality – a double crime in the period of mounting tension before Germany invaded Poland last September.

I raced back to Dortmund to enquire from the Gestapo of my father's whereabouts. Instead, I was interrogated in the usual manner; one officer interrogating, the other typing the statement, the third just watching every expression on my face. I explained that there must be a mistake, that my father was Catholic like my mother and me, that he had spent nearly all of his life in Germany, that he had served in the Austrian army where he had received decorations, that he had been a prisoner-of-war in Italy. I was given to understand that my father had told a similar story, but that he had been stripped of his clothes for a further inspection and that in his flesh he bore the sign of the covenant, although the gentlemen of the Gestapo did not put this observation in those terms. Neither was I told where I could find my father.

It took me three days to find the right prison. When I finally got there, the gate was slammed in my face with the comment that I'd missed the visiting hour for that week. I returned a week later and saw my father behind two wire grilles, a warder between them. My father, unshaven and in striped clothes, twisted a prison cap in his hand. There was not much to be said. Not much that could be said. I stood and looked at my father and never have I been more proud of him than during those brief moments."

Franz-Theo paused, his eyes brimming with tears. He shook his head, fumbled for a handkerchief and finally breathed a long shuddering sigh. He couldn't speak. Anita took his hand in both of hers, watching him.

"Seeing him there, it became clear why he had never discussed his background – in a vain endeavour to protect his family. It became clear why I had seen him so often studying a certain newspaper that published employment and business opportunities abroad, but my mother had wanted to stay in Germany near her sisters.

A month later, my father returned home. Something must have gone wrong with Nazi organisation and precision timing. Suddenly, there was a lot of coming and going in our home. Strange visitors called, with whom my father would walk restlessly in the park-like garden for the sake of secrecy. For the first time, I heard my father speak Polish. He had no time to lose in preparing his escape from Germany. The risks involved did not permit him to take me with him.

And so it was not long before I went with him just as far as Köln where we waited in a dingy café for a rendezvous with a man wearing a silver ring embossed with the Lion of Judah on his finger. When he finally appeared, he mentioned an address to my father. We made our way there and waited alone in the front room of a house for a knock on the window. A woman was to pass by, and my father was to follow her to an unknown destination. The time passed uneasily. Then we heard the knock. We stood and embraced for the last time. I still see my father's solitary figure walking down the street, carrying only a satchel and disappearing from my view. I was seventeen and alone in Nazi Germany. I took the train back to what had been home.

A few days later, the telephone rang and my father's voice assured me that he had arrived safely in Brussels. Anne the housekeeper was no longer needed and the school had to be notified that I would not be returning to complete the last year and that I would not be going to university to study medicine as planned. Tante Tine came from Aachen to be what help she could. It was very little.

Our business and our home were confiscated by the Gestapo. Somehow, I managed to send a consignment of furniture and the more treasured family belongings to Brussels before selling the rest for a song. There was no lack of vultures looking for a bargain.

The police issued me with a Fremdenpaß giving my nationality as Polish. My movements were restricted to a circle of 10 kilometres from where I was registered to live. Three times a week I had to present myself at police headquarters to sign a record. This I did, but little did the police know that I was not to be found at my registered address in Dortmund and, in fact, had to travel for hours by train from the place in the country where I was staying with friends of our family.

With some difficulty, I eventually convinced the German authorities that my links with Poland were rather tenuous, that I had never been in Poland, nor did I speak Polish. My Polish Fremdenpaß was replaced by another, giving my nationality as "stateless". It meant that I was free game, outside the protection of any government.

Tante Tine, who would have done anything for my mother's sake, offered me asylum and so I moved here to Aachen. I don't know why my father decided to abandon the faith of his family or his reasons to become a Catholic. I am certain his reasons were not religious, but rather his love for my mother. And knowing my mother, who would reproach him for that?

It was difficult to find a job here, but I found work as an assistant in a photographic studio for which I earn a pittance. I am determined to get out of Germany, one way or another, and that is what brought me to Professor Bauman's English classes – and to you."

Exhausted by this unburdening, having re-lived all the traumas of loss, love, injustice, confusion and bitterness, there was silence. Anita looked at him, her face tear-stained, too choked to speak, struggling to understand how this young man could endure wounds so deep, so raw and yet maintain a gravity and composure that so belied his years. At last, quietly, she spoke.

"What has befallen you is almost too hard to contemplate. How you have survived, I do not know. But that you have shared all this touches me profoundly. There are a thousand questions, but at the moment, I have no words, except to say how sorry I am, how sorry that you have had to suffer so much."

"No, I thank you for having heard me out – and I'm sorry if I have upset you. These are things I have not entrusted to anyone - as you may well imagine. Forgive me burdening you like this."

They stood together and Franz-Theo took Anita's hands in his. It was not a gesture he would normally have dared, but confession had brought both relief and intimacy.

"You see a man who has nothing and who has no prospects in this country. I would understand if you said you would not see me again, though I pray that it not be so."

Anita looked into his face, met the sad intensity of his eyes and recognised the man within. She squeezed his fingers, released her hands and folded him to her briefly. Stepping back, she said, "We will meet again."

A Tale in the Forest

Throughout the following days, she replayed again and again the images created by the photographer – the son standing helplessly by his mother's bed as she died in agony; the son watching his father walking into darkness, perhaps never to be seen again. A kaleidoscope of close-ups: a man's hand with a large ring on his finger; a woman's face at the window; striped prison clothes and a gaunt, unshaven face; a twisted prison cap; birds in a cage. She heard over and over the soft resonance of his voice, the hard gutturals of interrogation, the agonised cries of a dying woman, children calling in the snow, the insistent ring of a telephone from far away.

Thereafter, the frequency of their meetings gradually increased beyond the regular classes for interpreters. Theirs was a translation far more bewildering and perilous, no rules to guide them, but judgments that could destroy them at a whim. They would stroll through the small park behind the Elisenbrunnen - its famed waters having attracted such luminaries as Handel and Casanova – or retire to a café or the Bols Stube where the sweet liqueur partly assuaged the bitterness that came with parting.

On one such occasion, they agreed they would meet the following afternoon to take the tram west from the city and head to the nearby Friedrichwald near the Belgian border. In the forest, away from the public gaze, they might temporarily displace the uncertainty of the war and the apprehension of betrayal or impending disaster.

Clear sunshine blessed their rendezvous. Light of heart and light of step, Anita took Franz-Theo's hand to climb aboard and they sat together on the wooden seats. To the comfortable clatter of the wheels, Anita would remark on the passing landscape, a couple walking their dog, a garden yet showing flowers, the shapes of clouds. Sensing her happy mood, Franz-Theo said, "Perhaps now is the time to tell me a little of your childhood."

She smiled at him. "Do you really want to know?"

"Of course. It's why I asked. Tell me – tell me everything."

"It was a happy time. You already know that I was born at about 3 o'clock in the afternoon of a hot summer's day, on the thirtieth of July in 1911, in Böcklingstraße in Düsseldorf, and that my mother's family is descended from the Ritter Hilchen von Lorch. My father was born in Comberg but his family is obviously Italian and boasts a grandfather who, we are told, was the mayor of Milan – or maybe just a government official. None of that is really important because one of the first things I actually remember is having fallen asleep under my father's desk in the Herren Zimmer he used as a study. It was a favourite place, to nestle between the pedestals with the chair pulled in, safely hidden away. I was woken by my father who entered the room in his uniform, pulled aside the chair and lifted me out. With both hands, he held me high, looked at me very intently and then, with tears in his eyes, he hugged me tightly before setting me on my feet. It frightened the wits out of me somehow. Then he left for the war – Hauptman Gallo. Obviously he survived - and was twice decorated."

"That must have been a bewildering moment for you, to see your father's tears without any explanation."

"It was, and I still remember it clearly for its impact, but what explanation could he give to a child? I only understood that something important was happening and, when I look back, it was a rare show of emotion for a man so rigid and conscious of his duty."

"What happened then during the war while he was away?"

"My mother kept the apartment in Böcklingstraße because she thought the war would be over in a few months, but by 1915 it was considered too dangerous for women and children to stay in the cities and so, together with my mother and sister Erna, we went to live with my grandfather, Karl Hilge, in Bad Schwalbach. He was the most wonderful man. He died just three years ago in the town in which he was born."

"You were close to him?"

"Oh yes."

Anita paused, smiling as she remembered the years and the loving kindness of the man. Already it seemed very far away. She looked at Franz-Theo and thought to herself how easy it was to talk to this man who listened so attentively. He, caught in the web of her narrative and this woman whose girlish enthusiasm so belied the initial aura of unapproachability, marvelled at the revelation even as he marvelled at the images that emerged in the fluids of his darkroom.

Arriving finally at the end of the line, they alighted, Anita on Franz-Theo's arm, and headed into the forest where dappled light spilled through the leaves onto the forest floor and the meandering path. Anita took up her narrative once more.

"I don't know much about my grandmother on my mother's side, but I do know there were always mixed marriages. She was Catholic; my grandfather was Protestant. When my mother married, she was a Protestant who married my father who was a Catholic – but we were brought up as Protestants. Such marriages have existed throughout generations and it's probably one of the reasons I could never understand why there had to be conflict and why I have always been tolerant of those with different faiths.

My grandfather married Francisca Diefenbach and they had three children: my mother Anna, and her two brothers, Ernst and Wilhelm. Ernst was killed in the war and three months later his mother died because she couldn't survive the death of her son. Wilhelm married Tante Lena, but they had no children. They owned the Hilchenhaus, a lovely guesthouse with big rooms, nicely furnished and perfectly run as a guesthouse near the Kurpark. They adopted a fourteen year old girl called Gertie and, in their Wills, left everything to her. When Uncle Willy died, with his affairs in disarray, and people heard rumours of Gertie's inheritance, they believed the girl must be his illegitimate child. She ended up marrying an Italian, Peppi Marchetti, and they had two children – Tristan and Isolde, believe it or not. They tried to get rid of my aunt and take over the magnificent house, leaving her with a pittance. It finished up in court and, in the end, they had to pay her a small monthly amount so that she could live in a little apartment in the town.

It was a sad story really. Tristan died from an overdose; Isolde married a racing car driver and moved to Wiesbaden. Peppi couldn't cope and committed suicide. When they sold the Hilchenhaus, they got a lot of money for it and built a house somewhere in the Taunus Gebiet, thinking they would live happily for the rest of their days. But then tragedy struck their son. The father committed suicide and she died from a broken heart, having lost first her child and then her husband. That was the end of the family."

For a while there was silence while they each digested the misfortunes of the truncated lives in this abbreviated saga. Strange how history had a knack of upending the fortunes of those seemingly favoured; how avoiding one's destiny meant encountering it coming the other way.

The shadows were lengthening when Franz-Theo noticed a tall wooden structure through the trees. It appeared to be a watchtower, presently unmanned, but affording a view over the forest and across the border.

"What do you say Anita? Shall we climb up and sit above the tree tops?"

"Do you think we should?"

"There's no-one here – and it cannot do any harm. Come."

As they approached, they saw it was really quite a substantial structure. Four massive posts reaching through the trees, cross-braced, enclosed four flights of wooden steps with a handrail. Cautiously at first, together they climbed the treads, counting as they went. The last flight led to an open trapdoor in the floor at the top. A balustrade surrounded the platform itself, against which was a long wooden bench. Here they sat and surveyed the scene. Above the woods, the sky appeared much lighter, though streaked with the soft pinks and yellows of evening. They could look over the landscape as birds might do, seeing the open fields between the copses of trees, the roads snaking across the terrain and, in the distance, the spire of a church rising through its bower of trees and into the dusky sky.

They sat quietly together. Presently, Franz-Theo reached across and took Anita's hand in his. She did not resist and he gently squeezed her fingers.

"Tell me more about Bad Schwalbach, but this time not such a sad story."

"We lived in the Goldenen Engel, an old three-storey house with an attic. My sister and I shared a room that looked out over the Marktplatz. Behind us was a small yard, with a well and a pump, and there lived a huge dog. Everyone was frightened of it. Being wartime, food was rationed and not even Bibo the butcher who owned the dog could afford to feed it properly, especially when there was hardly enough for people. Being hungry, the poor beast was vicious. One day, I climbed into his kennel to clean it out for him because he was neglected. Nobody cared for him, although he did have a trough for water.

On an earlier occasion, he had slipped his chain, gone into the slaughterhouse and retrieved a big piece of meat. It was a catastrophe. They had to get the meat back, but the dog was so vicious, no-one could come near him. He had at last got something to eat and nobody was going to take it away.

My mother was terrified when she couldn't find me. She went to the gate and called, 'Anitachen, Anitachen' – das gute Kind, the good child she used to call me – and there I crawled out of the huge dog kennel. She was horrified. But I loved that dog and I had the habit of going secretly to the kitchen and rummaging in the cupboards to see if I could find something to feed him. I did things that were utterly outrageous.

My grandfather, with his connections around the farms, occasionally managed to get a calf or a pig that was brought to the house and slaughtered and then they got Bibo to make sausage. In secret, in my grandparents' private home, I can remember the sausages hanging in the bureau, or over the bathtub where they had arranged a big rod. One day, shortly after, my mother heard the back door closing and she caught me on the way out with a ring of sausages I had somehow managed to take down. She asked, 'What on earth are you doing with those sausages?' and I said, 'They're all hungry and they have to eat.' So the whole neighbourhood was supplied with sausage, the most secret thing of all."

There were many more tales to tell, but the two of them fell silent, listening instead to the birds settling to roost for the night and the first stars appeared. Between the wisps of cloud, a crescent moon rose as the chill air descended. They had been oblivious to the time that had slipped away so easily but, with a shock, realised they would now have to abandon this eyrie above the world of men, machines and malevolence. They stood, rubbing their hands and stamping their feet to restore circulation and paused to take a last lingering look over the landscape. Then, gingerly, Anita lowered herself backwards through the trapdoor,

Franz-Theo following till they stood on the landing. Thereafter he led the way down till at last they stood again on the forest floor. Darkness enveloped them. Perched above the trees it had seemed much lighter, but here not even the pale moon could penetrate the heavy foliage.

Anxious, Anita asked, "Which way is the path?"

"I'm not sure. I think we have to go to the right."

"You think so? I think we should go left."

They debated this briefly, then turned left. Around them, vast trunks loomed out of the uneven earth, disappearing into blackness. In front of them, an ever-deepening sameness until, after about twenty minutes, Anita, pointing to a large shape rising out of the gloom, exclaimed, "What is that?"

"It looks like the watchtower we left a little while ago."

"But how can that be? It's impossible. We can't have walked in a circle."

"It sometimes happens when one is lost."

They came closer and, certainly, it was the very place from whence they had started.

"What will we do now?

Franz-Theo smiled. "Perhaps we could try going in the other direction."

They set off again, into the same blackness as before, with no path or light to guide them. Anita experienced an odd mixture of elation and apprehension. What if they became lost again? What would her poor mother think? How would her father react? Perhaps it would be morning before they could find their way out of this maze and, by then, perhaps her parents' fear would have instigated an even more dangerous response, one that could transform this seemingly benign adventure into a catastrophe.

Several times they stumbled and had to re-direct their steps. It seemed to Anita that they were moving further away from the path that would lead them out of the trees and towards the road they would now have to walk all the way home. There would be no tram at this hour of the night.

Suddenly, miraculously, the trees parted and, with their eyes now accustomed to the darkness, they could discern a trail that seemed vaguely familiar. Relieved, Anita reassuringly tightened her grip on Franz-Theo's arm and with easier steps, they followed it.

"You were right," she said. "I should have listened to you the first time."

"At night, in unfamiliar surroundings, it's easy to become confused. But look, what do you see along the edges of the path?"

"In patches, it appears as if it's glowing, and there are tiny lights, like fireflies. It's as if they were leading us out of here."

"There are fireflies which create a bioluminescence from the luciferase they contain – little lucifers that have fallen from heaven. But there is also the phosphorescence of the fungi that grow in the rotting wood of trees that have fallen in the damp undergrowth."

"It's beautiful, mysterious and magical."

"Just as the day has been, so too the night."

She smiled and squeezed his arm again. Shortly after, they emerged from the woods and set off for the long walk home. It would take them another two hours before they stood breathless at the door of the Postamt. They bade one another a gently restrained good night and Franz-Theo waited till Anita had let herself in before making his way home to the cottage he temporarily called home.

Anita tiptoed up the stairs and, knowing how anxious her mother would be, crept into her parents' bedroom. She approached her mother's side of the bed and, leaning towards her whispered as quietly as with moth's breath, "Everything is all right. I'm safely home and there is nothing to worry about. I'm sorry it's late, but all is fine."

She felt her mother's hand reach for her and gently touch her arm in acknowledgement. Her father made no sound or movement and Anita slipped quietly away. When she had gone, Carl Gallo spoke to his wife. "Come. Lie in my arm. Das gute Kind, the good child has come home and you can now go to sleep."

CHAPTER THREE

A Growing Threat

There had been other times of commotion in Bad Schwalbach as little Anita grew up. Two incidents in particular had overtones unrealised until much later. The first concerned a story told by her mother about her brother Ernst when just a boy. There lived not far from the Goldenen Engel a Jewish shoemaker whose custom, in between his labours, was to sit at his open window and survey the world as it passed by. He was a quiet soul who kept his own counsel, performed his work with care and some pride, and maintained a kindly disposition to the villagers who provided him with a livelihood. They, in return, humoured his eccentricities, sometimes questioned one another about his origins and largely accepted his quiet ways.

Young Ernst, for reasons that can only be surmised, had selected the unfortunate man as the target for his latest discovery, which was his talent for shooting dried peas through a hollow tube with astonishing accuracy. Concealed in a doorway opposite the cobbler's window, he took delight in catching his victim on the cheek, or striking him in the ear and then watching as he flicked his hands in confusion across his face as if brushing away an annoying insect. Eventually he was forced to retire indoors without ever discovering his tormentor.

Opposite the Goldenen Engel on the other side of the Marktplatz was the Goldenen Kette. A gate, often left open, led into the enclosed yard behind the building. From the cobblestones one could look up to the verandah that led along the rear wall on the first floor that was the home of another Jewish family. Like the shoemaker, they minded their own business and traded like anybody else in the village but were known for the close observance of their faith.

In the third week of October 1916, in the month of Tishri in the Jewish calendar, it was the time of Laubhüttenfest, or Sukkot. It was an occasion for joyous celebration when it was customary for families to sleep, eat and entertain outside in a makeshift shelter as recognition of their ancestral exodus from Egypt through the desert. The family from the Goldenen Kette had constructed a simple bower, draped with hessian and garlanded with leaves and branches, on the verandah overlooking the hinterhof. At a time when nobody was about, Anita's sister Erna ventured across the Marktplatz, through the open gate and stole her way up the wooden steps to the festive bower. There, she tied the leftover pork bones that had formed part of the previous day's evening meal, before scampering back home and telling nobody.

It was some days later that the ructions this event caused stirred her conscience to confess to her mother.

"But why, why did you do such a thing?"

"I don't know. I really don't know. It seemed like something to do, for fun."

"Did anybody tell you to do it?"

"Not really. They just said that Jewish people don't eat pork and I thought 'why not?' There is no harm in it – and we eat it whenever we can."

"Not everybody has the same customs or beliefs. And who gave you the idea to do something so offensive? Was it your friends, people from school, other children in the village?"

"It was nobody in particular. Just something I heard at different times from different people. I meant no harm. Some people who heard about it thought it was amusing."

"But in the tradition of these people, it is considered unclean. You have desecrated their special place and destroyed the happiness of a family grateful to be alive, living peacefully among their neighbours and celebrating their custom. I cannot believe that you didn't think."

Erna's lip trembled and she began to cry, dismayed by her own foolishness and upset by her mother's reprimand. "What will happen now?"

"We will go to their house, knock at the front door, and you will apologise. You will say how sorry you are, that you did not understand and you will ask them to forgive you. You will also offer to help them in any way you can to make amends for your foolishness."

Thus chastised and the punishment fulfilled, the matter itself was resolved, though not without leaving a stain on the lives and memories of all who knew.

When, many years later, Anita recalled these incidents in the light of more recent events, she understood that the mutant seeds of the Führer's anti-Semitism had been planted in her countrymen long before.

Carl Gallo, Director of the Central Post Office in Aachen, inquired not from his daughter, but from his contacts in the Gestapo why the healthy young man calling on his daughter was not in uniform. It did not take long to discover the reason. The following day, Herr Metzger received a letter, its tell-tale postmark a premonition.

"It has regrettably come to my attention that you have established a friendship with my younger daughter, Fraulein Gallo. Circumstances dictate, and I must insist absolutely, that you immediately cease all contact with her or any members of her family. Grave consequences will ensue if you fail to heed this directive."

The pressure and stroke of the handwritten signature underlined both the tone and the intent.

Given the tensions and political allegiances of the time, the wisest course might have been acquiescence. As he filed away the threat, Franz-Theo understood that matters would go most uncomfortably for his confidante and he regretted involving her in such a perilous situation. Just how perilous, he learned later.

Carl Gallo summoned his wife and daughter. He motioned them to sit. In the circle of light he raised an angry shadow, despite the softness of his prelude.

"These are matters we need to discuss as a family. I ask you Anita, do you know what you are doing?"

"I am doing nothing. If you are referring to Herr Metzger, I have made his acquaintance through our mutual interest in an interpreter's language class. We share a friendship through common interests. There is nothing more – what could there be?"

"I presume you know his situation?"

"I'm not sure I understand what you mean, but yes, I know that he is a good man, a victim of misunderstanding and circumstances totally outside his control. I know he has just lost his mother to a terrible death, that his father had been imprisoned without just cause and that he has been made homeless by an unjust regime that has stolen his house and all his belongings."

"You cannot, will not say such things under this roof. You endanger not just yourself, but all of us here." He took several deep breaths, shook his head slowly and began again. "Do you know how old this man is?"

"Yes, but his years bear no relation whatever to his maturity, his intelligence, his dignity or his suffering."

"He's eighteen for goodness sake! And you're twenty-eight. He's still a raw youth and you're a mature woman, a German with your whole future in front of you. You have good prospects, intelligence and beauty, your family has position and influence. You can make something of your life. He has nothing, can offer nothing. Can you not see it?"

"I see perfectly, but are you not getting ahead of yourself? We are simply friends who ..."

"There is no place for friendship with this man! I will not tolerate it; Germany will not tolerate it! You have already seen what can happen. I will not let it happen to us."

"Then what sort of world are we living in?"

"The only world we have; and I will not allow you, or anyone else, to take it away from us. Think. If you should dare to take this further, if you even survive, he will be a young man in his prime and you will already be old. He will not be interested in you then. You have had ten years more life experience than he has, know things he cannot, nor ever will. Whichever way you choose to look at it, this friendship is doomed to failure. In fact, if you do not end it immediately, I shall be forced to take further action."

"What do you mean?"

"Let me make it perfectly clear: if you do not cease all contact with this man, then, for the sake of my position and the security of my family, I shall personally hand you over to the Gestapo!"

Anna gave a gasp and held her hands to her mouth. She could neither move nor look up. Tears welled in her eyes and presently her body shook with sobs.

Anita was stunned. The world she thought she knew spiralled away into a funnel of black fear. As the storm above her subsided momentarily, she looked up, wide-eyed and whispered, "What have you done?"

"I have written to Herr Metzger, instructing him to sever all contact with you or our family and have warned him of the consequences if he ignores my directive. It is the same for you." Then, with great deliberation, "You must understand that I have absolutely no choice in the matter."

Gathering himself, he pressed his lips together and with a fury that shook the air, he shouted, "And that is the end of it!" Stiff with rage, righteous anger making his one eye bright, he turned on his heel and strode from the room, slamming the door behind him.

Never had Anita's father spoken to her like that; never had such an unbridled fear assailed him. Alone together, Anita and her mother held each other and sobbed till the shock abated.

From then on, with the passing of each day, it became incontrovertibly clear in Anita's mind that she too had no choice. She would not relinquish this man. His years of innocence had disguised the legacy of his past, the yellow star in the blood, betrayed by a history more vast than his own. Fear had entered his door without so much as knocking, and unpitying death had already struck deep in his trusting heart. The jackboots that trampled his inheritance now strode unchallenged across the lives of countrymen and marched unchecked across borders. Anita, whose own privilege had shielded her from the clutch of real fears, had been admitted to a new reality that beckoned outside herself. She had heard and understood the voice behind the words confided in her. She was being called to a role she could not imagine but understood could not be contradicted. No threat, no government, no authority could alter the path that had led to this convergence of events. She was at a crossroad, her family at one corner, her past on another and her future opposed. Germany, nay the whole world, faced a similar crisis, driven by blindness that would end in tears and smoke. The idea being formed, it generated a momentum all its own, gathering speed with the inevitability of self-immolation.

The untenability of Anita's situation clarified and resolved itself in two seemingly simple and unrelated events. On a crisp winter day in an afternoon of watery sunlight, Anita and Anna were walking together past the Elisenbrunnen, collars turned up against the chill air woven through the bare branches of the trees. United by a common fear, they found solace in each other's company, the mother in her daughter, the child in the mother – kindred spirits in a purgatorial suspension. After all their hushed and urgent words, there now remained only silence and their even footfall on the pattern of stones.

The two women were utterly unaware of the tableau they created, elegantly dressed against the classic background of the rotunda's colonnade, as they crossed Friedrich-Wilhelm Platz on their way home. It made a pretty sight.

From the end of the street, the jolt of recognition arrested Franz-Theo. His heart thumped in his chest, his mind instantly crowded with a thousand confusions. They had not yet seen him and he debated whether to turn away or run the gauntlet, despite knowing that his situation made it impossible to pause for even the slightest courtesies. Anita looked breathtakingly beautiful, tall, refined, unapproachable – and yet he had long sensed an inner fire, a strength and a tenderness that intrigued and bewitched him. With slower steps and an assumed airiness belied by his inner trembling, he walked towards them, drawn to the flame.

Anita looked up. Involuntarily, her step hesitated. It was enough for her mother to observe a smartly dressed, rather handsome young man with deep brown eyes coming towards them. As they passed, barely turning her head, Anita smiled at him, a smile returned. She read both elation and sadness.

The remainder of the walk home passed in silence. Pausing at the front door, Anna turned to her daughter and quietly asked, "That was him?"

"Yes."

"He did not stop to speak with us."

"He knows what will happen if he does."

"So, what will you do?"

"For now, Mutti, I will do what I have to do."

The ambiguity of her answer was deliberate, but the surge of knowing in that passing encounter had galvanised in Anita's mind that, come what may, her allegiance lay with the man without a country of his own.

⁓

When next they met, Anita sensed immediately something was wrong. Troubled, she looked into his face, searching for some sign that might assuage her fears.

"What is it? What has happened?"

"I have received a letter, a most disturbing letter."

Anita waited, the air stood still.

"From your father."

She swallowed but said nothing. Her eyes welled with tears. The implications of this news terrified her. If the SS should come after him, if he was discovered, he was surely doomed. Even more horrific, she would be directly responsible for whatever consequences befell him. It was her intransigence, her wilful disobedience of her father's orders that had precipitated his anger. It was she who had imperilled not just her own family, but the life of a man she had barely met. She struggled to emerge from the suffocation of guilt and fear, finally asking for what she already knew.

"What did he say?"

"In short, that he would turn me over to the Gestapo if I were to see you again. Has he spoken to you? Does he understand what he is threatening?"

She answered both questions at once. "I am afraid so. For his security, his position, the sake of the family, he has forbidden me to have any contact with you as well. He is frightened – for us as well as himself. It is terrible, just terrible."

"Is he likely to act upon his threat?"

Anita turned her face to him and, with a sad despair so profound that it startled the man, replied, "He would even offer up his youngest child to safeguard the well-being of the rest of his family. He made the same promise to me."

"You are certain of this?"

"Indeed. Let me tell you why. My father had a sister, Minna. She married a man who frittered away his fortune on gambling and horses, getting deeper and deeper into debt. Her grandfather was nearly bankrupted by constantly covering his excesses and eventually Minna came to my father with a document she wanted signed. When my father asked what it was for, she said it was to make him guarantor over the debts of her husband. Outraged, my father refused categorically. Minna persisted, entreating him to be reasonable for her sake and making promises that everything would be all right. My father argued that he would under no circumstances put himself in the position where his hard work and savings would be swallowed up by a spendthrift. Forfeit his salary to pay the debts of her husband? Not ever would he put his name to such a document.

Minna's pleas fell on deaf ears until finally she said, 'If you do not sign this paper, I will throw myself into the Rhine!' And my father's answer to this? 'Then throw yourself in where it is deepest.' He never spoke to her again, nor did he mention her name.

Later, when she was dying, she approached him to make her peace. He refused to see her."

"He is perhaps a harder man than I imagined."

The winter chill bit at their faces. The darkening street was not a place to be seen in anxious conversation. They headed to the Postwagen for privacy and warmth.

"He has not had it easy. Even though he came from a happy family, wealthy people, by the time he was ten or eleven years old, he was sent to Wiesbaden to the Humanistische Gymnasium where he learned Latin and Greek. He missed his mother terribly and he looked forward to going home for the holidays. He would sit with her and cry when the holidays ended and it was time to return to boarding school. During the war he was sent first to Russia, on a dangerous mission from which he returned to tell my mother how appalled he was at the gulf between rich and poor. No wonder there had been revolution. Later he fought in the west, taking with him a photograph of my mother, my sister and me, so as to have his family with him. Sometimes I sense that, were it not for my mother, he would be a very lost and lonely man."

"That may well be, but I am now concerned what he might do to you and to me. It is no longer safe for us here. What do you intend to do?"

"For the moment, I can do nothing. For us to have time together, it will have to be in secret until we see what direction the war will take and what opportunities we have."

"So you do not intend to obey your father's orders?"

Anita looked at him and smiled ruefully. Her heart had spoken, but her words were ambiguous. "What choice do I have?"

These times of great uncertainty were deeply troubling for both of them, even though it would be some time before the events taking place in Auschwitz, Bergen Belsen, Buchenwald, Bamberg and Treblinka in the spring of 1941 would cloud the skies and minds over Germany. When talking about the precariousness of their plight, Franz-Theo would revert to questions of philosophy and religion, trying to find some metaphysical dimension to the real and temporal world that had snared them. Perhaps the Buddhist notions of impermanence and detachment might somehow offer hope.

"Attachment brings loss and loss brings grief. So we suffer."

"That sounds a very negative way of looking at the world."

"You have only to think of your broken dreams, your crushed hopes, or I my family destroyed, home and ambition lost, to know how great our pain and disillusion."

"What we had, what we believed in, is still important, and gave us great happiness. We can work to have it back again – but how do you reconcile this with the faith of your father, or your Catholic upbringing?"

"To compare is really pointless, because we are not comparing like with like." He paused to think, before adding, "Now is not the time to talk about these things when we need to save ourselves from a more dynamic existential threat. There is much to know and little enough time to discover it. I may spend the remainder of my days searching."

"Franz-Theo, you're a remarkable man, far wiser and more serious than your years. What you speak of is not some light-hearted nonsense, but of things that shape the way we live, that give meaning to the day."

"It's kind of you to say it, but recently there are indeed events that make me question the God of my childhood."

This conversation stayed with Anita many days, giving her pause to question the turmoil in her family, her own ambitions. It made her aware as never before of the traditions she had hitherto taken for granted. Most of all, its silken thread had begun to weave a cocoon which she knew would embrace the two of them in its dark interior.

The next time they met, Franz-Theo, for all his subdued pensiveness, appeared excited, boyish. He had news to share.

"You probably know," he began, "What is happening at the Staadttheater?" It was more a question than a statement. Anita feigned surprise.

"No, tell me." She smiled.

"You of course know the conductor, Herbert von Karajan. Does Irmgard Seefried mean anything to you?"

"Not yet, but I think it soon will."

"Irmgard Seefried is a soprano who will be making her debut, singing the role of the Priestess in Verdi's Aïda. Naturally they need publicity photographs. And yes, I have been chosen to take the portraits and, I cannot help but say, I am not the only person pleased with the results."

"My, oh my, that's wonderful. Tell me, how was she? How did she look? What did you have to do?"

"She was friendly and engaging. I used both the Rolleiflex and the Leica. The lighting was good and I managed some shots that were both flattering and dramatic; perfect for the program and the posters. She's young, only two years older than I am, but very talented. This concert will be a very important event to launch her career. Best of all, as we concluded the portrait session, she told me she had a rehearsal to follow. I was unsure whether to ask whether I could stay to listen, but she was spontaneous and kind enough to ask. So, there she was, on stage with just a piano for accompaniment… and I was the audience."

He smiled.

"But how was her voice?"

"Lovely. It was sweet, lyrical, clear. She has good control. She will be famous, I'm sure. You will hear it for yourself, with all the spectacle of the theatre to go with it."

He paused, before adding, "I fear however that it may be the first and the last time for me. Given my circumstances, it would be difficult to appear in the concert hall; and impossible to attend with you and your family, for obvious reasons. Who knows if that can ever happen, given the world we now inhabit."

There was silence. Anita looked at him, his lipped pressed together and his eyes suddenly sad. Quietly, he recited:

> *"Oh patria mia, mai più ti rivedrò!*
> *Mai più! mai più ti rivedrò !"[4]*

She placed her hand on his arm. For the moment, there was nothing further to say. And neither of them could imagine their impending roles in the theatre of war, an opera whose voices would be the wail of sirens, the clatter of bullets and the deep pounding of bombs on a stage piled with the hapless bodies of the dead.

⌒

By December 1940, snow was falling around Aachen while bombs were falling on London. The countryside lay under its blanket; the city burned.

---

[4]Oh my homeland, I will never see you again!
 No more! Never see you again!

(Act III, Aida)

Once more, Franz-Theo and Anita had risked meeting and travelled again to the outskirts of the town and into the forest of Friedrichwald. They found the observation tower, deserted today, each wooden step capped with a mound of snow. Carefully they climbed up, through the tops of the trees and surveyed a very different landscape from the one before. No moon or stars to gently light the shadowy contours, but a sullen grey that brooded over a silent, troubled world.

Franz-Theo cleared an armful of snow from the bench and they sat together, each wrapped in a thick coat, pulled tight against the chill air. For a long time they were silent. It was as if, being suspended in the firmament, they understood the vastness of what they were faced with, and their powerlessness to change events that were changing the world. Despite the nationalistic propaganda, they had heard enough to know that, even in impossibly far away North Africa, the Italians were desperate for more German support. They were aware of the fall of Tobruk and whispers of an impending assault on the Soviet Union. Events so far removed still reverberated in the everyday lives of the most innocent, their means, their food, their safety, their survival. And to whom did one turn when God was so deathly silent?

When they turned to each other, sadness met sorrow. Whatever might have been, now seemed futile. He saw in her steady gaze and the contours of her face a beauty he hardly dared imagine. He had heard her voice, sensed her searching, touched the aliveness of her mind. He had brought her to the precipice of his own life, tempted her from her family, threatened her life merely by knowing her. If he cared for her at all, he could not ask for more.

Gathering himself, he stood and motioned towards the stairs. Once they reached the landing, they descended together and stepped out on the path. Anita held his arm and they walked slowly, her mind full of unknowing.

Gradually, it began to snow – light flakes drifting silently through the branches, soft, so soft. Calm and unhurried, it laid its crystals on the dark branches and the glimpses of green still visible by the track, building a slow drift that guided their steps. On either side, the trunks receded to whiteness, the canopy lost in the union of snow and sky. The only sound was their soft footfall on the frozen earth.

At last, Franz-Theo paused. He disengaged his arm and turned to meet Anita's questioning gaze. He stood perfectly still, looking at her upturned face, the snow falling on her cheeks, her hair, her mouth, his eyes exploring hers, searching for the answer he knew was his, his heart suddenly pounding in his chest. And then slowly, with exquisite gentleness, he cupped her face in his hands and felt the unutterable softness of her lips on his mouth. She raised her arms around his neck, holding him close, feeling the bewildering recognition of the kiss of a man. Suddenly giddy, she felt his arm around her waist, soft kisses on her face, her eyes, her lips, her cheek, her hair and again he found her mouth.

Around them, the snow fell gently, pure witness to hope and desire, all the inexorable seasons of life's pulse. When they parted, tears stood in Franz-Theo's eyes as he struggled under the avalanche of his emotions. He wanted to laugh, to cry out, to thank God for this moment of sublime ecstasy that obliterated all knowing, except for the soft abandon in which he might happily die.

Anita stood quivering in his arms, her eyes wide, her heart flooded. As she tried to breathe, she was filled with such a certainty as she had never imagined, a conviction that for her no other choice would ever exist. In this forest, under these stars, in the arms of this extraordinary man, she had, for better or worse, met her destiny.

He watched her, waiting for the intensity within to subside so that he could find a voice that would somehow encompass the meaning of the moment, of his need to speak the impossible. Finally, with startling gravity, he said most quietly, "You have beguiled me from the day I met you. I cannot see you, or think of you without feeling that the very impossibility of our situation is there for a purpose. The reasons are unfathomable. Come what may, only in you have I placed my trust, only with you do I feel whole again, only with you can I live my life. Whatever divinity has shaped our days, it is asking that you will go where I go, that I will live where you live, that your people shall be my people."

He paused, and Anita gently laid her hand over his heart. She spoke slowly, deliberately.

"Whatever befalls us, we will always have one another – of this I am certain." She reached up and, smiling, kissed his cheek.

In this forest, under these stars it seemed the air held its breath, for it had stopped snowing. As they brushed the flakes from shoulders and sleeves, a winter robin splashed vermilion on a snowy bough, hopped thrice and was gone. Now, with arms around each other, they resumed the path in silence, re-living the enormity of each minute detail. Both were exultant, and awed, by the implications of what had transpired.

"Do you remember the story of Johannes and Weli?" asked Franz-Theo presently.

"I do, I do. It moved me very deeply. In many ways it reminds me of us, and I remember you telling me how much it meant to you – almost as if you knew then what would happen today."

"Perhaps I did, but nothing imagined is ever reality, either good or bad. This, I could never have imagined. This is a transfiguration – neither of us the same person as before – and it is why I mention Johannes and Weli."

Anita paused before asking, "Are you suggesting we should assume these names?"

"With each other, just between ourselves, our own private mythology that reflects who we have become, an intimacy to share. What do you think?"

"Well," she tried it in her head first, "Johannes, it seems a lovely idea. We can try – and if it begins to sit comfortably – we will know."

"To all the world, you will be Anita – and in the world we inhabit, you shall be my Weli." So saying, he hugged her close, then wanted to kiss her, but instead remarked, "In a few days it will be Christmas. I think we should have a tree."

The idea was as impractical as it was spontaneous. Maybe it was the headiness of the moment, maybe the sight of a small tannenbaum[5] a few metres from the path.

"How can we possibly have a tree? How will you cut it? How shall we take it home? Where will you put it?"

So many questions, but now, all things were possible. The stem was small enough that the struggle was short-lived, despite getting covered in snow, falling over and finally emerging victorious. Meanwhile, Anita stood with her hands to her mouth or shaking her head, smiling at the mischievous improbability of the situation. Her Johannes then held up the prize, reciting the verse,

"O Tannenbaum, O Tannenbaum,
Du kannst mir sehr gefallen!
Wie oft hat schon zur Winterszeit
Ein Baum von dir mich hoch erfreut!" [6]

---

[5] A fir tree, known in German as a "Weihnachtsbaum" or traditional Christmas tree, favoured for being evergreen.

[6] Loosely translated as:

"O Christmas tree, O Christmas tree,
Much pleasure dost thou bring me!
For every year the Christmas tree,
Brings to us all both joy and glee."

As it turned out, the tannenbaum asked for nothing more than a suitable container to stand in and its origins to remain discreetly concealed. Once secured in the corner of the living room, the family set about decorating it, unpacking the fine glass baubles from the tissue in which they had been preserved since last year, and hanging them where best they would catch the light. The remaining red candles, for there were none to be had this year, were inserted into the clips shaped as cockleshells and fastened where they would be least likely to set fire to either the tree or the house. Finally, a tinsel star was mounted at the top and a Christmas cloth draped beneath the tree. Everybody stood back, admiring the symmetry, the freshness of the needles, the ability to make something special out of so little in times of struggle.

In Franz-Theo's mind, another struggle was taking place. How could he not share this with Anita, his accomplice, his beloved? How would he broach so precious and delicate a subject; how would he risk revealing something so potentially dangerous? Then, abruptly, the cloud of doubting evaporated and he realised that after all that had been revealed since that terrible phone call in Gantenberg, these were the people he could most trust in the whole world. Had they not also shared fear, grief and the loss of family – bewilderment and anguish?

Resolved, and suddenly serious, he said, "There's something I have tell you. Quite a lot to tell you in fact." His aunt and uncle, immediately concerned, motioned him to an armchair and took up their places side by side on the sofa. "It concerns a young woman." Onkel Willy smiled ruefully. With that, his nephew began the story with his need to leave Germany, the opportunity to improve his English at the class for interpreters, and the remarkable Fraulein Gallo he encountered there. Soon, not only did they meet chez Baumann, but on his way to the atelier, or the library, or the Elisenbrunnen park, the Bols Stube – wherever and whenever they could, while trying to be as discreet as possible so as not to draw attention to themselves. He realised the last escapade may have jeopardised that somewhat.

He also told of the letter he had received and the threat made to Anita, the risks of remaining in Aachen. He also confessed why he had arrived home after three in the morning, having missed the tram late at night on the outskirts of the city. When, at last, he was done, all three realised that they were sitting in the unlit gloom of an evening that had arrived unawares while he talked.

Suddenly, it was time to turn on the lights, draw the curtains, set the table and find something to make a meal. As they set about their tasks, Tante Tina turned and asked, "Franz-Theo, would you like to invite Fraulein Gallo here? We don't have much, but we understand it is not possible to be together with her family and you have nowhere else. I'm sure we will be happy to meet her. What do you say Willy?"

A man as jovial, happy and lovable as Onkel Willy could only be delighted by the prospect – and so Franz-Theo received his answer before he needed to find the courage or the opportunity to ask his question.

⌣

When Anna Gallo arrived home the next day, she met her daughter coming down the stairs on her way out. They greeted one another with familiar warmth and affection but, caught in a confusing pang of guilt, each recognised the other's submerged uneasiness. Silence hung momentarily on the air. Oddly disconnected, there was nothing to say until, finally, Anna tipped her words into the void.

"I saw the young Herr Metzger today, carrying a pile of books. He must have been coming from the library. He looked very solemn and thoughtful."

"Did you speak with him?" Anita asked, suddenly anxious.

"No, no. I don't think he even noticed me. He was pre-occupied. He seems very serious, and, quite a handsome man."

"He is Mutti. He is not just some young fellow in a well-tailored jacket, but a man with a very deep understanding. And he has suffered a great deal. Much has happened to make him introspective, but there is also a great deal about him that is very charming."

"You really are fond of him, aren't you?"

For a moment Anita hesitated. It would not do to reveal more than was prudent, although she yearned to share the joy she felt. She knew her happiness came at a cost she was not yet ready to admit, either to her family, perhaps not even to herself. Instead, she stepped closer and hugged her mother to her, holding her close, holding in her words, and letting her feelings flow with silent tears. As they stood together, Anna sensed the impending weight of loss, the immensity of love for this girl grown to a state of womanhood, the child whose blood was blood of hers, whose life she had shared so intimately and whose lives would be wounded and torn by this war.

At last, they relinquished their embrace and, very gently, Anita said, "Yes, Mutti, I am fond of him – more than I am able to say."

They looked at one another, leaving unsaid the immensity of what they each knew and did not know. Then, Anita straightened her coat, checked her hat and her hair and turned to the door. Her mother, stifling tears, climbed the stairs, each tread a step from tenderness to uncertainty.

In the street, the chill air bit at Anita's cheeks. She took a deep breath and then stepped briskly across the road and headed up Kleinmaschierstraße towards the Dom. The encounter with her mother distressed her and though she replayed the scene again and again in her mind, she came to no explanation, only the discomfiting turbulence of her heart. What else could she have done? What else might she have said? There was nothing that could be done, nothing to undo what had been done, or to avert what was to come.

She turned right, traversed the Hühnermarkt and saw ahead the Postwagen where she was to meet Franz-Theo. She corrected herself: Johannes. She whispered it to herself and smiled. Johannes.

He was already waiting beneath the lantern hanging from its arm with the coach and horses in painted silhouette. He waited, watching as she approached, taking in the swing of her coat as she walked, the tall gracefulness of her bearing, the line of her, the turn of foot. Her eyes were bright, her cheek flushed, her lips moist, so soft, so briefly on his cheek. He looked at her, smiling, slowly shaking his head, almost in disbelief.

"It is wonderful, Weli, wonderful to see you. Now, eternity exists in an hour. Come, let us go in where it is warm."

He held the door and they made their way into the snug intimacy of the painted panels, the timbered ceiling, the lead-lighted panes and stained glass. They hung up their coats and sat opposite one another at a covered table, holding both hands across the embroidered centrepiece.

"Johannes," Anita began, then stopped.

"Yes, Weli?"

"Nothing. I just wanted to say it. Johannes." She smiled.

"You are so lovely. But I have things to tell you, things I must ask." And so he proceeded to tell her of the arrival of the Tannenbaum and its decoration, of his conversation with Tante Tina and Uncle Willy, and of the invitation to be their guest.

At that moment they were interrupted. The patron of the

establishment had materialised beside them at the table. Behind him stood a young girl, presumably his daughter, drawn into service as a waitress when stifled trade precluded the hiring of outside staff. She held her hands together in front of her, a supplicant reflecting her father's discomfort.

"Excuse me. I am sorry, but if you are here because you would like something to eat or drink, I am afraid we are unable to help you. You must know already how difficult things are for us with the war progressing the way it is. Food is impossibly hard to get and we certainly have no proper coffee, let alone anything resembling cake. I am sorry."

"No, no, we understand, completely," said Franz-Theo. "We were looking only for a quiet place to sit out of the cold and where we might talk in private. Please, do not concern yourself with trying to bring food."

Sensing he was speaking with good people, the patron continued, "Sometimes, you know, we are able to ...", he made a gesture with his hand receiving anonymities behind him, "find some small things on the black market. " He nodded slowly, letting the gravity sink in. "If you have any coupons, any Marken, I might be able to make you some soup, something to warm your insides."

"No, thank you. It's very kind of you to offer, but with things as tight as they are, we really couldn't ask you."

"What about some Ersatz Kaffee? We have some ground acorns that are not too bitter. At least it would be something. Let me get it for you, please."

So saying, he departed, his daughter in tow.

⌣

CHAPTER FOUR

Arbeit Macht Frei

In the living room on the second floor of the Postamt on Kapuzinergraben, Carl Gallo called his family together. He looked tired, diminished, uncertain how to find the words for a situation now larger than himself, his position or his authority.

Into the space between the turmoil of his thoughts and the news he had to impart, Anna quietly asked, her eyes full of concern, "Are you all right Carl?"

He looked up. "Yes… yes," he said. He gathered himself, "You know things are not going well, with the war I mean. Despite everything that is being said and all we are asked to believe, there is dangerous talk that Germany's forces are in too many places at once. Rommel was in Tripoli, the Luftwaffe are bombing in Britain; there have been protests about the killing of the disabled and mentally ill. All Jews older than six years now must wear the Star of David with 'Jude' written on it. Germany has troops from Yugoslavia and Greece to Russia."

He paused, suddenly fearful he had said more than he should as a servant of the Reich.

"There is more, much more that I cannot say. But," he turned to look at Anita, his words detonating directly at her, "when Polish writers and scientists have been murdered by our troops in Lwów and plans are being put in place for a final solution to the Jewish question, you need to ask yourself what on earth you think you are doing."

Anita stared at him, her heart suddenly thumping so she could not speak. She saw his anger, sensed the unspoken knowledge he had withheld, his fear of what the future would reveal. The shards of her own dread skittered through her mind; what would happen to Franz Theo, what would happen to her, to her family? What was the "final solution"?

At last, as both a question and a statement, she quietly said, "The final solution is death."

"It will be death; death for the Jews."

"Death comes to all of us. It is only the manner that need concern us."

"I am not here to discuss philosophy, or death; I have seen enough of it. I am here to tell you that after ten years in this place, we are being asked to move. The building is needed for offices and for the administration of the Reich. We will have to find somewhere else to live."

"But where?" asked Anna. "Already Aachen is not as safe as it once was. Last winter, bombs hit the cloister. There are children in there making sure that if it is hit again, or there is a fire, they can put it out and clean up; keep it safe."

"Aachen is a fortress. The Führer has commanded that it be protected at all costs. After all, it is the city of Charlemagne, the First Reich." Suddenly he stood tall, his chest filled with pride and his eye bright. "We have roadblocks, minefields, the dragons' teeth anti-tank installations, ditches and bomb shelters and bunkers. If it comes to it, every door and window will become a blockhouse, a gun emplacement. We will not surrender this city, precisely because we know how much it means to our enemies."

That was that. He had spoken, his doubt blitzed into subjugation. He waited a moment and then, in more measured tones, continued.

"I have been told there is a first-floor apartment nearby that will soon be vacant. I want you and Anita to have a look to see if it is suitable. My work keeps me here and it is important that you feel comfortable and can make it a home."

Home. What was home anymore? A place you could feel secure? A shelter against the winds of change? A warm bed, soft lamp light in the evening, the familiar smells of cooking, pictures on the wall and photographs on the sideboard and mantelpiece? A clock on the wall that measures the pulse of each day; a pendulum whose every sweep erases the hours that remain?

As she lay awake in her bed that night, Anita replayed again and again the harsh anger of her father's words, the bitterness in his voice. Gradually, the hurt she felt for herself gave way to her fear for Franz

Theo. What would happen to him? Where would he go? Where would they meet? Could they ever be together, or would she, once the "good child", bring devastation and death on all around her? She was trapped, pierced through her very being like a butterfly pinned to a board by forces beyond her comprehension or control, caught between the yellow Star of David and the Swastika.

In the next room Carl lay on his back in the dark staring at the ceiling. Though he could see nothing, it pressed down on him, suffocating him. His chest hurt, his head hurt; this was not how it was meant to be. Beside him, Anna lay awake, her tears dried. When she spoke, her voice was gentle.

"You are too hard on Anita, Carl. Like you, she no longer has a choice. As for all of us, her world too is shifting. Already we are losing our home; let us not also lose our daughter. Let us not lose each other."

She turned towards him, her hand on his arm. "Please Carl. It will be all right. Tomorrow, we will go and look at the apartment and begin to pack up things in the house. We will do what we have to do, however hard it may be. We will do it together."

So saying, she kissed him gently on the cheek, felt the stubborn stubble of his silent resistance and said, "Now we must sleep if we are to have the strength to face a new day."

She turned away, burying her face in the pillow. In the darkness, the ceiling pressed ever lower.

〜

The following morning dawned bright but with heavy clouds drifting low in the Spring sunshine. A chill breeze ruffled the new leaves and shimmered the few pools on the pavement from the overnight drizzle. As Anna and Anita stepped outside, they pulled their coats more firmly around their shoulders before heading in the direction Carl had given them.

They finally arrived outside a narrow building wedged between the more ornate facades of the street. Blinds were drawn across the two windows on each of the first and second floors. A doorway on the right opened to a vestibule and a staircase leading to each of the four storeys. Cautiously, the two women stepped inside.

"He said the apartment on the second floor. We should go up."

As they climbed the stairs, it seemed they were entering another world, smaller, narrower, infinitely removed from the imposing façade and generous proportions of their apartment on the Kapuzinergraben. Here, people lived private lives outside the edges of the bustling city centre; quiet lives, undiscoverable.

They stepped out on the landing and were confronted by a polished wooden door and its doorbell. Anna paused a moment, hesitating, and then rang it. Inside, a distant tinkle. Then silence.

"Perhaps we should knock?" asked Anita and stepped forward. She waited, head turned to listen and then rapped four times. Despite the heavy door, it sounded hollow; then footsteps on the wooden floor. A key turned in the lock and cautiously the door was opened. A gentleman in his early forties, dressed in jacket and tie, his hair already turning silver and wearing glasses on a face written with fear and unknowing, peered out at the strangers. He opened the door wider and standing behind him in the gloom, Anita and her mother saw a woman and a child of about ten standing beside a small pile of boxes and two suitcases. They were dressed as if about to embark on a voyage, a hat, coat and gloves; sturdy shoes and a folded umbrella. Bewilderment rained down.

Nobody spoke. Inside the apartment, a few pieces of furniture, stripped of their embroidered cloths, ornaments and photographs, stood naked against bare walls in the light that seeped between the curtains. The remaining pieces had been gathered in the centre of the room; a world collapsed to just these few sacrificial belongings and suitcases packed with futile hope.

Anna put her hand to her mouth, choking. "I'm sorry. We've made a mistake. We're sorry to have disturbed you. We should go."

"No. You have come to look at the apartment, have you not?" He spoke kindly, thoughtfully. "We were just waiting for the authorities to come and collect us. You will have to excuse us; we were confused when we saw you. We expected somebody else."

"Thank you, but no," replied Anna. "We have already seen more than we needed to see, and..." her voice trailed off as her eyes stung with tears, "we can only pray that you will be safe. Please forgive us; forgive us all."

She turned back onto the landing with Anita close by. From behind them, a child's voice piped, "Good-bye", its echo bright in the darkened space.

⌇

"So what did you discover?" asked Carl when the women returned home.

"There is no way on God's earth that we could live there," replied Anna. "It was the most terrible experience. The poor man thought his hour had come." She proceeded to tell her account. "It would be impossible to build our lives on the suffering of those poor people, the silent mother, the wide-eyed child. They have no idea what will happen to them. Do you have any idea what will happen; where they will go?"

"You obviously recognised they were Jewish," replied Carl. He paused to consider before continuing. "Germany is now deporting Jews from Aachen, Duisburg, Düsseldorf and Essen to Theresienstadt. It's a model Jewish settlement."

He was interrupted.

"Theresienstadt? Where is it? What is it? A ghetto?"

"Theresienstadt is in Czechoslovakia, now occupied by Germany. It's in Terezin, a garrison city. From there, they may be relocated elsewhere. You don't need to worry or to know any more and anyway, it's all for the best. Be glad we don't have to go there; but we do need somewhere else to live since we cannot stay here."

By the time the family had found its new house on Boxgraben at the beginning of summer 1942, over 2,000 Jews had been transported from around Aachen to the Theresienstadt Ghetto. Those who hadn't perished from disease or malnutrition, or hadn't been executed, ended up with thousands of others who had been removed to Treblinka and Auschwitz. Into that swirling tide of dispossessed humanity was washed a small family whose bewildering misfortune had struck the heart and mind of a woman whose history would take a different path, ever remembering, to a death for the moment, prorogued.

The move to Boxgraben complicated life for everyone, especially Anita. She had already found secretarial work at Veltrup Werke on Jülicherstraße, not really aware of the extent to which the factory was producing war materials, from armour to pressure pumps and parts for Junker aircraft. Her previous three kilometre walk had now become four, taking more than three-quarters of an hour and requiring her to get up at 6 o'clock each day to confront a job that was increasingly troubling her conscience as her allegiances shifted.

Then, a stroke of fortune. A letter from Tuttlingen in sister Erna's handwriting. Chiron-Werke, the manufacturer of precision mechanical and surgical instruments, had asked her whether Anita wanted to come back and work for them. They had rented a big place on the corner of the Hauptstraße as accommodation for the workers, so there would be no problem.

As she held the letter, Anita looked up, the mythology not lost on her. Chiron the demi-god centaur, wise and just, the constellation in the heavens, had offered reprieve. Had the stars aligned? In that moment, she had already forgotten there would be a price to pay.

Having shared the news, she retreated to her room, opened her writing desk and prepared to compose a response. Where to start? What to say? She was thankful for the opportunity, but the reasons were complicated. She was exhausted from the tension with her father; the fear of what he might do to imperil both her life and that of Franz-Theo. He had already threatened to hand her over to the Gestapo, his own daughter. She felt sick to her stomach. She no longer felt any allegiance to the Reich, but God forbid anyone should divine that. The work she was doing was innocuous, but she had not fitted easily into the office and didn't really care for the company she was obliged to keep or the pretence she needed to maintain. There were other things, more pressing on her mind.

If she left Aachen, it would be good to be close to her sister Erna and her young family, but she would miss terribly the love and support of her dear mother. She had already lost the additional comfort of the family's maid, Maria, for whom there was neither the money nor the room to retain her loyal service and companionship; kindness that only amplified her mother's goodness. And, now that they were re-established in new premises, she still had her room with its furniture and books, fine curtains, the plumped comfort of her big featherbed, a wardrobe of elegant clothes and pictures on the walls. Would she leave all this for the unknown functional blank of worker accommodation?

Ever cautious after the bombing in January 1941, it had been agreed that the most precious items would be carefully packed into two trunks and secreted in the cellar – too small and dangerous in the event of an attack should the door be blocked by fire or rubble. The Limoges porcelain dinner set, long-stemmed crystal glasses, Meissen vases and the engraved family silver, together with boxes of photographs, were all wrapped and painstakingly arranged before being secured and carried downstairs. Carl had reviewed the whole exercise with meticulous efficiency; Anna had turned over each piece recalling its special place in the family history; Anita had wondered whether she would ever see any of it ever again.

As she faltered between two worlds already divided, she heard her father's footsteps pass her door. The thump in her chest provided the answer; hope would triumph over fear. She would return to Tuttlingen and take her chances there. She drew the paper towards her, dated the sheet and, never one to write long letters, summarised her thoughts.

Aachen
September 3, 1942

My Dearest Erna,
Thank you for your kind letter and news about the children. I am especially glad to hear of the offer from Chiron-Werke and will write to them to accept the position.
It will take me only a few days to pack my things and catch the train to Tuttlingen where I will first come to you. From there I will make the further necessary arrangements.

With all my love,
Anita.

Stuttgart

Given that the Earth rotates anti-clockwise once every 23 hours, 56 minutes and 4 seconds in relation to the stars, while hurtling around the sun at 30 kilometres per second, it's perhaps not surprising that the astral alignment was brief. The heaven-sent peace Anita had hoped for was soon scattered across the firmament.

As he watched each image slowly swim into focus in his dark room developing tank, it also became clearer to Franz-Theo that staying in Aachen brought with it risks, both to his own safety and to Anita's. Whenever they met, he saw beneath her beguiling smile a watchfulness of their surroundings; a wariness when someone passed close by. He sensed her anxiety carried from the tension at home and the unpredictability of her father in the face of his thwarted discipline. He was, after all, trying to protect his position and the safety of his family;

he didn't need his daughter's recklessness to become exposed. As he worked, Franz-Theo recognised the irony of him bringing the latent images to light, while Carl Gallo attempted to keep his daughter's friendship in the dark.

With his photographs achieving recognition from a growing portfolio of portraits and intimate cityscapes and armed with a letter of recommendation from the Kuphalts for whom he had worked, Franz-Theo set out for Stuttgart. It was an odd choice. On the one hand, there was an artistic community in a large city stitched between the hills and valleys between forests and vineyards, so it appeared relatively safe and was well-protected by heavy anti-aircraft batteries; but on the other hand, much of the Jewish population had been deported by train to Riga years earlier. On top of that, there had already been a number of Allied bombings that had wrought increasing destruction.

There were, however, two defining considerations. Without work, there would be no money, no food and little chance of survival, sheltered by sympathisers or sleeping in barns, while trying to evade the authorities. The other was Stuttgart's proximity to Tuttlingen and to Anita. He would take his chances.

He arrived in the evening when the silhouettes of branches stood black against a sky smudged with grey clouds, their underbellies a dusky pink as the light faded. Despite the chill air, he strolled leisurely to the address he'd been given, taking in the architecture, the chimney pots against the deepening sky, the ornate facades, the contrasts of light and dark, the line and shadow of the street.

Once he arrived, reality and doubt became his companions. The photo-studio of the highly respected Adolf Lazi had no need of another amateur photographer, no matter how talented. Other ateliers were struggling to survive but, most of all, he was met with the same questioning look: why was a young man with a camera wandering around looking for artistic work while Germany was at war?

After two days of rejection, the whole city felt hostile. He wrote to Anita.

My dearest Weli,

Hopefully, you are well and you have found yourself in a more comfortable environment in Tuttlingen, albeit far from your family. At least you have Erna, Emil and the children nearby.

Having come to Stuttgart with high hopes for work in any of the photo-ateliers, I appear to have stumbled into a brick wall. The city is on edge and I have heard some terrible stories of deportations to the Riga Ghetto and thereafter to Kaiserwald. Gunshots had been heard throughout the day and later it was discovered that thousands of Jews had been massacred by the Einsatzgruppen and Latvian military police in the Rumbula forest. As I learn more, especially about the bombings in September last year, the situation here becomes more unsettling by the day.

I now find myself in an uncomfortable predicament. Each time I have presented myself for work, the continued refrain is, 'There is no work like this for you; you have to work in the war industry.' Although I am not interrogated verbally about my situation, it is plain that people are suspicious. It is possible that someone may say something to the authorities, in which case it shall not be interrogation, but a gunshot to the head.

If, in your position at Chiron-Werke, it is possible to enquire discreetly on my behalf if there is any work, it might yet be possible to escape unscathed from my overly optimistic decision to try my fortune here.
To be away from you is unbearable. You can barely imagine how much I need your company, how much easier this struggle becomes when we are together.

Johannes

By the time the police had tracked Franz-Theo to the rented room in Stuttgart, he was already on his way to Tuttlingen. Anita had spoken to her supervisor, Dr. Schoenler, saying only that a friend had found it difficult to find continuing work for the war effort in Stuttgart and would take whatever employment was available. Enquiries were made, the situation was resolved and, "yes, there was work for him in the surgical instrument laboratory in the factory further up the hill".

Since no further accommodation was available on the Hauptstraße, Franz-Theo set about finding accommodation elsewhere, finally alighting in the tiny attic of a modest house owned by Frau Manz. Despite life's unkindness, she was a kindly soul, generous of heart. Her thinning hair was coiffed to be as bouffant as possible; atop a face lined with loss and care. Even so, her eyes were still lively and it was possible to imagine a life filled with happier times before the death of her husband and the alienation of her family. Better still, as far as Franz-Theo was concerned, she asked few questions.

What misguided angel directed Anita, in a letter to her mother, to reveal that Franz-Theo was now residing in Tuttlingen, was a mystery beyond comprehension. Perhaps it was simply the unshakeable bond of love and trust between a mother and daughter; perhaps it was relief to have him nearby, or unabashed simple honesty. Did she imagine, even for an instant, that her father would not hear of it?

Hear he did. So apoplectic with fury was his response that Anna feared he would have a heart attack, would explode in a torrent of shouting that not all the bombs that fell on Germany could silence. He stamped about the place, fulminating, slamming doors and then sitting with his head between his hands, exhausted by his own anger. Finally, he spoke.

"They have deceived us; they have cheated us. They have conspired, against my clearly expressed demand, to be together and, in so doing, to put us all at risk."

He stopped, lips compressed, breathing heavily through his nose. He shook his head.

"I have written to the fellow and told him I will turn him over to the Gestapo. And he has defied me! A Jew in Germany – and he has defied me! And Anita – what does she think? Does she have no idea?"

He paused again, as if trying to understand what idea she might have. Then, suddenly resolute, through clenched teeth he made his staccato pronouncement.

"I will put an end to this. I will write to Erna. I will let her know. I will tell her that her sister has betrayed us. She will know that I have informed soldiers in the SS. It will not be the end for me, but it will be the end for him. And it will be the end for Anita."

He took a deep breath. Sitting on the floor, her head in her hands, Anna silently sobbed her heart out.

It was not Erna, but Emil who wrote back.

Herr Gallo,

If you have any concern for your daughter, it is concern first born out of love. No father who ever loved a child would do what you are proposing, because the consequences are certain death, and death that will not go unpunished. Your daughter will be shot – and you will have pulled the trigger. Her blood will be on your hands, and your wife will never let you lay those hands on her ever again. You will lose everything you ever had, all in a fanatical effort to save it.

As for Franz-Theo, you know what will happen to him. He will be sent to a concentration camp where he will undoubtedly perish. And while that might not particularly trouble you, he has done no wrong other than to be caught up in a tragedy of time and circumstance outside of his own making.

Meanwhile, you have another daughter and a son-in-law. You have three grandchildren. Their lives will be forever scarred. Here in Tuttlingen we are a well-respected pharmacy business with a considerable reputation. The Müller family is highly esteemed and we will not have our name besmirched by your selfish havoc involving the police and the Gestapo.

If you proceed with this madness, we will make sure you alone will be made responsible for the inevitable disaster that will follow. We are warning you to desist. The situation will resolve itself, one way or the other, without your interference.

If you retain any shred of self-respect, you will do nothing.

Emil Müller

When she learned the consequences of her unwitting revelation, Anita was devastated. On top of that she was feeling sick, whether with migraine or flu or both. She excused herself from work, closed herself in her room and retreated to the sanctuary of her bed.

For two days, fever gripped her and the pressure behind her eyes was relentless. Whichever way she turned there was no comfort, till in the end she lay still, her breathing shallow and her eyes closed.

Finally, on the third day, the distemper subsided to be replaced by hunger. Having surrendered her coupons so that she could have the meals provided downstairs, there was nothing to be had here. Completely washed out, she tried to sit up. Her head swam and the room appeared to close in on her. Again she tried. This time she managed the pillow behind her and leaned back, pulling up the covers. Breathing hard, she realised she was still too weak to get up, shower, get dressed and go downstairs. She sat there, staring ahead. What now?

As if in answer, there was a gentle knock at the door. A pause. Then another tap and a woman's voice called, "Fraulein Gallo?"

"Hello?" Anita cleared her throat. "Hello, yes, you can come in."

The door opened and Anita recognised Erna's maid Hannah. She was carrying a covered basket and wearing a look of misgiving.

"I'm sorry, excuse me," she began. "Your sister asked after you and was told you were not well. She was concerned and thought you might need something to eat or drink. I have brought you this."

She folded back the cover to reveal some bread, schinken, wurst and cheese; even a small cake and some apples, together with a glass bottle of water.

"She would have come herself, but they are busy in the shop," she apologised. Then she added, "We hope you will be better soon. Is there anything else we can bring you?"

"Thank you, but no," replied Anita. "This is lovely and will keep me going till I can go downstairs again to the cafeteria. Please thank Erna and tell her not to trouble herself. It is probably best she doesn't come here herself. I will visit when I am better. Thank you. Thank you for coming."

Hannah set the basket on the chair by the bed. Then, with a small bob she turned and let herself out, quietly closing the door behind her.

Anita sat there, worried. What enquiries had been made? How did they know she was not well? Why did Erna send her maid when she could surely have come herself? It was probably better that she didn't come, that she didn't become involved. Nobody else should become implicated by her decisions. She had made her mind up, dangerous as it was, and would accept the consequences. She felt a surge of defiance. Hannah had appeared uneasy; so she must know something. Perhaps people in the factory were whispering. Perhaps her father had already made a move. And where was Franz-Theo? Was he in contact with Emil and Erna? Who had come to visit him in the attic at the house of Frau Manz?

She turned over the questions again and again until, finding no answer, she reached for the basket to replenish her strength.

The following afternoon, it was a Sunday, there was again a gentle knock at the door. Anita was resting, just dozing; her mind for the moment at rest.

"Yes, hello; who is it?" she called.

"It is only me," came Franz-Theo's voice.

"Come in; come in. What a surprise! Oh my dear man, how wonderful."

He entered and closed the door carefully behind him. Anita sat up, pulled up the sheet and plumped the featherbed. She looked at him, suddenly revived, eyes shining. He crossed to the bed and gently kissed her before pulling up the chair and sitting by her side. He looked at her, saw the tousled hair, the sudden flush of colour to her face; sensed the urgency of her love. She was so happy she wanted to cry. Instead, she blinked and then reaching for his hand, asked, "So how are you? How is everything? Are you all right? Are you safe? What has been happening? How did you know where to find me? Tell me."

And so he told how, not having heard for several days or having seen her, he had asked among the other workers who had given him the worrying news; how he had avoided going to the pharmacy; how he had kept to himself while trying to find out about the progress of the war by listening to radio broadcasts. It was, of course, illegal. If the attic were raided and his shortwave radio discovered, he would most certainly be shot. The BBC was an enemy radio station, as were those German radio frequencies whose traitorous broadcasts 'weakened the resistance of the German people'. But they persisted anyway, even if it meant imprisonment or death. The German broadcasts played triumphant military music and marches, only to be interrupted by repeats of Hitler's speeches and claims that Germany was acting in self-defence or was only bombing military installations. It seemed, said Franz-Theo, that things were only going from bad to worse.

Behind him, the door crashed open.

As he spun half round in his chair, his raised hands open in front of his face, Franz-Theo saw the uniforms. Schutzstaffel. The knee-high leather boots; the red swastika armband; the sig-runes on the collar patches; the black leather shoulder cross strap to the belt buckle with its swastika and imperial eagle; the words "Meine Ehre heißt Treue". Blinding.

Two of them. Impossible. His heart thumped in his chest; blood roared in his ears.

In the same instant, Anita jolted upright in her bed, clutching at the covers. Her eyes were wild; her scream silenced by terror. She felt her heart in her throat. A wave of despair washed over her. So this was it; this is how it would end.

They stepped into the room, taking in the scene: a young woman respectably attired in her bed; a younger, well-dressed man in a jacket and tie sitting in a chair nearby; the room tidy, everything in its place. The taller of the soldiers turned his head to the side and looked at them intently, inwardly looking for answers to an unasked question. Finally, he asked, "Is Frau Fischer living here?"

Anita shook her head. It took a moment to find her voice. She swallowed and took a breath.

"I'm sorry, I do not know a Frau Fischer."

The soldier looked at her again, testing her answer in his mind.

"Very well," he said. "That is all." He looked again at Franz-Theo. Then, with a small click of his heels, he turned and left the room. His colleague marched after him.

Footsteps faded down the hallway. The world stalled. For several minutes they sat in silence and then Franz-Theo stood up and closed the door.

"They were looking for something; and it was not Frau Fischer," said Franz-Theo at last.

"They were looking to see if there was an excuse to arrest you. To see if there was something improper, if we were doing anything wrong or immoral. Instead, they just saw two people quietly talking."

"But somebody has said something. How else did they even know I was here? I cannot be certain, but..." he paused. Anita finished the sentence for him. "You think my father had something to do with it, yes?"

"It is possible. He has threatened exactly this. But it could be anybody. There is such fear everywhere; children are turning in their parents; neighbours are inventing stories about each other to show their loyalty to the Führer. Loyalty, 'Meine Ehre heißt Treue' – My Honour is my Loyalty – and for what? Loyalty to a regime that has rained death and destruction across Europe? There is no honour in that."

He paused, before continuing, "We cannot go on like this. I cannot put you again in the position you found yourself today. It is not fair to you, to your family. I am tired of the war, and this is no life, not for either of us.

When you are strong enough, I think you should visit your parents in Aachen. You need to make peace with your father and be nurtured again by the love of your mother. I will go back to Stuttgart, to the authorities there, and plead my case once and for all."

They were quiet for a while before Anita replied.

"I will return to Aachen to do as you suggest. But you will not go to Stuttgart alone; I will come with you. Together we will have a better chance; together we will know where we stand. And, if it comes to it, together that will be the end of it. There is no other way."

She took his hands in hers, looked him in the face and said, "Without you, there is no way."

Returning to Stuttgart was high risk. For a long time they sat in silence on the train. Franz-Theo recalled the emptiness of his last visit, a sense that the city had closed itself off, a premonition of failure. Only this time, they would be walking into the maw of the beast, Gestapo headquarters and putting their lives on the line. What could they possibly hope to achieve? To have their relationship sanctioned? All he wanted was to be left in peace, to have the constant threat removed – to be free of the fear that at any moment he would feel a pistol pressed against the side of his head and be arrested. And for what?

Beside him, Anita squeezed his hand and looked into his troubled face. He marvelled that she appeared so calm; appeared so lovely. What would they do to her? What would become of both of them as they leapt off the precipice together?

"It will be all right," she said. "We are doing nothing wrong; we wish no harm to anyone. We will tell them the truth and we will know where we stand. We will do what we have to do. And then we shall see."

By late morning they arrived under sky that seemed not to have made up its mind and, having found the place, waited on a bench in the hallway. Portraits of the Führer hung either side of a clock that ticked interminable minutes. Franz-Theo wondered for whom time was running out.

Finally they were ushered into an office and the door closed. The officer was a small man, thin lips, square face and an immaculate uniform. His eyes were grey and his movements considered and precise. He wore a wedding ring on his right hand. He returned to his seat behind a large mahogany partner's desk, pressed the ends of his fingers together and said,

"You may sit."

There was a moment of awkwardness as chairs were shifted and suddenly the whole situation seemed to lurch out of control towards futility.

Anita spoke.

"We have come here to explain our situation ..."

"Names?" she was interrupted.

"Fraulein Anita Gallo and Herr Franz-Theo Metzger." The officer looked at them, not moving. There was no paper, no pen. While he wrote nothing, it was clear he had recorded the information.

"And so, Herr Metzger, what is the situation you wish to explain?"

"There appears to be some bureaucratic confusion about my ancestry which makes my position in Germany now more difficult than perhaps it should be. In particular, it makes my relationship with Fraulein Gallo exceptionally difficult, given that she is the daughter of a high-ranking government official. Under no circumstances do I want to put her in an uncomfortable position."

"So you are Jewish and you want to marry a German girl." The tone was clipped.

"That we wish eventually to marry is true, but that I am Jewish is not entirely accurate. As you are no doubt aware, Jewishness is matriarchal, passed down from the mother. My mother was Catholic and I remember as a child we would visit the cathedral in Köln, for her a particularly sacred place. I had no idea about my father's religion until I learned that he had been arrested in March 1938. It was not something that was ever talked about."

"He was arrested for being a Jew."

"So I understand. But I am not. My mother was German as I said. As for my father, he lived much of his life in Germany, he fought in the First World War on the side of the Germans. He put his life at risk for this country. He has worked hard, built a life for my mother, paid his taxes. He has been a good citizen."

"But he is a Jew and you are his son, no matter how you try to argue the question. And now you have complicated your life by your relationship with this woman."

Anita spoke again.

"I see that you wear a wedding band. Does that not say anything about your understanding of the love between two people? This is not some frivolous 'relationship' and I am not just 'this woman'. We would not have come here, putting ourselves at risk, if this were not fundamentally important to both of us. There are some things in life that are bigger than politics, race or religion and we both have made sacrifices to try to make a life together. Herr Metzger no longer has a family; I have been obliged, for the sake of peace, to forsake my own. We are alone in Germany and we have come to you to find a way that we can be together, without persecution and without the constant threat of arrest or execution."

She paused, flushed by her own forthrightness. The officer sat immobile, expressionless, totally devoid of emotion. He looked at them, unblinking, with his steady grey eyes. It seemed there was nothing more to be said. Finally, Franz-Theo asked,

"Is there anything we can do, any information we can provide that will assist you to make a decision? Are there others with whom we might speak? Do you have any advice for us?"

After a long pause, the officer folded his hands neatly in front of him.

"Yes, this is my advice. These liaisons are frowned upon in Germany, in fact they are not tolerated. If you cannot accept that, then you should shoot yourselves."

So saying, he pulled open the top right hand drawer, took out a nine millimetre Luger pistol and laid it on the desk.

"If you cannot do that, then I will do it for you. This interview is terminated." He picked up the weapon, toying with it. "Now leave."

There was nothing for it but to stand, collect their things and go. Franz-Theo opened the door and Anita passed though, turning back to look directly into the square face, the expressionless eyes, the man holding a gun.

"What man are you?"

She turned on her heel and they were gone. The gun clicked.

As they stepped into the street Franz-Theo asked, not unkindly,

"What were you thinking? To challenge him like that. He could have shot us."

"He would not have wanted our blood spattered over his office."

"He could shoot us in the street and have his lackeys clean up afterwards."

"He is a small man whose manner is to appear larger than he is. His pistol is larger than he is. He is bound by rules. Anything outside the rules would simply confuse him. Besides, he was rude. He has to know I am not someone who can be interrupted or treated like a nobody. We have done nothing wrong and he threatened us."

"There was certainly no hope in trying to convince him. We can only hope that Germany will lose the war and that will be our salvation."

They walked back to the station and waited for the train.

"We came here," said Franz-Theo, "to learn where we stand. There is obviously no hope for us in Germany and I suspect in the short term things will only get worse. In fact, I think we are lucky to even get out of here alive – and we don't yet know what consequences will come from today's encounter. And trying to leave Germany has its own problems. We have no money; we would have to find work. You would have to leave your family completely; your mother would be heartbroken."

"Johannes, my dear man, you already know that wherever you go, I will go with you. Even today, we had no idea where we would find ourselves."

"You are a brave woman. Every day, you amaze me. But where we might go, I have no idea. It seems nowhere is safe and no-one can be trusted."

"Do you not remember your friend in Aachen, Albert Steiner? He is a man of influence, leader of the Catholic Youth with lots of international contacts. He is a good man and has said already that if we needed help, we could come to him. If anybody is to be trusted it will be him. What do you think?"

"It's a good idea. I will write to him – but of course will have to be discreet – to arrange a meeting as soon as possible. It will not be easy, especially now that we are being watched."

Just how hard it would become to slip the tightening noose was yet to be revealed.

On the Thursday after their return from Stuttgart, Thor unleashed his thunder. It began as a sharp flash of light and dread. Franz-Theo looked up from his lens polishing workbench in the factory to see three Gestapo soldiers walking towards him. Three together meant their intentions were serious. Were they here to arrest him, drag him away? There was nowhere to run, nowhere to hide. What did they know? Who had sent them? What did they want this time?

"Herr Metzger?"

"Yes." He looked from one to the other, saw the same implacable determination in their faces, an expression of cold satisfaction that came from unassailable authority. They were not much older than him but had experienced life's cruelty as perpetrators rather than the quarry. A universe separated them from Franz-Theo, and yet here they stood face to face.

The tallest of the three reached inside his coat pocket and withdrew an unsealed envelope. From it he drew a sheet of paper, unfolded it and laid it on the bench.

"You will read this and then you will sign the document."

Franz-Theo picked up the page. His hand was shaking. He put the sheet down again and rested his hands on either side, trying to mask his fear. He tried to focus on the words. At first he only saw the official letterhead *Geheime Staatspolizei* in the top left hand corner, then the typewritten date inserted on the right. At the bottom was a stamp with the eagle and swastika. It took him a moment to focus on the typewritten text.

> *Effective immediately, any further contact with Fraulein Anita Gallo is denied, no matter for what purpose. I, Herr Franz-Theo Metzger, whose signature appears below, swear that I will make no attempt to communicate with her or her family, under pain of arrest and deportation to a labour camp.*

There was a dotted line on which he would sign.

He read the words again; no further contact, no communication. He looked up at the soldiers.

"I cannot sign this document. It is unreasonable; it is not fair, not just."

The second soldier flipped open his leather holster, took out his Walther P38 and uncocked it. Stepping across to Franz-Theo, he pressed the muzzle to the side of his head.

"You will sign, or I will blow your brains against the wall."

Franz-Theo sank to his knees. He saw nothing but the blood behind his eyes; heard only a roaring in his ears. If he could not see her again, he would be better dead. To sign would be death. Not to sign would be death. What did it mean to sign? What part of himself would he give away? What if he signed, but disobeyed the order? Signing was a betrayal, betrayal of Anita, betrayal of himself. Being shot here would be the final betrayal of his love for Anita, a betrayal of his hope for their life together. If he died here, he would not even had had the chance to say good-bye. How would she hear the news? What would she expect him to do?

The sharp press of cold steel jabbed against his temple decided him. He would sign, but the mark he made would not be the man who made it.

He rose to his feet and held out his hand for a pen.

The first diagonal stroke of the 'F' was a shield. Under it, two short strokes completed the letter. Then a dot. The top of the 'T' was another diagonal shield, the stem hidden beneath it. Another dot. The

'M' was drawn up from beneath the line into a jagged sawtooth, then a hesitant gap before the next three letters, another pause and the tail of letters condensed to three short strokes. That was it; a disconnected hieroglyphic. He looked at it and could not find himself.

The second soldier put away his pistol, picked up the letter to inspect the autograph and then looked at Franz-Theo. He shook his head but said nothing as he handed it to his comrade. After a cursory glance, he said,

"You know that if we come to see you again, it will be a very different story."

All three turned on their heel and marched out of the building.

⌒

That evening, Franz-Theo returned to his attic too disturbed to know his next move. Sensing he was under increased surveillance, the best thing to do was keep an even lower profile than before. If he was seen heading out, it had to be by himself, only going to work or getting food. Even posting a letter now could appear suspicious. He thought about asking Frau Manz to deliver a message to Anita at the factory, but that would unnecessarily involve her, invite suspicion at Chiron Werke and potentially backfire. Even to send her on a mission to Erna and Emil would drag her family back into the conflict. The safest option would be for him to report to work as usual and hope that Anita would make her own cautious enquiries within the organisation so that he could explain his absence and his silence.

Meanwhile, he tried to unravel what had happened. At first, he imagined it was Carl Gallo again who had been making trouble in his obsessive belief that his life, future pension and the security of his family, would be preserved if he could remove the troublesome Jewish youth from his daughter's attention. It was a ridiculous delusion, for the simple reason that the progress of the war and the likelihood of Germany's defeat was a far greater factor in destroying everything than the short-term danger he might be. Then again, the simplistic reasoning of the Stuttgart Gestapo had made it abundantly clear that being the son of a Jew, no matter how loyal a German subject, was sufficient to collapse a house of cards.

The more he thought about that potential suicide mission, the clearer it became that the cold little man with the Luger had made his move. They had challenged his administrative authority, appealed to reason and compassion. That had failed. Anita had challenged him as a man. She had seen through the mask of detachment, saw the weakness hiding beneath the inflexibility of rules. Recognised the vanity of the man climbing through the ranks with controlled precision. Unable to pull the trigger, he had sent three of his henchmen to do his vindictive work. And he had won. For the moment and from some 130 kilometres away, he had the upper hand.

Steiner

Steiner's letter of reply was brief, giving away nothing.
Dear Mr. Metzger,

It would be a pleasure to again share your company, with friends, when next you are in Aachen. I am sure you will remember where to find us over the next two weeks.

Travel safely,
Kind regards,
Albert Steiner.

Franz-Theo recognised the implicit meanings: there was no reference to his own letter that might raise suspicion; 'friends' could include Anita; the address was not stated and safe travel meant that he understood there were risks of being followed. He only had a window of two weeks. To not invite questions at work, it would mean travel only during the weekend break. He questioned that thought and a possible alternative.

It was not the only good news that day. It was already dark outside when he was interrupted by a gentle tap on the attic door. He got up to answer it, expecting Frau Manz, and opened it to see Anita standing there wearing a long coat and with her head swathed in a scarf.

"Weli," he whispered in disbelief. "Weli, how wonderful to see you. Come in, come." He stood aside and looked over her shoulder to see there was no-one on the stair and then quietly closed the door.

"Does anyone know you're here?"

"Only Frau Manz who let me in."

They looked at each other and then held one another in a long and silent embrace. Suddenly, all the promise of life was re-kindled as he felt the press of her body against him, the softness of her cheek against his face; smelled the sweetness of her skin; the wisp of hair on her neck. He wanted to laugh and cry at the same time.

They parted and he took her coat and scarf and pulled up two chairs.

"Tell me, what brings you here?"

"When I had not heard from you for some days, I asked the girls in the factory whether anything unusual had happened. Nobody knew anything, so I casually asked Dr. Schoenle how things were going in the lens manufacturing department and, because he knows you, asked whether he had seen you at work. He told me you were there, but that the Gestapo had also been to the factory, although he was unsure why. Of course, I imagined the worst, but knowing you were still alive, I came to see how you are."

"You know, it's now more dangerous than ever for us to be seen together; even for you to risk coming at night. But thank goodness you came wrapped up in the dark."

He then proceeded to tell her of the ordeal in the factory, the impossibility of having to sign a document he knew he could never honour and his conclusion that the visit to Stuttgart had been the stimulus for the ultimatum.

"See, I knew that man was an ambitious weakling without a soul. The way he just sat there, smug, self-righteous, giving away nothing. But of course now, it means we must be even more careful."

"You are absolutely right. I no longer see any way we can remain in Germany if we are ever to be together. I think it best that I leave Tuttlingen and go to Freiburg where I might find some accommodation and perhaps work. Nobody must know where I am. In the meantime. I have written to Steiner in Aachen asking for help. You will remember he has offered support before because he understands our situation. He has contacts internationally in his role as leader of the Catholic Youth Organisation."

Franz-Theo paused, watching the expression on Anita's face. In those shifting clouds he sensed her apprehension that he would be gone; saw that she was piecing together the yet unspoken plan that might untangle them from the web being spun around them; admitted the risk between fear and hope. Leaning forward, he took her hand.

"It will be all right. Today I received a reply from Steiner. He will see me – see us, if you want – in Aachen. It is only there that we can speak freely without fear of correspondence being intercepted or any arrangement being exposed."

"But we cannot travel together. That would be too dangerous and we have very little time. We cannot risk inviting suspicion."

"Let us make our way separately. We have the address and we can make a time to meet at the house. You will have to find an excuse to be absent from work. After what has happened to me, I shall simply disappear. When my absence is noted, people will draw their own conclusions as they piece together the events of the last few days."

He paused, trying to shut out the grim alternative to the already impossible choice he had made. Anita kept her silence. Her heart ached as she regarded the man weighted not only by his layers of grief but by the precariousness and uncertainty of the road ahead.

It was late and eerily quiet by the time she left. No moon, but heavy cloud lay over the town as she made her way silently through the dark. Her mind repeatedly churned the arrangements they had made, testing the detail, alternately anxious and exhilarated. Things could not stay the same and while the progress of the war and Germany's fate, including the repercussions for her family, were beyond her control, she would embrace her destiny with all the strength and hope she could harness. After all, had she not already made her choice?

⌢

As he had planned, Franz-Theo slipped unnoticed from Tuttlingen, heading the ninety kilometres west to Freiburg. Separated from Anita, he found himself in a world between worlds, disassociated from reality, suspended in isolation. Even so, he reasoned they would both be safer without being seen together, subject to the whispered gossip among co-workers or the covert scrutiny of the police or Gestapo. Anonymity might bring indemnity.

A small sign in a window – Zimmer frei – a vacancy in a modest house, afforded inconspicuous accommodation. The owner was a young woman forsaken with two young children while her husband was away in the war. Left with the responsibility of managing on her own, she had cleared out a room to earn a little keep that might put food on the table and quell the crying of her infants. Franz-Theo's reluctance to leave the house afforded her the opportunity of his company while she regaled him variously with tales of woe and her hopes for the future – if ever her husband returned alive and sane. With surprising patience, her lodger listened to her stories without telling anything of his own.

Meanwhile, feeling ever more isolated in Tuttlingen, Anita was devastated by the absence of the man she loved and for whom she had forfeited her family. Erna with her husband and children living in the same town only made the pain of separation more poignant, reminding her of what once was and how brutally unfair it was that her life – and the whole world – was ruptured in war. There were moments of grief in which she questioned her choices, fleetingly tempted to be reconciled, to resume her life from where it had been broken. Just as quickly, she recognised that the plans she had dreamed had been swept aside as life took their place; how being forced to remain in Germany had now led to the necessity to leave.

She decided to abandon the factory accommodation and move into the attic of Frau Manz. It would distance her from her co-workers, afford the isolation she needed and affirm the continuity of their plan. Besides, Franz-Theo had lived here, slept here, needing to be close. She saw his face, heard in memory's ear the soft cadence of his voice, recalled the warmth and urgency of his embrace, felt herself engulfed in the sureness of his heart and mind. Yearning tore at her being, releasing tears enough to fill the void of his absence and threatening to drown her.

In Freiburg, Franz-Theo had secured work in the factory of Fritz Kuhnert, making prisms for antiaircraft guns. He struggled with the moral dilemma of contributing to Germany's war effort by shooting Allied aircraft from the skies, while at the same time wanting the war, with all its sickening nationalistic idealism and brutality, to end. He had been entrusted to do a job and owed loyalty to his employer, but his work, if imperfectly done, could sabotage the effectiveness of the defensive weaponry. And, potentially, that could bring an earlier downfall of the Reich. Preposterous to think in those terms. As if, in the face of Armageddon, a lens grinder could influence the course of history.

Having spoken with Kuhnert, Franz-Theo found him to be not just a businessman, but intelligent and intuitive – someone who would say less than he knew and understood more than he might reveal. Even so, it would take time to grow the seeds of trust, and even then there needed to be a little light of exposure. Franz-Theo asked whether, in view of his temporary accommodation, any correspondence could be directed to the work address. Kuhnert looked at him, divining the sub-text of the request, and gave just the hint of a smile of understanding.

"I believe we can probably manage that."

With his situation now established, Franz-Theo called Aachen 31671 and spoke briefly to Steiner. "Please send correspondence to Rheinstrasse 62, Freiburg in Breisgau. Heartfelt thanks." When he replaced the telephone, he felt his heart in his mouth and found he was shaking.

A week later, Kuhnert handed him a letter. When he turned it over, Albert Steiner's stamp was on the back. Franz-Theo thanked him and secreted the envelope in the pocket of his coat. He would have to wait till he returned to his room before opening it.

No lens manufactured that day would be as focussed as the kaleidoscope of thoughts that formed and swirled and re-shaped themselves in Franz-Theo's brain. Tension lay in the waiting; not in the action. Delay only meant there was more time for other events to intervene, to de-rail the carefully assembled wagon of hope and liberation.

Once in his room, Franz-Theo locked the door and carefully opened the envelope.

On letterhead and typed:

Albert Steiner, Aachen, Dietrich-Eckart Str. 10
30.August 1942.

Dear Herr Metzger,
I was unlucky in Berlin. I travelled all night and arrived at Russischen Hof at 8:30 in the morning. Because I wanted to travel back the following night, I didn't take a room. For 13 years, I've been a regular visitor at the hotel. I thought I might at least leave a letter for you here. The porter wouldn't take the letter, despite my friendly insistence. He remained obstinate; polite, but cold as ice. I explained that I had no alternative but to give him the letter and asked he could make an exception. The answer: the fundamental consideration is that he must refuse. Others would come; the hotel was not a post office. I then spoke to management and got the same answer. I then gave the haughty German a piece of my mind and left. Because I didn't have your address, there was no possibility to contact you. By 9 o'clock

I had to be at another meeting. When I was finished at 5.30 in the afternoon, I went to the post office on Potsdamer Platz and sent a telegram to Dr. Krone at 649041. In it I asked Dr. Krone if he could please arrange a meeting place and give you the letter in case you called by. I also asked that my telegram should be sent from Berlin to you in Tuttlingen. Dr. Krone's address is Kaiserstrasse 43, Berlin-Friedrichshagen and he could help you with good advice.

From Dr. Krone I learned that Frau Dr. Luckner is in Freiburg (im Breisgau). You can ask for her address from the archbishop at the cathedral. She would be able to give you good advice in the matters that concern you. From Tuttlingen, a trip to Freiburg would easily be possible.

Now to your letter of the 28.8.'42. I thank you wholeheartedly for the trust both of you have invested in me. I am obliged as a man and a Christian to offer you my hand. But there are questions.

Firstly, why not wait? Current events are coming to a head. In deferring your ultimate purpose, nothing will be lost. Love knows no boundaries. Secondly, is this the time for the fulfilment of such a proscribed young love? If a child is brought into these uneasy times of one's life, under huge emotional strain for the mother, it may see the light of the world in circumstances that will not make life's journey easy. A child can mean endless joy for the parents. It can also bring much sorrow. Then ask yourself, in light of your own life, whether now you should just wait?

Thirdly, both your lives are precious, without danger, though you risk an undertaking that would destroy them. ...

2. September 1942

I have just returned from a trip to Magdeburg. There was not time for me to finish the letter I previously started.

... You would find the words "without danger" very curious because for you it's a real problem, you face real questions. I know how you could answer me, however – there is a virtue called PATIENCE. Therefore the question: why now bring your life into such peril? You must live your life by your own inner principles, but also avoid every confrontation with the civil law along the way. It's not easy, I know, but it is less dangerous.

From what I know and my inner conscience, I must say something else. Just as there is only one centre to a circle, exactly the centre, so there can be but one centre point for the conscience. I call it the three-part God: the Father, creator of all that is seen and unseen (the lawmaker who set the stars in motion; gave mankind its conscience) – the Son, light of light, who lived as Man amongst us and, by the will of the Father, lived out his holy law – the Spirit that is all Love and binds the father and the Son.

Do I believe in you? Yes, I believe in you because I know your upright character and your true inner strength. My foremost wish is that you never stray from the mercy and call of God.

Dear Herr Metzger, you are considerably younger than your lady who I hold in the highest regard. But you are also possibly more mature than others of your age. You are both travelling an extraordinary path. God will demand a lot from you, yes, a great deal. Much human strength and great compassion. Your ties will be fundamentally spiritual, the most loving symbol of this holy bond. With your growing years, ever greater. Only in this way will you be, and stay, happy. God bless you!
May God lead you.
Heartfelt with all my love,

Albert Steiner
And family.

Handwritten below:
Herr L. answered that he is currently travelling and cannot do anything for you at present. He will explore your concern. He is not hopeful because regulations have tied his hands.

Franz-Theo read and re-read the letter several times. There was less than he needed and more than he wanted, but enough in the potential contacts to keep hope alive. There were names and there were places. He needed only to make his introductions and wait.

He looked again at the three questions. Why not wait? Even if it were true that current events were coming to a head, how could there be any guarantee of the outcome once the end was reached? Besides, how long was the present situation able to be sustained? How long before the knock at the door, the tap on the shoulder or being marched into oblivion? Love might wait forever, but the Nazis would not.

As for the fulfilment of young love in these times, that is always a risk. How is this argument different from Carl Gallo's opposition to the relationship? Do they imagine my younger years or my ancestral heritage will make me less responsible, more restless, less capable of loyalty, love or support? Do they doubt the absoluteness of our commitment to one another? Just witness the trials to which we have both been subjected in this crucible, where the cruellest fires might lead to the creation of something new. And while Germany now forbids such marriages as we might make, whatever children are brought into this world will be as innocent, as sacred and as precious as the five you and Christa have conceived in this valley of the shadow of death.

As for danger, you are right. Every shadow, every noise, every anonymous face on the street, every footfall on the pavement behind me reminds me of the danger. I have felt its cold steel against my temple; I have seen it in the eyes of young men suited in uniforms bearing the twin lightning bolts of the SS. I have heard it in the arrogance in the voices of men inflamed with unchecked power. I have been on my knees with the fist of danger above my head. Yes, indeed: God has demanded much of me, but I fear God is busy somewhere else and I doubt I can wait for Him to rescue me now. Whatever gifts He has given me, and whatever help He has put in my way, it is my responsibility to seize it while I yet may.

❧

Five pairs of children's shoes were neatly lined up in the entrance porch of the house at Dietrich-Eckhart Strasse 10 in Aachen. Since Franz-Theo had travelled some days earlier, he met Anita at the railway station and together they walked to the Steiner's house, glad that their rendezvous had gone largely unnoticed. It felt strange that they should be here, in this town that had brought them together and that could just as easily tear both their lives apart. While the familiar city was indifferent, their presence here, on this day, made it feel hostile, menacing. What had once been comforting now felt threatening.

The door opened and there stood Albert Steiner, immediately warm and reassuring. A man in his late thirties, hair beginning to recede, his face kind and wearing spectacles. He spoke softly.

"Herr Metzger, Fraulein Gallo. Wonderful to see you have arrived safely. Come in."

He stood aside, gesturing into the hallway. Sanctuary. In the subdued light, on the wall by the door hung a small wooden crucifix inlaid with mother-of-pearl. A modest oriental rug on the parquetry floor softened their tread as they made their way to the living room. Christa Steiner rose to meet them, extending her hand and receiving the customary kisses on both cheeks. Her hair was tied up in a bun and her blue eyes were bright, but she looked tired and concerned.

"It is so nice to see you again," she said. "I understand that things have not been easy of late. You must be exhausted not just from travelling, but with all the things on your mind. Come, sit and I shall bring tea. I'm sorry we cannot offer you coffee, but you understand how difficult it is to get anything much at all with the way the country is at present." Graciousness and understanding remained as she left the room.

As they took their seats, Franz-Theo spoke. "You will please forgive me Albert – I can still call you Albert? – for this intrusion. I understand that our presence here constitutes a risk for you and your family. If the Gestapo knows I am here and imagines that you are somehow collaborating, it would mean considerable unpleasantness. Our lives are in danger; we do not want to imperil yours."

"Franz-Theo, we live in troubled times, but that should not stop us doing what we should – indeed, what we must. But we are also called upon to be careful."

"You will understand when I tell you," said Franz-Theo, "that we have tried to talk with the authorities, pointing out that in the Jewish diaspora my Jewishness is not even recognised because it is on my father's side. They simply do not understand the distinction or the argument. Perhaps what upsets them most is that I am seen with a German woman – and one from an important family. Or perhaps it is just Anita's father who, being against the relationship, seeks to destroy it through adherence to the Fuhrer's fantasy of a Herrenrasse, a pure Germanic race."

"What is even more disturbing," replied Steiner, "is the failure to understand the Abrahamic tradition. If I remember correctly, you said your mother was Catholic – as are we – your father Jewish and Fraulein Gallo Evangelische, in itself a federation of Protestant Christian denominations including Lutheran, Reformed Calvinist and United Russian. Judaism, Christianity and Islam all claim Abraham as their first prophet. Prophets mentioned in the Bible, the Torah and the Q'ran all lived in the Holy land, the same geographical region over the last four thousand years. We are all one – and what has happened in the meantime is an unfathomable tragedy. We use the term 'brotherhood of man' but it is a brotherhood, a sisterhood, of humanity – under one God."

While the men talked, Anita surveyed her surroundings, taking in the bookshelves that lined the room, the heavy drapes, the vase of flowers on the polished side table, the paintings on the walls and the photographs on top of the piano. Set into a niche was a Hummel figurine of the Madonna with a candle set in a blue crystal holder beside it. The calm elegance of the home, the soft light, books and music, all suggested harmony and a peace belied by the events outside its walls. She had noticed, as they walked the hallway past the children's rooms, that above each bed was an icon of their patron saint and a crucifix, their guidance and their defence. Five little ones in a line; five organ pipes playing from the same music.

Christa returned, shepherding three of the children, the eldest carrying a plate with home-made biscuits while she brought a silver tray with tea and cups and saucers. In approximate unison they chimed "Good afternoon Herr Metzger; Good afternoon Fraulein Gallo."

They set their offerings on the small side table.

"Hello, hello. Don't you just look lovely," said Anita, captivated by both their innocence and their good manners. Looking at the eldest, she asked, "Tell me your name again?"

"Hedwig," came the reply. Her blonde hair was tied into plaits either side and she wore a deep blue dress with the white collar simply embroidered around the edges. Her big blue eyes looked up at Anita, recognising the kindness in her voice while taking in the tall, elegantly dressed woman with the grey-green eyes.

"And what have you been doing today?"

"Reading," came the simple reply.

"And look at you," Anita said, turning to the boy. He looked up, bashful, unable to find any words.

"This is Norbert," said Christa. "He's a little shy, but he's a good boy; aren't you darling?" She stroked his cheek. "And this is little Walburga, not yet four years old. The other two, Mechthild and Roswitha are having a sleep."

"You are blessed to have such good and lovely children," said Anita. "I'm sure you have your hands full looking after them and keeping them safe."

"Yes, we are very fortunate and can only hope that they grow up in a world less troubled than the times in which we find ourselves now."

"Amen to that," added her husband.

"Let's leave these good people to talk," said Christa. "We shall come back later. Say good-bye." The three children's voices piped "Bye-bye" and were bundled ahead by their mother.

"And now," said Steiner turning to Franz-Theo, "to the matters that bring you here."

"The situation here in Germany has become impossible, not just for me, but for Anita." He proceeded to briefly outline the events in Stuttgart and in Tuttlingen, the ever-present fear that he was being watched and the inevitable consequences if he were to be apprehended again. Steiner listened, occasionally shaking his head in dismay. When he looked up there were tears in his eyes.

"Those are horrific events and I cannot understand how you survived them or how they must haunt your waking and sleeping. I am aware that there are continual deportations of Jews and have heard some of the accounts about what happens in the labour camps. I can see that life is precarious – and that your choices have made it more precarious still. But I am not here to judge; only to help as best I may. I begin to see that you wish to find a way to escape – perhaps to Switzerland. Am I right?"

"I see no other choice. I could try to make contact with the French Resistance or take advice from you where to find either a safe house or a way out. Where we have friends in Austria or France or Poland, there is no safety because of the occupation. Switzerland seems the most promising."

"While that may be true, I have also heard that betrayal exists everywhere – not just here where neighbours turn in their fellow Germans, where children betray their parents, but also abroad where fear or opportunism drive the worst of human behaviour and treachery. It is hard to know if anywhere is safe. However, if you are resolved on this course of action, I will need to make some enquiries and devise a plan that will see you secure. If I have an address, I can write to you, couching the substance in more innocent matters – you will have to read between the lines – and hope that you can avoid any repetition of the events that have beset you recently."

"I understand only too well the need for caution. Your own safety and that of your wife and children is paramount – for who you are as a family and for the work you do helping others. I would not wish to compromise that for anything."

Anita added, "We place ourselves in your hands, Herr Steiner, without putting you under any obligation. For whatever you can safely manage we shall be grateful. If there is no alternative, we shall have to deal with that when the time comes."

"Let us see," said Steiner, "In the end, we can but do our best and trust in God."

PART TWO

A LOVE COMPELLED

CHAPTER FIVE

Fall of the Axe

When Anita returned home there was a letter waiting on the hall table. The brown 'Deutsches Reich' postage stamp with the face of the Führer – oddly facing right she noted – had been over-stamped with the Freiburg postmark. The handwriting addressed to her was that of Franz-Theo. No return address on the back. She took it up to her room and opened it.

My dearest Weli,
You know only too well how much I would prefer to have you near and speak with you than to have to write. For reasons I have yet to understand, I have been obliged to find alternative accommodation, the details of which I cannot share here, other than to say I am safe and well.

The train to Freiburg is no longer an alternative for you and I suggest a similar rendezvous but at Immendingen. It will be a much shorter journey for you. Maybe you could leave some sign that you have arrived.

I trust that all is well in Tuttlingen.
ftm

Anita understood the need for brevity and caution. She wondered however what had happened. Her first thought was that her visits had somehow triggered suspicion and, even if they could not see their pursuers, they were still being shadowed. It would not do to become anxious; now was the time to hold one's nerve and remain resolute.

On the usual weekday, and at the same time, she took the train. It seemed no time at all before she arrived, the place teeming with German soldiers. Her heart sank. How would she negotiate a way through the crowd and how would she find Franz-Theo? Then she corrected herself: she was a good German citizen, doing nothing wrong, simply a woman with a parcel, her handbag and a red umbrella. She stood tall and stepped onto the platform.

Immendingen was busy. Trains changed direction, shuttling civilians as well as the military. She headed towards the waiting room, avoiding the shouts and stares of the soldiers. People were pushing past, but above the hubbub, out of the darkening western sky came a distant hum. Some of the soldiers paused, heads turned, listening intently, instinctively questioning the sound. Quickly it became a low growl, becoming steadily louder.

Suddenly, panic. British aircraft. Shouts. Run! Get down! Find shelter! Men foresaw yet again what they had so far managed to survive: strafer fire, shells exploding off the iron rails, plumes of earth, flashes of fire, smoke and streamers of light lacing the sky; heard the staccato rattle of the machine guns before the rising scream of engines as planes climbed the air again. Feared the flying shrapnel that whined past, splintered stone and wood or tore the flesh from bones.

The drone became louder, chopping the air as people ran, stumbling over one another, cramming into the building or fleeing across open ground into the nearby forest. Above them the air trembled as the heavy bombers made their way towards Mannheim and Augsburg. Wave after wave they came, flying low, sowing terror.

Anita rounded the building to the east, away from the approaching threat. With her heart pounding, she leant against the wall and tried to draw breath. Insane she thought, here we are trying to avoid being shot by the Germans and instead, we will be bombed by the Allies. Aircraft roared overhead. She placed the parcel of washing she had brought on the middle window sill and propped the umbrella next to it. Sufficient for her Johannes to recognise; then made her way out towards Bahnhofstrasse calculating that any attack would be on the rail lines rather than the street. She kept to the shadows, pausing in the recesses of the building. Only a few stragglers remained visible as the aircraft receded eastwards taking their immediate terror with them.

She rounded the building and cautiously scanned the platform. Nobody. Best to return the way she had come. Worried now that she may have missed him, or that he had caught a different train, she tried to work out what to do next. She could probably walk back to Tuttlingen – it only seemed a few kilometres and she would remain unnoticed. Or she could wait in case there was another train. For the moment, there was no need to do anything except to remain watchful.

Although clouds had obscured any winter moon, her eyes had accustomed to the dark. She pulled her coat tighter against the cold and rounded the corner of the building. Then she saw him, by the window where she had left her signal. Relief washed over her; she wanted to laugh, wanted to cry, wanted him to hold her, to be safe. Overwhelmed, she abandoned the customary caution and embraced him, felt the press of his body, smelled the skin of his neck and the comfort of his arm around her.

"Come, my darling Weli. We cannot stay here where bombs and machine guns might strike. We can head into the forest and find shelter there. Take my arm. Anybody who sees us here will not care who we are or where we have gone."

They headed across the road and up the hill into the trees, stumbling over the uneven ground till eventually they found a cluster of boulders behind which they might take cover. Franz-Theo gathered some of the forest floor litter and laid his coat over it that they might be more comfortable as they nestled together. They talked quietly before hearing again the distant onslaught of bomber aircraft. As before, they filled the sky with thunder as they passed overhead, their black silhouettes stamped against the sky or slipping between the layers of cloud.

"One can only wonder what destruction they will have brought before they rise and turn back," said Franz-Theo. "But I have to tell you what has happened in Freiburg and the latest from Steiner."

He then proceeded to recount his eviction from the house and his conversation with Kuhnert who had offered him sanctuary.

"But can he be trusted?" asked Anita.

"He had every opportunity to surrender me to the authorities, but I suspect he is sympathetic to my situation, though he knows nothing – or at least so I believe – about us. He does not question my allegiance, the quality of my work or ask about my family. And while the war serves his business well, I feel his conscience is troubled by what he knows. Like us, he waits for an end to this conflict that has conflicted him.

However, there is better news. I followed the trail laid down by Steiner and have now secured this."

He took from his coat pocket an envelope which he handed to Anita.

"You will not be able to read it in the dark, but there are two documents. The first is a letter from Steiner that confirms what he has already told us: that, as a Christian, he feels it his calling to help us and that we can rely on him. He acknowledges there are dangers for us – without referring to the dangers for him, which are equally terrible – and that he has also enclosed a letter to Swiss people he knows. A safe house. Once we have crossed the border, and hand over that letter, he assures us we will be safe."

Anita held the letter in her hands, sensing the kindness and the danger behind it. She remembered again the warm and intimate peace of the Steiners' family home, the faces of the children, the soft voices and the reassurance that came with authority and respect. If she questioned the risk, she had only to look skywards to know that remaining was riskier still.

She handed back the envelope. "So, what do we do now?"

"During the week, because you can move more freely than I, you will go alone to Singen and look for a place along the border where we might cross. You will need to look at a map first so that we are not at cross purposes. I will attempt to do the same, by myself so as to avoid any suspicion, and we will try to meet again in ten days' time, here at Immendingen, to share what we have found."

"And when we leave, do we bring anything with us?"

"Nothing. We can bring nothing at all. It must look as if we are simply walking in the forest and then we vanish. I have nothing except my camera. The few possessions rescued from my family home are in a box I sent to my father in Brussels. Who knows what has happened to them? Anything you want to keep you will have to pack into a crate or a suitcase and leave with Erna at the Engel Apotheke. They can put it in the attic or in the cellar. If ever we return, we can see what is left – and if we don't, then it won't matter anyway." There was a grim quiet.

"I have only my mother's letter with me in my handbag. Whenever I am most alone, I read it again and am reassured by her love. Even though she has it hard, I feel her mother's concern and her prayers for our safety and happiness."

They sat in silence for a while, resting against each other, carrying the weight of hope and uncertainty.

Pale dawn saw them cold and stiff from not moving, crumpled against the reality of a new and overcast day. Together they walked back to the station, the streets quiet, the terrors of the night temporarily dissipated.

Anita decided she would walk back, an hour or two at the most. It would give her time to assemble the events of the night into something less chaotic and prepare herself for the uncertainties that lay ahead. Franz-Theo tucked his parcel of washing under his arm and found a corner in the building to rest until the train came to take him back to whatever waited for him in Freiburg.

Each of them carried in their pocket a letter that would either condemn them to death or offer them salvation.

In the Tuttlingen library Anita pored over the clearest maps of the region she could find. Being a border town, Singen would be heavily patrolled and river crossings particularly perilous. She traced her fingers over the lines, creating a pathway she could remember. Southwest towards Büsingen am Hochrhein and Schaffhausen seemed to be the safest and thereafter into the forest just north of Gailingen. Then perhaps it would be easy enough to follow the path towards Buch or, better still, Ramsen.

As the train trundled southwards, Anita turned their plans over in her mind. Switzerland was neutral but protected its border. If they were captured before finding sanctuary, it was just as likely they would be shot by Swiss border patrols or returned to Germany and who knew what would happen then? There had been stories of Jews who had escaped being rounded up and handed over to the SS only to meet the same fate as those loaded onto cattle trucks and sent to Poland. The same would happen if they tried elsewhere. France was occupied and therefore even more dangerous. Steiner suggests Switzerland as the best alternative, and he has connections with the Polish Resistance, the French Underground and other cells to escape deportation in Belgium and Yugoslavia. His network is his faith and his trust in God; our only choice now is to trust him.

And what if we make it safely across? What then? We sit in hiding and wait for the war to end, maybe for years. What will happen to my family left behind in Germany? My dear mother; or my father unable to understand how or why his world has been turned upside down.

Even to imagine that sending Franz-Theo to his death might mean a reconciliation with me or a return to the life that has long disappeared in a world gone mad. Impossible. And Erna, always older and more clever, yet she still believes that somehow Hitler's promise of a strong and proud Germany is possible. As an upright German, she has nothing to fear from the Ordnungspolizei or the Gestapo. Her family is strong and her children are safe.

Maybe I will never see any of them again; never see my home again. The past will cease to exist except in memory. She paused. Looking out of the window, the present replaced the uncertain future as the train pulled into the station at Singen.

The day was still early and there were few people about as she stepped onto the platform. Pulling her coat tighter around her against the late winter chill, Anita headed out of the building and turned left onto Bahnhofstrasse before finding a seat in the nearby park. It was going to be a long walk, but far safer to try a crossing where the border ran through the forest than traversing open fields and farmland where one could be seen, stopped and questioned.

She set off again, keeping away from the main roads and weaving her way steadily in the direction she had planned. By late afternoon, she reached woodland and a narrow path between the trees. She followed it and then spotted the stone border posts with their line across the top, a letter D on the German side and S on the Swiss side. That was it; as simple as that. One stepped across the imaginary line between the posts and one was in Switzerland. Could it be so easy? Once through the forest and out into the countryside, what then? What if we are stopped, with no papers, no belongings. Do we just say we are lost? No good to think that way. She looked again, then listened. Just the soft soughing of the wind in the trees; not even a bird calling. She stepped forward between the posts and stood, waiting. Here I am, in Switzerland, safe. She stepped back again, out of the land of hope and imagination and into the urgency of escape.

She surveyed her surroundings once more, taking in the lie of the land, the trees around her and the path leading away. Resolute, she turned back the way she had come. By nightfall, tired and footsore, she sat on a bench in the dark and waited for the train that would take her back to Tuttlingen and the familiarity of her little attic.

In the days that followed, Anita began to pack her few belongings together, just a suitcase with some clothes, her copies of Schiller and

Rilke, a small document folder of letters and photographs and her travelling alarm clock. She debated whether to leave it with Frau Manz or take it to Erna at the Engel Apotheke where it might be stored in the attic. She wanted to avoid any explanations, but then thought it might be the last, perhaps only, chance to say goodbye to her sister, Emil and the children. Too risky to reveal anything of plans to flee or even hint of an absence. A careless word could be magnified; a question contrived into conspiracy. Revelation to Carl or to Anna Maria might well bring the Gestapo. Safer to say nothing and just disappear.

She sat on the edge of her bed with her problem packed in front of her. Her eyes welled with tears. Germany was lost, her family was lost; even her room seemed empty. Franz-Theo was a hundred kilometres away in Freiburg and wavering hope lay over the border to the south.

"Why am I doing this? I am no Glückskind, a lucky child; I am Anitachen, das gutes Kind, my mother's little Anita, the good child." She scoffed at the thought. "Not even in my childhood. Headstrong, stubborn. No, I am the black sheep of the family, chasing a dream, disregarding the advice of all who love me, save the man I love. Can I help it? Do I have a choice?" She looked at her case, reminding herself of what she had packed away. Then it came to her, Schiller's "Hoffnung", the lyrical pursuit of happiness in a better world. She recalled the lines, speaking them aloud to the door opposite:

Hoffnung
Es reden und träumen die Menschen viel
Von besseren künftigen Tagen,
Nach einem glücklichen gold'nen Ziel
Sieht man sie rennen und jagen,
Die Welt wird alt und wieder jung,
Doch der Mensch hofft immer Verbesserung.[7]

She had made up her mind. She would take her case to her sister Erna.

---

[7] *Hope*
People talk and dream on end
Of some better and fairer day
Towards some glittering golden goal;
Seen running and chasing.
The world grows old and then grows young
But the hope of man is betterment still.

The visit began awkwardly until the two boys came in, happy to see their Tante Anita and asking what was in her suitcase.

"Nothing important," she replied. "Just some summer clothes I don't need at the moment and I have very little room to hang them at my place. I can always come to collect them later. Now show me what you've been doing." Ottokar and Eberhard led her away to their room, talking excitedly and asking could she take them skiing next time it snowed. Little Hannelore was asleep in her cot, rosy cheeked and angelic.

Erna interrupted. "Come and have something to eat and drink; you look pale and tired. Is everything all right?"

"Yes, just tired from working long hours and wishing this war would end. It's no fun living alone, though I prefer my own company, especially in these dark winter months. It will be better in the spring."

"You know, you can always stay here. We have spare rooms. You can eat with us and the children are always happy to see you." She watched her sister's face, then added, "Is there something else troubling you?"

Anita was careful. "You already know, Erna, how difficult it is with our father and how I have had to leave home, for his sake, for Mutti's sake, and yours. Of course that is upsetting, but nothing stays the same and we can only hope that things improve."

"If you were to give up your relationship with Franz-Theo, or if something were to happen to him, you would be forgiven and we could all be a family once again. It hurts us all you know."

"God forbid that anything should happen to him. That, for me, is unthinkable. Even not knowing where he is, or if he is safe, is hard enough. Please, let us not talk about things we cannot change."

Erna sensed she would not learn more and they retreated to share supper. When it was time for the children to go to bed, Anita prepared to leave and little five year-old Eberhard asked, "Tante Anita, when will you come again?"

She touched his cheek. "Darling boy. I will come to see you as soon as I can and you can show me how well you can ski." Tears stung her eyes and she blinked them away, bending down to give him a hug. "Good night little man; sleep well."

She embraced Emil and Erna in turn, longer and more closely than a casual visit might merit. When Erna looked into her eyes again, she sensed something deeper, more serious. "Are you sure everything is all right?"

"It's fine. You know I was planted close to the water, so tears come easily. I have much to think about, beyond what I can speak. Maybe, in time, we can share more."

So saying, she turned, cutting a lonely figure as she walked into the swallowing darkness. She had left behind a suitcase of worldly things and brought with her a heart full of loss and longing.

The winter evening settled over Immendingen as the train from Freiburg pulled into the station and spilled its passengers onto the platform. Franz-Theo threaded his way clear looking for Anita or the tell-tale umbrella that would signal she had already arrived safely. In her absence over the last week, he had become withdrawn, retreating into the unremarkable anonymity of his work. His few possessions he had packed into a suitcase; he didn't expect to see them again. These were simply steps towards the unknown, steps taken in the belief that whatever he might intend, forces outside his reckoning would shape the outcome regardless. In what seemed only yesterday, how could he ever have imagined finding himself where he was now? He felt remote, detached from himself.

Then, standing in the shadow of the building, he caught sight of her wearing a long dark coat and a hat, her upright elegance undeniable among the departing stragglers. Impossible for her to remain unnoticed, he thought. He wanted to call out, to watch her walking towards him, savouring the anticipation and the warmth of her embrace. But for now, such enchantment was to remain suppressed until they were safe. He strolled casually past, knowing that she would follow him silently to the dark seclusion of the nearby forest.

Alone, together at last, they talked in hushed tones, eager for each other's news. In the fading light, Franz-Theo watched the outline of her face, the stray hair that brushed against her neck, listened to the cadence in her voice and heard nothing of what she was saying. She took his hand in both of hers.

"Johannes, are you listening? I have been to Singen. I had to walk for ages, perhaps because I was confused by what I remembered of the map, but then in the forest, there it was, the mark between Switzerland and Germany. One has only to step over the imaginary line and then, in another fifty or hundred metres, one is safe. I saw no-one there; there is nothing to it. What do you think?"

"It sounds promising. I too looked at a map but couldn't decide the easiest or safest place. Besides, for me to make the trip twice would attract attention, take much longer to and from Freiburg and therefore be too dangerous. I knew you would find a way."

"And when we are on the other side, what then? It will be dark, we don't know the way and we will have nothing to eat."

"We ask. There will be strangers to help us, perhaps even offer us a place to sleep or some food. We can say we are lost, that we are heading towards Ramsen. If there is nobody, perhaps we can find a barn. We just need to be careful, appear honest and friendly and trust that people are open and kind."

"So what shall we do?"

"We go. We have no other choice."

Their decision resolved, they talked quietly under the night sky, agreeing to travel separately; Franz-Theo from Freiburg via Immendingen to Singen and Anita from Tuttlingen, arriving as early as possible but at different times to meet in the park where Anita had rested before her journey. From there, they would reconnoitre together to find the posts that stood as sentinels to their freedom.

It was a cold, grey morning when they met again just outside Singen. Franz-Theo, as ever, appeared casually well-dressed wearing a long coat and scarf and carrying his Rolleiflex camera in its leather case with a shoulder strap. To the casual observer, he was just another young man taking a leisurely promenade. In his pocket burned the letter from Steiner.

Anita too had dressed with understated elegance, wearing a hat, coat and scarf against the late winter chill. In her handbag she carried a letter from her mother, a purse with a small amount of money, an embroidered handkerchief and the key to her attic in Tuttlingen. She wondered if ever she would use it again.

Together, they set off, first arm in arm and occasionally separated as they made their way along narrow or steep paths till, some hours later, they found themselves surrounded by trees and walking on the soft forest floor under dappled light. The world seemed strangely quiet, holding its breath; no birdsong, no sound of water or soughing of wind in the trees. They walked silently, occupied with their own thoughts, looking into the shadows, searching for a sign.

Abruptly, Franz-Theo stopped. He turned his head to listen. From nearby came the hollow ring of an axe resonating on the still air. It came again, a blow to cleave the heart. Anita looked at him, her eyes full of alarm and questioning.

"A woodcutter?" she whispered.

"Possibly." He waited and listened. It came again, irregularly, unevenly.

"Should we turn back?"

"If we turn back, our chance to escape is over. If it is simply a woodcutter, we have nothing to fear. Besides, we are merely taking a walk. If he stops to talk with us, we can simply ask for directions to somewhere nearby, or towards Schaffhausen."

Gathering themselves, Anita took his arm and they walked on. Ahead lay a clearing. In it stood the woodcutter. He waved a greeting, rested his axe against a log and walked across. An amiable conversation followed before the inevitable and obvious question.

"So, what brings you here, to this part of the world, walking in the forest? Are you going somewhere?"

Franz-Theo responded as casually as he had planned. There was much nodding and pointing before he finally gestured a farewell and they took their leave. They waited till well out of earshot before Anita asked in hushed tones, "Did you notice his hands? They were not the hands of a woodsman. They were not hands used to hard work. And his voice? He was not a simple farmer from around here. You could tell by his accent. Besides, he was trying too hard to be friendly."

"You may well be right. But look!" Franz-Theo pointed ahead. "That looks remarkably like the border post you described. And there's another beyond that one."

Anita's heart quickened. "Here we are then."

They stopped and looked about, checking they could not be seen, before making their dash for freedom. In that instant, from behind, came a man on a bicycle, pedalling hard. A man in uniform. He shot past and then wheeled around to face them. He dropped the bicycle and with head raised, pulled a pistol from his holster. It was the woodcutter.

"So, you thought you could trick me? No, no. You are not who you say you are. And I am not who you thought I was. I am here to trap birds like you; birds who think they can fly south for the winter."

He seemed impressed by his own cleverness. "And now you are coming with me to Singen and then we shall see what the Gestapo has to say."

Anita felt the blood drain from her head. She closed her eyes and tried to contain herself, drawing deep breaths. Then she drew herself up and looking the soldier in the eye said, "You have no right to do this. We have done nothing wrong. We are good German citizens simply going for a walk. Now let us go."

For a moment he was taken aback by her tone. Franz-Theo sized him up. Bigger, stronger, a fighter and with a gun. Could he overpower him; shoot him? Or would he call out, perhaps to another soldier hiding nearby; shoot Anita; shoot him? The imposter must have sensed the rush of adrenalin because he turned the pistol at Franz-Theo's head.

"It can end here in the forest, or you can come with me." He released the safety catch with his thumb, his finger curled on the trigger.

Franz-Theo put up an open hand. "You can put the gun down and we will come with you. Having committed no crime, done no-one harm, we have nothing to fear."

They turned to retrace their steps, the soldier between them. Along the path, Franz-Theo contrived a story that would ensure they did not contradict each other during the interrogation they knew would take place separately. Meanwhile, in his pocket he carried the death sentence for Steiner and his family and, just as certainly, his own. Anita knew it too and saw already the terrified faces of the children as the Gestapo burst through the door and summarily executed their parents before one by one blowing their brains out.

As they walked, Franz-Theo slipped unassumingly out of his coat and hung it over his shoulders, his hands behind his back. Anita guessed his intent and directed her attention to their captor, engaging him in conversation before pausing to adjust her shoe while the soldier looked on. Franz-Theo carefully took the letter from his coat pocket and held it under his coat behind his back as they continued. Piece by tiny piece, he tore it up, occasionally running his hand over his mouth with a scrap to swallow. Each fragment he dropped returned safety to his friend while bringing the hope of his own freedom to an end.

Gently it started to rain.

⌣⟩

"You were trying to escape." The interrogator's tone was smug. "You were in the forest along the border with Switzerland. You have no papers, no other reason to be there and you thought you could outwit us and escape."

Franz-Theo looked at him and saw a man in his mid-thirties, self-assured in the authority of his uniform but with little to recommend him by way of intelligence. He would bludgeon his prisoner by repeating the accusation and ignoring the answer.

No longer fearful, but patient, Franz-Theo's dogged persistence matched his captor's. "As I have already said numerous times, we do not come from these parts, we are taking a break from our work heading first towards Stein am Rhein and perhaps, later, Schaffhausen and the Rheinfall before returning north. We have done nothing wrong; if there is a border, then we have stumbled into it. I know nothing more. There is nothing more to tell you, no matter how many times you wish to ask."

"You were trying to escape. Admit it."

"There is nothing to admit. I have told you what you need to know."

"You are carrying a camera. Show it to me. Open it."

"If I open it, the film will be exposed and the photos I have taken will be lost."

"Do not test my patience. Open it so that I can see whether you have hidden anything inside."

Resigned, Franz-Theo handed it over. The soldier fumbled with the case and removed the camera, looking for the catch to unlock it, his frustration growing.

"Let me do it before you break it. It's not a gun; it shoots pictures, not bullets." He gently opened the back, exposing the interior before handing it back. The soldier slipped his finger behind the film and pulled out the roll before holding it up to the light and then throwing it on the floor. Nothing else inside. He handed it back.

"If you had not destroyed my pictures, you would have had the evidence of our innocence. Had I been the criminal you take me for, there may have been images that could have compromised me or, for that matter, Germany. Now, by your own actions, you will never know."

The soldier looked confused but decided he didn't much like his captive.

In an adjacent room, Anita had been subjected to much the same treatment; arrogant, self-righteousness backed up by a pistol and a soldier in the doorway with a rifle. She had already explained that they had been living in Aachen and had decided to go for a walk here in this unfamiliar part of the world. As for a border, they were apprehended by the woodcutter before they could cross any imaginary border line. That was it; there was nothing more to say.

The Gestapo officer began again, "You will tell me why you were in the forest."

"Herrschaft noch mal; enough already!" Anita banged her fist on the desk in front of her and stood up. Fierce with anger, she faced her accuser. "You have no right to talk to me like this. We have done nothing wrong. Look at you; you hide behind those lightning bolts on the collar of your uniform. I don't care how shiny your boots or how powerful your pistol, how many good people you have killed, you have to ask yourself who you think you are. You are no longer men; this war has made you barely human. You have forgotten what it means to be a good German. You have forgotten the homes from which you come, have forgotten decency and justice; and you have forgotten your manners as well." Her eyes blazed. "How dare you behave like this? I will speak with your commanding officer."

Stunned and disarmed, the Schutzstaffel officer stepped back from the fury and indignation that confronted him. He looked at the woman, tall, proud, strong, inwardly boiling with rage and completely unafraid. He shook his head as if to free himself from the spell and made his way to the door. The soldier with the rifle stepped aside. In the silence that followed, the room remained electric.

Moments later, the officer returned with a second Gestapo officer wearing his cap with its eagle insignia and swastika. He stepped behind the desk and faced Anita.

"Oberführer Richard Donnevert." He clicked his heels. Voice clipped, he asked, "What is the matter?" His eyes narrowed as he surveyed the woman holding his gaze unflinchingly. He seemed to be trying to remember something.

"I am a good German citizen and I will not be spoken to as if I were a criminal. It seems these men of yours do not know their place. We have done nothing wrong and have been arrested for no good reason. You have interrogated us and found nothing and so now I demand that you let us go."

Donnevert looked at her, saying nothing. Then he raised his head and signalling to the chair said, "Sit down." Turning to the soldier at the door he ordered, "Bring in the man."

Franz-Theo was ushered in, a chair placed next to Anita at the desk, and the stage set for the next scene.

"So you demand, you demand that you be released. On what authority do you 'demand'?"

"The authority of self-respect."

Donnevert paused, then slowly nodded his head in acknowledgement. There was a long silence before he asked, "What is in your handbag?"

"See for yourself."

Anita placed her handbag on the desk and pushed it forward. The soldier opened it and tipped the contents out before him. Pointing to the letter, he asked, "What is this?"

"From my mother."

He drew out the letter and unfolded it, looked up at Anita and then read to himself.

Aachen 1942

My dearest Anitachen,

Life has changed now that you are no longer living at home. Your father is very busy and has to attend many meetings with important officials. He doesn't tell me what they are about and mostly keeps to himself.

It is very different from the days we spent together in Wiesbaden, when you and I could walk through the gardens or enjoy our strolls along Wilhelmstraße. Do you remember the wonderful musical evenings in the Staadttheater? The organ recitals in the Marktkirche? Those days seem so carefree now, before the war changed everything.

For you, my darling girl, I understand how life has become even more complicated. Your innocent hopes and dreams have not materialised. The world of language and literature and travel is now confined to a smaller, narrower world of work and survival. Despite all the prospects you had with fine young men from good families with money and position, your heart has chosen life's hardest course. I understand how you need to share your life and how difficult your situation is, but you will never be satisfied with anything less than what you know is right for you. Your strong will has always made you both rebellious and courageous.

Of course I am worried for you. Your father too is worried, but as much for himself and the family and our security as anything else. He knows that we live in uncertain times and he does not want to see you hurt. Perhaps he does not yet understand that there are some choices we make because we have no choice.

Although we stay here together in Aachen, we do not know what will happen. I miss you and imagine you alone so far away, unable to share the stories that make up your day. There is no-one to keep you company, to help you when you are sad or anxious. I understand that you must keep to yourself, but it is hard for a mother to look on and know that there is nothing she can do.

I pray every day that God will keep you safe and that we will see each other again.

I do not have words to say more clearly how much I love you, how precious you are, how good and kind. God bless you always my dear Anita.

Your loving Mutti.

It took a moment or two before he looked up again and saw the calm, impenetrable face of the woman opposite. Then gently, he said, "I thought I recognised you. Anita Gallo from Wiesbaden, yes? You attended the Lyceum Höhrerstudienanstalt, near the Martkirche, opposite the palace. You have a sister. Your father was Oberpostrat, Director of Posts and Telegraphs. An important family."

He waited for a response, then quietly asked, "You do not remember me?"

"I once knew a man who resembled you. He came from a good family and studied medicine in Gottingen; but I do not recognise the man in uniform wearing the swastika and the badge of the SS."

He watched her face, her grey-green eyes steady, allowing what she had said to sink in. Finally, he admitted, "We do what we have to do to survive."

Franz-Theo had watched the exchange, waiting to see how it would unfold, before quietly adding, "That applies to all of us, as long as we do not lose our self on the way."

Donnevert turned to the voice, judging the man by his face, young, but serious, thoughtful, high forehead with his hair combed back, his gaze even.

"Am I to assume you intend to marry? Because you know marriages such as yours are frowned upon in Germany; there is no way you can marry or live together here."

"Love is patient. If it is hard now, we can wait. We will endure what we have to endure."

"Then I will tell you this. Knowing who you are, I accept that you mean no harm and will give you the benefit of the doubt. We will let you go this time but, if ever you should try to escape and we catch you again, the consequences will be very different. You know what I mean." He stood up. "Now, collect your things." He pushed the letter and the contents of the handbag across the desk. "Good afternoon Herr Metzger," and then turning to Anita, with a slight bow said, "Good-bye Fraulein."

He walked to the door, the soldier stood aside and he disappeared leaving behind his order, "Let them both go."

Outside, in the fresh air, they both breathed deeply. The aftershock brought stinging tears and a long silence. Anita hooked her arm through his; for the moment, nothing could touch them. Then, together, they walked away.

A while later, in hushed tones, Franz-Theo said, "You were magnificent."

"Not really." She allowed herself a smile and, squeezing his arm, added, "But I am Anita Gallo."

CHAPTER SIX

Eviction

Autumn was turning the leaves russet and gold; days were becoming cooler. Anita confined herself to her work and her little attic. Sometimes when she returned home, Frau Manz would stop her at the foot of the stairs to ask how she was feeling. Was she well? She looked tired and sad. Was everything all right? Was there anything she could do to help? She fluttered her hands and fussed with her apron, earnestly looking up at Anita who quietly reassured her that she was fine and simply wanted the war to end.

In her room she lay on the bed, watching the light creep up through the curtains. Soon it would be dark and in the gloom her fears would rise. Where was her Johannes? Was he safe? What was he doing now? For more than a week she had heard nothing, the silence eroding her confidence, enlarging her anxiety. As the weeks passed, the morning mists became her tears; her hopes falling with each fading leaf as it fluttered to the ground.

Finally, she received a letter from Franz-Theo reassuring her that, so far, while he was waiting for further news, nothing untoward had happened. Perhaps she could arrange to meet him in the evening at the station in Freiburg.

Suddenly she felt alive again. Fears were dispelled in the need to act. The next two days at work crawled by until, at last, having returned home, she slipped downstairs, told Frau Manz that she would be gone for a couple of days and then headed for the train.

The woman who emerged from the station in Freiburg wore a long coat, the collar turned up, a woollen scarf and a hat with a wide brim that shielded her face. It was already dark and her clothes had less to do with the cool night air than the guise of anonymity. She walked casually along the platform and recognised Franz-Theo's outline ahead. She wanted to run, to embrace him, have him hold her close, feel his mouth on her cheek, on her lips. He had turned and calmly walked away into the shadows. She knew she must follow, but independently, as if they were strangers.

Eventually she drew up to him. They spoke quietly, without touching, as Franz-Theo led her to his rented room. Once inside the house, it was a different story. Weeks of abstinence had grown an insatiable hunger, to have and to hold, to share the news, to be exhausted and be happy.

"You must stay the night. I have told my landlady I have a friend coming to visit and she has made up a room for you. We must be seen to be observing every propriety and we cannot risk a hotel or anywhere you would need to register. So far there has been silence, but I am ever fearful that it is a silence before a storm."

Autumn turned to winter and there were two more visits until, one evening as he returned home, his landlady approached him in the hallway. She was agitated, avoiding Franz-Theo's look and breathing heavily between her words.

"Is something wrong?"

"Today, two men – one of them from the police I think – came to the house and asked whether I had a boarder. I didn't know what I should answer, but I said yes. 'Just the one?' they asked. Again, I said yes. 'Are you sure?' they asked again. 'Of course I'm sure,' I replied. Your friend does not have a permanent room here and has just been a visitor two or three times. I didn't tell them that, because it's none of their business. They asked to see through the house and I had no choice but to let them look. Of course they found nothing suspicious. I have two children, have little money and am simply renting a room while my husband does his duty fighting in the war."

"Did you tell them that?"

"I did. And then they said, 'You must tell your lodger that he can no longer live here.' What am I to do? What could I say? I asked whether I could have another person here after you left and they said yes; but you were not allowed to stay. I didn't dare ask why. Is there something wrong?"

"There is a lot wrong, but nothing that you have done. You have no idea who has said anything? Who knows I am here?"

"Not at all. You are quiet, you make no trouble. Everything seems fine and then, suddenly, this. My friends have asked me did I let the room. I said I had, to a quiet young man who keeps to himself. No more. I'm sorry. I don't know what has happened."

"I am sorry too, but somewhere out there is someone who knows more than you or I. You have no need to worry. In the morning, I shall be gone."

Through the night, Franz-Theo felt a rising anger. Who are these people who whisper behind their hands and talk to the police or the gestapo? As Steiner had said, there was treachery everywhere: neighbours spying on neighbours, imagining every unfamiliar face to be a threat, interfering in the lives of others about whom they know nothing. Was it the casual remark of a friend, or was it the ongoing watchfulness of the gestapo who had tracked him to this unremarkable bolt-hole far from anyone he knew? Or, more frighteningly, had someone linked the arrival of the lady in the dark hat and coat to the man staying in the rented room?

It was a giant leap of faith, but the next morning Franz-Theo approached Kuhnert and told him that he had been obliged to give up his rented room for reasons he did not understand. Was there any place he might stay until things settled down and he could look elsewhere? Fritz Kuhnert looked at him steadily, deliberating whether to play safe or say what he suspected.

"Herr Metzger, I think you are in trouble. I have observed enough to know that you are not in uniform, that you do not seem to have any family and that you are wary of visitors to the factory. I make no judgements. You do not have to tell me anything, but I suspect you are hiding and you are waiting. And now I will tell you something else. I do what I have to do for the sake of my family and my business – and from what I see in your face I think I can trust you and I am prepared to help you."

Franz-Theo looked at him steadily for a long time before he said anything.

"I had hoped my demeanour was not quite so transparent, but I cannot contradict you. If you had wanted to alert the authorities, you could have done so by now; but you haven't. Neither would you have engineered my removal from my previous lodgings. That would have been pointless. It seems, therefore, that our trust must be mutual."

Kuhnert smiled. "Come with me; let me show you to your room."

Together they climbed to the third floor of the factory to a section that was locked and unused. From his pocket, Kuhnert took a ring of keys, separated one from the bunch and opened the door before handing the key to Franz-Theo.

"You will find a bed and a mattress, and sheets and pillows in the cupboard. Next door is a sink, a table and chairs and, at the end, a toilet. We will have to make some arrangement for meals but, for the moment, that can wait. I believe you will be safe here."

The two men looked at one another before Franz-Theo, swallowing the choke in his voice, said quietly, "I do not have words sufficient to thank you."

Welschingen

Just as air bubbles to the surface, so Franz-Theo's thoughts turned to his father in Brussels. In the autumn of 1940, Belgium complied with the Germans to register all Jews, even though it was contrary to the country's constitution. Then, in December of that year all Jews in official positions were removed from their jobs. In December 1941, Jewish children had been expelled from schools. In wry disgust he knew why - you don't need to be educated if you are to be exterminated. He had also heard reports that some thousands of Jews had been deported to labour camps in Poland, despite some fractured resistance from the Belgian authorities. Where had that left his father?

Franz-Theo was very aware, from newspapers, clandestine BBC radio broadcasts and radio Italy, that over the years there had been mounting evidence of Hitler's urge to purge Germany of everybody from political criminals to the disabled and people described as sub-human: the deformed, the sexually perverse and those considered racially inferior, undeserving of life. And none more so than the Jews. These were the degenerates whose very existence polluted the pure Aryan gene pool.

The events of Kristallnacht on November 8, 1938 still reverberated in memory as Nazism's unshackling of Germany's pre-existing pent-up anti-Semitism. The prejudicial night curfews imposed on Jews so that they couldn't molest Aryan women were simply the precursors to further abuses such as the auctioning of possessions of detained or murdered Jews in March 1941.

Collaborators, fuelled by religious hatred, blind obedience or opportunism and xenophobia, continued to aid and abet Hitler's death squads, the Einsatzgruppen. It was beyond comprehension that neighbour could turn on neighbour; that customers would turn on shopkeepers or even members of the same family could so betray one another. Through any number of speeches and public rallies, by the following year Hitler had made his position absolutely transparent when he maintained, "We shall regain our health only by eliminating the Jew". Germany's security was dependent on everyone supporting the Führer's pathological hatred of the sons and daughters of Abraham.

In his attempt to understand the motivation behind such widespread and virulent loathing, Franz-Theo had already dismissed the simplistic belief that the Jews had killed Jesus and must therefore be made accountable. After all, it was the Romans – Pilate under Tiberius. Better to avoid political unrest and the concerns of Caiaphas. What was more disturbing was the detail with which the Reformation's Martin Luther had argued[8] that Jewish schools and synagogues should be set on fire, prayer books be destroyed and rabbis forbidden to preach. It was not only justified, but necessary, to raze homes and confiscate property, show no mercy and offer no legal protection. Jews were "poisonous, envenomed worms" who could be made slaves or exterminated.

It now seemed to him that the deep anti-Semitism of Luther's Christianity had become shackled to the emerging nationalism of Hitler's Germany.

While these cogitations troubled his waking hours, Franz-Theo's nights were punctuated by recurring nightmarish concoctions of brutality: pursued through darkness and wind, stumbling over uneven ground; abandoned buildings harbouring only the spectres of former inhabitants; the cold gleam of a pistol, the undiscoverable face behind it in shadow; a shovel ripped from a worker's hand to be smashed against the side of his head, shattering bone and spraying blood; the tap on the shoulder from behind and turning only to be confronted by the eyes of the Gestapo saying, 'Now you follow me', to oblivion; disoriented families herded into trucks; visions so clear he would start from his bed, choking the cry in his throat.

Such was the growing unease everywhere that, one morning, Fritz Kuhnert approached him at his workbench.

---

[8] Martin Luther, *Von den Juden und ihren Lügen (Jews and their Lies)*, 1543

"You know, things are becoming increasingly dangerous as the war progresses. Allied aircraft are now threatening German towns, especially where there are factories suspected of supporting the military. Roads, bridges, transport and communications are disrupted and our workers are no longer safe. I have decided to relocate some of our operations to Welschingen, about 100 kilometres to the east, where we will be less conspicuous. It is mostly farming country and forests and not far from Immendingen and Tuttlingen. You will, however, need to look for accommodation."

Franz-Theo met the news with a mixture of concern, relief and sudden optimism – concern that what little security there had been was being eroded, relief that there was a removal from further potential scrutiny by the SS, and optimism that he would now be much closer to Anita in Tuttlingen with the possibility of spending more time together, albeit secretly.

The following week, he took the train to make an exploratory trip to Welschingen, arriving in the afternoon of a late autumn day, the last of the leaf colour caught by the soft light. It was quiet, serene after the bustle and tensions of the city. He walked leisurely, wondering how he might find accommodation without drawing attention to himself. He had learned to trust no-one.

There were few people about, but presently he noticed figures ahead. As they approached, he noticed a man walking a dog on a leash. Beside them was a young boy absorbed in conversation with the man. For a moment, he was unsure, but dismissed his fear; he needed to appear completely comfortable. Besides, such a situation was hardly threatening. As they drew close, the man doffed his cap in greeting.

"Good afternoon. A lovely day for a walk, don't you think?"

"It certainly is. And that's a fine specimen of a dog you have there."

"He is. His name is Max, just 3 years old." He patted the dog and turned to the child. "This is my son, Asher."

"Hallo," piped the boy. He looked up from under a mop of dark hair, his brown eyes bright.

"And I am Jakob Weiss. What brings you to our village?" The question was light, interested rather than inquisitive. Franz-Theo searched his face and saw the beginnings of a smile.

"I am Franz-Theo Metzger and I hope soon to have work here. I will need somewhere to live, at least to the end of the war. We have no idea of course how long that might be. These are insecure times."

He had said more than he intended and turned the conversation back to the dog.

"For a German Shepherd, he appears well bred; taller in the back legs than many and his ears are really alert. He has a good head; lovely colour; a fine animal."

As if he understood, the dog looked up to his master to see if he agreed and then looked back at Franz-Theo, steady, accepting the stranger.

The conversation continued easily. Jakob was a farmer, living nearby, married with two children. He was stocky, fit from hard work and long hours outdoors. He milked a few cows, grew vegetables and kept hens and ducks. It meant food on the table with enough left over to share or barter with the other villagers. He stopped.

"You said you needed to find lodgings. Have you secured anything yet?"

"No. I have just arrived and haven't yet had the time, or even known where to ask."

"I have an idea, but I must first speak with my wife, Mindel. She is waiting at home. If you care to come with me, I shall see what might be arranged."

There seemed little point in resisting the engaging humanity of the man and so Franz-Theo succumbed to the prospect of a roof over his head and the kindness of strangers. With the dog trotting beside them, they walked amiably towards the farm, turning in at a wooden gate and following a path in whose borders the first bulbs were beginning to push their soft green shafts into the waiting world.

At the door, Jakob turned to say, "Please wait here. I'll be back in a moment. Come Asher." As he ushered the boy inside, Franz-Theo remained suspended between the past and a flickering hope. An unusual sense of calm familiarity, a common humanity, had been the unspoken dialogue woven into the easy conversation, a connection beyond the spoken words.

He looked around him at the stone and timber-clad farmhouse, shutters on the windows, a long woodpile neatly stacked along the side wall, an axe wedged into the chopping block. Smoke wreathed from the stone chimney. Alongside the house was a large half-timbered barn under a tiled roof. A large stone trough with a water spout above it was attached to the wall, with a collection of rakes and hoes under the eaves. Nearby was a four wheeled wooden farm cart. A path led away to a kitchen garden with a few herbs, leeks ready to harvest and the remaining carrots, kohlrabi and cauliflower. Here was a way of life predicated on the rhythms of the seasons, honourable toil and a respect for what the earth might yield.

His contemplation was interrupted by Jakob inviting him to come inside. Mindel Weiss wiped her hands on her apron and smiling, shook his hand. "Welcome to our home," she said. Her voice was kind. "Yaakov tells me you have just arrived in the village. You must be hungry and you will need a place to stay. I hope you will join us, even if just for a few days to get settled." She looked at him, her head tilted, waiting for an answer.

"That is most kind, more than I could expect and more than I can thank you for. You must tell me if there is anything with which I might help."

"There is certainly plenty to do," replied Jakob. "We will start by finding you some boots and then we will bring in the cows and the sheep before it gets any darker. They stay in the barn overnight. The hens will already have settled into their roosts. The children will come with us."

Across the fields, the animals were already making their way home, unhurried in the pattern of their days. The doors open, they filed into the dimness in some bovine hierarchical order that needed no other human intervention than the supply of chaff in their stalls. The children rounded the sheep from the fold to their place in the barn and secured the doors. A barrow load of wood was brought to the house and the evening settled down with lentil soup, freshly baked bread and conversation that carefully unwrapped the lives of those sitting in the lamplight around the table. In the warm, timbered interior with its tiled kachelofen in the corner and the steady ticking of the longcase clock, the rhythm of life assumed a different, gentler heartbeat.

Encouraged by the sanctuary of his new circumstances, and with the warm endorsement of his hosts, Franz-Theo wrote to Anita inviting her to join him at the farm. The weeks of separation since the cautioning of Singen may have served to quell the immediate urge to take risks, but reinforced the absoluteness of their destiny together, come what may. They met at the station, Anita wearing a buttoned blouse with a scarf tied at the neck, the splash of white in her hair catching the light and a smile that felled the composure of her man utterly. He pressed back the tears of relief and elation and held her close, breathing in her scent, feeling the curve of her body against his, aware of the physical reality of this moment only imagined for so long. They parted and he held her face in his hands, kissing her gently on the mouth and then on her forehead before offering his arm. Absorbing the moment, they walked in silence, recognising again why they were together, knowing that this was all that mattered in the world.

Presently Anita asked, "So, tell me about the family I am going to meet."

"Good people, kind. He, German, she from a Polish background, married before the war; both Jewish and with two young children. Happily, they have so far escaped the terrors that have uprooted this country and sown such fear into the hearts of so many good souls. Perhaps it's the isolation or simply the unremarkable normality of their farming life. You will find them charming, I'm sure."

There was more about feeding animals, forking hay, cutting wood and evenings around the table or music as the children practised their piano.

They were met at the gate by Max who bounded out, ran a circle around them and promptly sat at Franz-Theo's feet as if waiting for an introduction.

"What a darling dog; he's beautiful. Can I pat him?"

Franz-Theo tousled his head. "Of course; this is Max. Max, meet Anita."

Formalities over, Max leapt away, escorting them to the house.

"I see we are already friends," said Yaakov, smiling, as he met them at the door. "Welcome. Please come in."

Stepping into the home of strangers, Anita's natural reserve would normally have evinced some formality. Already disarmed by the dog - and his master - she found herself quickly charmed by Mindel and the children as well as by the warm intimacy of the space and concerns for her wellbeing and comfort. The travel had been uneventful, the break from work welcome, being reunited with Franz-Theo just wonderful and she was grateful for the kindness of the family's hospitality.

Later, during a simple meal together, Asher asked, "Can you play the piano?"

Anita looked at him. "I can, but it's been a little while. I may not be very good at the moment."

"Oh, but you must," cried Rachel. "We have to practise every day, so it will be good to hear you play something different. Please, after dinner, you must play for us."

The matter settled, the meal completed and the dishes put away, the family retreated to the living room. Rachel pulled out the piano stool, lifted the lid and said, "You must choose something you like from the music here – unless you know something by heart."

"No, I'm not confident enough for that, but I notice you have some Chopin here. Let me see."

Embarrassed, but tempted by the instrument, she selected a Nocturne and sat down, running her fingers above the keys, before gently playing a chord and then a soft arpeggio. Into the hushed room, she began, hesitantly at first but then gradually allowing the music speak for her.

When the last note had faded, there was silence before suddenly, the children clapped and everyone joined in. "Amazing, wonderful; so special; thank you."

Franz-Theo looked at her disbelievingly. "I had no idea. That was extraordinary. You are amazing, more than amazing." He shook his head to escape the spell. "Come, let me turn the page."

"More," said the children – and the melodies continued till it was time for bed.

The day had begun with the clickety-clack of iron wheels on iron rails and had ended with a different music; a lightness of touch and a wellspring of feelings.

As she lay in the bed that had been made up for her that night, her mind filled with the kaleidoscope of images from the day, Anita marvelled at the good fortune that such difficult circumstances had wrought in bringing them together in this place. Just as lamplight had filled the corners of the room, so too had this family brought hope and light into the darkened corners of anxious uncertainty. A warm and comforting present had supplanted the precariousness of an uncertain tomorrow.

She visited the farm again in the late summer and autumn, walking in the fields with Max by her side, taking in the air and the sky, watching the scudding clouds. Often she was reminded of her childhood years – so far and so innocent – in Bad Schwalbach, walking through field and forest with her grandfather as he contrived stories of the birds of the air and animals of the field where the complexities of war and suffering were far less troubling than they had now become. Franz-Theo would bring his camera and capture the wind in her hair, flowers at her feet or washing her hands under the tap by the farmhouse wall.

Days would draw to a close and she would again take the train to Tuttlingen and her little attic above Frau Manz, the space confining her life again to solitude and the bitter reminders of separation from the family she loved but whose very existence she threatened.

In the months that followed, as Franz-Theo became absorbed into the life of the mishpacha, only one troubling thought persisted. For how long could this good, kind Jewish family remain untouched by the events that were shaking the world?

Aachen

The return to Aachen was a long, slow fuse sputtering towards an unknown detonation. Countless conversations churned over in Anita's mind. She played out the arguments and counter-arguments. Yes, it's risky. I understand that in your position you have to support the Reich. I know you have worked all your life for the good of the family. Yes, we have had enormous privilege. There has been money, fine clothes, music and theatre, 'kaffee und kuchen', walks in the Kurgarten. I have not changed that; the war has changed it. Hitler has changed it.

I am as certain as I have ever been of any single thing in my life, that the man you are so opposed to shares the same values and interests that I do; that we all do in our heart of hearts. He is intelligent, sensitive, widely read and fighting for his life. His family, like ours, had everything: money, position, respect. And from the age of seventeen, he found himself alone, homeless and persecuted. He did not ask for that; the war gave it to him. Hitler gave it to him.

Does his Jewish background make him less vulnerable to hurt, less capable of love, less able to live a good life? Does his heart not beat the same as ours? Does he not bleed the same red? Is he not swayed by the same fear; impelled by the same love? He does no-one harm, he wishes none harm and, in truth, for all the grievances thrust upon him, he has been kinder than you have been to him. And to me.

I ask for nothing more than for you to leave him alone. The more you enquire or interfere; the more people you question or to whom you talk, the more you scratch at your own wound, the more you put all of us at risk. In fact, the less you know, the easier it is to avoid a disaster. In your world, he need be no more than someone your daughter met at a language class and who has gone off to do work for the war effort.

I am coming home to try to make peace with you. I do not understand how, with the example of my mother's love, you can put the life of your own child at risk. It seems as if you do not care about me, or her, or even Erna and her family. I understand that I cannot live under the same roof; I cannot put my feet under the same table if I do not abide by the rules of your house. I know that I will have to leave, and I know that it will break Mutti's heart. But in these times, it may also be that I will never see you again and, if that is the case, what memories will you be left with? What legacy will I inherit? Guilt? Remorse? Never ending grief?

Her thoughts shuddered to a stop as the train arrived. She collected her case and her coat and stepped into the cool night air. The imagined monologue gave way to the reality of the long walk through familiar streets that already belonged to an alien world.

Arriving at Boxgraben, she hesitated. Should she use her key and let herself in? No. She knocked. Eventually, footsteps. Her mother.

For a long moment they clung to one another in silence in the hallway.

"My darling Anitachen. You cannot imagine how wonderful it is to see you. Thank you. Your room is ready. Take your things and freshen up after your long journey and, when you are ready, come down. I will let your father know – and he will be quiet."

Anita hung her coat in the hall and took the stairs to her room. The light was soft, the familiar framed pictures on the wall seemed somehow removed, as if she were in the house of strangers. Her room was as she had left it, the bed made, the chair by the secretaire, the lamp on the small table with a bookmarked copy of the poems of Rilke. She sat down, picked up the volume and randomly opened it. What were the lines for today?

The page opened at the Sonnets to Orpheus, number XI, where she read of the enigma of death and killing, but it was the last two lines that were the evening's talisman:

"Rein ist im heiteren Geist,
Was an uns selber geschieht." [9]

As always, there was more and she read the next ten sonnets, letting the cadence of the verse carry her amid the images of the world and time, before she finally closed the book, for the moment replenished.

---

[9] *When the spirit stays serene, / whatever happens to us is good.*

Carl Gallo rose to greet his daughter as she entered, kissing her formally on each cheek before returning to his chair. There was a prolonged and awkward silence before he asked, "So, what is the news from Tuttlingen? How is Erna and the family? How is work?"

Her mind raced. Sick in bed; the visit from Hannah; the visit from Franz-Theo; the Gestapo; questions in the factory. She wanted to ask a thousand questions of her own. What have you said? What have you done? Where have you been? To whom have you spoken? What do you know? What will happen now?

Instead, she calmed herself, deliberately erasing anything that might reveal the turmoil she had endured. Tuttlingen was fine, the factory was fine, her room was adequate, she had been too busy and too tired to see Erna or the children. The weather was getting warmer, she had kept to herself because talk of the war was distressing; she just wanted things to end so that life would return to normal, whatever that new 'normal' might be.

The rising wail of an air raid siren cut off Carl's next and more dangerous question. Again and again it rose, an insistent cry fading to a dying moan to be resurrected ever louder, ever more urgent.

"Oh my God, not again, no – not again!" Anna put her hands over her ears. "Every few nights now there have been more and more bombings. Just a few days ago. We have to go. We cannot stay here; the cellar is not safe. There is a bunker on Goffartstraße; we must go, now."

As they plunged outside into the darkness, they could already hear the low rumble in the distance; the harbingers of death. They struggled into their coats as they stumbled along the street, joined by others, whole families shepherding children, some running, others walking, some in tears. Behind them, the drone of engines became louder, a dull and heavy thunder. Then a series of muffled explosions pounding the earth. Louder wailed the sirens, the vibrating air thick with the roar of engines, the vault closing in, the whine of bombs and the concatenation of thudding detonations. Behind them, fire lit up the night sky.

Then they were there, jostling their way into the cavernous maw to huddle between death and burial in a tide of displaced humanity.

⟿

It was not the first time Carl and Anna had been forced from their bed, hearts beating wildly in the dark, fearing their end in the cramped cellar, imprisoned under the rubble and asking themselves 'how has it come to this?'

Tactical Fighter Squadron 425, flying Vickers Wellingtons, together with the *Alouette* unit of the Royal Canadian Air Force, went into action overnight on October 5, 1942, bombing Aachen with a small number of aircraft. The border city was a strategic target, not only the western entrance to Germany but also historically and culturally important; its fall would break the spirit of its people. Leaving RAF Dishforth in Yorkshire, England, they attacked again overnight on July 13, 1943.

But there were yet more lives to be lost, more cruelty to be inflicted, more destruction wrought, more hope abandoned, before retribution on April 11, 1944.

∽

They hear the distant rumble of aircraft even before the sirens begin their baleful cadence, rising and moaning, drawing people from everyday tasks, evening meals, anxious conversations or fitful sleep. This time the approaching growl is heavier, more menacing. Preparatory thunder for a storm whose thunderbolts will reverberate in the turgid air, tearing at the fabric of the trembling city and its trapped inhabitants. Fear already sown in the belly rises to panic.

Seconds turn into minutes, an age to find a coat, a bag. What to take? What to save? The descending whistle of a falling bomb turns to a blinding crash nearby, shaking the earth. Carl, Anna and Anita blunder to the door and stumble into the street. The air is thick with noise. A crazed cacophony of multiple sirens, the roar of engines, the shriek of falling bombs punctuated by the crash of detonation and exploding masonry. Flames roar, smoke fills the air and a series of explosions blows apart the buildings behind the house.

Transfixed, the three of them stand in the street and watch as another bomb whistles towards them, piercing the roof of their home before exploding, sending streamers of flame through the clouds of fire and smoke. A second detonation blasts out the remaining windows, tearing away part of the wall in a shower of masonry. Roof slate scatters skywards before clattering across the roadway. As part of the roof caves in, the front wall seems to slowly detach itself and lean into the street before finally collapsing in a crashing waterfall of disintegrating bricks.

Mesmerised, Anita watches the chandelier in her room swing crazily from the remaining ceiling before crashing to the floor in a cascade of glass. A ball of fire careens down the staircase as flames claw their way up the drapes. In the updraft of the firestorm, pictures and books are sucked into the air, like the birds who flame briefly before floating lightly into oblivion.

Another piercing whistle and thudding explosion behind them punctuates the rising scream of engines as the planes soar skywards again. Clouds of fire and smoke rise after them and all around are shattering blasts as buildings and gardens and flower pots are hurled to destruction.

Nearby, a child is crying.

Over the thunderous noise around them comes the sound of the next wave of aircraft bringing Armageddon. Suddenly galvanised, the now homeless family turns to find its way blocked on all sides by rubble.

"I think the easiest way is probably through the hospital," shouts Carl above the uproar.

"But it's been hit; it's on fire. How will we get through?"

"I can't see any other way. We have to try."

Hanging onto each other for support, the three of them clamber over piles of rubble and skirt burning debris looking for a way through the destruction, their path illumined by flames. Still the sirens wail and the whistling bombs burst and thud under the roar of machinery filling the sky. Acrid smoke and dust claw at their throats.

Rounding part of the building that has been blown open, they see they have stumbled into the morgue. Before them on slabs of marble lie the bodies of those whose death has preceded the slaughter that this night has brought. In the turmoil that rages around them, they appear strangely still; part of a world to which, mercifully, they no longer belong.

Her flight for the moment forgotten, Anna looks on these personal deaths, each one its own loss to family and friends, and feels a disturbing mixture of compassion and envy. Turning to Anita, she says, "They look so still, so peaceful, so calm while the world crashes down around them. They can be thankful they do not live through this infernal horror as we must."

So saying, she turns to follow Carl who is steadily making his way towards the bunker, leaving behind those who had found the still centre of a turning world.

Between flames and rubble and under a sky on fire, they make their way to the Goffartstraße bunker, stitched into a thickening thread of dislocated humanity. Many are injured, struck by flying stone or glass, others coughing or weeping. A few they pass lie in the road or among the rubble. Sometimes, the white gleam of bone protrudes through their clothes.

At last they arrive and are drawn into the bowels of the shelter. The relentless roar and shocking thud of explosions outside are partially replaced by the hubbub and confusion within. People crouch in terror or are numb with shock. Some huddle in groups, others sit alone, dazed, uncomprehending. Again and again, Anita sees the house torn open, smoke and flame devouring the fragile sanctuary of her room. Sees again the grey faces of the rigid dead. Hears the startling bang of the explosions that spew fire and gas and shards of steel.

Inside the vault, Anna sits with her back to the wall staring blindly into the middle distance. What will be left? Where will they go? And how will they get there? Carl sits beside her, lips pressed together. What have we done? Has it really come to this?

Outside, the world is being blown apart in walls of fire; the ever-present sirens sounding like the wailing of the dead. Above them, 352 British bombers pound the city into submission.

The next morning, when the sirens died and the drone of aircraft had retreated, people began to venture outside. They were greeted by a city in ruins and a sky smudged with smoke. All around were eyeless buildings, their windows blown out. Charred rafters reached starkly into the sky; walls had collapsed revealing half a room with its wardrobe still against a wall or a bed protruding above the splintered floor. A singed rag of curtain flapped idly against a broken wall. Smoke rose from the twisted wreckage of broken furniture and piles of rubble.

Already, people were fleeing: mothers with prams; two gentlemen pushing bicycles; a couple carrying a baby carriage loaded with blankets. Bricks, stones and smashed chimney pots littered the way. A black dog, looking for its owner, stood mutely in the roadway.

In the re-aligned landscape, Carl, Anna and Anita tried to orientate themselves, the windowless shells looking down on them. Landmarks had been obliterated; streets were blocked and fires still burned, acrid smoke stinging their eyes. The pungent stench of gas and leaking sewage engulfed them. Slowly they picked their way back along the path they had come the night before. Staring blankly, people came towards them carrying suitcases or satchels; others leading children by the hand. In what might formerly have been a laneway sprawled a body on a pile of bricks. Blood leaked from his ear onto a half-buried wooden beam. Further on, a boy perhaps ten years old sat on the step of what may once have been where he lived. With him were his two younger sisters, sitting on the ruins. They were waiting for their parents. They would wait forever.

Finally, Anita and her parents arrived at what had been their home. Half of it was still standing; the rest a smouldering ruin. Shards of glass were strewn with smashed porcelain and broken furniture amongst the bricks and timber. They picked their way over the stones and debris and stood in what had been the kitchen. Miraculously, part of the wall remained and on it hung the porcelain clock that had kept the hours for as long as Anita could remember. To her amazement, it was still ticking.

Across the city, throughout the centre and south, and in the outlying suburb of Burtscheid, fires burned. Those killed would number 1,525. In what had been Dietrich-Eckart Strasse, a devoted housekeeper, Hildegard Imdahl, together with Albert and Christa Steiner, lay dead in the devastation of their home, with five little organ pipes under the rubble, their prayers unanswered.

CHAPTER SEVEN

Expulsion from the Garden

Something was wrong. As he approached the farm, Franz-Theo was caught by a sense of unease. He slowed his stride, looking about him, trying to fathom what had happened. The air seemed foul, stained, though not by the smudged colours of the fading sunset. An unnatural silence smothered the place. As he approached the house, he saw that the door was open. He listened. Nothing.

"Hello?" he called.

He strained into the emptiness. Still nothing. Where was everyone? Normally there would be voices, or the playful laughter of the children. Max would have sensed his approach and come bounding out, tail wagging to greet him. No sound; no smell of Mindel's cooking.

He called again. Where was Jakob? Had he stayed in the field later than usual? Was he in the barn? Had the children gone with him? Suddenly cautious, the fear rising in him, he walked quietly to the open door and stepped inside, waiting for his eyes to adjust to the gloom of the unlit room.

Familiar shapes defined themselves – the comfortable chairs around the fireplace, but no fire in the grate. The piano against the wall, open sheet music on the rack; bookshelves sharing the space with framed photographs of the family and a pretty painted papier-maché box of keepsakes. Framed pictures on the walls. In the dining room a simple menorah sat in the middle of the sideboard, the table covered with a hand embroidered cloth and a vase of field flowers in the centre. The curtains had not been drawn.

He stepped into the kitchen, the sound of his shoes suddenly loud on the stone floor. A noise – and then the heavy beating of wings flapped past his head in a flurry of fear and confusion. Heart beating wildly, Franz-Theo stepped back, struggling to make sense of what had just happened. Then silence again. On the bench he noticed the makings of a meal that had been scattered about. The bird, a raven he guessed, had come through the open door in pursuit of food. It seemed the bird had not been the only intruder; Mindel's preparations had been interrupted leaving dishes and bowls and half prepared vegetables on the table.

Cautiously, he made his way to the back door. Outside on the flagstones lay Max, his muzzle smashed and black blood dried around the wound above his eye where the bullet had drilled the bone. Franz-Theo closed his eyes against the dawning conviction that this was the work of the Schutzstaffel. Somehow, the Weiss family had been betrayed. Was it by his presence? Had the Gestapo followed him here and then discovered this good, kind and loving family, snatching them as the prize in his absence? Or had there been other Germans aware that this family should have been wearing the yellow star?

To confirm his fears, he retreated inside and climbed the unfamiliar stairs to the bedrooms. Wardrobe doors were open, clothes strewn on the bed and on the floor. No time to prepare for a destination that could only be feared.

Filled with a sudden dread that his room at the back of the house may have been searched, he descended to find the door still locked. Was it intentional? A trap? He fumbled for the key before cautiously inserting it, listening intently before turning back the latch. Only the silence of betrayal, loss and death. He opened the door. Everything was as he had left it: the bed made, a room seemingly unoccupied, waiting for guests, relatives or friends. Relief, but tinged with doubt. What did they know; why was nothing disturbed?

Darkness now enclosed this fractured sanctuary and there was no time to try to reassemble the disembodied pieces of people's lives. That would have to wait till morning when daylight could diminish the possibilities of surprise; not that the darkness of what had taken place would dissipate with the rising sun. He gathered a spare blanket and pillow from the cupboard and made his way to the barn where he might find a hidden corner to come to terms with the new circumstances in which he now found himself.

Sleep didn't come easily and when it did, it was filled with the flapping of wings, the smell of blood and a look of bewilderment in the eyes of a dog already dead on its feet.

At first light, Franz-Theo emerged with a shovel and set to digging a hole big enough to accommodate the loyal affection of the family's defender. Max would not have stood by while strangers dragged crying children and stunned parents out into the yard, prodding and beating them on a path from their home. His bark could be silenced by a gunshot; his bared teeth could be broken.

Franz-Theo picked up the already stiffened body and gently lowered it into the grave. He could think of no words, and so shovelled his sadness with the clumps of earth that gradually covered the fur and the wounds.

The rest of the morning was spent tidying up the kitchen, putting things away and sweeping up the scattered food. While he worked, he wondered why it was necessary; would these people who had become his friends ever return? Probably not, but it was a mark of respect, an act of gratitude for the hospitality that had been extended to him. Who would live here in the days to come? Who would be the custodians of memory for the lives that had been lived within its walls, around the table? With the music stilled, what ghosts would haunt the silence? Who would inherit the fruits of honest labour, curious minds and loving hearts? Had this wild, unpredictable storm of suffering rendered human endeavour futile?

The answer came as he recalled his mother's love, undiminished by her suffering and death; his father's courage and dignity even when dressed in the striped uniform of his imprisonment. It came as he remembered Anita's words in the face of arrogant power and the clarity and tenderness of her love for him. A surrender to despair would be a betrayal of all that was possible, of all that mattered even in the face of death.

He set about ensuring his own safety, firstly by establishing a safe place in the barn and ensuring his access to the house would be as invisible as possible. Doors closed; no lights; no smoke from the chimney. He would leave by the fields; return by hedges and trees. How could he defend himself? The sudden thought occurred that he might find a weapon concealed in some cupboard or drawer and so began a search over several days until, as if by some benevolent legacy, he stumbled upon the false bottom of a drawer in a chiffonier. Opening it he discovered what he was looking for: a pistol.

Wrapped in a scarf was a Walther PPK snub-nosed handgun, together with a magazine of seven bullets. Next to it, a small box of 9-millimetre shells. Franz-Theo gingerly unwrapped the weapon, feeling its weight in his hand. The wooden grip was elaborately carved and bore the trademark Walther banner. Though he knew little about guns, he would quietly familiarise himself with its mechanism and felt grateful that this piece was small enough to conceal in a coat pocket. He wondered how Jakob Weiss had come by it, and when he imagined he might need to use it. It felt strange, emboldening, to actually hold a gun when, so often, one had been pointed at him or pressed against his head. And while he hoped he might never have to use it, he felt a grim satisfaction knowing that, were he ever to be caught again, he would not die alone on that day.

Meanwhile Jakob Weiss and his family had been herded towards a cattle truck with another seventy or eighty prisoners. Fear and confusion reigned among them, disoriented as they were, pushed and prodded under the barked instructions of the soldiers. Rachel and Asher, wide-eyed, clung to their mother's skirt. Jakob clutched Mindel's hand and the small suitcase of spare clothes among which he had pushed Rachel's favourite doll and Asher's stuffed teddy bear. In front of them, people stumbled as they tried to climb into the wagon, while behind they were jostled and pushed.

Suddenly, over the shouting and voices, came a cry. "No! No, I will not!" There was a scuffle. Soldiers dragged the man aside.

"No, I'm not going! Not going!"

The soldier pulled his pistol.

"So, you are not going? No, you are not." He nonchalantly swung his arm and pulled the trigger. The bullet entered the man's unshaven cheek, smashed the bone and sprayed blood from the back of his head. As his legs crumpled beneath him, his wife fell to her knees in a wail of despair.

"And neither are you." His second shot struck her in the side of the head.

Guards pulled the bodies aside. There was no further resistance; the silence only broken by the hushed sobbing of the children.

The doors shut and bolted, the world they had known was locked out and an incomprehensible realm of half-darkness, human sweat, excrement and putrescence would envelop them for the next three days.

As the carriages trundled through the countryside, Jakob tried to glimpse what he could through the cracks between the boards. He noticed the shadows cast through the trees were long and guessed that it was late in the day. If the sun was in the west, then the shadows pointed east, in the same direction as the train. They were heading towards Poland.

❧

"The world has surely gone mad." Fritz Kuhnert's voice was hollowed out by futility. He closed his eyes, shook his head and continued. "It's as I feared. Last Monday, November 27, Freiburg has been destroyed. The only thing left standing, miraculously, is the cathedral."

Franz-Theo looked at him as he struggled to absorb the impact of his loss. What to say? The course of the war was clearly coming to a head and it was complete madness to persist in a folly that would lead to ever more destruction and death.

"To say I am sorry is not enough; it is but one more tragedy to add to a litany of sorrows. Thousands will have died and a beautiful city, a medieval town, has been sacrificed. Do you know what happened?"

"Apparently it was all over in less than half an hour. Allied aircraft, British I think, must have dropped hundreds of tons of bombs. And yes, thousands are reported dead, homeless and injured. It was bad enough in May 1940 when the Luftwaffe mistakenly bombed the city, but this..." his voice trailed off.

Franz-Theo waited, concerned for the man who had become both employer and friend. Kuhnert was not a man to surrender easily. Presently he asked, "Do you know what you will do?"

"I still have to find out how many workers are left, but I have access to the Arbeitseinsatz, labour deployment, to fill the spaces when soldiers are called away or workers are killed. Civilians who have been rounded up fill the vacancies – they can be political prisoners of the Gestapo, foreign citizens or Prisoners of War – you know how it is."

"You have the workshop in Welschingen, but it's only small."

"There's a factory in Berlin – but who knows how long that will last with the way things are going at the moment. You could come with me; I could do with your help." He paused, thinking. "You know, it would be a good way for you to keep a low profile, hidden away among the forced labour."

Franz-Theo considered. While Welschingen had been a welcome refuge, it was also unsettling to know the Weiss family had never returned and he was there, alone, not knowing whether he was safe or would be the next to vanish. A moving target would be harder to hit. Apart from proximity to Tuttlingen, there was nothing else to hold him there and here was a situation that might well provide a little certainty in an uncertain world.

"That's probably a good idea. Thank you."

The matter agreed, it was only a week before they were on a train heading north to the capital.

In Berlin, much of the population had already realised that it was only a matter of time before the city would be overcome. A week of raids in February 1944 had been followed by another series a month later and yet again in May. The Luftwaffe had been drawn out and while it inflicted losses, it suffered losses it could not replace.

Franz-Theo questioned the wisdom of coming here. Buildings smashed, their eyeless gaze onto rubble-strewn streets where, in some deluded belief that Germany could prevail, hardened nationalists had hung flags with the swastika or left placards declaring 'Unsere Mauern brochen, unsere Herzen nicht', our walls broken, our hearts not.

He wandered amid the rubble in some hallucinatory daze, past houses of death in a city of death. No street intact; buildings gutted amongst isolated facades. The corpses, for the moment, cleared, but the stench of destruction and decay abundant and foreboding. The corrupting canker of war.

Christmas, less than three weeks after arriving, was a desultory affair. There seemed little point in trying to celebrate the birth of a new order when the world was being blown apart. Tradition, folklore and custom are wonderful things, but Franz-Theo's heart was too heavy, too alone and alienated from the quiet reflection of the past. While some may have suspended hostilities for a day and wished for a silent night, a holy night, there were very few apart from the dead who slept in heavenly peace.

Winter was hard: cold and depressing, seeming to hold the city suspended. Then, on the Saturday morning of the third of February, a massive bombing raid set the city on fire, the flames spreading eastward. Franz-Theo set out to find Fritz Kuhnert.

"Surely this is the end. I see no point in trying to remain here, putting our lives further at risk. Either I will be killed by the Allies or I will die at the hands of the Gestapo. Presumably they are too busy to deal with the likes of me – and I imagine they will have their own lives to protect.

Their dream has turned to a nightmare from which not even fanaticism can wake them."

"I suspect you are right, even though here you are doing no wrong – in fact, helping the war effort. Once you leave, you are on your own."

Franz-Theo forced a rueful smile. "You already know how much I am on my own – and have been for some time. And yet there is one person, one hope that sustains me – and for her sake I will take my chances. I shall return to Welschingen."

As he turned southwards again, Franz-Theo weighed how the brutality of the conflict made manifest in the broken stones reflected the brutality of power, ideology and blind ignorance. How human weakness could cause such horrific destruction.

〜

Escaping the city did little to dispel the premonition of what was to come in the next six weeks. In particular, he worried about Anita's safety in Tuttlingen. More and more of the country was now vulnerable, especially to air strikes, and with Russians and Americans from the north and French from the south, it was impossible to tell from where the next assault would come. It was clear to him, as it was to most Germans, that the war was over. Isolated pockets of resistance, sporadic and unpredictable, could not keep at bay the combined determination of those sensing victory against the depleted resources of the Reich.

Back in Welschingen, he took the familiar route to what had essentially become his home, the garden still subdued under the chill of winter, the buildings hunkered into the landscape under the bare trees. He wondered if all would be as he had left it some two months before. In some places, whole villages had been abandoned. To where did those people flee? Had opportunists or looters stumbled into the isolated farmlet, found refuge, found something worth taking when everything was lost?

Out of habit, he approached cautiously. Silence, No signals of life; just stillness. He searched for the key he had hidden beneath a rock by the door. It was there, but in the back of his mind, an unformed idea, a sense that something was not right. He tried the door. It was unlocked.

He trawled the memory of the day he left: no tell-tale sign left inside, windows closed and latched, the door closed, locked, checked to make sure, key hidden away under rock and earth. Barn doors closed, gate closed, a final look back to confirm all was as it should be. So, what had happened?

He reached into his coat pocket and felt the familiar weight of the pistol. With his left hand he carefully opened the door and called out.

"Hello? Anyone there?"

Silence. He called again. Another echo of silence. He entered, straining for a sound. Nothing. He called again at the foot of the staircase before carefully taking each tread to the landing. Just stillness. He checked the rooms and made his way back to the kitchen. Then he saw it. Left deliberately in the middle of the bare table was an envelope with his name on it.

Taking a knife from the drawer, he slit open the envelope, unfolded the letter and was confronted by the letterhead of the Geheime Staatspolizei. Dated February 5, 1945 and effective immediately, it was a summons to report for deportation to an arbeitslager, a labour camp. Above the signature, the words "Heil Hitler!"

Breathing heavily, Franz-Theo pulled out a chair and sat down. With his elbow on the table and a hand over his mouth, he stared into the vacancy before him, waiting for the room to clear. So this was it. He knew perfectly well what the order meant – he was destined for a death camp. After all this time, just when it was nearly over. Even when their own futures were in peril, they had pursued him to this. He took a deep breath and pulled the letter to him again, trying to make sense of the words, the typed hieroglyphs that spelled despair and death. He looked at the date: the fifth. What was today? Wednesday. The fifth was Monday. As he was leaving Berlin, soldiers of the Gestapo were entering his house. They had missed him by two days.

Doubtless, they had come before, only to find the place deserted. How did they know he had been here? Who had given away information that was not theirs to give? He wondered again whether it was his presence that had betrayed the Weiss family. And now he would pay the price, together with those who had offered him succour. What was certain was that he would not obey the order. He had in his pocket the means to rob the police of their capture, just as the Jews of Masada denied the Romans their victory. But no, he had learned once already, on hearing of the arrest of his father and the imminent death of his mother that shooting himself was not the answer. Friends had torn the rifle from his hands and the moment of blood and blindness had passed. Even alone and pursued through Nazi Germany, there had been moments so sublime and full of promise that he was grateful his impetuosity had been stilled. There would be other ways to die, at some other time.

Again he would hide, marvelling at yet another escape from evil while being captured by the heart of love.

⌇

Tuttlingen

Their home in Aachen blown apart, Carl and Anna Gallo had little choice but to find their way to Tuttlingen to stay with Erna and Emil and the three children. By now, the Engel Apotheke was becoming crowded; on the first floor above the shop lived Erna and Emil, and on the next floor, Emil's mother and her unmarried brother with a heart condition. On the third floor, the third and youngest married brother lived with his three girls, including Helga who also suffered a failing heart, and a boy Klaus who was severely autistic.

Carl Gallo struggled to understand what had happened to his life, so meticulously planned and so ruthlessly undone. Beautiful, cultured, historic Aachen, home to Charlemagne, the first German city to fall, and he having to flee for his life as the bombs rained down, flattening everything. Two thousand, eight hundred and ten bombers dropped 10,097 tons of explosives and fire before the American First and Ninth Armies rolled in with their tanks, shelling anything that might harbour a sniper or a family. The Allies were counting.

Emil had long ago made up his mind where his loyalties lay and his quiet non-compliance with orders to surrender rubber, gasoline or steel meant little to the failing war effort, but a great deal to his conscience. Erna too had shifted her position from early headiness about the power and mystique of the Führer. She had been holidaying in Berchtesgaden when she heard that Hitler was in his mountain retreat and had joined the throngs of people eager to glimpse the man who would be Germany's saviour. Even before the war, while the whole family was in Koblenz, Hitler came along the Rhine by boat and the crowd was so frenzied the first rows were nearly pushed into the river. Emil and Erna were at the front, being held back by a line of police, when Erna suddenly ducked between two of the guards to get closer. One of them grabbed her coat, but she slipped out of it, stopping just a few metres away. There was much commotion and Anita, who had remained deliberately inconspicuous at the back, witnessed her sister emerge as if hypnotised, unable even to tell whether the great man was wearing a hat or not. The only thing to capture Anita's imagination was the fact that he had his two big Alsatian dogs with him.

Now, even though the family was thrust together in the same city, Anita kept her own counsel, careful to avoid any conflict with her father, but glad for the opportunity to occasionally share some of her own anxiety and heartbreak with her mother. She hadn't heard from Franz-Theo and could only hope that it was the increasing chaos that had disrupted mail and transport, but that he was safe. Every day she nevertheless feared the advance from the south and west and its inevitable progress towards Tuttlingen. Then, surely, one way or another, it would all be over.

That progress came sooner than expected in a series of five bombing raids in February and March. The Eighth Air Force sent eleven of its two hundred and seventy-four B-24 bombers during Mission 863 to destroy the railroad marshalling yards. The roar of aircraft overhead rekindled all the terror experienced in Aachen, compounded again by the insistent wail of sirens. The old and the ill, already facing an uncertain end, were overtaken amid the panic of terrified men, women and children as they ran scrambling for shelter. It was not over yet.

After the turmoil of Berlin, Franz-Theo – despite the shock unwelcome of his summons – was glad to be back in the countryside. Over the next six weeks, the spring clusters of daffodils, wildflower fields of edelweiss, red vanilla orchid, blue monkshood, vetch, rampion and buttercups had brought colour back into a world both bleak and charred. Cows grazed on green fields and farmers were turning the rich soil in hope of better times. It seemed that only in cities and towns did war still have a place, streets empty or filled with rubble, occasionally saved by white flags limply hanging from fearful facades. Resistance as tanks or infantry rolled in was sporadic, with most folk surrendering their weapons in the knowledge that the war was all but over. Those who chose, inexplicably, to fight on, did so at deadly cost.

On 19 March 1945 the First French Army finally breached the Siegfried Line. Twelve days later, they crossed the Rhine at Speyer and Gemmersheim, advancing through the Black Forest. The Fourth

Unit under the command of General Jean de Lattre de Tassigny left Strasbourg on April 23 on its way to Freiburg, Villingen and Tuttlingen.

Franz-Theo, ever watchful, but buoyed by blue skies and new growth, made repeated forays to high ground in the expectation that liberating troops and armour could be seen as they made their way nearby. He planned to become their ally; Germany's enemy would become his friend.

He heard the heavy machines before he saw them. For a moment his heart beat wildly. He knew the danger. He was a German who would most likely be taken as a prisoner of war, especially if he was armed. These soldiers were meant to be his nemesis; they could not know how much he welcomed them. He scrambled down the hillside and, near a clump of shrubs and trees found a rock large enough for his purpose. He cleared away the grass and, struggling, tried to roll it over, his hands slipping on the wet stone until he could get his hand underneath it. At last. He clawed at the damp earth to make a hollow and then took from his pocket the Walther pistol that had been his insurance. He looked at it, assessing the wisdom of what he was about to do and then placed it in the shallow hole before rolling the stone over it. Some sticks and foliage shrouded the burial.

He wiped his hands on the grass and dried them on the inside of his coat before heading down toward the convoy.

The soldier driving the tank saw a man in an unbuttoned coat with both hands in the air standing in the middle of the road. Was he crazy? Did he imagine he alone could stop the advance? He slowed the machine and stopped.

Above the heavy noise of the engines of war and liberation, Franz-Theo had to shout. He chose French.

"I am a friend. I need help. Where is your commanding officer?"

Two soldiers jumped from the armoured vehicle following. They had drawn their pistols. Franz-Theo turned to them, his hands high.

"I have no weapon. I am a friend. Please, you must help me."

He was frisked and a conversation in French followed. To anyone watching from a distance, it would seem a bizarre spectacle: an animated conversation; pointing along the road and then north; a young man shaking hands with members of an invading army and then being invited to climb aboard a truck, before the whole convoy re-engaged and headed into the countryside.

Franz-Theo was heading to Tuttlingen.

The deep stone cellar of the brewery, the *brauerei keller*, had become an improvised bunker repeatedly offering shelter as the attacks on Tuttlingen escalated. On Thursday April 26 there had been constant alarms and a rising panic and, as dark descended, Anita with many in the town had once again descended into the depths to hide among the vats. As they huddled under the thin light of a stuttering globe, unfamiliar shadows thrown against the cold walls, they could hear the continual retreat of the German troops along Neuhauser Straße and the muffled drone of passing aircraft. The shuddering outside world sent its vibrations throughout the night to those entombed in the bowels of the earth. Sleep, if it came at all, did not come easily.

By the next morning, the night's restlessness brought frustration, bodies stiff with cold and cramp and children crying with tiredness and hunger. Voices were raised as anger replaced fear. The noise outside seemed to have abated but had been replaced by a deeper rumble and the growl of heavy machinery. A voice called out.

"Enough. I have to get out. We can't stay buried here forever."

He pushed past the weary bodies, trying not to step on hands or legs, made his way to the ladder and clambered out into the sunshine so bright after the gloom of the cellar. Others stood up, stretched and began to gather their few things. The damp air was fetid with the smell of sweat and urine. From the street above, a voice called.

"It's safe to come out. French troops are here on the street."

As she made her way to the exit, Anita dared not hope. She stepped into the light, blinking as she tried to re-establish her bearings. In neighbouring streets she could hear noise and confusion and wondered whether her family was safe. They had doubtless stayed in the cellar beneath the Apotheke, each separately struggling with conflicting fear, hope and despair.

Rather than be caught in the confusion, she decided to return to her attic, the better to stay safe and absorb the magnitude of what was happening. She turned into a lane and, in a haze of emotion, made her way between the buildings. Suddenly, the light was blocked out and the huge noise of heavy machinery assailed her. A tank had turned into the narrow street, filling the space, rearing in front of her, cutting off her progress. Stunned, overwhelmed, she stopped. The monster slowed but continued its advance. Panic, then, to her right, a doorway alcove. She slipped into it as the tank clattered past her.

From his open turret, the young soldier saw a startled, pretty woman with her hair dishevelled, and smiled to himself. The spoils of war. From the doorway, Anita saw a young soldier, wearing a beret instead of his helmet, and smiled up at him. The liberator. For a moment, the world stood still, each of them making their own sense of the moment.

Then he was gone. Anita stepped out into the lane, suddenly joyous. Ten minutes later, she unlocked the door to her room, took off her shoes and coat and lay on the bed. She hardly dared breathe; her eyes filling with tears. Finally, finally the world was righting itself. There would be struggle, but it would be different. Now there was a path out of the valley of the shadow of death.

Exhausted, she fell asleep.

Some hours later, she was woken by a gentle tapping at the door. She sat up ruffling her hair.

"Yes, Frau Manz? Is that you?"

"Weli. Thank goodness you are here."

She leapt to the door, opened it and stood staring in wonderment at the man before her.

"Johannes, is it really you?" She tried to make herself believe, looking at him, convincing herself he was real. He reached out his arm and she folded herself close, felt the press of his body, the stubbled cool of his cheek, the softness of his mouth. They clung together in silence, drinking deep from the well so long denied.

After a long moment, she unfurled herself from his embrace and said, "Come in. Come, sit down and tell me everything. Look at you. You haven't slept; you have to eat. What can I get for you?"

"It's fine; everything is fine. I'm all right and here you are, safe and well."

They sat opposite one another, holding hands across the table and, in an avalanche of questions and amazement, recalled for each other the events of the previous months – the suspended mists of autumn, the bombed infernos of winter and the burgeoning spring that brought with it fresh hope and this day of deliverance.

As the evening descended, it enveloped them in a new, exhilarating wonder.

"We made it. We really made it. We are saved. At last, we are saved and we are free."

CHAPTER EIGHT

Breathing Anew

As the tanks of the French army moved in, Germans ventured out of their homes to witness what was happening. Emil Müller emerged from the Engel Apotheke onto the Obere Hauptstraße and found himself quickly rounded up with a dozen or so others. Erna and young Eberhard watched in shock from the door. This sudden, unexpected action created a great deal of angry confusion with much shouting and struggles as citizens tried to break free. More soldiers carrying rifles arrived and fired shots into the air. From the sidelines, people were calling out that these were unarmed civilians and not to be taken as prisoners of war. Arguments and jostling broke out and, in a moment of distraction, Emil risked everything. Ducking out between the others, he sprinted left onto Stadtkirchstraße, slipped left again down the alley and, through the gate, bounded left down the stairs to the cellar door. Breathing heavily, he waited to hear if he was being pursued. He could still hear the noise and confusion in the street, but no footsteps nearby. He waited till his heart was stilled before making his way into the building by the rear entrance. Finding Erna, he confessed both his impetuosity and his good fortune, to which she replied with some relief, "You had a very lucky escape."

Anita had resolved to go alone to the Apotheke to see what had happened to her sister and parents. While she was now free, she felt more than ever that she was the black sheep in the flock. Somehow, her wilfulness had prevailed in the face of all opposition and her mother's heartbreak at the rupture of her family.

Erna, grim and unsmiling, met her at the door and took her up to the living room before going to fetch her parents and Emil. Anna greeted her daughter without words, but tears and a long hug before everybody sat down. Anita looked from one to the other: Erna in charge but confounded by the unknown of the new order; Emil who appeared relieved but concerned for what would happen next. Her father sat resolute, refusing to accept that the world had changed; and her mother, tearful with relief that at least Anita was safe. Collectively, there was great lamentation – Germany had lost the war. What would it mean for the future? How would they be ruled? What would happen to their security, their future, their wellbeing? How would they live? How would they even survive? Would there be food? How could the country rebuild after the devastation; whole cities bombed, villages razed and untold hundreds of thousands dead? And what further retribution for the devastation inflicted by Germany across Europe? How would the Allies divide the spoils of war?

The more she listened, the more remote Anita felt. She heard their distress, their fear of the unknown, the grief of loss and she knew that healing, if it were to come at all, would take time, for everyone. For her though, the past few years had already been a crucible to distil the essence of what she believed, faced with risk and loss and death at every turn, fearing for the life of the man she loved beyond words.

When the conversation finally turned to her – and the relief that she was safe and well – her father quietly asked, "And what about Herr Metzger?"

Anita looked at him steadily.

"He is alive and safe."

"Where?"

"Here, in Tuttlingen."

"You have seen him?"

"Yes. He arrived with the French troops from Welschingen. Now he is resting."

"So what do you intend to do?"

"From the beginning it has been our intention to marry and now that the war is over, that is what we shall do. If that offends you, then I am sorry, but what we have had to endure has only made us clearer and more determined to follow the destiny laid out before us. It is no longer a question – for anyone."

"Where will you go?"

"That will depend. I understand the French have already asked Franz-

Theo to interpret for them, so where they establish their headquarters, we will go."

Anita looked at her father, recognized the stubbornness in his defeat and knew that underneath his challenged pride dwelt a lonely man whose authority had shrivelled to nought. No longer could he engineer the pursuit that had vexed and endangered them for so long. She saw his isolation, sensed his vulnerability.

"I'm sorry you cannot be happy," she said. Carl Gallo looked at his daughter and did not reply.

⸏

"How was everyone?" asked Franz-Theo when Anita returned.

"Upset, of course. As you can imagine. Now that Germany has lost the war, nobody knows what will happen next. Erna and Emil will be all right because they are well established and have a good reputation, important citizens in the town. Business will pick up again. How many more people will need the pharmacy now?"

"And your parents?"

"Mutti is simply relieved I am safe. She had no idea what would happen if the Gestapo should arrest us. And I think she has understood for a long time that I have made up my mind. Hard as it is, for the sake of my happiness, she accepts the situation. What else can she do? She loves me."

"What about your father?"

"Sadly, that is a different story. He has always been a loyal German, doing his duty. He was well-rewarded for many years. Now, that loyalty has, in his eyes, been betrayed. He has heard rumours of German concentration camps, atrocities towards Jews, and simply says they cannot be true; Germany would never do such things. I think he believes in basic human decency – and what has happened to him is an injustice."

"And will he now give peace as far as you are concerned?"

"I don't know. I don't think he acknowledges the connection between the war and the perverse ideology that created our situation – the whole idea of the unpolluted Aryan race. It was simply a rule that had to be followed and he became fixated by it."

"But what about your wellbeing? You're his daughter."

"I think that's the problem. He has always wanted the best for me

– perhaps not my happiness – but the best security, the best position in society. Two years ago, just after he retired, they were on holidays in the Black Forest and I was having a break in a sanatorium nearby, so I went to visit them. In the hotel where they were staying there was a family with their son, a young man in the SS. There was a great fuss made about how outstanding in appearance and how impressive his behaviour. What a son! My father saw him as the model German citizen, a promising man with a promising future. I could not have been less impressed."

"Well, you certainly made a point of choosing the opposite."

"More than happily, as you well know, but my father sees that almost as disobedience. Then he makes it worse by using the difference in our age, or religious background, as he imagines the future – all with no understanding of who you are; closed off from even wanting to know. It's tragic – because it makes him unhappy, and my mother unhappy. I can only hope that, with time, he will soften. Otherwise, he will die a very lonely man – and that would make me sad."

"Now is not the time for sadness. Even though everything is uncertain until victory is declared and a new order established, it is time for us to make plans for our future together."

⌒

During the next week, as arranged, Franz-Theo caught up with the French soldiers who had brought him to Tuttlingen and learned that they would set up interrogation headquarters in Freiburg. It would be to his advantage to move to the city where he would be employed as an interpreter and translator. Having French and German was already helpful; having Polish, Italian, English and some Yiddish was better still. He would be busy.

In the meantime, he would need to find accommodation. He smiled grimly to himself. This would be a very different challenge from the last time. First he would have to find a building that was still standing. Then, given how many people had been displaced, their homes smashed or uninhabitable, every cellar, shed and outbuilding would be occupied. This time at least, it would not be a hiding place he was looking for.

He decided to return once more to Welschingen to pack a case with some clothes and retrieve his cameras – the Leica and the Rolleiflex. Who knew when such things would be available again, and there was no point in leaving them behind? He would leave some things with Anita to pack into a trunk to be stored at the Engel and bring just the necessities with them to Freiburg.

It was a difficult trip. In the late spring, the garden flushed with colour and the house abandoned, the place had been at once a refuge and a scene of tragedy; where music had been replaced by gunshots; where a loving family had been transported to certain death and he had concealed himself for weeks in the cold darkness of the barn. Whose story would play out in the now empty rooms, or who would tend the fields and garden, would remain for him forever a mystery.

He closed the door, picked up his suitcase and, without looking back, took the road by which he had come.

Germany's surrender came in stages: on May 2 Berlin unconditionally surrendered to Soviet forces; thereafter north-west Germany fell to the British and the Canadians and Bavaria surrendered to the American 6th Army. By May 8, victory in Europe was declared and Franz-Theo was on his way to Freiburg.

It was as he imagined – a city in ruins. Ravaged remains of buildings, gable ends without a roof; stark skeletons of trees, charred and twisted, protruded from the rubble. Fallen walls leaned out of piles of brick and stone, timbers charred, no windows to reflect the afternoon sun. In the distance, a group of people stood among the remains of a building, searching for he knew not what. Nearby, a man in black picked his way precariously among the stones that once led to home.

As he turned the corner he saw the historic Bertoldsbrunnen had been destroyed. He headed down Kaiser-Joseph-Straße towards the Münster, its spire rising above the flattened city, and he marvelled how it had survived so nearly unscathed. Could it have been spared as a landmark for even more destruction? It certainly wasn't out of respect for sacred sites. The magnitude of devastation around it was overwhelming, mesmerising. He sat on a block of fallen stone, a man marooned amid the unchartered obliteration that swam across his vision. He no longer knew what he was looking for.

Gradually, the fog of hopelessness lifted and he set out once more, turning left to where the Rathaus once stood. Unsure at first but heading towards him was a familiar figure.

"Fritz Kuhnert! What on earth? Imagine seeing you here."

"Indeed. But what are you doing, wandering through the ruins?"

Franz-Theo explained how he had returned to Welschingen only to find the letter from the Staadtspolizei but had travelled to Tuttlingen with the French forces instead. Happily reunited with Anita, the French had offered him work in Freiburg and expected him to find accommodation. So, here he was at his wits end with nothing to show and the day drawing to a close.

Fritz Kuhnert looked at him and smiled.

"You know, someone is looking after you. I have been here all day trying to find out what is left of my factory – next to nothing as it happens – and then I run into you looking for a roof over your head. Berlin had become impossible – you left just in time – and so I came home. I have a house in Merzhausen, just four kilometres from here. We can walk there in less than an hour. We live downstairs; upstairs is currently vacant. What do you say?"

Franz-Theo did not know what to say. He pressed his lips together and slowly nodded his head.

"Come. Let us walk. It may not be much, but some warm food and a clean bed will be all the words we need."

⌁

The letter, when it arrived, brought a quickening of the heart and a sigh of relief. It also brought a potent reminder that there were yet unseen hazards embedded in the path ahead. Handwriting on the envelope was studiously, deliberately clear and Anita subconsciously registered the effort. Inside, the lettering was small, irregular and disconnected. Some inner sense told her that it would be forever so after the crazed scratching he had been forced to make at gunpoint – the unfair bargain he had made with death, a bargain that disconnected him from himself but gave the hope of a life together, no matter the odds.

Whatever liberation had been brought, it came with a price, the irrevocability of memory and loss. Anything the future held would contain the past.

Pushing aside the foreboding. Anita unfolded the pages and slowly began to read.

My dearest, most precious Weli,
Firstly, how are you? I can only hope you have not been distressed by

the silence since last we spent time together. Much has happened and I have good news. Seemingly by a miracle, we have accommodation in Merzhausen, just outside Freiburg.

As the war progressed, Fritz Kuhnert had worried that ever more properties would be seized, including those in villages outside the main cities. He was even more concerned that now, after the devastation that had left tens of thousands homeless, his house in Becherwaldstraße would be compulsorily acquired to mitigate the crisis. Voluntarily accommodating an additional family might well reduce the risk. Completely by accident, we met in Freiburg – another story – and so, in sharing our respective situations, he has made the very generous gesture of the upper storey for us to start our new life together.

The family is wonderful – his wife Eleanor and their two children, Hans and Peter. The house itself has been spared the devastation of the cities. It sits on a slight rise against a background of trees and is surrounded by a small garden and then mostly by fields. I'm sure you will find it very lovely, especially at this time of year.

You will, of course, need to make arrangements to leave your work and Tuttlingen. I imagine that it will not be easy to leave the sanctuary of your dachstube above Frau Manz, and even harder to be removed from your family at the Engel as they struggle to come to terms with this new, occupied and unknown Germany. Given all that has happened, there will not be very much to bring with you and, on top of that, we don't know what will transpire in the coming months. Unless it is needed now, anything else can be stored with Erna and Emil.

Now, the French have me busy as they round up sympathisers and try to make sense of the chaos that is the result of the madness that is war. I have been given a motorbike, a Zündapp commandeered from the Germans, to get from Merzhausen to the city and back, but that will not help very much to bring even your few things. In a week or two, we shall fix a date to bring you here.

There was much more – words that not only emphasised the reality of a new beginning, but the understanding of why beginnings bring about endings, and why endings are a necessary transition to something unknown. As she surrendered to the pledges of love and longing, hope dissolved her fears and yearning shored up her day.

Concern about handing in her notice or abandoning her attic was replaced by a surge of impatience to move, to grasp a yet mysterious certainty.

It was late afternoon on a spring day, the middle of May, high clouds against an intensely blue sky and the gentlest of breezes, when Franz-Theo and Anita finally stood outside Becherwaldstrasse 1. The door was opened by a tall woman in her mid-thirties, her dark hair parted in the middle and falling to her shoulders, a cream blouse buttoned to the neck. She smiled, warm and relaxed, obviously expecting them.

'Hallo. So here you are at last Fraulein Gallo. As you might imagine, we have already been introduced in your absence.' The voice was kind.

'Please, call me Anita.'

'Then you must call me Eleanor.' A small face appeared by her side, eyes wide. She tousled his hair. 'And this is Hans, always curious to see what is happening. Come inside. We can manage your things later.'

With the windows open and the curtains pulled aside, the room was surprisingly large. On the oak sideboard, a vase of flowers from the garden added a splash of colour and informality. On a side table, a modest afternoon tea had been set out and soon they were joined by the boys and their father. He was wearing round, metal-framed glasses and a modest moustache; his face more angular and more pensive than Anita had imagined. He approached and, with a slight bow, proffered his hand in welcome.

Soon, they were seated, Anita quietly taking in her new surroundings, the comfortable room, the children's voices and the unfamiliar normalcy of a family seemingly less troubled than might be expected. Beside her sat Franz-Theo and she sensed how already he had become relaxed and engaged with the family who had embraced his quiet and serious ways. She slipped her arm through his and stole a glance as he listened to the plans being made for them. She allowed herself a deep breath of acknowledgement that this was all good and once more she could feel safe, grateful for the kindness of strangers.

The upstairs quarters that were to be their new home comprised a living room with a fireplace, a big bedroom, a kitchen and a bathroom. Given that so many families had been forced to live in cellars and outbuildings after the destruction wrought by the war, this comfortable, light-filled space with its shuttered gable windows, lace and dormers represented a degree of luxury barely imaginable. Out of deference to the new guests, twin beds had been made up, each with pillows and eiderdowns in white cotton covers. Two small, painted armoires would take their clothes and few possessions.

With just the hint of a smile, Fritz Kuhnert had remarked, 'You may re-arrange the furniture as you feel inclined.'

⤳

What until now had been the unambiguous intention to marry assumed a more complex perspective in the practicalities. While religion had often been discussed, primarily from a philosophical and historical point of view, the formalisation of a relationship required something intensely personal as well as something that could be documented. Anita's religious upbringing had largely passed her by until, at the age of fourteen, she was expected to be confirmed in the Protestant tradition, dressed entirely in black. On the day of her confirmation, her father was sick in bed and she went to say goodbye in her black stockings, black shoes and black dress. Propping himself up on one elbow, he blinked and stared before dropping back to his pillow. Unable to digest such severity for so important an occasion, for his blessing he simply remarked, 'You look terrible'. Accompanied by her mother and sister, the ceremony had taken place in Wiesbaden in the Marktkirche.

As for Anita's family, Carl Gallo was Catholic, but never talked about it. Anna Gallo, like her mother, was Protestant, so mixed marriages were simply accepted. Upon Carl Gallo's first posting to Emmerich am Rhein, a Catholic priest had presumed to re-align the couple's religious allegiances, only to be unmistakeably told, 'We are perfectly all right, and will be so as long as you keep out of it.'

Perhaps unsurprisingly, Franz-Theo's father had not spoken at all about his Jewish heritage. There were signs enough already that cancerous pockets of anti-Semitism presented dangers. One led a quiet life by keeping quiet. His mother, on the other hand, was Catholic and she would often go to the cathedral in Köln with her son who surrendered himself to the contentment of his exclusive time with her and the solemn traditions played out in that vast monument to the glory of God.

Two related events clarified their position. On a sunny Saturday afternoon in Freiburg as, arm in arm, they approached the cathedral, they observed a large wedding crowd milling on the forecourt in preparation for the emergence of the bride and groom. A deep blue carpet had been rolled out and strewn with red and white rose petals. Stationed some twenty metres from the Gothic arch beneath the red sandstone tower entrance was a gleaming black Mercedes Tourenwagen with the top down, its chrome headlamps catching the sun. A chauffeur in black cap and uniform stood waiting by the running board. Elegantly dressed women in hats and gloves, some with strings of pearls and fingers carbuncled with rings and precious stones, others clutching leather handbags and all carrying that air of self-assurance that comes with wealth and privilege, sashayed from one group to another. Gentlemen in suits and immaculately polished shoes, their waistcoats occasionally revealing a glimpse of golden fob chain, chatted and laughed about the prospects of the newlyweds, how fortunate it was that the war was finally over and the world had righted itself in the spring sunshine.

To a jubilant cheer, the young couple finally emerged, posed for a moment on the step and then proceeded along the avenue of well-wishers tossing confetti, rice and roses. The photographer danced his way among the jostling crowd to clip the moments of joy and frozen smiles that would be the keepsakes of this most special day.

'She does look lovely,' remarked Anita.

'Yes indeed, but who are these people? Where did they come from? The war is barely over, the country in ruins and people desperate, yet here are families who seem untouched by the last few years.' Franz-Theo tapped his forehead as if trying to wake from a delirium or unlock an answer.

'It certainly seems strange. Where does one conceal such a car? That jewellery has not been hidden under a mattress.'

The families now formally united, the throng gradually dispersed till only a couple of ladies with brooms were revealed, sweeping up the symbols of love, life and fertility.

Anita glanced up at the troubled man by her side. 'Shall we go inside to have a look?'

After the brightness of the sunshine, the vast interior seemed dim despite the candles still burning at the altar. 'I'm amazed it's still standing,' whispered Franz-Theo.'

'Beautiful.'

A sacristan materialised with a brass snuffer on a long pole. One by one, the flames were replaced by curling columns of grey smoke. Two more women appeared and began removing the white bows from the ends of the pews. Following them came the priest in a long black cassock with a white surplice. He approached and with a slight incline asked, "So you must be the couple for the next wedding, yes?"

Taken aback, they looked at each other before Anita spoke. "No, there must be some mistake. We simply came in to have a look inside the Münster."

"Ah, my apologies. There is another wedding to follow. In fact, I think I see them coming." He looked over Franz-Theo's shoulder and stepped aside to greet a young couple, simply dressed and accompanied by two others who Anita guessed may have been relatives or parents.

The young girl whispered a greeting and apologised, hoping they were not late.

"No, no. Everything is in order. We are just getting prepared."

Franz-Theo hesitated before stepping forward to calmly interrupt. "If you are getting prepared, why are the flowers and the wedding decorations being removed? Why are the candles extinguished?"

The priest turned to him and hissed quietly, "These people cannot pay. The flowers, the carpet, the decorations all belong to the people who were here before."

"But they have already gone. What will you do with all this?"

"It will be thrown out." He corrected himself, annoyed. "Or they will be given away."

Franz-Theo turned his back on the servant of God, took Anita by the arm and, as he passed the embarrassed couple, said quietly, "May your love be strong and your life together be long and happy." With eyes full of tears, Anita whispered, "Bless you. May God bless you all."

As they stepped back into the light, the rich blue carpet had already been rolled away.

〰

As they settled for the night at home in Merzhausen, Anita remarked, "On Kristallnacht, while the synagogues burned, the Catholic church closed its doors and closed its eyes. Today, the Church closed its heart."

"I would not ask you to change your faith for what we witnessed today. Whatever god exists sees us for who we are regardless of our inherited allegiances. There is no church where we might marry, no church that would welcome us. But marry we surely will."

On Saturday June 16, 1945, in the registry office of the Standesamt in Merzhausen, Franz-Theo kept his promise and Anita Gallo became, indissolubly, Anita Metzger. There was no ceremony, no crowd of well-wishers, just a small family sharing a house by a field.

In Tuttlingen, Carl Gallo still wondered what had become of his younger daughter.

Regeneration

"You can be thankful you're not in Berlin." Kuhnert's voice was grim.

"We are thankful to be here," replied Franz-Theo. "Why? What have you heard?"

"We have friends there. We received a letter this morning. They're struggling, like everyone else. Starving. The city in ruins. Orphaned children running wild in the streets, looking for food; stealing whatever they can find to trade for a bite to eat. No wonder." He shook his head. "So many men, husbands, sons, brothers, killed in the war; mothers left behind to fend for themselves. And the Russians," he shook his head again trying to push away the disbelief. "Women and young girls raped; what hasn't been destroyed is smashed in anger and retribution. Appalling."

Franz-Theo stood there, searching for words, his mind in turmoil. It's what war does. Brutishness and violence is part of the struggle and the aftermath. Berlin might be far away, but Germany is occupied. Are we safe here? I leave home every day to go into the city, itself struggling to re-build. Anita is by herself, isolated here, even with Eleanor and the children. So far the French have been kind. And no, we don't have much food either. Perhaps we are just far enough away to be safe. Better to be in the countryside than in the cities.

Kuhnert interrupted his thought. "Germany has been an industrialised country. We have always had to import most of our food. What little farming we did has been devastated by six years of war. Machinery broken up for the war effort or destroyed, farms burnt down, fields laid waste, livestock slaughtered. And the workers. All those foreigners brought in from countries we occupied have gone home to their own despair. Even if we could buy food from outside, we can't transport it because the roads are damaged, the railway lines torn up. No wonder people are starving. And they're sick and dying. Disease everywhere; no sanitation. Sleeping in sheds and barns and ragged buildings that are barely standing." He rubbed his hand across his face and pressed his fingers in his eyes.

"What can I say? The killing has stopped, but not the dying. And with winter coming, it will be even harder. Is there anything you can do for your friends?"

"Not really. They have family in other parts of the country and will try to make their way where it is safest. They may be able to get some supplies through the black market. With money and the right connections, it's apparently possible to get suitcases of everything from caviar to chocolate. They'd be happy with some schinken or kassler to put on their bread."

Franz-Theo gave a wry smile. "Yes, some salami would be nice."

Spring had already surrendered to summer and thereafter, in turn, the days became cooler. The occasional thunderstorm had rolled across the hills bringing a pang of sudden fear, a reminder of heavy aircraft low in the sky, the crash of falling masonry or the blinding flash that threw the horizon into stark silhouette. On such nights, Anita would cling tightly to her husband as the house trembled, waiting for the time between the flash and the boom to grow longer and the edge of the thunder to abate. Franz-Theo lay awake counting the seconds, measuring the distance for the noise to travel its 343 metres per heartbeat, pushing away the pain of the past.

Germany's defeat brought even more severe rationing. Vouchers allowed only fifty grams of meat per week. Likewise, only fifty grams of butter; a quarter of a litre of milk and two slices of bread per day. Only once did Anita, with her stomach clawing for food, leave her bed in the middle of the night and eat one piece of the bread reserved for the next day. Immediately, she regretted it, knowing that one slice alone would only make her hunger worse. And then there would be less for the next day. Tea and coffee did not exist, but ground acorns infused in boiling water became something of a substitute until rose hip, clover or elder flower could be found again.

In Freiburg, Franz-Theo continued his secretarial and translation work at the Délégation Supérieur, the regional military government answerable to the central authority in Baden-Baden. Questions of public security and justice were fraught by a contradictory stew of politics, long-held resentment and a desire for rapprochement. In prosecuting war crimes, ordinary German citizens felt more punished than the real offenders, with sporadic outbreaks of hate and anger on both sides – acts of banditry by the occupiers and acts of deceit and obfuscation by those now wanting to hide a bitter and shameful past. The reconstruction of post-war Germany teetered between opposing ideologies and competition for the spoils of war – a struggle that both intrigued and disillusioned the man once hunted, now riding with the hunters.

Soon it was Christmas, though it served only to remind Anita of the happier times of her childhood in Wiesbaden. Every year her father took it upon himself exclusively to decorate the tree in front of the bay window of the dining room, hung with baubles that caught the light of flickering wax candles – and a bucket of water outside the door in case anything should go wrong. The large table, with its embroidered Yuletide cloth, was laid out with presents and, together with Erna, she would play the piano and the family would sing Christmas carols. And the maid Johanna, where was she now? She had been asked by Anna Gallo what she would like for Christmas, but she was too embarrassed to say, even though it was finally divined she would love a watch. When she opened her present, there it was. Beside herself with happiness she put it on and kept looking at it, turning her wrist, checking the minutes and smiling even while she went off to the kitchen to prepare supper. Yes, *Bescherung* had always been a lovely time of gift giving. Such a long time ago. And now? A family riven, a home reduced to rubble, estranged in an occupied country. When all things pass, is anything everlasting?

Despite the excitement of the children and the Kuhnert's kindness, the Christmas days were subdued. Outside it was cold, with sullen skies and flurries of snow. The countryside lay silent and still under its blanket, waiting for the world to turn. In the privacy of the house, Franz-Theo and Anita found in each other a quiet companionship, made all the more precious by shared hardship and enclosed spaces.

Spring brought the children out to play. When they heard Franz-Theo's motorbike at the end of the day, they ran up to greet him, suddenly serious in front of the big machine. He cut the engine and removed his goggles.

"Come, Peter. Do you want to hop up?"

He reached down, hoisted the boy beneath his arms and sat him between his knees on the petrol tank. Hans was jumping up and down. "Me too; me too."

"Just a moment. One at a time."

They played the game, pretending to be flying along, leaning from one side to another, the boys calling "faster, faster!" though they weren't moving at all. The freedom of the road; the freedom of childhood. Franz-Theo smiled.

Anita, unobserved, watched from the door, her heart full of knowing. She marvelled at his ease, so often clouded by seriousness or cramped by memory. Here, at peace in the flush of the spring garden, he had allowed himself to disentangle the cords that bound; had surrendered more absolutely to her love. She saw anew the freshness of his face, the dark brown eyes, laughing today, his full mouth, felt the resonance of his voice. For a moment, he looked his age, just 24, but older, wiser, deeper. She felt a surge of wonder and longing. She stepped out of the doorway.

Franz-Theo looked up, saw her and smiled. He gently prised Hans from the bike and lowered him to the ground before dismounting and walking over. Anita hugged him, kissed him lightly and put her arm through his.

"Come. Let us walk."

Franz-Theo looked at her, enquiring. "What is it? You look different. You know something."

She smiled and squeezed his arm. "Walking will be good for us."

"Why are you being so mysterious?"

"Because I want to tell you something." She stopped, turned and looked at him long and steady. He searched her face, read her grey-green eyes and sensed a sudden wordless awakening. "We are going to have a child."

A wave of dizziness engulfed him. He breathed deeply, holding in the stinging tears. He found himself shaking and wrapped his arms around this woman he adored. There were no words, only swimming clouds of amazement, wonder, gratitude. And then questions. They parted and he held her at arm's length, looking at her, drinking in the calm beauty of her face, the new knowledge, the sudden realisation that there was another life sharing the path on which they stood.

"How long have you known?"

"A few weeks; about six I think. We will need to see a doctor soon to confirm. But I'm sure. A woman knows these things. And you have noticed, even though you didn't know what it was you noticed."

"I did think you have become more lovely each day," he smiled. "And yes, you seem clearer, more still, more sure. Something has changed, but I had no idea why – or what this will mean."

"We can hope it will mean a very happy Christmas!"

Professor Doctor Keller wore wire rimmed spectacles and a shock of greying hair swept back from a high forehead. He was, perhaps, in his late forties and smiled with his cheeks and perfect teeth. He looked like a man who could be trusted, his friendliness undiminished by his status, or his faintly pinstriped suit and mauve tie. The following week, in Freiburg, he confirmed what they already knew. But it came with a warning: times were hard and food scarce. One could not be lured into complacency by summer and autumn, because winter again promised to be hard. Children in Germany were dying through disease and malnutrition. One needed to maintain one's health and strength, make provision for unknown times ahead.

"You must look after yourself and see me again in four weeks. We will make sure you are well and that the baby is safe."

Notwithstanding the exhortations of the good doctor, the demands of feeding two when there was barely enough food for one became ever more worrying. During the long nights, Anita would often lie awake, anxious about the irregular movements of the child within. She would take Franz-Theo's hand, placing it on her belly and ask what he could feel. In the dark, he sensed only a miracle, not daring to think beyond the precious fragility of the moment.

By November, it was deemed necessary to move Anita into preparatory care at the Lorettoberg sanatorium where rest, food and medical attention could hopefully give her the physical strength for what was looming to be a difficult final term. The greater Anita became with child, the more Franz-Theo became filled with even greater anxiety as he watched her struggle. Mopping up the spillages of war became the actions of an automaton until he could sit by her side again in the evening, holding her hand, talking quietly and feeding mother and child with all the energy of hope.

With snow on the ground and winds laced with ice in the depth of winter in mid-December, Anita was moved from the Lorettoberg to the private rooms of Professor Keller now entrusted to deliver the child in Freiburg. The baby had turned and then was still.

"What's happening, Doctor?

"I don't know. We have to wait and see what will happen next."

The doctor was not there to see what happened next. It was a Sunday when the first contractions plunged Anita into a sweat of apprehension and pain. She knew it was no longer simply a cramp; she felt it in her lower back and abdomen, increasing in intensity and becoming stronger and more regular.

Professor Keller had been to church, had lunch and his post-prandial nap before disappearing for the rest of the day. It fell to the midwife to make the decision.

"We will have to stop the contractions until the doctor can be here tomorrow. We will have to give you an injection."

The resulting backwash of hormones created chaos. Her blood cried out as her body heaved until, eventually, she was sedated. Exhausted, she slipped into oblivion.

In the middle of the following night, her waters broke. The midwife was woken by the cry and appeared, dishevelled, by her side. A torrent of questions: contractions? How often? How hard? How do you feel? Weak, confused and in pain, Anita struggled to understand what was happening and could find few words.

"You must call Franz-Theo. Please."

"First I will wake the doctor. All will be well; you must stay strong."

It was morning before Franz-Theo could see her and then only briefly between the bouts of contractions and pain. Confined periodically to a chair in the corridor he struggled to contain the storm in his head. He had seen birth and death, but here the two seemed locked in a struggle beyond his grasp. He paced the carpet and returned to the chair, his head in his hands. He tried to pray. Dear God, whoever you are, God of Abraham, whatever force you are in the universe, whatever it means to implore for help… I know I can ask for nothing; others have implored in vain and yet here we are, so often saved, searching for we know not what. Who am I asking? What am I asking? Let it not end this way. Here, at the most critical time of my life, I am powerless. Nothing I know, nothing I can do can change what is happening. Everything we have endured, everything we hoped for, everything that matters is taking place on the other side of that door.

A wave of stillness followed. Then a muffled cry from the room. Distant voices of comfort and encouragement.

Eventually, Keller appeared, his face drawn.

"The situation is not easy. Anita is exhausted and the contractions have, for the moment, stopped. We can only hope that she is able to regain some strength before she tries again."

"And the baby?"

"The child has turned and appears to be in an awkward position. We don't know yet how, or if, we can turn it again."

"But it is alive?"

"It's probably best if you go and sit with your wife until the contractions resume. Then we will see what we can achieve."

Throughout the night, Franz-Theo sat by the bed holding the hand of the woman he loved, his head sometimes resting on the bed by her side. There was silence. Occasionally he placed his hand on her swollen abdomen as if, somehow, he could breathe life through his palms.

Outside, the day resumed with its watery light. In the room, the lamp burned steadily as Franz-Theo watched the shallow rise and fall of Anita's chest. She opened her eyes and looked at him, exhausted, pleading, lost.

Keller entered, looked at his patient and turned to her husband.

"Come with me." Once outside and the door closed, he continued. "The situation is grim. We will have to intervene if we are to save the mother and, hopefully, the child. Your wife is now in deep distress and exhausted after three nights of struggle. She is unable to continue without assistance. I am proposing an instrument assisted birth. It is too late to try anything else and your wife is now precariously weak. We will try to turn the baby and use forceps to draw it out. We will do what we can to ease the pain but I cannot promise that the child will be unharmed." He waited for the words to make sense. "I need your permission to proceed." Despite the urgency of his words, the voice was kind.

Franz-Theo understood the alternatives: the life of the mother or the child; the woman he had come to know and love, without whom his life was fruitless – or the unborn life, the unknown child. Without the intervention, both are lost.

"There is no choice. You must do what you can."

"I must ask you to leave and come back in an hour or so. It will not do to have you nearby when I need to focus so completely on what has to be done. Please, I hope you can understand."

In that long hour in the birthing room, the whispered instructions were interrupted only by the distressed cries of the exhausted mother.

"If you want your child alive, you must push."

Anita reached into the space by her bed, seeking a hand to grasp. Instead, she met the cool steel of the lampstand, clutching at it as she cried out with what enfeebled strength she could muster. Then, at nine-thirty on the Wednesday morning, December 18, the baby was finally turned and drawn out head first, slippery with vernix and blood, before being held aloft by his heels.

Silence.

Time moved slowly as the seconds ticked away suspended breath. Nothing. Keller slowly shook his head.

Was that a movement? A twitch? A shudder? Perhaps a cough?

At last a cry. Again, a cry.

Suddenly the world had righted itself. Routine resumed. Five kilos; fifty-three centimetres and wrapped to the nose to preserve a precarious beginning.

When Franz-Theo returned, his three-dimensional world had become four. Incomprehensible. Relief, gratitude, elation. He buried his head on Anita's pillow and silently wept. Somehow, his need had reached into the universe.

They named the child Michael Gerson - Gerson being the German variant of the Jewish Old Testament 'Gershom' from the Book of Exodus – a "stranger in a strange land", a status that applied to them all.

CHAPTER NINE

New Difficulties

Someone was pounding on the door. Impatient. Eleanor looked up from her embroidery, startled and angry.

"They'll wake the children. What on earth?"

"It's all right. I'll go."

Fritz opened the door to a stout man wearing a cap and a heavy coat that had previously belonged to a larger man. His eyes were small and his nose and cheeks bore the signs of someone who had enjoyed his glass of wine when it was there to be enjoyed. He carried a notebook and pencil which he had removed from his satchel.

"I'm here to inspect your house." The accent was French; the tone adversarial.

Kuhnert knew exactly why he wanted to see inside – it was something he had long dreaded. Anticipating the worst, he had been fortunate that Franz-Theo and Anita had needed roof over their heads and, in the weeks after Christmas, his mother had also needed support and moved in. Monsieur had seen a large house, was sceptical about the Bosch and saw an opportunity to wield some authority without the need to show any respect.

"You had better come in then." Kuhnert held open the door and calmly stepped aside.

The Frenchman removed his cap and entered, counting the rooms aloud as he walked about. He peered into Hans' room and then Peter's, noted that each had a separate room with toys and a train set and suddenly a steam of indignation burst his proverbial boiler.

"Germany has lost the war," he roared, "and look how these children live, while our children live in cellars!" His face flushed and the veins in his neck bulged. "What do you think it is? These children have a whole room to themselves? Unbelievable! Things will change, believe me!"

"Perhaps you should look further before you damage your health," said Kuhnert quietly.

"How many people live here?" shouted the official, flicking open his notebook and licking the end of his pencil. "How many?"

"There are eight of us in six rooms," replied Eleanor in a voice edged with ice. "Two families; an aged parent; a newborn child – and you have managed to upset all of us."

Half an hour later, the tide of anger had ebbed, only to expose deep undercurrents of resentment and the lingering hazards of shipwreck if he should return.

"One doesn't need bombs to destroy someone's home when you have a man like that," said Franz-Theo, shaking his head.

"Just as well you could speak with him as you did. I think he understood you might have some influence. You could make his intrusions and bluster uncomfortable." He patted his friend on the shoulder. "Now we should set about putting the place back together again."

In Tuttlingen, Erna received her sister's telephone call, time and distance suddenly collapsing. Prolonged absence had served to make them strangers, unaware of the grist of their separate lives, the connections with family and friends, the daily challenges or the progress of ageing parents or growing children. It began guardedly. Anita had long been hesitant to expose the choices she and Franz-Theo had made, decisions that had so fundamentally contravened the wishes of her father and which fell so far outside Erna's linear comprehension. It had been a long silence of self-preservation, not wanting the bright, life-giving moments of her new freedom to be tarnished by corrosive judgement.

Though her mind teemed with questions, Erna instead told of young Eberhard's playful mischief and enthusiasm for all things, how Hannelore was now six years old, eager to be involved in whatever the boys were doing and how Ottokar was flourishing at his Gymnasium schooling to one day maybe follow in his parents' footsteps. Emil was fine, busy with the pharmacy and she had plenty to do looking after the household and trying to feed everyone when food was hard to come by.

"Is Mutti there? Can I speak with her?"

"Sure, she's upstairs; I'll get her. Just a minute."

While she waited with the hum of static on the line, Anita tried to unravel the seemingly ordinary normality of ordered lives. In truth, what else did she expect? Erna had always calmly and steadily followed what, for her, was a pre-ordained path, its milestones measured by duty, a quick mind and a conviction that all was for the best. War may have disrupted the timing but not the order of events. Whatever divinity shaped Anita's ends had hewn an unforeseeable path, an upending of expectations; a crucible whose alchemy had produced a harrowing miracle beyond the aspirations of youth.

"Hallo? Anita?"

In the gentle warmth of her mother's voice, all the love that ever existed flooded her heart. Every tender moment, every kind word, each day shared, was distilled into an embracing aura of understanding and trust. No single moment, no particular event, just the overwhelming abstract that is the inextinguishable bond between mother and child, mother and daughter. She blinked, trying not to cry.

"Anitachen?" Softly.

Her mother's face swam into view – the kind eyes, her silvering hair swept up from a high forehead, her gentle smile. She wanted to hug her close, bury her face against her shoulder, tell her everything, share all the pain, all the joy, all the confusion.

"Mutti. It's been too long. I'm amazed to hear your voice."

"It has been a long time, though you are never far away. The world may have changed, but some things never do. How are you?"

All that had happened since departing Tuttlingen more than a year before was somehow compressed into words of wonderment, laughter and tears. As she listened, Anna marvelled at the transformation that had taken place. Her gutes kind, the good child, having left the nest, had not fluttered helplessly through the canopy to the forest floor, but with strong wings had beaten against the storm to build a nest of her own.

"I will speak with your father and he will come to understand. Then you must visit us, you, Franz-Theo and little Michael. After all, you have made us grandparents, again – blood of our blood, bone of our bone."

"In the summer, it will be easier. Life is still precarious. There is not enough food for me to make sufficient milk for our little boy. He is not well. We struggle with feeding. He also has a persistent cough which worries me. He is not yet strong enough to leave the safety of his cot."

She paused, concerned, doubtful for a moment. "We shall see how he is in the summer."

As she replaced the receiver, Anna understood that great conflict, which had brought such fear and uncertainty to so many lives, had brought a luminous clarity to the path her daughter had unflinchingly chosen.

During the next anxious weeks as summer struggled to break free, young Michael's condition deteriorated. What little solid food he was given he hamstered in his cheeks, unable to swallow and digest it. He fell sick with what was locally called *der Englische Krankheit,* English sickness, because of his pallor, but properly known as rickets. The cough that racked his feeble frame turned into pneumonia. From Merzhausen, he was moved to the hospital in Freiburg. There, in answer to what might possibly be done to save him, the doctors suggested they could perhaps try the new drug penicillin. However, trials had been inconsistent and there had been evidence of adverse reactions, from vomiting to nausea and diarrhoea – all of them risky in this particular case. In fact, angioedema – swelling of the face and tongue – would complicate things further, even if one assumed no further hyper allergic reaction. That said, there was also evidence of seemingly miraculous cures.

"And if we do nothing, then what?"

"He will probably not make it. The infant mortality rate in Germany is, as far as we can tell at the present time, double that anywhere else in Europe."

Struggling to make sense of the situation, Franz-Theo thought his question aloud, "The risk of an adverse reaction, when there is nothing else left to do, is less than doing nothing, am I right?"

"Correct."

"Then we have no choice."

"Probably not, but supplies of penicillin are short and there is none to be had readily."

Franz-Theo gripped his forehead in his hand, his eyes closed. He breathed heavily. Was there no way out? What was he supposed to do? How could he tell Anita? What would happen to this young, struggling life? In despair, he looked up.

"Somewhere, anywhere, there must be something. Where is it? Where can I try?"

"Maybe the French, at their headquarters, among their medical supplies, they may have something. Perhaps. Who knows?"

He returned to Becherwaldstraße without looking back on the sick child in its hospital cot. Now was not the time for good-byes. Anita heard the news, her face set against the fear of infinite loss, her heart pulsing hope.

"I'll do what I can. It may be some hours."

"Be safe. To lose both of you is unthinkable."

With no other choice, no money for medicine, he left the house, mounted the Zündapp, dropped his weight onto the kick-start and headed north. Inside the house, time stalled, suffocating Anita. She needed to act, to get out, to face the world, to confront whatever fate awaited. In the street she waited for a tram to take her to the hospital where she would meet Franz-Theo when he returned. It was a grey, summer day, dour and uneasy. Presently a tramcar rattled towards her. She put out her hand, signalling it to stop. The driver steadfastly ignored her waving and passed by, the young woman's entreaty superfluous to his full carriage. Frustrated and angry, she tried to compose herself, hoping desperately there would be time enough for their audacious hope to be realised. Presently she heard the next tram. She stepped into its path. It stopped and she boarded.

When Franz Theo returned, he carried several vials in his coat pocket.

"Is it possible?"

"Come. We must hurry."

It seemed the doctor had been waiting. He nodded his understanding as, with a mixture of gratitude and relief, Franz-Theo handed over the precious drug.

"It's all right; all is well. Thank you. Knowing that you would replace our supplies, we have already administered the first dose. It was not a risk we could take."

Distraught and bewildered, both parents stood looking at the doctor. Suddenly, tears welled in Anita's eyes. Franz-Theo shook his head, swallowed and turned away.

The nearby French *potager* may not have been laid out as an elegant parterre bordered by neatly clipped hedges – after all, it had once belonged to a German farmer – but it was a vegetable garden of size and substance to feed the occupying army. On her way home, Anita stopped to ask whether she could have a few carrots or silver beet, whatever excess there might be, to feed her small family. Knowing who she was, the workers didn't begrudge her the few beans, kohlrabi or green leaves that might supplement the meagre rations by which they tried to survive. But, at home, no matter how she boiled, mashed, fried or combined what little there was, Michael turned his head away and refused to eat. Each cry of hunger tore at his mother's desperate heart.

Franz-Theo, ever watchful, had observed that cigarettes were currency. He also noticed that it was not possible to smoke the last portion of an unfiltered cigarette, and rarely did anyone smoke all the way to the filter. He began to collect the stubs from ashtrays, the footpath, wherever the dregs had been carelessly flicked. At home, to Anita's consternation and dismay, he would unravel them to extract the precious tobacco.

"What on earth are you doing?"

"This will become food for the child."

"That's crazy – but how?"

Franz-Theo took from his pocket a small packet of cigarette papers and proceeded to roll a cigarette, thin, uneven and crooked. He looked doubtfully at his handiwork.

"The next one will be better."

"And do you expect Micha to eat it or smoke it?" She suppressed a laugh.

"It may seem a bizarre jest, but ten of these will buy me a handful of grain. Another five will pay the miller to turn it into meal. Even without one of these, you will turn that flour into a gruel that Micha will eat and he will grow into a strong boy." He smiled. "Hard times call for desperate measures. Besides, the blend in these firesticks is one a smoker is unlikely to find anywhere else."

She kissed him. "I hope you are not tempted to try one for yourself."

"Not when your kisses are free."

In the afternoon of the following day, he left the house with some carefully tied bundles of currency and a pillow case. He had noted, during his travels to and from work, which farmers grew grain, who kept sheep or a few cows and where he might best try his luck. His second foray brought results: half a pillowcase of oats, though it cost him twenty of his best rolled creations. Finding someone to grind the grain was harder, but the advice of his benefactor eventually yielded the desired result, albeit now with a much depleted bag. As he proffered his thanks, the good miller, well dusted from his efforts, hesitated before asking, "Would you be interested in a puppy?"

Franz-Theo looked perplexed. "A puppy? You mean a dog?"

"Yes. We have a German short-haired pointer. She whelped just a few weeks ago. Five little ones – two male, three female. We can't keep them all, even with the farm." He thrust his head forward and looked expectantly at the new father. "We would give you whichever you chose. I don't want payment."

"But…" Franz-Theo paused, uncertain, "but how would we feed it? It's difficult enough – as you can see – to feed ourselves."

"That's not such a problem. If you go to the abattoir, they will give you the bits of carcase they don't want. The beast might have a disease, or bloat, or infected lungs and that meat would just be thrown away. You can boil it – it takes time, I know – we do it all the time. But you will have another addition to your family … and I can supply you with flour from time to time." He raised his eyebrows expectantly.

Franz-Theo didn't know what to say. He could return home triumphant with a pillowcase of milled oats and be thanked. Or he could add a puppy to be met with consternation and concern. Then again, he remembered Anita's stories of affection for the massive hound she befriended as a child in Bad Schwalbach, or the happiness with which she greeted dear Max in Welschingen. Besides, the promise of flour and possibly other farm produce was tempting. It would be churlish to refuse.

Anita's response was less contradictory than he feared. Whether it was simply her deep love of animals, or the heightened need to nurture, she was delighted by the bright and lively eyes, the intelligent face and his one cocked ear. She was less delighted when, overcome by excitement, he emptied his bladder on her foot.

With the same concerns about food and care as had troubled Franz-Theo at last explained, the adoption was given the imprimatur, "He will be a good companion for Micha as they grow up together."

"So, what shall we name him?"

"I thought perhaps *Jemo*?"

"That's very unusual. Why?"

"If I remember correctly, it's a German variant of Jakob, a man I am happy to remember, although I think he had a sad end. Doubtless there are other interpretations in other languages, but what do you say?"

"I think we should call him Jemo – Jemo of the Puddles."

"And this," said Franz-Theo holding aloft his pillow case, "makes it a most successful day."

Just how successful was measured by the appetite Michael showed for nourishing food. His cough dissolved, his crying abated and slowly he began to gain weight. Like the drifting leaves of autumn, Anita's worries fell away, though the stark and naked branches against the shortening sky presaged the harsh cold of another winter.

Then a letter arrived.

Since he had last seen his father walking away down that dark and narrow street to an unknown destination, Franz-Theo had said little of his suppressed grief. He recalled the shadowy café, the furtive wait for a stranger, his face turned away under the shadow of his hat, his stature cloaked under a long coat. One ungloved hand. Whispered words. Then he evaporated. Long moments seethed with bated apprehension before a cautious retreat to a strange house, the door unlocked and an empty room that faced the murky street. Silence. What was there to say? Sometimes there are no words, the moment being all.

Finally, a tap on the glass. A knock that would lead to another world, a narrow door, a long passage into the night. He felt again the bewildering embrace that held the past while abandoning it for an unknown future. And a man with his life in a satchel, his son marooned in a hostile land.

44a Rue Leys
Bruxelles
3 Septembre 1947

My Dear Franz-Theo,

I do not know where to begin. Eight years may have elapsed, but they have barely separated us from a past that has washed us to the shore we now find ourselves. A war never ends, it merely changes shape.

You will have noticed the date. My best wishes for your anniversary. I can only hope that your survival has not come at too great a cost. You were, after all, left an orphan to make your way as best you could. Thankfully, you have been blessed with a quick and curious mind, sufficient tools one would hope, to enable what must have been a perilous journey. You must tell me all that has happened.

For my part, I have – unsurprisingly perhaps – made a modest living doing what I had previously accomplished with your dear mother.

A small clientele keeps me busy, provides a roof over my head and food on the table. Apart from that, I remain anonymous.

A photograph of how you have grown would gladden my forgetful heart.

Your loving father.

Franz-Theo read the letter twice, handed it to Anita and quietly descended the stairs to the garden. She watched him from the window as he stood among the fallen leaves; understood he needed to wrestle the breaking tide of grief alone; that she would be there for him when he returned. She herself was no stranger to love and loss.

Winter arrived, and with it a warm woollen coat, beautifully cut and crafted to the measurements Franz-Theo had quietly forwarded to Brussels. Anita put it on and turned slowly, the line highlighting her tall elegance, the collar accentuating her face. "It's beautiful." She looked at her husband, hushed by the generosity from someone she had never met. "How did this happen?"

"We have written frequently to each other to find the lost pieces of our lives. I told him about you and Michael and our life here. He asked how he could share that in some practical way, a way that only he could. This is the result."

He looked at her, clothed in the work of his father's hands – love and kindness magnified. "You look lovely."

"When next you write, I will add my thanks. When we can – when we can get a permit – we should go to Belgium. It is important for you to see one another again."

As the days grew shorter, food supplies became even more irregular. Soon, there was little left.

"I don't know how we can stretch what we have any further. Perhaps potatoes, but we don't have any. What do you think?"

"There is a field nearby, between the road and the forest. The farmer seems an angry, suspicious man. He has his contracts to supply the French and shops where people must present their vouchers. I doubt he would simply hand anything over."

"So what can we do?"

Franz-Theo sighed before taxing his conscience. "There's food there. If he won't part with it, we will have to work for it."

"What do you mean?"

"We go, at night, and dig. With a bright moon and a clear sky, we can see. Without a moon, I have the little dynamo torch. It might help."

"And how do we carry them home?"

"I have a satchel. If we are seen walking along the road, it will be less suspicious than carrying a bulging sack - or a pillow case."

"Do we dare?"

"How can we not?"

The night was chilly; the air still. Moonlight waned as fingers of cloud drifted across it. With no other light, their eyes adjusted to the darkness until, at last, they came to the corner of the field and crept in. In silence, on their knees and with bare hands, they pulled away the damp earth and felt for the precious tubers. Some ten minutes later they had enough to fill the satchel, quietly clipping it shut. They raked over the disturbed soil with their fingers and then half crawled to the road. Upright again, and with no-one about, they rubbed the dirt from their hands and walked home as nonchalantly as it is possible when heavy with guilt.

They sinned again, many times, complicit in survival.

In answer to his father's request, Franz-Theo sent pictures. They were just contact prints he made without an enlarger, but sufficient to reveal mother and child and such images as are typical of baby photos everywhere. He hesitated, but finally added one of father and son.

Over the next few months he was unexpectedly rewarded with small parcels of clothes, all beautifully made, but also a disquieting reminder of happier days when a prosperous, well-dressed family spent comfortable times at home or holidaying with friends by the lakes in Austria.

"Perhaps we could save some of our coupons for a treat at Christmas," Anita suggested. "What do you think; what would you like?"

"It's not a traditional Christmas treat, but a small salami would be nice." His eyes twinkled above his crooked smile. "Yes, I know, it's an odd way to be optimistic about the future."

"If that's what you would like, that's what we will do." There not being anything sensible left to say, Anita began wondering how she would make ends meet until they could go to the butcher.

That day arrived a week before Christmas and they returned home with their present to each other, quietly pleased with both their sacrifice and the prospect of a minor luxury after the seemingly interminable hardships in securing food.

"What do you think of hanging it on the window catch by the sink?"

"An excellent idea. Cool enough, and a tempting reminder."

Silly how a sausage could bring such simple pleasure, albeit for such a short time. Returning home on Christmas Eve, they let themselves in and climbed the stairs. Something seemed odd.

Uneasy, Anita asked, "Is something the matter?"

"Not sure." Franz-Theo looked around, standing Michael on the floor next to him. "No, everything is as we left it." He looked again. "Did you move the salami?"

"No. Why?"

"It's not there." Together they went to the window. Certainly there was no salami. But what remained was the strunk, the stump with its piece of string.

"The dog. That's what was wrong. He normally comes bounding to meet us. He's hiding."

Jemo had secreted himself between the two lounge chairs. He looked up, his eyes big, unsure, but definitely knowing that he too had sinned.

Anita stood with her hands to her mouth, unable to say anything – torn between her disappointment and her affection for the beast that had devoured Christmas.

Franz-Theo spoke to the dog. "It's all right. What could we expect? How could you know; you're just a big bundle of affection following your nose. We were foolish to forget. Come here." He patted his thigh. Jemo rose and approached tentatively to have his head scratched.

"I'm sorry," said Anita. "We didn't think."

"It's fine. Everything is fine. Perhaps we simply asked for too much, though I'm not sure Jemo thinks the same." He turned to the dog. "Frankincense or salami?"

The four of them stood together, two parents, a child and a dog. It was a silent night, a holy night – calm and bright.

Anita stood waiting by the front door, the birch trees dappling the spring light that splashed the walls and turned the window panes to mirrors. In the distance she could hear the Zündapp approaching. As had become his habit, Franz-Theo was home for lunch, separating himself from a persistently lingering history to harvest each moment of this new and intimate reality. It wasn't the simple raisin sandwich that brought him home, but the precious moments with Michael and Anita's soft kiss.

"Darling man, tonight you must write again to your father. He has already said that he will try to visit us. Evidently it's easier to enter Germany than to leave it. It will be hard for him after what the Germans did to him – locked him up, stole his home and forced him to flee."

Once betrayed, trust never comes easily. Cruelty eats away forgiveness. Haunted by loss, Franz had secured an unobtrusive sanctuary in his narrow house. One said little, remained close. Venturing over the border would be straying into what was now unchartered territory, a geography of the heart where the border posts had been removed. A creaking rowboat had taken him at night, on black and swirling waters, across the Rhine, away from watchful eyes waiting on bridges. A perilous passage in the dark; somewhere he feared to go again.

Somehow, he had been made a grandfather. The son, named after him, had miraculously crossed another river to a precarious shore. And a woman, Anita Helene, had borne him a son, a stranger in a strange land. Together, somehow, against all odds, they had clung to the flotsam of war and built from it a new home, a new life, a new hope. He summoned his resolve; he would go to Merzhausen bei Freiburg.

Franz-Theo understood it would not be easy. Even with the beast slain, he would not step across its maw without trepidation. How would his father have changed? Sorrow doesn't make one younger. In the age of innocence, age is irrelevant. Now his father would be in his sixty-eighth year, nine years alone, nine years to grieve. How could they not be strangers? How could they not be father and son?

"I will, my darling. We cannot let fears of the past drown our gratitude for today or the sunshine of tomorrow. We must believe we are safe again."

An hour slipped by. Suddenly, it was time to go.

"Johannes, it's late. You have to fly." She kissed him. "Be careful." A moment later she heard the roar of the bike as he sped away. She tidied away the lunch dishes and sat Michael on a rug in the playpen. Jemo jumped over the rail and lay down in the corner before the two of them tumbled over each other – a delight to themselves and the mother who looked on.

Only a quarter of an hour later, Eleanor Kuhnert called from the bottom of the stairs.

"Anita? Are you there? I'm coming up."

She arrived, agitated and breathless. "Here, give me Michael. There's someone at the door for you. You have to go."

Anita didn't recognise the woman at the door. The stranger was flushed from her exertions to reach the house, breathing heavily, strands of hair across her face.

"I live up on the hill by the forest. I think your husband has had an accident."

Eleanor appeared behind her at the door, Michael on her hip.

"It's all right. I'll look after him. Off you go."

The two women headed back along the road, half running, stopping to catch their breath before rushing onwards. Anita tried to quell the dizziness, the nausea of not knowing. Is he hurt? How badly? Between her gasps, she turned to ask, "What happened?"

"The road to Günterstalstraße. It's one way for part of it. He went the wrong way. Another car. Coming towards him. Swerved at the last minute. He must have braked hard. Hit him anyway. Over the bonnet. Don't think he was killed. People came to help."

Finally they reached the place. There was little to see.

"There are marks here on the road. I can't see any blood and there's no broken glass. They must have taken him away and removed the bike. You better come in and use the telephone."

It seemed nobody knew anything, except that perhaps Franz-Theo had been taken home. Frantic, Anita retraced her steps, burst into the house and rushed upstairs.

"Johannes? Johannes, are you there?"

Franz-Theo emerged from the bathroom, his face scratched and bloody, his nose badly swollen.

"What on earth! What happened?"

"I think I've broken my nose." He sounded as if he had an exceptionally bad cold.

"You need to go to hospital."

"No, no. We don't need any fuss. It's still straight, just a bit swollen. It will get better."

"But you could have been killed!"

"As you can see, I wasn't. Lucky yes; but killed, no."

"And the bike?"

"It's here. It will need to be straightened and has some scratches. Amazingly, nothing that cannot be fixed."

"But what were you thinking? What happened?"

"My mind was elsewhere. I followed the path of our conversation instead of following the road."

Later, after the dread had subsided, Anita couldn't help but shake her head each time she looked at his face. He simply turned away and nursed his bruised ego. In comparison with the perils they had endured, Franz-Theo had at least retained a sense of proportion – one to which his nose finally returned.

With the Zündapp repaired and a more cautious journey to work, life resumed a sense of normality. Flowers nodded in the warm breeze of the garden where bees hummed and Anita walked with young Michael. It was slow progress as he stopped to inspect a stick or a pebble before rocking onto his little legs and running into the grass. Sometimes Eleanor would join them, holding her own newborn, the perhaps predictable result of witnessing new life under the same roof. She had called the child Eva and, though she didn't know it at the time, was already carrying another.

One day, as Anita returned to the house, a courier arrived with a telegram, an omen rarely bearing good news. She returned upstairs, set Michael down and unfolded it.

REGRET TO INFORM DEATH OF FRANZ THEO METZGER 21 APRIL 1948 AT 44A RUE LEYS BRUXELLES STOP

Contact details of the notary followed.

Anita found a seat and sat with her hand over her mouth. In shock, her mind repeated "no", again and again. "No." How could she tell her husband? What would he say; how would he react? With all that had become possible, this was impossible. Hope and expectation swept away without warning, utterly obliterated. Why? How? His arrival had been only weeks away, a day that, now, would never materialise. The time for reunion had become a time of separation, a time to mourn. How could she be of comfort in the face of inevitable devastation?

She heard the bike. Her chest thumped with dread as she rose to meet the man she knew would be broken when she handed him the folded paper. She had no words but the tears that stood in her eyes as she passed him the news.

Franz-Theo read the message, each word draining the life and colour from his face; his shoulders slumped, his hands limp by his sides. Finally, he raised his head and, looking at Anita, simply stated, "And so it ends."

Caught by Charybdis against the cliffs of Scylla, the room swirled, his mind shutting away the crackling thunderstorm, sucked into the vortex of wordless sorrow. Shipwrecked, unable to think, unable to speak, he sank helpless into a chair. He could find no tears.

Presently, Jemo rose from his *hundeplatz* to sit at his master's feet, resting his muzzle on his thigh. Inside, only silence; outside, the darkness descended.

The next day, Franz-Theo emerged from a sleepless night where the past had replayed itself through a kaleidoscope of memories: his mother's face turned to him; his father's voice; the shared days in the sun by the lake. A prism of childhood radiating possibility, before the world turned to black.

Disoriented as day broke, he had nevertheless distilled a pathway.

"I will have to go to Brussels to sort out my father's estate. I will have to get papers and permissions. Given my past, that will not be easy."

"Of course. I can stay here to look after Micha and Jemo. It will be easier on your own – but I know it will be hard."

It would be foolish to imagine a bureaucracy would make life easy for anyone, except perhaps those able to serve their own interests. The jumble of records after the turmoil of war only made things more difficult. Requests for information depended on other information that had been lost, misplaced or didn't exist. Both Germany and Brussels seemed intent on creating an ever increasing mountain of obstacles and demands.

During the interminable periods of waiting, Franz-Theo would get out the bike and ride through the hills, the wind on his face, the machine liberating him from the claustrophobia of inertia. Having wound his way through the countryside, past open fields with the late afternoon sun casting long shadows, he returned home calm, his anger and frustration stilled. Sometimes, Anita would be waiting for him in the garden with Micha. She would sit him on the tank, between his father's legs and the two of them would ride a stretch along the road and back. When they stopped in the yard, Micha's small voice would pipe, "Again, again." And his parents smiled, even through their submerged sorrow.

Six months later, as the first snows dusted the landscape, the necessary papers arrived and Franz-Theo left behind his small family to follow his father's footsteps. History has a way of repeating itself, however imperfectly.

He found the house, wedged between two taller buildings. It was a contrast from the villa in its own gardens, to a prison cell and then this pinched space with its banded red and white brickwork. A paradoxical prison that enabled a guarded freedom. On either side, there was a third floor under an attic. Here, the third floor sat under the roof with a dormer window, a smaller one to the side. The second storey had an enclosed balcony facing the street, a modest architectural ornament affording a private outlook. The curtains were drawn. He tried the front door. It was locked.

At the nearby notary's premises he secured a key and returned. He hesitated at the door, unsure what he might encounter, before inserting the key and stepping into the entrance hallway. It was gloomy and smelled musty. He walked carefully through the unfamiliar rooms and wondered at the spaces where furniture might have been. It appeared the ground floor had been consigned to the business: a cutting table, a pair of sewing machines, two cheval mirrors and an adjustable tailors' mannequin. Rolls of fabric and samples of material were set out along one wall. Nearby were empty hanging racks.

Upstairs was a sitting room with a small settee, a walnut bookcase, and a small oak secretaire with a chair. Pictures hung crookedly on the walls. Somehow it felt the room was incomplete. He opened the curtains, dusty now with the motes hovering in the sudden shafts of light. In the empty space along a wall, he noticed marks in the carpet, marks where furniture had stood.

Beyond was a small kitchen, the cupboards mostly bare. A cup and saucer had been left in the sink; a tea towel hung over the back of a chair. A narrow staircase led up to the attic which had been used as a bedroom. The wardrobe doors were open and clothes were laid out haphazardly on the embroidered coverlet. Again, Franz-Theo opened the curtains, as if trying to shed light on what had happened. Who had been here? He could imagine how his father might have lived in the house, could construct a routine of his days and his habits, but who else had invaded his space, had violated his privacy? His father had been adept, organised, meticulous in his dress and manner. He was uncomfortable with surprises, interruptions to his ordered ways. External habitude allowed his mind to explore ideas, history, poetry, philosophy and the creative flair that demanded the discipline of his craft.

He returned to the sitting room and pulled the chair from the desk. On either side he drew out the supports and folded open the front.

Inside, a row of pigeonholes and two small drawers contained oddments of stationery. Papers that had been taken from drawers lay scattered on the desktop. People had been looking for something.

He took out one of the drawers and sat it next to him. One by one he removed the items, among them a small bundle of letters tied together with a length of bias binding. He recognised his handwriting. From between them, photographs slipped out and he saw Anita, saw himself holding his newborn son. Saw his father sitting at this desk, the pictures beside him as he wrote his replies. He sat for some time, his elbow in the desk, his cheek on his fist, and looked beyond the scene in front of him to some distant, invisible horizon.

Presently, he returned the items and brought out the second drawer. It contained what he judged to be incomplete business documents and some scraps with notes. Several pages, written in pencil, had been folded together. Opening them, he found they contained an inventory of the house contents. Immediately he recognised that he had not seen some of the listed pieces: a walnut, mirror-backed credenza; a round cedar folding table on a turned pedestal; a two-door glazed mahogany bookcase; a rosewood salon cabinet; a Junghans mantel clock.

Later, he left the house, locking the door behind him, and walked the streets till he found something to eat. It felt disconcerting when he imagined how it might have been, walking beside the man, hearing his voice as he pointed out the landmarks that had become familiar in this unfamiliar, adopted locale. Now, his questions would not be answered by his father, but by strangers in an office in a strange city where the remnants of his father's life lay scattered on a desk in an alien place.

He returned to the house before nightfall. In the dimness, he climbed the stairs to the attic, cleared the garments from the bed and hung them back in the wardrobe. There being no lighting, he folded back the coverlet and lay on the bed looking up at the darkening ceiling till night invaded the narrow window and consumed the room. Like a young Hamlet, he would have been pleased to see his father's ghost, to hear what had happened; to learn what he must do. But no, only the fading voices from the street and then silence. In that hour, like his father, he was utterly alone.

The next morning, he returned to the offices of the notary. He was obliged to wait before it suited the convenience of the solicitor to grant him an audience. It did not begin well, the man assuming a haughty authority that was obviously misplaced. Leaning back in his chair, he pressed his fingertips together, peered over his glasses and asked, "And how may we help?" He brushed imaginary lint from an expensive suit.

"You could begin by telling me where my father's body has been taken and then let me see his Will."

"Ah," he paused. "He has been buried in the cemetery where his grave has a number. I can look it up for you. As for a Will, there wasn't one."

"What do you mean there was no Will?"

"As I said, we didn't find one and nothing had been lodged with us."

"My father is not a man," he corrected himself, "was not a man, to be negligent in such matters. He was meticulous in his affairs; he would have left clear instructions in the event of his demise."

"We went through the papers in his desk and found nothing."

"I don't know that. But you found something. There were documents relating to his business that were incomplete, invoices, receipts."

"I should be careful making any insinuations of misconduct, Herr Metzger." He leaned forward. "We have gone to considerable lengths to ensure your father's affairs have been properly managed, especially since it has been more than six months before you appeared to finalise matters." The tone was smug.

While his blood boiled, Franz-Theo dropped his voice and, very deliberately and quietly said, "Were it not for the infernal delays created by your office, and the Belgian and German authorities, I could have been here months ago."

The tone became increasingly adversarial as Franz-Theo asked persistently detailed questions only to be met with increasing obfuscation. Where were the details of his banking and financial transactions? What had happened to the clothes that had been made for clients? Why had the pieces of furniture been removed? Where were they now? The answers, such as they were, came with a deal of hand waving and suppressed agitation from a man caught between his own hubris and the disarray of his formerly coiffed hair as he ran his frustrated fingers through it. Each time he swerved from the answer, Franz-Theo would ask the question again with the patient insistence he had acquired working for the French.

What he learned included the implausible assertion that there were debts to be paid and items had to be sold to recover costs. Clients had collected their items, though some of them hadn't paid. Rent was owing for the six months since his death and there were funeral costs. In effect, there was nothing left. On top of that, there would be an invoice for the settlement of the estate.

"And, as I remember Herr Metzger, he was buried in the Cimetière de Bruxelles on the Avenue du Cimetière some five kilometres from here. You may retain the key until you have cleared the apartment, when you will return it to us."

"From what I observed as I came into your offices, some of the apartment seems to have been cleared already. The walnut credenza, for instance. And the mahogany bookcase. They correspond to items on a list you apparently overlooked. Tell me, monsieur, what are they doing here?"

"They were sold and are being retained until they can be collected."

"After six months?"

"I am asking you to leave now. You have exceeded your appointment time."

"And you, sir, have sweat on your brow and have much exceeded your authority."

With that, Franz-Theo stood and turned to leave. At the door he looked back. "There are many ways to steal, but to rob a man of his inheritance, however modest, is among the most despicable of all."

Outside, the fresh air was welcome.

He walked off much of his anger on his way to the cemetery, though the bitterness remained. He arrived in the late afternoon, only to find the gate locked. Closed at 4pm. Frustrated yet again, he walked back to the house to sort through what could be retained or abandoned.

The process was cruel. Here were things that mattered to his father but bore no relevance to a shared life. Given what had been destroyed or stolen during the war, did anything matter at all? The world moves on, things are lost and soon forgotten. Relevance comes by association, and if those memories are unhappy, why do we cling to the reminders? Besides, how to transport anything? Where to keep it?

All the signs revealed his father had lived a modest life. There was little of value left in the apartment, but two things in particular caught Franz-Theo's attention. Upstairs, in the bottom of the wardrobe were three sealed boxes. As he opened them and carefully undid the heavily wrapped pieces, he was startled to see again part of a Meissen coffee set that had graced the dresser in the house in Dortmund. Bewildered and with stinging tears, he wondered how on earth these things had been saved? Who had rescued them? How had they found their way to this dark corner of a cupboard in an attic in a foreign land?

He held a hand-painted saucer to the light, marvelling at its translucency, its delicate fragility. Unbroken. A delicate fragment of the past still intact. The scene arranged itself. He saw the room, saw his mother, recalled the table set for *kaffee und kuchen*, the silver cutlery, the damask cloth, flowers in a crystal bowl. The smell of the still warm apple *streuselkuchen*. And the light, warm daylight filtered through lace curtains. He packed the pieces away carefully and the tableau faded.

In the salon, stowed in the bottom of the bookcase, he found the black box containing the portable Remington typewriter. It too had come from Dortmund through some mysterious form of translocation. He remembered sitting at it as a young boy writing up his schoolwork or typing letters to friends. Two fingers may have been slow, but it allowed him the time to order his thoughts as he wrote. It was a happy reunion.

After three days, he had sourced a trunk which he carefully packed with the boxes, the typewriter, letters and photographs and the few clothes that fitted him. The rest he offered to a second-hand dealer, a whining, miserable little man offering an opinion as to why things weren't worth much and how the trade was difficult and he barely made enough to keep a roof over his head. Avarice is always ugly.

"Just take it," said Franz-Theo. "I wouldn't want you to have a troubled conscience knowing you too had robbed me."

He went again to the cemetery, carrying a towel in his satchel. There was some confusion as to where Franz Metzger might be interred. Was it Franz or Francis? When did he die? Do you know the date he was buried? Was there a monument?

"Ah, at last I think we have it. It's been a busy time. Lots of people dying. The plots are numbered." A sudden idea illuminated his commentary. "Like our days. Come with me and I'll show you."

Not all the plots had numbers, but at the end of the row it was possible to step out the distance between the graves to find the mound, or the collapsed indentation where a body might have been consigned. Having found the place, the attendant in a moment of deference, said, "I'll leave you to it. Pretty sure this is the place." He looked at Franz-Theo, a lonely man with a satchel, before adding, "I'm sorry, sir." He stood aside and then walked back the way they had come. Strange, he thought, everybody has a story – and usually a sad one – but this young man, well, he was very serious. Didn't say much; very intense. He'll probably be all right, but there's a lot going on.

There was. Franz-Theo stood there trying to imagine his father in a coffin, already collapsed in the damp, dark earth. He could see only his face as he last remembered him, serious, thoughtful, reserved. He had not witnessed how death had touched him, though the notary had revealed it was a heart attack in the bathroom that had claimed his life. Mortality had surprised him, uninvited, when he was unprepared. There was to be time before an afterlife. No more.

He knelt at the foot of the grave, opened his satchel and removed the towel. Carefully, he scraped a few handfuls of earth into it, before folding it again and locking it away. A keepsake. Maybe he would plant a tree and spread the soil around its base so that the living thing would be a reminder of the dead. He knelt for some time. No prayer came.

His return to Merzhausen was met with relief. Anita understood that one cannot bargain with death and its ways are hard. She waited for him to set out the burden of his grief in his own time. Besides, she had sad news of her own to reveal.

"Where is Jemo?"

"I'm sorry, Johannes." Tears welled.

"Tell me Weli, what has happened?"

"He's outside. Covered with a blanket. Poison; fox bait. He came home yesterday, very sick. Before we could do anything, it was over."

They went downstairs and Franz-Theo lifted the blanket from his head. The body was cold and stiff; the eye veiled. Not Jemo, but still Jemo. Death had been cruel, painful, unremitting.

"I wanted you to still be able to see him, to say goodbye. Fritz offered to help, but I couldn't bury him. After what you have just endured, this...." She couldn't finish.

The snow was deep, the ground cold and hard. As he dug, hot tears blinded him as the hole went deeper. He couldn't think, couldn't speak; felt only hopelessness and overwhelming loss. Each shovel of dirt only made the burden seem heavier, an answer further away.

At last it was done, deep enough to bury a dog. They laid a blanket in the earth and arranged the corpse as best they could in the cramped, dark hole. Words would sound trite, so they wept tears of sadness onto his fur before covering him and shovelling the ground over the grave.

During the night, it snowed again, sealing the tomb.

Farewell

"There's nothing left, not here, not in Germany." Franz-Theo's voice was tired, a man lost in the wilderness. Anita saw how he had shrunk into himself, heard the futility in his words.

"My poor darling. I don't know what we can do." She sat closer, putting her arm through his. "Everything that was important to you has been taken away – I understand that. Life has not been kind, not to you, not to your family."

"No." He paused, remembering. "Once, we thought we might escape to Switzerland to begin a new life. Just as well we didn't make it. The Swiss were just as likely to hand us over to the Germans who would have made an end of me. We always suspected something was wrong, but only now do we know about the labour camps – Dachau, Sachsenhausen, Buchenwald, Auschwitz-Birkenau." He shook his head. "It's not *what* happened there, but *that* it happened. What have we become?"

"It's as if, in the beginning, we were hypnotised. Then… who knows how it could happen?"

"It was allowed to happen. Germans were complicit. They did these things. Every day I work in Freiburg I hear people shifting the blame, claiming their innocence when they should have said no."

"To refuse was to be shot."

"I know, I know. I just see everything I value lost in the smoke from the chimneys of Birkenau. When that can happen, appropriating the family home, the bank accounts, the imprisonment and the persecution is all just a prelude that serves a greater moral bankruptcy."

"What do you want to do? You still have me and Michael."

"I don't know. I can't stay here. I can't hear German spoken anymore; I never want to ever see another swastika. I can't face the bureaucracy, the rules, the police. I've seen the effect all this has had on others, on my family, the cancers that flower in body and mind."

"Then where should we go?"

"It's not as simple as just running away. What opportunities are there for us now if we stay? People are leaving all the time – a huge post-war migration to the States, Canada, to Argentina, to Australia. America and its allies are assisting."

"You want to leave Europe entirely?" Anita was incredulous.

"I'm sorry Weli. I know you still have your parents and Erna and Emil and the children. Your father has not been kind to you – on my account I know – and I know life has not been easy for all of them either. It's really a question of where you want to make your life."

There was a long silence as each of them tried to digest where their conversation might take them. Eventually, Anita put her hand on her husband's cheek and turned his face to her. She looked at him, long and steady and then said, "Wherever you go, I will go with you. Wherever we go, we will make our life together, both of us with little Michael."

"I said to you in the very beginning – as I hesitated to tell you my story then – that I was a man with few prospects and I would understand if you chose to not see me again. By some miracle you have stood by me and saved my life countless times. All that, despite your father who, in some perverse way, imagines that with me arrested you would be happy again. My prospects are no better now."

"We have always known, from the moment we sealed our destiny with that kiss in the snow so many years ago, that there is no other way."

Anita looked at him, her grey-green eyes clear, certain that nothing – not war, hunger sickness or hardship – could threaten the bindings of her heart.

In the weeks that followed, Franz-Theo set about discovering what he could about The United Nations Relief and Rehabilitation Administration, UNRRA. Roosevelt had already used the term United Nations in 1942 to represent the forty-four allied countries whose mission it was to re-settle displaced persons. Many were survivors from Nazi concentration camps, labour camps or had been prisoners of war. They had witnessed rape, murder, looting and death. Mistrust and trauma accompanied them wherever they went, whether they were repatriated to the fragments of their families and villages or hazarding the remnants of their lives in a foreign land. Sickness and suicide abbreviated hopes already lost.

Knowing that Germany could never be his home – after all he had been declared Polish and then stateless - Franz-Theo had secured forged Polish passports for himself and Anita. There might well come a time they needed sanctuary other than in the country of his birth, the fatherland that had rejected him. How this would play out with UNRRA was yet unknown, but as always, it would be wise to be cautious – nationality meant politics, and religion meant prejudice. Perhaps it would be safer in the moment to embrace Catholicism. Why, in the world, did the labels pinned on us by others, so define our identity? Why the swastika? Why the yellow star of David?

On Christmas Day the Kuhnerts were blessed with another daughter, appropriately baptised Christine. The burgeoning household served as a potent reminder to Anita that there was a family in Tuttlingen from whom she might be separated for some time. She resolved to visit, relieved in a way that she would be unable to define any more than a general intention. Now was not the time for interrogation, but to create the memories that would sustain her in the times to come.

With snow still deep, it proved a pleasant time. She went with the three children past the cemetery to the gentle slopes around Burg Honberg where she delighted in watching them slip by on their little skis, arms waving, a leg in the air, their happily accidental version of a *Schuhplattler* folk dance. The laughter of children was something she would miss. Their voices calling Tante Anita.

At home, in the warmth of the Engel, there were tales of the French Officer who had lodged there briefly. The occupiers were as much in need of accommodation as the displaced locals and it would not do to create animosity by refusing hospitality. His stay had come to a more abrupt end than anticipated when one day there was a disturbance in the street below. In his haste to establish what was happening, the soldier rushed to the window and poked his head out. Unhappily the window was closed at the time. A most serious affair, but with the window temporarily boarded over and the damage to his skull less injurious than his punctured ego, the man left for less hostile accommodation. For the family, the brief discomfort was replaced by a wry and lasting amusement.

The days passed quickly, each one bringing a growing awareness of loss that Anita tried to conceal. Her mother sensed the underlying sadness.

"What is it Anitachen?"

"Nothing Mutti. We are not sure that we can stay here in Germany any more. Even with the war ended, the memories are cruel – especially for Franz-Theo. It might be a little while before I see you all again."

"Where will you go?" The question was gentle.

"Not sure yet. But I don't want you to say anything. It would only upset Papa, Erna and the children. Better to wait until we know more clearly what will happen." She looked at her mother, then turned away as tears filled her eyes.

Anna Gallo harboured the uncertain news in silence. Her daughter's choice was not wilfulness, the simple assertion of an independent spirit. It was born of loyalty and a fierce commitment to a shared destiny that surpassed either understanding or expectation. She feared its consequences out of compassion for her child. Carl Gallo had only ever seen the limitations of his daughter's choice.

In Merzhausen, winter was relinquishing its grip. Michael missed being taken for walks by the dog and pulled his little wooden cart around the garden instead. Sometimes, Franz-Theo would hoist him onto the tank of the motorbike and they would ride slowly around the mountain roads in the evening light.

A steamer trunk with wooden bindings had been found and into it were packed the few possessions that would provide the essentials for a new start. Some precious items from home – tablecloths monogrammed with "AG", hand embroidered bed linen, some porcelain and silver were too precious, too personal to leave behind. Clothes that had been made by Franz-Theo's father – a coat for Anita, some suits and shirts - were packed into two suitcases. One single Australian pound note had been bought on the black market.

Furniture had to be abandoned – the dresser that had been made for them, the table and chairs, kitchen utensils. All those things that had been rescued from the past or that had formed the beginnings of their new life together, were relinquished. Hardest of all was yet to come.

"What do we know of Australia?" Anita asked as they closed the catches on the trunk.

"Probably as little as Australians know about Germany. Apparently they play tennis there. That suggests something – I'm not sure what - about the quality of life. And it gets hot in the summertime. I was told that apples bake on the north side of the trees."

"How on earth will we cope with that? What will we do for work, to earn enough money to live?"

"I have no idea. If I have to break stones by the side of the road, that's what I will do."

"You are not made for that. There must be something else. But why Australia; there are other countries?"

"Australia is furthest away. Argentina is about twelve thousand kilometres; Melbourne in Australia is around sixteen thousand. The other end of the earth and probably far enough away from everything that has happened here."

Anita looked at him and shook her head. How deep the scars. She had witnessed the periods of withdrawal, had woken him in the night when nightmares had torn the fabric of his sleep. She had seen the look on his face, dark in his eyes, as he met the reminders of his past. Does one ever recover? How far away is far enough?

It was time to say goodbye. Cruel to leave when tulips are pushing through the violets, the sky blue and spring sunshine on fields. Looking back is hard. A farewell has few words to harvest shared lives. They said adieu in the garden and Fritz accompanied them to the station to catch the train to Tuttlingen. With the luggage stowed, he turned and said, "So there it is. I wish you good luck my friends. I admire your courage – but then again, I've seen enough to know you can survive."

Franz-Theo reached out to shake his hand. "You asked few questions and you gave me work and shelter. I can offer you no more than my deepest gratitude." He paused, considering where to go next. Best to say little. "Your kindness will be long remembered Fritz. Give our love to Eleanor and the children."

So saying, his emotions harnessed in the formality of his words, they boarded the train and it drew away from the platform to head east for one last time. A small family, two suitcases and a trunk, on a train in Germany, heading into the unknown.

Erna and Emil met them at the Apotheke and, leaving their luggage in the entrance hall, proceeded upstairs. Ottokar, about to turn fourteen, was happy to see his Tante Anita, but was at that age when a more respectful formality seemed appropriate, especially in the calm before something portentous. Eberhard had lost nothing of his boyish optimism and happily gave his aunt a hug of welcome. Hannelore, shy, stayed close by her mother. Franz-Theo, despite his smile and kind greeting, was not familiar.

It was Emil who confronted the awkwardness of polite greetings, the weather and the journey.

"So, you are going to Australia. Why so far away?"

Franz-Theo had anticipated this was coming. He knew the deep reasons would be impossible to explain to those who didn't know him. Caution and diplomacy permitted him only to say that UNRRA had assured him that Australia offered the best prospects for work and a new life and that there would be opportunities for Michael growing up in a new land.

Anna's voice was sad. "You have given us a grandson. We barely know him. How can you take him away from us, from his own flesh and blood, from his cousins?"

Anita looked at her mother, understood the hurt. "I'm sorry Mutti. I can see how hard it is for you. And it will be hard for Micha too, having to make new friends; not having an extended family around him. It will be hard for all of us."

"Why leave at all? The war is over and Germany will rebuild." Carl Gallo turned his good eye toward the stranger who was his son-in-law.

"The war is not over. No war is ever done; it reverberates through history. The shelling may have stopped, but a war persists. A German is still a German and memory runs deep."

There was silence. Emil, earnest and persuasive, took up the argument.

"There will be work, lots of opportunities. So many have died, returned to their homelands or been injured. We need workers, doctors, teachers, businessmen and women. You can stay. We can make room here."

Carl turned to his daughter.

"Anita, you would leave your family? Leave your mother, your sister?"

"Papa, I have already left home because I was given no other choice. It breaks my heart to leave my family and God alone knows whenever I will see you again. But I have made a promise and it is one I will not break, not for anything on this earth."

In reality there was not much more to be said. During the meal later that evening, Erna quietly regarded her sister and knew that she was not for turning. Why, she did not understand, but there was a growing respect for this woman who had chosen such a perilous path and who so unshakeably knew her own mind.

In the morning, they would catch the train to a transit camp south before another train journey to the International Refugee Organisation's embarkation centre Bagnoli in Naples more than a thousand kilometres away. There were promises to write letters and send pictures and such good intentions as would console those leaving as those left behind.

Despite the generosity of the breakfast, nobody shared any appetite for eating as they faced the imminence of departure. Finally, in the hallway against the backdrop of the Müller stained glass window, the children watched bewildered as their parents cried and hugged one another in an outpouring of sadness and grief. As she held her daughter one last time, Anna whispered, "My darling Anitachen. How can I say goodbye when I already know I will never see you again?" Tears were her only answer.

And so they parted. Emil took them to the station and loaded their cases. He embraced them once more, turned and walked away, his head down. He did not look back. From the window of the carriage, Anita scanned the platform as the whistle blew and the heavy iron wheels began to turn. It was then she saw her mother, a solitary figure with her hand raised in farewell, her white hair caught by the wind.

⸏

The Displaced Persons Camp at Bagnoli was originally designed to support young people in need and had included a school and workshops, together with dormitories and an infirmary. It later served as a German Officers Training School before reverting to an orphanage. By 1944 it had been made home to a US Squadron before becoming the IRO's Processing Centre.

Families were segregated. Anita and Michael found themselves in Block D, room 39, in a vast, bare concrete building with only a bunk for any comfort. Nearby was a canteen that would keep them fed for the three weeks it took to process the required documentation. Names, date of birth, DP Card number, nationality claimed – an interesting term given the personal histories of many – and the level of education attained. For many answering the question about addresses of relatives or friends in Australia, the answer was 'nil'. How many admitted to 'Civil Offences' would never be known. Applicants were also required to pass a literacy test and submit to the IRO's Resettlement Medical Examination.

Entry to the Commonwealth of Australia came with a caveat. Each refugee had to sign an undertaking written in English and German.

UNDERTAKING: I hereby certify that the personal particulars supplied by me to the Australian Selection Officers are true in every respect and that I have made myself familiar with the conditions under which displaced persons can emigrate to Australia. I fully understand that I must remain in the employment found for me for a period of up to two years and that I shall not be permitted to change that employment during that period without the consent of the Department of Immigration.

"But Johannes, they can ask you to do anything?"

"They cannot ask me to do anything that has not been done before.

It will be all right. I don't think they can ask a photographer to be a blacksmith. I am more concerned that we were told families would not be separated, yet already – for reasons I can understand here – we have been."

Anita befriended a Latvian lady, her blond hair swept back, her face open and kind. Her husband was quiet and gentle – a well-educated family with a boy around three years old. The children were playing when suddenly, in a moment of inexplicable jealousy, he threw a clockwork toy striking Michael in the left eye. Thereupon the spring broke. Blinded with blood and pain, Michael's screams brought parents running. Unable to properly assess the damage, and terrified her child would be blind, Anita demanded an urgent trip by taxi to the hospital in Naples.

At first, the entrance to the city appeared quite beautiful to her with the Piazza Giovanni on one side, the waterfront on the other, but quickly the streets became narrower with bookmakers, seamstresses and workers having to move out of the way as the car threaded its way through. Arriving at the hospital, she was horrified by the chaotic disorder, voices raised as staff rushed past each other, blood everywhere on cottonwool, in dishes, on the floor and the aprons of doctors and nurses. Eventually a doctor arrived and removed the handkerchief that had been held over the wound. Close inspection revealed that scratches to the eyelid would heal with time as would the tears to the cornea. There was nothing more to be done and Michael would grow up learning to compensate for the damage to his sight. A patch would protect his eye for the next few days.

Despite his concerns, Franz-Theo tried to make light of the situation. "If we are travelling by boat, it's just as well we have a pirate on board." Michael didn't understand and Anita was not amused.

Isak Skaugen, in 1948, had purchased the incomplete vessel *Ostmark* to refit as a cargo carrier. However, when he learned the International Refugee Organisation was seeking a charter of suitable tonnage to assist the resettlement of displaced persons, the ship was renamed Skaugum and provision was made for 1,700 passengers. Conditions were austere at best. Sea trials of the 11,626 tonne twin screw vessel were conducted in April 1949 and she was deemed ready to begin service between Italy and Australia.

As passengers began boarding it became evident that luggage was going to be an issue. Among the more practical, people had packed boxes with things they could sell when they arrived, microscopes, precious artefacts, tools and equipment. Boxes, crates and steamer trunks took up precious room, with the ship's master becoming increasingly alarmed and agitated about the numbers he had to squeeze onto his boat. But Italians are good at packing sardines – and so it felt to those pressed into the tin can set upon the water. Many were sick and still malnourished from their wartime hardships, especially children among whom disease spread quickly – measles, scarlet fever and whooping cough. The next four weeks would test them all.

On Monday the second of May 1949, with 1,619 passengers on board, the *Skaugum* steamed away from Europe to the other side of the world. Anita Metzger (817), Franz-Theo Metzger (818) and Michael Metzger (819) were among those on their way to the Promised Land.

ALL LOVES EXCELLING

AUSTRALIA

Intermezzo

The sea is a stranger bearing foreigners on unpredictable waters. It tries their stomachs, tests their legs. It does not pay to watch the shifting horizon from a heaving deck. Coracle or cargo ship, the ocean is large and deep, beset by gales or shrouded in mist. On a clear day it is a sheet of glass stretching to an unbroken line, a precipice at the edge of the world.

"Where are we?" ask those who have never before seen the sea; those who have emerged from bunkers into the light of a changed world. Many are unable to surface from the visions of darkness and smoke. They see the faces of loved ones gone; hear their voices in memory's ear. Cramped in the narrow hold, in the fetid sweat and smell of sickness, their past accompanies them across the waters. Wasted children cry. Some will die. Even those buoyed by the DP camp posters depicting Australia as the "Land of Tomorrow" find themselves more threatened by the perilous conditions in the bowels of the vessel than the pitching world beyond.

But it is hope that pushes the boat forward from Naples into the waters of middle earth, then onto Port Said and the narrow neck of Suez into the Red Sea. Against the unknown, many have made provision by stowing away seeds in the cavities of clothing and children's stuffed toys, fearful that what sustained them in the past will be taken from them in the future. Salami and olive oil are insurance against the plain and unremarkable ship's rations of potato, meat and wilting vegetables. Alfonso Bialetti's stove-top mocha pot will, in days to come, brew the

---

[10] ...yet now behold the New World o'er the wave!

espresso coffee from the beans now buried in the linings of clothes.

The vessel is re-stocked in the port of Aden before heading into the Arabian Sea. Those who have found their feet are playing cards or chess, gambling or making music. New alliances are forged and some are consummated in dark corners above decks or in a lifeboat under starlit skies. There will be children and, sometimes, a wedding.

Colombo's exotic atmosphere carries the spices of curry and stifling heat. In the cramped bunks below it is impossible to sleep. Like fish drowning in air, passengers gasp on pillows dragged from their cabin into the sultry night. As the sun lifts from the sea, they retreat again to the stifling darkness.

The journey south cannot escape the equator. Neptune's court will test these novices making their maiden voyage, their pleas and prayers for safe passage. Mercifully, a bargain with superstition is not a bargain with death and the *Skaugum* crosses the line to head into the Southern Ocean.

The weather is calm when Franz-Theo finally coaxed Anita from the sullen dimness of her cabin. She felt weak, wracked from seasickness and separation. Michael had cried with fever until exhaustion overtook him. It was to be the beginning of something worse.

The sun is an elixir and she sits on the blanket laid for her and the boy. Despite her suffering, she is a picture under a wide sun hat, a halter top, her long legs tucked to the side. Franz-Theo captures the moment of her smile with the Rolleiflex, Micha beside her.

"Look, Weli," he insists, "flying fish!" He knows they will never see such sights again. Anita sees only the horizon, gently heaving, and turns away.

Night comes again and Micha is consigned to the medical quarters. His eyes have become inflamed and the insides of his cheeks have white spots. His cough is dry; he has a fever and his face is spattered with a rash. Others share the same symptoms as rubella rages unchecked, the air heavy with droplets of contagion.

As the ship heads south, night storms light the chopped silver plate of the sea with growling sheets of luminescence. Gusts of wind fling broadsides of spray as she pitches into the current, forging downward, alone in the expanse of water and sky.

Days pass till, distant on the port side, a faint line materialises darker than the vault, lighter than the sea. Slowly the line builds to a coast, adding pieces to its identity, beckoning those crammed to the railings. Fremantle sends a tugboat to bring the ship safely to harbour. Is it imagination? The air feels different, the light is brighter, the ship is still. Passengers step with sea legs. There yet remain eight days and one thousand, seven hundred and twenty nautical miles across the Great Australian Bight. But the mood has changed, the music played with more gusto, the friendships more intimate, the hope more urgent. Small lives cling in the dark.

A wide, opposing arc charts the perilous south coast littered with the hapless wrecks of sailing vessels claimed by rocks, reefs and storm till, at last, the Skaugum turns to enter the Heads of Port Phillip Bay and steams to Station Pier. Myth and hopes, dreams and despair will find their owners on a new shore in the days and years ahead.

CHAPTER TEN

Transitions

The wharf is crowded, as much with emotion as by swarming customs officials, baggage handlers, photographers and welcoming parties. Thousands mill in a cacophony of orders and greetings, shouts and cries, a smorgasbord of tongues, Babel on a railway pier. Cars and ambulances weave between buildings. A train is waiting. Some are on their knees, thankful for safe passage. Others stand in awe, wide-eyed, their hearts full, searching for a sign that says not my end, but my beginning. Tears of relief are also the tears of parting, forsaking the brief camaraderie of lives that clung to one another over thirty days across the unknown seas.

Families with small children and those plagued by measles or wasted by diarrhoea are the first to disembark, the most fragile taken by ambulance to Melbourne hospitals. Those who have family to meet are given a blue button; single women a white one, and those going to Bonegilla have yellow. A moment of hesitation, but this time the badge is not a sentence to oblivion.

The train is long, the access high. It is a scramble to lift the battered cases, the parcelled lives, into the wooden compartments. A steam locomotive pants in readiness. Franz-Theo prepares room for Anita to sit, Michael lying limp and listless across her lap. He regards his son but says nothing and his face is grimly set. What have we done? What have I asked? We left what remained that we might live, might make, for this frail scrap of mortality, a better life. To save myself, what must I lose?

Ahead, the commotion resolves itself with a rising head of steam, a harsh whistle blast and a waved green flag. Iron wheels turn, couplings clank and Franz-Theo is momentarily uncoupled from his fears.

Passengers lean from open windows, shouting their goodbyes, waving to those now slipping behind as the wheels gather pace and the engine settles into its rhythm, beating the iron rails.

It is not long before they leave the city at Broadmeadows and head north-east into ever widening countryside. It is a strange land. Emerald fields have been replaced by paddocks, some still brown or bare after the baking heat of a summer barely alleviated by autumn's cooler days. The landscape is punctuated by stark skeletons of ringbarked trees thrusting into a blue sky; a ploughed patch of red earth. There are scraps of bush, the dun-coloured leaves of the eucalypts an alien green. Some believe the bark that falls away means they are dying. Grey sheep stand in the wide open spaces, gather around a concrete water trough, or clump in the shade under a solitary crooked red gum. Sometimes a low weatherboard farmhouse emerges, and occasionally a ramshackle barn, its timbers slipped and its corrugated iron roof stained with rust against the background hill.

It is late afternoon when the train stops at Benalla and disoriented passengers straighten, stretch and stumble to toilets and water. Food has become a priority. Those who had imagined they might disappear, melt into a landscape to make their own way, have seen enough to accept it would be futile. Having come this far, what would be the point? They had forgotten in the moment that the running was over.

As shadows lengthen, the journey continues, clattering through the landscape. The air is cool. Anita enfolds Michael more tightly in the blanket from his grandfather in Brussels. Franz-Theo takes his coat and wraps it around her shoulders and they huddle against each other, draining as the day drains.

After eight hours and pushing into deepening darkness, the journey grinds to a standstill. As the engine subsides, silence rises around them. Where are we? There is nothing. No building, just an island platform, a siding by a spur rail in the bush. There are brackets of withered grass. As eyes become accustomed to the dark, they are surrounded by looming silhouettes of trees reaching to unfamiliar stars.

Buses are waiting and more arriving to take them to the processing centre. The camp is vast, a former army training facility now repurposed for one of the largest migration programs in Australia's history. Twenty-four blocks with twenty families in each and sharing a common kitchen, bathroom and mess room. The huts are low, corrugated iron, three steps to a wooden door and a four-pane window to the side. Enter and find an iron bed with a base of wire mesh, a thinly stuffed kapok mattress and pillow and a pair of grey woollen army blankets; a folding camp table, a canvas chair and a chest of drawers The walls are thin and there is little shelter from the either the neighbouring inmates or the elements.

Here, in this sprawling enclave in the middle of nowhere, it will be easier to maintain control, away from the pockets of migrants in the cities. Isolation and austerity ensure the migrants will not live better than Australians. The men will be sent to work as labourers on nearby dairy or tobacco farms at Myrtleford, or vineyards along the Murray towards Mildura. There are other unskilled jobs in factories, harvesting sugar cane in Queensland or cutting timber in the logging towns. Women will find work as domestics or, if they have good language skills, will find secretarial employment. As they wait, disoriented and homesick, the authorities will not hear them quietly sobbing on their chicken wire beds under black blankets in the endless night.

Amendments are made to the documents. Franz needs Theo added and his stateless nationality augmented by 'Pol' in brackets, Anita has 'German' added to hers and her religion has become 'r.c.' – it may be easier that way. Although families were promised they would not be separated, Anita is not well and will be sent to Cowra in New South Wales where there are additional medical facilities. It is three hundred and sixty-four kilometres away to the north-east. Franz-Theo will be sent to the Department of the Army in Albert Park in Melbourne, three hundred and thirty-seven kilometres south-west.

Michael, also 'stateless' has (Pol) added and has, at once, become both Polish and Catholic. Perhaps it won't matter. He is now so ill that he will require urgent medical attention in the camp infirmary. Even wrapped in his Brussels blanket, his temperature has dropped alarmingly.

"Do you know what is the matter with him? Why he is so sick?" Anita's eyes are wide with fear.

"There are lots of sick kids, but this one's unusual. Not much of him either. Most of them have high temperatures. Could be scarlet fever, but we don't know."

"What will you do?"

"Take him in; keep an eye on him." The doctor's tone was matter-of-fact. "Not much we can do really. If he dies, we'll let you know."

He holds out his hands to take the bundle while Anita and Franz-Theo try to understand the words. "We'll let you know?" This is a human life, a precious child. Our son. Is this why we left Germany? "If he dies?" We thought the Nazis were cruel. Heartless. And you say this to us, as if it means nothing? Where have we come? With her heart breaking and her eyes full of tears, Anita turns to her husband and clings to his arm. Franz-Theo looks at the doctor who is already turning away as he hands the child to the nurse beside him. The blanket falls away exposing the fragile frame, the face ashen, his eyes closed. "If he dies." What choice is there? What else can we do? Hopefully there will be medicine; food. Once more, it has come to this; caught by forces beyond our control, even here at the other end of the earth. And we must trust strangers with this most precious life in the world.

Together, they stand silently bound by dread, before turning away to find their room. Anita, sitting on the edge of the bed, feels numb, empty. She has no words; her child taken from her. An abyss of unknowing as the night closes in, cold, unremitting. The washed out light of day is welcome relief from the sleepless night. Wrapped in the warmest of their clothes, they make their way to the hubbub of voices in the dining hall. The lingering smell of baked mutton floating in vast trays of fat drowns the frying of sausages and eggs. Will there perhaps be porridge? Hesitantly, they join the queue, unable to attempt conversation, taking in the simple wooden structure of the building, the bare tables, the animated faces of those who have already made acquaintances or found friends. Someone, unshaven, eyes sunk in his drawn face, wanders aimlessly with a tray, solitary, lost in an alien world. Franz-Theo recognises a fellow traveller.

Even after weeks of transit and barely digestible food, the strangeness of the camp's offerings is mostly inedible. Waves of nausea force Anita into the fresh air. Where have we come? What is happening to us? How will it change? What do we have to do? They have to go back into the kitchen to wash their dishes, together with everyone else at the communal sink where the filthy water contaminates the plates and people's hopes.

Daily visits to the hospital bring the same response. "He's still with us, but he's very sick. Maybe his measles didn't come out properly and that's caused his temperature to drop. We'll keep an eye on him." It is cold comfort, but hope is kept warm by the improvised braziers fashioned from tin drums and wire mesh. Whatever sticks can be found or brought back from walks to the Hume Weir, feed the coals that stave off the autumn chill and encourage memories and conversation. Sometimes an accordion or violin ruffles the air and brings perhaps a smile or a pang of homesickness as a familiar tune plays the chords of the heart. Those plucked from neighbouring villages in now distant lands, find themselves shoulder to shoulder in the same kitchen, sharing the same bathroom, huddled around the flickering light of a fire, or asleep on the other side of a partition wall.

It is the carolling of magpies that brings Anita out into a day of bright sunshine. The camp is already busy and children are playing in the dust between the serried huts. She listens to the accents as people pass, trying to guess their origins: Polish, Latvian, Yugoslav, Dutch. Behind her, a voice in German. It is Ilse Traumanis from the neighbouring room in the hut. She is smiling, her blue eyes bright, her short brown hair freshly combed. She has been kind, united by having her own three-year-old Michael. Her husband too has been traumatised by his past and ragged dislocation from home and hearth. She hopes everything will work out for the best. Today is special; the men have decided to go to the weir and try to catch fish. One can only stomach so much of the food here, the interminable mutton, the all-pervading smell. "Just imagine, fresh trout. How long has it been since we have had such a treat?" Anita is curious, but uncertain.

"How will you cook it?"

'There is always the kitchen, but one has to ask and they might think it rude. We can always try on one of the braziers or in the coals. I've heard the aborigines wrap the fish in wet bark or clay to cook it."

"I don't think there are any aborigines here to help us. Lots of refugees, but not many native Australians."

"No. I wonder what happened to them." She mused for a moment. "So you don't want to come today?"

"I'm not sure. We have no fishing rod and have never tried it before. We wouldn't know what to do and I don't think Franz-Theo would like to kill a fish. It's a nice day, so we might try to go to Albury or Wodonga to see what we can find. I think there's a bus we can catch."

It turned out there was no bus, but a green Bedford truck carrying a load of firewood that stopped for them as they walked arm in arm along the road. A battered hat with its dark stained sweatband appeared at the open window. A stubbled weather-beaten face appeared below and a voice called, "You all right? Where you off to?"

The New Australians struggled for a moment to understand the truncated sentences before it suddenly became clear.

"Oh, yes, thank you. We are fine. We are walking to Albury."

"Too far to walk. Twelve miles. Wanna lift?"

"We do not know how far that is. Are you going there?"

"Yeah. Here, hop in."

He leaned across to the other side and pushed open the door. Franz-Theo helped Anita step onto the running plate and up into the cabin before squeezing himself in beside her.

"That's very kind of you. Thank you."

"You from the camp are you?"

"Yes, we are. We have been there for three weeks."

"Migrants. Where ya from?"

Again, a pause as they tried to decipher the question. "We come from Europe."

"That's a long way." They heard, "Thassalong why?" It seemed an odd query.

"Why? It was no longer possible to live there after the war. Everything was destroyed."

Franz-Theo thought it wiser to reveal as little as possible, even if the farmer in his truck seemed friendly and uncomplicated. For all the English classes in Leipzig or Aachen, there was little that corresponded with the Australian version, especially when delivered with as little movement of the lips as would make it intelligible at all. The conversation continued with some difficulty over the noise of the engine and when talking loudly failed to clarify much of the meaning. Nevertheless, they learned that Jim was married to Esme and they had a son David who had left school early to work on the farm where they milked a dozen cows, had three hundred sheep and grew all of their own vegetables. Three hundred sheep sounded a preposterously large number but went some way to explaining the staple food of the camp.

Albury came as a surprise, a rural city with substantial buildings – including a magnificent Italianate railway station opened in 1882 – made roads, houses with gardens and a sense of history untroubled by war. It came as a blinding contrast to the migrant camp stuck in a vast paddock removed from civilisation, one whose inhabitants were mostly the dislocated victims of war. Here, despite the odd looks from passers-by at their formal dress and bearing, they began to feel a glimmer of hope. Others had succeeded in making a life for themselves, growing their children and contributing to the commerce of their world. There appeared no reason they couldn't achieve the same. Later that afternoon, they stepped more lightly onto the bus at the station, exchanging one world for another.

During the next two weeks as the weather grew colder, they explored more of the camp, checking for any mail at the post office, visiting the Catholic and Lutheran churches and spending some time in the recreation hall listening to the musicians who occasionally came together recreating the melodies, and even folk dances, of their homeland. People had brought their past and their expectations with them and so this 'little Europe' swung between a concentration camp and a detention centre; from a place of no hope to a first home.

On a morning in early July, an announcement was broadcast across the public address system. "Would the parents of Michael Metzger please report to the camp hospital." The public naming came as a shock as much as the dread thought of what they would find when they arrived.

"Johannes, what do you think?" Anita's eyes were wide with fear.

"I don't know. After so many weeks without bad news, we can only hope everything will be all right. I know that's not a rational argument, but we must choose to be optimistic."

When Michael saw his mother, he reached out his emaciated arms to be picked up, his eyes big, full of surprise and wonder. Anita gathered him up and he clung to her, his head on her shoulder. Her heart repeated again and again, "My darling boy, my dear, darling child." Tears streaked her face. Franz-Theo looked up, holding in his emotion, silently giving wordless thanks for this reprieve, this living reunion. Finally he turned to the doctor.

"Thank you. Thank you for saving him."

"That's okay, but he's still got a long way to go. He's out of the woods for the moment, but he'll need some good food and sunlight."

It was a difficult message to digest, but the essence of it was understood. Anita asked, "Do you have his clothes? His woollen blanket?"

"No idea. All that will have been lost amongst the stuff that flies around here. You've got your boy back; you can be grateful for that."

"We are thankful, very thankful." Anita wasn't going to be dismissed so nonchalantly. "It's a pity. We brought his things halfway across the world. They were gifts from his grandfather and now they are gone." She waited for him to perhaps say something. Nothing. "Still, we have Michael and are grateful for that much care."

"We'll make arrangements now to send you both to Cowra where there are additional medical facilities. You've now become too sick to stay here. You'll get the chance to become stronger until you can get settled in Melbourne. We're stretched to the limit here. Our paperwork says that you, Mr. Metzger, will go to Albert Park for work and to find a place to live."

They carried Michael back to the hut, his stick legs too weak to stand properly let alone walk. As she changed his clothes, Anita counted the ribs poking through his skin, worried about his wasted muscles, his silent clinging to her.

No sooner united, the following day they were separated again. As he kissed Anita good-bye, Franz-Theo knew that he would remain with her as she held their child close, the fabric of one another. Parting only strengthened the urge to be together, whatever the unseen future. As he held her to him, he promised, "I will find the place that waits for you."

⤳

A Proposition

AHQ Signal Regiment
No 1 Area
Albert Park Barracks
MELBOURNE, 1949

My dearest, best, beloved Weli,

Yesterday morning at 5 o'clock we left Bonegilla and after much trouble the time has come when I can write to you. Throughout it all, I thought of you, but I have to tell you we could not have found a better place. Close to the city, railway station and the sea sits this military area; when one steps out of the door there lies before one a wide street with a large grassed area and beyond it the sea. I wouldn't have believed it had I not seen it.

The officers welcomed us to the camp and introduced us, clarifying that we were free civilians and not under the authority of any of the military. After work we can go where we wish, at night sleep here or elsewhere as we want. Most importantly, we will be in contact with the soldiers, we will eat with them and have access to their canteen. They want to make us Australians as quickly as possible, force us to speak English and so on. The officers, like the soldiers, are great fellows and easy to get along with.

The soldiers and the kitchen hands do all they can for us. In short, so far I have had a lot of luck. There are forty men in the barracks, in sixteen living quarters and there are eight designated camp staff, of whom I am one. We are not required to work or live outside the camp and thus I am in comfortable quarters with good people (two doctors, an orthodox clergyman, and so on). The duties of "mess orderly" have fallen to me; that is, I am responsible for the cleanliness of the mess, supervise the food distribution, give out the bread, jam and cheese and look after the tables. It also means I am last in the kitchen and must speak English – sorry – Australian and hear a lot that is not clear. Understanding only half is stressful. But "noise=nice", "täum=time" and so on. One is supposed to know, but at first it's hard to understand.

I am now called only Frank by everyone, but I cannot tell the Bobs, Bills and Georges apart. The officers are all very kind and casual, though the behaviour of soldiers towards their 'boss' is not particularly respectful. It's not for us to question it. The head chef is unfortunately unable to understand a single question from those who can't speak Australian, even though I am assured they want to do everything they can, finding themselves unfortunately in such a foreign land.

When a DP comes to polish an officer's shoes, a soldier will come to make sure he has the right colour. If he sees that the DP-shoe shiner isn't good, he does his own – that's how it went today with the Russian doctor. Everyone is unbelievably kind to us dreadful foreigners, who have barely arrived in this madhouse, but one quickly becomes accustomed to the treatment - not good.

There was no trouble on the first day and we wanted to see how it would all work out and how we would be paid. It can't be much, because we work so little, and I the least. My designated work doesn't specify hours, which is, to foreign eyes, disturbing. So we drag ourselves from one meal to another while the in-between times are interrupted by tea breaks.

Tomorrow, I want to make myself at home, look around and get organised, so that on the weekends I can find a job. With Saturday and Sunday being paid, I can perhaps earn some money – dishwashing at £2 per day, I've heard. That way I can specialise in the kitchen when I find a hotel.

I am incapable of intelligent work; my thoughts always turn to

Cowra and I have to stop my tears. I love you so much, both of you, and am so unhappy without you. And I worry about coming to Melbourne because I fear the city will bring back memories of Brussels. The discrepancy between what one has lived and the uncomplicated life one makes here, are in stark contrast. The simple, free and straight core in me is encrusted by old and strong inhibitions which obstruct my uncritical and easy access to this world. It feels painful and oddly complex.

At the moment I want no other work than what I have and will learn it from the chaps in the kitchen. Let me tell you, today in the office I worked with a Major (Liaison officer between the Employment Office and the Army, dealing with DPs from the whole of Victoria). It was only work for today, as a backstop and, unless two clerks are needed, an ex-serviceman will fill the post. All I care about now is to learn English and the important things about the Australian way of life by being in constant contact with as many people as possible. If the dishwasher works, we will be good to save.

Let me for today go to sleep my love. It's bitterly cold; where you are as well. I wait impatiently for news from you having now left my Bonegilla address. Perhaps Monday. Now I will try to find a letterbox. Good night my dearest, my love, my all. What am I without you? Good night; write soon. Write also to your parents, everything is in order and we will soon have our affairs made right. Don't be influenced by the deliberate undertone of my letter and hold to that well and truly. I'm sure that the worn and swinging pendulum will rebalance. It has been for a while.

Check with your camp leaders; here, just a few miles from Melbourne, a Holding Centre is to be constructed. Who knows when it will be finished? Then you can come here with Micha. How are you feeling and how is Micha's health? Is he slowly getting stronger?

I am always and totally yours,
Johannes. aka Frank

Cowra seethed with hundreds of east European refugees struggling to communicate and with long histories of conflict, arguments that continued to spill over throughout the camp. During the summer, temperatures had been so unfamiliarly hot that the fire brigade had to hose down the huts. And though it was now winter, the subterranean Vulcan of long held grievances erupted unpredictably. Misunderstandings could only be quenched by an as yet unformed common tongue and less chaotic delivery of health care and removal to outside jobs. Mothers with sick children didn't know what to do, didn't know what to say and kept them in their huts, away from the doctors and the help so desperately needed.

Scarlet fever took hold. Anita succumbed and Michael with her. Distressed as she was, Anita nevertheless had the comfort of Frank's letter – 'Frank', it sounded so odd – and her spirit was stirred by the music that occasionally emanated from first one hut nearby and then another far away, a dismembered orchestra searching for a common voice. Each day she would watch through the glass of the hospital ward, each day she would ache to hold her fevered child, to urge his strength, make him better, hear him laugh, watch him play. Five weeks later, a doctor took her aside.

"Your boy is well enough to be released, but he cannot stay here because of the risk of re-infection. You need rest and you won't get better looking after your son. We advise that your husband collect him until you are well enough to join them. He will, of course, first need to find proper accommodation."

With Anita hospitalised, it was Ilse Traumanis, her friend from Bonegilla, also relocated to Cowra, who looked after Michael until Frank could travel north to collect him. As the train rolled and swayed through the sombre countryside, patches of sunlight on dour green and stands of trees that coalesced into clumps of bush, Frank struggled between anticipation and bewilderment. How to look after Micha and keep working at the barracks? How would he find somewhere for them all to live? He longed to see Anita, hold her, surrender to her, lose himself in complete abandonment. Would she be well? Would there be time to be together?

When they met, it seemed the other end of the earth was not just upside-down but back to front, dislocated. They clung together on a precipice at the edge of the world, finding themselves in each other as the past ebbed away. For a long time there were no words; then a torrent as they stitched their separate lives together again. Hope barely had time to breathe. And then came Michael, a shadow. Frank caught him up, felt the thin arms around his neck, the tousled hair on his cheek.

Alive. Frail. Somehow held together by the tenuous promise of better things to come. But there is no primrose way to happiness, no broad and simple path; just a maze of undiscovered connections that will reveal themselves in the unlikeliest of ways.

⤳

Back in Albert Park, Frank had no option but to hide Michael away in his room. While the soldiers and migrant workers seemed not to mind, there were whispers that this was neither a satisfactory solution, nor one that could be sustained for any length of time.

"It's just until I can find suitable accommodation," protested Frank.

"There are returned servicemen who'll get priority for anything that comes up. There's not enough housing for us as it is. You'll just have to wait your turn." Frank couldn't tell whether it was Bob, Bill or George who explained it, but the consensus wasn't helpful. When it came to it, these jovial Australian fellows would invariably pull rank over an Orthodox priest or a Russian doctor. He was trapped, just like the child in his room.

The trap was sprung one afternoon. The Regimental Sergeant Major, that "first among equals", had been on leave. His return signalled a tightening of discipline and that necessitated a general room inspection. With officers in tow, the door to each room was opened while the occupant stood aside, each of them conducting a mental checklist of what had been either hidden or left exposed - a tell-tale drink stain, a stained magazine. Is it the smell? Do they think I'm disposing of a corpse? Are my boots polished?

Frank stood aside. The door was opened. Sitting on the bed was a child, his brown eyes wide. The RSM held his position because he was an experienced soldier, capable of managing critical situations, calm in the face of the enemy. He stood there, eyes narrowed, trawling through the rule book of combat and valour for a reasoned response. Behind him, his staff struggled to hide their smirk, anticipating either a detonation or a tactical retreat. Instead, he turned to the DP.

"Can you explain what the hell is going on here? What's your name?"

"My name is Franz-Theo – sorry – Frank Metzger, and that is my son. He is here because we have no home."

The RSM was not a tall man, but drew himself up, taking a deep breath. His moustache was more than Hitler's toothbrush and to

Frank it looked like an affectation he could ill afford, despite the over-arching arrogance of his authority. Having survived the Gestapo, the re-branded Franz-Theo knew this was not a man he needed to be afraid of. Nevertheless, the words were harsh and angry.

"You foreigners just don't get it, do you? This isn't a crèche, it's a military barracks!" He centred himself again. "What do you do here?"

"I'm the mess attendant."

"The mess attendant, 'Sir'. Well, you've certainly made a mess of that. You're dispensable. I'm not having you here. You can't look after a kid and do your job. You'll pack your things and report to the front desk before leaving. Effective immediately."

"I'm not sure you understood me. We have nowhere to go." Frank was calm. "You have just turned us out onto the street, in a foreign city, knowing no-one and without money."

"You should have thought of that first. Your pay will be ready for you when you sign out." He turned and strode away, his muttered anger still audible. "Bloody migrants; no idea. Can barely speak the language, expect us to look after them – and their bloody kids! Turn the place into a kindergarten! We're soldiers, not nursemaids." And so it went on till the steam turned to laughter.

With his suitcase in one hand and his child holding the other, Frank stood in the street. At least it wasn't raining. In just a few hours it would be dark, the air chill and a little boy would be hungry. They crossed the road and walked towards the sea front. Perhaps there would be a room, a hotel, someone he could ask. He checked his pocket for the envelope containing his wages. Perhaps it would last a day or two. Quite unexpectedly, they arrived at a medical centre. Should he ask here first? They entered and sat in the waiting room until the receptionist was free. She was young, her long hair tied back, a blouse and a jacket. She looked up.

"Can I help you? You need to see a doctor?"

"I hope you are able to help, but at the moment perhaps not a doctor. Maybe that will come." He then proceeded to tell his story, having been sent from Bonegilla, his wife sick in Cowra, unable to remain in the barracks and with the responsibility of his young son. It was a long and hesitant account that ranged outside the narrow job description of the girl behind the desk. Besides, there were others waiting to be attended to.

"Look, I'm sorry, but I really don't think we're able to help you. I can make an appointment for tomorrow if you want to see the doctor, but there's really nothing more I can do." She looked at him, shrugged her shoulders and spread her hands. "Sorry." So that was that. Frank picked up his case, put out a hand for Michael and turned to leave. As he neared the door, a woman approached.

"Excuse me." The voice was kind. Frank paused and looked at her; early forties, well-dressed, hair in a bob, her face open and her eyes smiling. "Look, I'm sorry, but I couldn't help but overhear your conversation. I was sitting just over there waiting for the doctor. I hope you don't mind, but I think I may be able to help you." She crouched down to meet Michael's gaze. "Hello little man. What's your name?" Michael looked at her without understanding a word. He said nothing. She stood up again. "Look, my name's Mrs. Ardley. I work for Dr. Merry. I've got two children and I live in Hampton, not far from here by train. There's a spare room with a couple of beds and you can stay until you find something for the three of you. What do you say?"

Frank had no idea what to say as he tried to absorb this sudden and unexpected act of kindness. He played the words over again in his head, testing whether it could possibly be true. Why? What is this country where, from one hour to the next, a door is slammed shut and another one opened?

"I'm sorry. My name is Frank Metzger and this is my son, Michael. I am overwhelmed and don't know what to say. Your offer is very kind. In the circumstances, I don't know what else I can do."

"There's nothing you have to do. Here, I'll write down my address; you can catch the train and see for yourself. I still have things to do and will meet you at home later this evening." She smiled at him. "It will be all right, believe me."

It was as Mrs. Ardley had said. There was the house with a path along one side to a gate. Frank opened it and tentatively made his way around to the back where a sunroom looked out over the garden. Putting his hands up to the glass, he peered through the window. There were children's toys on the floor. Suddenly, tears stung his eyes.

∿

Melbourne, 27th September 1949

My dearest, best Weli - this letter, which I hope is the last to Cowra, is once again "Australian". Yesterday evening, I was with the Ardleys where I met the husband of this much loved lady – a really nice fellow. I was barely at the door when it was suggested to me that instead of staying in the wretched bungalow you should come here until we can find some appropriate lodgings. Because they do not yet have the house readily available, they will sit down today with the Housing Commission to resolve the matter. In the end, it wasn't discussed, as - completely contrary to the usual "no hurry" – we ran after the bus to go to Dr. Merry who wanted to meet me. Schaffner, who already knows me, made the agreement – not at the stop, but right on the doorstep.

When Ardleys offered their home, I protested they didn't even know you. They simply need to know Micha, and they will discover the mother by the child. He is so well behaved and with such good manners, that their children cannot be compared. They are just crazy about Micha, seeing him with chubby red cheeks, dazzlingly handsome, asleep in his crib. Their 6-year-old daughter has been relocated from her bedroom because Micha has already taken over the house. He is far ahead of the other children in intelligence and independence. As for "technical understanding" (Merrys have a very complicated washing machine!) they have predicted an engineering career for him. Anyway, in my hurry to get to the heart of the matter, I have, as you can see, muddled the timing. In coming to the Merrys, I have come to a very nice house, and have now met the entire very decent family.

They called a relative to say that I was there and a short time later, a very distinguished English-looking lady arrived in her car and proposed the following: to the east of Melbourne lies a Bay, at the tip of which lies an island, Phillip Island, which I will now describe. It's about 45 miles as the crow flies; 90 miles by road from Melbourne. On this island, about 9 miles from the nearest small town, by the ocean where the penguins congregate, there is a boarding house on about 15 acres of land and a smaller allotment that belongs to the lady, Mrs Reith. (1 acre = 0.405 hectares; 1 hectare=1000 sq. metres). Because of a shortage of staff, the house is only open during the season from December to Easter for 35 guests. It's fairly remote; drinkable water is one and a half miles away and requires an electric pump. Electricity has its own generator. Now comes the "Australian" part; they proposed that, if I – and above all you – want to do it, we would run the guest house. That means you would run the kitchen and cook for the guests, two maids would keep the rooms in order and help in the kitchen preparing vegetables, washing dishes and serving; I would look after the house, the pump, the generator and so on - maintenance and schedules for those who venture to the house and, for what else is to be done, two family members will do the books, manage the purchases and finances, and show you how the hares run.

During the season, when we've worked out how the place functions – and that can't be too hard to learn – we will have the opportunity to lease the property, keeping it open throughout the year and then, of course, during the next season. The owners are not relying on making the maximum out of it and would apparently settle with a lease. If you don't want to work in the kitchen but somewhere else, your pay would reduce from £8 to £5/15, which is what the other maids would get. Also, were the kitchen job not appropriate for you, I don't feel it is so subordinate that it detracts from your independence and initiative. What I can't judge is the work performance required to cook for 35-40 people in the busy times! Accommodation and meals are free, so that together we would have at least £12-15 per week, which means that, over a season, we would have more than £200 saved, on top of which tips from the guests would be added. I will see if I can get the Gulajews – Stefania and Wanda from the camp – to come and help, then we could really run the whole show.

So, that's the proposal they are offering us, but I have to clarify it first with 2 authorities: my wife and the employment office. The first is fundamental: if the idea appeals to you, above all the idea of an independent acquisition, then we can undertake it, but if you have the least doubt, then we will let it be. We know how to get by, whether you work or not; I have often said to you that, no matter what the circumstances, I will not have you work if it is not congenial to you – factory or similar. There is no question, even if I have to work day and night. I don't think looking after a house, or even a small hotel, would be too demanding a job. We could even have sheep or a cow; perhaps Gulajew could milk it. The owners had considered bringing two cows. Because it starts in December, you've got time to make up your mind and then make your preparations. That would make it more efficient; but to balance that, maybe the physical work will be interesting and rewarding. Above all, once you're here, we must go and look at the place. It should be very nice; a surf beach at the ocean. Good. Enough. Amen. This is just for your information and food for thought. I can say

Wednesday October 5, 1949. At last. It would be a long day confined to the train, but finally free from the confines of the camp. Spring – sunshine and rain; a chance for renewal, to flourish once more. Anita would change trains at Albury before heading to Melbourne. Ever since the telegram arrived on Monday, waves of anticipation rolled over her, barely giving her time to breathe as she packed her things, checked the Hampton address, 182 Thomas Street, and cleared her departure with the camp authorities. She would be glad to leave Cowra behind her: the food, the chaos, the cold nights and loneliness. She struggled to fill some of her time trying to write to her family in Tuttlingen, but already she felt removed, isolated in some purgatorial existence, trapped between opposing worlds while yearning for reunion with her child and his father. Words didn't come easily as the detail of lives became more disconnected by time and place. How could she burden them with her doubts, the debilitating sickness that had nearly claimed their grandson? They had already disputed so much of what she had chosen, it would serve only to justify their opposition. So she asked questions, asked after the children and harnessed the uncertain fear that she would never see them again.

Now, from the window of her carriage, she watched the shifting light on the landscape, the sheep grazing in paddocks. Did they, as they nibbled at the green pick, question their existence, anticipate a future? Hopefully not. Perhaps one would do well to be as the beasts of the field, just quietly accept the day for what it is; embrace its opportunity. She drifted into sleep, lulled by the clatter and sway of the train.

In Melbourne, the freshly branded Frank counted the hours. He would take the train to Flinders Street and then change for the extra stop to Spencer Street to meet the country arrival. He had thought to bring something; flowers perhaps but sensed they wouldn't last. Instead, he chose the early daffodils and aquilegia from the garden and found a vase. He arranged the welcome in the room they would share.

He arrived early and found the terminus busy - city commuters scurrying for last minute departures, shoppers waiting with clutches of bags, some lost and checking their watches, a blind woman with her dog. So many individual lives thrust together in this anthill of urgency to be somewhere, to find someone. And he among them, just one anonymous heartbeat in the throng. Waiting for the one person in the world.

When he saw her, taller than those around her and carrying her suitcase, it was as if seeing her for the first time. Her elegance, her hair tied back in a chignon, the coat with a scarf loosely tied at her throat, the very way she walked. Her air of poise and authority. The intimacy of their shared life only served to make her approach even more startling. Then she saw him. All her self-contained calm dissolved in a smile bigger than the moon and stars. She put down the case and they held each other in wondrous silence as the world ebbed and swayed around them. Finally, they parted and looked at one another, reading each other's face, searching their eyes, and knowing their hearts had spoken.

"But where is Micha?" Anita's voice was suddenly anxious.

"It's all right. He's with Mrs. Ardley at Dr. Merry's rooms."

Frank picked up the case and she took his arm, squeezed it. He pressed her close.

"Wonderful to see you; have you near. You look well, but the trip was long, yes?"

"Exhausting, but it doesn't matter. I'm glad to be here."

"We can walk down Collins Street, maybe have a coffee and a bite to eat. You must be hungry. Then to Flinders Street station. From there, a train to Hampton."

The city was new. Anita was struck by the reality of it, the wide streets, the tall buildings, traffic and people. Apart from the bivouac isolation of the camps, she had only seen Albury, a country town. This was a place she could come to know, a place with shops and trams, banks and businesses. There were no shrapnel scars on the stonework, no rubble, no visible disruptions to the metropolis, but a place of promise. Some of the other migrants had gone to Sydney where they had connections and she had asked questions, but the dice had rolled differently. Here she was – and there were plans for work and a new beginning.

There was much to share, an abundance of questions until they reached Swanston Street and turned south towards the station. "Look at that huge building, what is it? The town hall? So much to see." Frank smiled at her enthusiastic surprise. There would be time, but soon a little boy would be waiting. Then a sandwich shop and a chance for a coffee. It was a modest affair and the food barely palatable.

"Remember in Aachen, at the Postwagen, we sat at a table – not like this – and even then the coffee tasted better." Anita screwed up her face.

"Maybe at Young and Jacksons, the hotel next door, we could get a meal one day, something different. I'm not sure. They are more famous for drinking - and a French painting of a nude - than they are for their food. But now we have a train to catch."

Anita pointed to the cathedral. "Look, it's amazing; beautiful. Next time we will have a look inside. And over there, that is a bridge, so there must be a river?" They passed under the station clocks and found their way to the platform for the Sandringham train. Hampton would be the second last stop.

"In your letter, you said that Kowanko's family was moved to Uranquinty. That's not so far from Cowra, but I've heard it's hard there."

"I think we were better off in Bonegilla to be honest. He says that the corrugated iron huts have no lining, so it's freezing at night. And every noise is amplified – children crying, arguments and the same monotonous food."

"It was the same at Cowra. When people complained, they were told if you want to become Australian, you had better just get used to it."

"He said he had to use his suitcase with a blanket over it for a chair. And resourceful fellow that he is, he found a metal pipe and stuck it into a block of wood for a lampstand. The trouble is, work is very hard to find and, without work, people can't find a house or a bungalow, so they can't be together."

"You were lucky that Mrs. Ardley heard your story."

"For sure. I had found a place in St. Kilda to rent, but both she and her husband said it was not a good idea."

"Why not?"

"Apparently St. Kilda has a reputation. She used the word 'seedy' – ladies of the night, drunks and sometimes there is violence. Bohemian, but not artistic. I got the impression they didn't think it the best place to bring up Micha. Anyway, we have another alternative to discuss."

It was early evening by the time they reached the house. Frank let them in with the key he'd been given. On the table was a note.

Dear Frank & Anita,
Welcome to our shared place. Please make yourselves at home and help yourselves to anything in the fridge. Tea and coffee on the bench. The beds are made up and we'll see you soon.   Stella

"So very kind." Anita was taken aback. Such generosity from people she had never met; kindness she would long remember.

No sooner had they settled than they heard voices. The family was home. As she opened the door, Mrs. Ardley ushered Micha in first and let go his hand. He stepped carefully over the threshold and looked up. Disbelief flooded him and he stood a long moment in silence, sifting reality out of confusion, before reaching out both his arms to be picked up.

"Oh, my darling boy." Anita gathered him and held him tight, smelled his skin, his hair; felt his little arms around her neck. Emotion drowned her. The others watched in silence as mother and son found one another again. Then followed a commotion of welcome and introductions: six-year-old Catherine with her legs in callipers from the polio that had afflicted her as a toddler, her older brother James looking awkward and shy with the stranger in his house and then the Ardleys with whom long-established European tradition made the informal greeting of first names uncomfortable, despite the protests that they should be called Stella and Tony – Anthony if you like.

For once, Micha was reluctant to play with the children, but climbed onto his mother's knee, curled against the comfort of her breast as the family sat and talked over their plans in the living room. Anita found herself on the one hand desperate to have some time alone with her Johannes, on the other to be intrigued by the possibilities of running a guest house. At the same time, she was distracted by Micha's need for attention and by such comforts of home as had been denied for so long: a settee with down-filled cushions, lamplight, pictures on the walls, thick carpet underfoot and the steady ticking of the mahogany longcase clock.

Over the next week as the household settled into its routine, the evolution of the relationships that enabled the Summerland venture became clear. The elegant English-looking lady who had arrived in her imported Ford, Elaine Reith, was in fact the sister of Dr. Merry's wife. Her husband, in turn, was another doctor, Alec Reith. In conjunction with a third family, Doctor and Mrs. Sambell, the three families had formed a partnership to own and manage Summerland House. Such a joint venture diversion was not without its problems as competing interests sought to make it a success. Hopefully, the injection of new blood in its management might lift it from stagnation and precarious viability.

Thus, a month later on a day that threatened rain, and again leaving Micha in the care of Mrs. Ardley, Frank and Anita were chauffeured, by Mrs Sambell and Elaine Reith, into the unpredictable wilderness, as remote and unfamiliar as the far side of the moon.

CHAPTER ELEVEN

New Beginnings

There is a vista at the top of the climb from the Anderson station turnoff that, even under a sky of mist and cloud, compels an intake of breath. It signals an arrival and an attempt to comprehend the vast expanse below that is Westernport Bay, today a sullen plane of water but, under the western sun, a shimmering, diamond-struck sheet between near and distant shorelines.

The car winds the descent to the fishing village of San Remo and the suspension bridge that crosses The Narrows to Newhaven and beyond. The car clatters across the 500 feet of boards hung above the fishing boats while the tide surges 40 feet below. They turn west towards the village of Cowes. It has started to rain and the landscape is flat, the vegetation scrubby and there is no-one about. Empty holiday shacks can be glimpsed through clumps of boobialla. Nearing the village, there are stands of bush, gum trees where koalas feed, and finally the turnoff into Thomson Avenue, its flanks bordered by cypress. Hardly a boulevard, but an entrance.

On either side, along the steep incline to the waterfront and the jetty are shops, a post office, a bakery and general store among them. Unfamiliar cars are parked outside. It's strange to imagine this place becoming home. Along The Esplanade, opposite the English styled Isle of Wight Hotel, is the jetty, with the Cowes Ferry Company vessel tied up. They decide the weather is too inhospitable to walk – there will be time for that later – and turn back to head out on the Ventnor road.

They pass the single room weatherboard primary school on their left and then the road to Grossard's point and Lonely Man's Grave. The place feels more desolate than ever, the rain driving against the beating wipers. "Just a short cloudburst," announces Elaine. "It will clear up shortly, I'm sure." Ahead on their right, sitting atop a modest sand dune and surrounded by tea tree, are two galvanised iron water tanks. "That's the water supply for the house. There's a bore nearby at the spring, and a pump. A bit brackish, but drinkable. Best if it's boiled first. There's also a tank at the house." Elaine seems to suggest managing water will be no problem at all.

"And here we are," declares Mrs. Sambell as they turn left up St. Helen's Road, the unmade stretch to the gate before it follows the windswept coast around to the Nobbies. "I'll just open the gate." She slips out of the car into the blustery wet, undoes the chain from the iron farm gate and lets it swing open as she returns and shuts the weather out. "We can wait till the rain stops before walking around outside and taking a look at the beach."

"Should I close the gate," asks Frank.

"It'll be all right until we leave later."

They pull up in front of the verandah, the house looming above them. It's an imposing building, but through the rain streaked window, Anita sees the arc of the bay and the distant headland shrouded in mist. Stepping out of the car, the smell of wet vegetation and the taste of salt on the wind and rain comes as a surprise, heady and exhilarating. From below comes the muffled boom of the breakers, the elements beating their pulse across the bluff. Oblivious to the drenching, Frank and Anita stand transfixed in the swirling gusts that inhabit this wilderness.

"Come on in. You'll be soaked and catch your death of cold." Elaine is impatient; besides she has seen this all before.

The spell broken, they climb the seven wooden steps to the verandah and turn to look back. The paddock stretches all the way down to the road and the wooded dunes beyond. To left and right, tussocks are tossed by the wind.

Elaine holds open the wire door with her foot while she rummages in her bag for the key and lets them in. The entrance is dark and the place smells musty. As their eyes become accustomed to the gloom, Frank notices the wall bracket beside each door, a candle holder with its stump of candle and a box of matches on it. The doors have numbers, a white enamel plate with the numerals in blue, like a French house number. Perhaps they have them in England too. A worn carpet runner extends the length of the passage to a swing door opening into a dining room. There are about ten wooden tables, each with chairs left haphazardly around them. Some of the tables have a kerosene lamp in the centre and there are others side by side on a dresser by the wall. In several spots water is dripping through the ceiling.

They enter the kitchen, low ceilinged and with a large wooden work table in the middle of the floor. In a vast brick and tiled chimney breach sits a cast iron, double oven IXL wood stove, an industrially scaled piece of engineering. To the side are several heavy smoothing irons of various sizes and on one of the hotplates, a huge black kettle with a brass tap and spout. Kenwick & Sons, Bromwich, England. No. 12. 6 gallons. Water trickles down the flue pipe as well as through the ceiling.

"Probably best to get some pots and pans under those drips," suggests Mrs. Sambell and rummages in cupboards to find them. "I'll see if I can find some dry wood and we'll light the stove; get it a bit warm in here."

She disappears while the others find whatever containers they can and distribute them under the heaviest of the leaks. Elaine has found some old newspapers and together the women open the firebox and attempt to coax a flame in the dampness. There is smoke and belching before, at last, the air clears and the chimney roars. Poor Frank is overcome with migraine and asks to retreat to a bed somewhere; just for a couple of hours.

"You could try room 5," suggests Elaine. "There's a fireplace in there if you want it warm – and there should be sheets and a blanket on the bed."

"For the moment, I'm done with fire and water. Thank you. I'll just lie down with a blanket. I'm sorry."

They hear the swing door flap back and forth and his footsteps as he treads the creaking boards to the room and the door clicks shut.

"Is everything all right?" asks Elaine.

"I think he's been worried and excited about coming here. He would love it all to work out, but he can see there's a lot to do. It's been a big day so far." Anita is apologetic.

"Won't be much good if he folds under pressure. Still, this is what we have and it's probably time for some lunch. I've made sandwiches and once the kettle boils, we can have a cup of tea."

With the day sorted, the weather clears and the number of leaking spots gradually diminish. Anita is taken on a more detailed exploration of the house and is relieved to learn that the laundry is picked up every couple of days and taken to Cowes. One less task to be managed, though she looks at the stove with both doubt and dread. Elaine has shown her the baking trays, reminiscent of Bonegilla, and explained how the lamb will need to be cooked.

Frank is woken and while he and Anita step outside to circumnavigate the property, the ladies make lists of what needs to be brought back. 'The season' will start in four weeks, supplies are minimal and there's a deal of tidying up to be done. And while the two women are unsure how the migrants will manage, they're a better proposition than having the place locked up and slipping further into dereliction. Such a brief and inauspicious beginning asks more questions than can be answered in a day and it's probably best to return to Melbourne until, together with the weather, their minds become clearer.

Limonis Rasa had come from a long line of Latvian farmers whose life and land had been seriously compromised by the fluctuating claims of geopolitical rivalry, most notably the Germans and Russians. Having escaped the roundup of kulaks to Siberia, he now found himself at the other end of the earth along with the tens of thousands of other displaced Europeans. Fortunately, he was both intelligent and industrious, qualities that, together with a boyish charm, had endeared him to his young wife Skydrita. She was the counterpoint to her husband's seriousness and, in addition to her skills with needle and thread, loved her music and the folk dances of her native land. She was also a necessary asset to the maintenance of a vegetable garden free of insecticides and fertilisers, something that had stood them in good stead in a time of war and dearth. They had also made a son, Andrew, just a year younger than Micha.

How Elaine Reith had found the family remained a mystery, but they were duly installed on the farm and entrusted with the responsibilities of milking the two cows, ensuring the hens were fed – and multiplied - collecting eggs and attempting to raise a pig. Such produce would feed the guests, or at least supplement the provisions, while the remaining spare time would attend to the domestic chores of housemaid and kitchen hand. Resourcefulness was an estimable quality.

The farmhouse was a rude dwelling, small, squat, with strapped cement sheet walls and a corrugated fibro cement roof. Two bedrooms, a simple kitchen with a wood stove, a table and chairs, a sofa and a dresser - and a lean-to with a toilet - the whole shambles embowered in boobialla. A tank on a low stand collected rainwater from the roof and fed the single brass tap. Various farm buildings accommodated the animals and a grey Ferguson tractor along with hoes, rakes, shovels and such impedimenta as would enable subsistence.

Up at the guest house was a simple separate bungalow whose prime feature was a picture window that looked out over Summerland Bay. Rarely is such a panoramic vista afforded from such a humble dwelling. It carried the prestigious title of 'servants' quarters', though it was to be occupied by a single woman with two children and no husband, his absence being a mystery at which one might only guess.

With most of the cast assembled in readiness, it remained only for Frank and Anita to confirm their intentions. With his fantasies of running a hotel substantially moderated – and having spent more time asleep with a headache than engaged with the demands of management – Frank nevertheless thought there was sufficient potential to make something of the place and their life together above a penguin rookery. How hard could it be? Anita, not having had to cook for herself until the war changed everything, wondered how cooking for 40 guests on that formidable wood stove could possibly be achieved. On top of that, one could only hope it didn't rain when the guests began to arrive.

In the end, it was a triumph of optimism that signed the lease. Elaine suggested that another visit would be in order and, to facilitate that, the simplest plan would be for Frank to drive the guest house car back to the island. It had been driven back to Melbourne while the place was closed during the low season but would be required again for trips into Cowes and to carry the mail and provisions. It was a singular vehicle: a 1928 Willy's Overland Whippet Tourer. Four cylinders; 30 horsepower – and a crank handle. While it had achieved venerability, it no longer demanded the fashionable driving accoutrements of the 1930s, such as a soft napped woollen cap or driving gloves. It was a car without affectations. Frank's literary, intellectual and artistic interests were about to be extended to the practical and ingenious.

They packed their things and one last time entrusted Micha into Mrs. Ardley's safekeeping. Elaine would come in a few days, bringing Micha, a stack of cookery books, lists of weights and measures; all the proper amounts that needed to be prepared for the guests, especially the roast beef and the roast lamb.

⏝

As the Whippet careered southward along the Bass Highway, its occupants were both terrified and exhilarated, as much by the motor car as by the prospect of what they were about to undertake. It was hard to talk with the wind whistling under the canvas roof and the hum of the motor, so they each tried to imagine what words they might use to welcome the guests, how to show them to their rooms. Should they be offered morning or afternoon tea on arrival? What information would they be expected to provide for the sightseers? What was the best time to set the table? How much wine should be served? Or did Australians drink mostly beer?

They drove directly to the house; there would be time to explore the rest of the island later. They opened up and brought in their cases and the boxes of provisions that Elaine had supplied. Packing it all had appeared more than enough; now that they were here, it seemed scant beginnings for a new chapter. Following the previous example, Anita had made sandwiches and so they sat in the dining room, campers in the vast, abandoned space. Fearing the stove, she had also brought a Thermos of hot tea. It brought some comfort to the anxiety they felt.

"What have we done, Johannes?"

Frank saw the trouble in her eyes, the moment of hesitation. He put aside his own flicker of doubt.

"If it is all too hard, we put a sign on the gate that says 'Closed' and we find something else. But," he summoned the rest of the argument, "we are not being asked to do anything that has not been done before. We have plenty of help – I'm sure there are good people to show us the way. We have lived through harder than this and, if that hasn't been preparation enough, then I would be surprised."

He reached out and took her hand. They sat in silence, while below, the boom of the breakers rose to fill the space.

That afternoon, the sky clear, Anita and Frank decided to take the path down the cliff to the beach. At the edge of the yard set among the boobialla bushes was a rusty gate fixed to a rickety post. The ground was slippery from previous downpours and Frank lead the way, stepping sideways, his hand outstretched to help Anita as she felt for the narrow footholds cut into the cliff. A few metres to the left stood a small brick structure, roofed, the door hanging open from a broken hinge. In the gloom sat a single cylinder Ronaldson-Tippett engine with its flywheel and a belt fixed to a generator. They had no idea what it was, or why it was there.

Further down, to each side of the path were cypress trees that had been planted some 20 years before. After them, the path flattened out a little and they came to the creek, a meagre stream that passed beneath a makeshift wooden bridge. With sand already filling their shoes they climbed the dune.

Before them, fringed with breakers, the crescent bay opened. An immensity of sky. To the right, waves crashed on the glistening basalt at the foot of the headland. To the left, a sweep of sand that stretched to a succession of promontories, each fainter than the last. Ahead, the ocean, unbroken to the horizon. Arm in arm they stood, breath suspended, silent, Anita's hair tousled by the wind. When, some minutes later, they turned to one another, they sensed they had entered a new dimension, one that would claim them and bind them to one another and this place.

Together, they made their way to the sand at the edge of the world. The incessant boom and crash of the waves displaced the distant echo of pounding guns, droning planes and the shock of dropped bombs. Here was a power more vast and timeless than any empire. Frank gulped in great lungfuls of air, face to the sky, incapable of thought, struggling wordlessly to reconcile a past with this present, this fearless freedom.

The wash of water at their feet loosened the trance.

"Let us walk."

Anita pulled her coat around her, hooked her arm into his and they set off along the sand. Occasionally clumps of kelp would block their path, or they would see pieces of driftwood, cuttlefish and the half-buried feather and bone of a vanquished muttonbird. Sandpipers progressed on clockwork legs and Anita remarked how, when a seagull alighted, there were three birds – the gull, its shadow beside it and its reflection below. It seemed as if all life was multiplied, was magnified.

Finally, at the end of the bay, they turned. Looking up, above the dunes, nestled into the top of the distant cliff, they could make out their new home. For the moment, its challenges were subdued by the immensity of water and air and an undirected gratitude for this communion with the elements.

Later, as dusk settled, a new sound emerged. At first a single cry, but then a gathering orchestra of guttural song, a diverse two-tone scale of call and counter-call across the dunes, at the foot of the cliff and towards the house. It was the return of the fairy penguins.

In the guesthouse, there were light switches on the walls, but they produced nothing. Frank and Anita rummaged through cupboards and drawers in the descending dark and finally found more candles and matches. The result was a struggle between the bleak and the romantic, but enough to enable them to assemble a cold meal before venturing to bed – a lumpy mattress on a sagging wire that creaked in protest. Together, they lay in the dark, the wind buffeting the house full of unfamiliar sounds, while below them the muffled surf and the continuous cry of penguins finally soothed them to sleep.

The morning came to consciousness with a confusion of questions. Saucepans, placed to collect yesterday's rainwater that had dripped through the ceiling, created an obstacle course. Water in the bathroom was cold. In the musty gloom of the kitchen, set into the chimney breach, was the vast black iron stove, heavy oven doors on either side of the extinct firebox. There was the smell of damp ash. Over the sink, the hot tap produced a trickle of cold water. To add to the discouragement, it had started to rain once more. The penguin calls had ceased. Presently, the plop of water in pots began again.

Wrapped in a coat, with a scarf against the morning cold, Frank discovered what appeared to be a boiler behind the kitchen. Beside it were the remains of a woodpile, sufficient encouragement to attempt setting a fire in the rusted grate. Nearby, an axe was wedged into the battered edge of a worn chopping block and so he set to work. Apart from choking smoke to begin with, the embers finally took with a promising roar and he partly closed the damper and retreated inside.

The trickle into the sink remained perplexingly weak but gradually felt warmer. It was time to try the stove. Again, smoke belched from under the hotplates and back down the chimney till, finally, the kindling blazed under a cast iron kettle of rainwater.

"Is everything all right? Are you not too cold? Your hair is wet, you poor man." Anita brought a towel and then set about laying a breakfast table with whatever she could find.

With a wry smile, a mixture of concern and relief, Frank asked, "And now, what do you think of our new Schloss, our castle in the wilderness?"

"It will be fine. We will make it fine. We have each other and we have a new start."

"A new beginning – at the end of the world." He paused, then smiled. With grim irony he added, "It appears we have reached the Promised Land." Anita could only look at him and shake her head.

They found a bottle of Bushells "Coffee and Chicory Essence", some bread they warmed in the oven and eggs left for them in the pantry. It was an improvised start to the day, but enough to hearten them for what was to come.

In the afternoon, as the wind rose, the chimney in the sitting room huffed and sucked like a distant muffled thunderstorm. And then the water ran out.

⌒

Frank remembered the two water tanks Elaine had pointed out on the dunes at Flynn's Beach, just over half a mile away. Not knowing what he would find, he chose to take the car in the event he might need tools. It was a judicious move. He parked by the side of the road and walked in, struggling up the sandy slope and investigated the plumbing. Simple enough: each tank had an outlet with a gate valve, and each was connected to a two-inch pipe that ran away to the guest house. Another pipe ran up from the opposite direction, evidently to the pump. He tapped the sides of the first tank, only to discover it rang hollow all the way down. Then he saw why. Bullet holes. There was no-one to hear, but frustration overcame him. "What on earth!" Then in German, "Verdammte idioten!" The holes were on the approach side from the road. "Couldn't even get out of the car!"

It wasn't the first time they had been the object of poor marksmanship. Repairs had been made in several places, primarily by cutting some rubber tubing and fitting it over a nut, washer and bolt, and then screwing it down. It would mean getting into the tank to first insert it and then tightening it from the outside. So much messing about for someone else's vicarious pleasure. Wasn't life already frustrating enough?

He tapped the second tank. Half full. That was a relief. A brief inspection showed why. Another bullet hole at the water level. That would be a more challenging repair. Making sure the first valve was closed, he opened the second. A pause and then some internal bubbling and a gurgle as the air was displaced. A promising sign. From there, it was a scramble down the sand following the pipe to the pump. It was sitting on a wooden cradle with a battered sheet of rusty corrugated iron that offered scant protection. An inlet pipe rose from a soggy reed bed that formed a natural well around the bore. There was, however, no electric motor, but another petrol engine similar to that in the shed by the house. For the moment, he had no idea how it might work.

In the hope that the simple change of taps might temporarily solve the problem, he made his way back to the guesthouse, resolving that tomorrow he would go to the farm to see what he might discover by way of tools and such bits and pieces as could secure a reliable water supply – assuming of course that there would be no more vandals with guns.

Anita met him at the door. "What did you find?"

"Let's just try the tap first and hopefully I can explain." It was some time before anything happened. Then, a distant whistling and finally a splutter and a few drops. A moment later a gush splashed into the sink.

"You fixed it?" Anita was impressed.

"You shouldn't sound so surprised." He then proceeded to recount the irresponsible stupidity that had caused the problem in the first place and how, if he couldn't prevent the cause, he could at least address the symptoms.

"You know, you could have been a doctor!" She kissed him and smiled. "Come." She took him by the hand and they headed to room number five.

⁓

It was late morning by the time anyone ventured into the kitchen and later still before Frank cranked the Whippet into life and headed for the farm. A bent piece of wire was all that held shut the sagging wooden gate. He dragged it open into the long grass before stopping front of the barn. A pair of weathered wooden doors greeted him. He contemplated them for a moment, seeing a tableau of rural life in the detail of the exposed grain, the lichen that had fixed itself into the open joins, the rusted latch trailing its ochre stain. He reminded himself to bring the camera next time. Inside was gloom, the only light coming from a small four-paned window above a work bench, the glass frosted with dust and salt spray, the frame hung with trails of web. Empty kerosene tins had been cut open and stacked to provide shelves and storage. Hessian sacks were piled in a corner, along with drums of petrol and oil. Old Arnott's biscuit tins and Vegemite jars filled with assortments of nuts and bolts, rusting nails and screws sat on the bench among the tools.

On the far wall, leather harness hung from nails and a wooden bracket. In a drawer under the bench, among old receipts and a ball of twine, he found what he was hoping for: Ronaldson & Tippett "CA" Type Crude Oil Engine Instruction Book, No 14. Out of the darkness there now shone a light. He stepped outside with his prize.

It was mid-afternoon before he returned to the house, his hands covered in grime, clothes oil-stained and smelling of kerosene.

"O my goodness! What on earth have you done?" Anita was incredulous. "Look at you. You can't come in like that; you have to wash first. You can't touch anything."

"I have learned something today." He smiled ruefully. "Blood may be thicker than water; but oil is thicker than both." He held out his hands, then turned them over to reveal his barked knuckles.

"You need to take off your clothes and have a bath and then something to eat."

Later, having obeyed instructions, Frank was challenged to further voyages of discovery with a simple question. "What can we do about the leaking roof?"

"First I must find a ladder and then I can find a solution. After that, we must go for a walk along the beach. Tomorrow is another day."

"And in four more days, Elaine will be here with Micha and we have to be ready."

"I will look for a ladder."

Resigned, he set off. The block sloped away on the ocean side of the house, meaning there was room underneath the floor. Access was provided via a door between scrappy plantings of hydrangea, coastal banksia and juniper. He slid the bolt and peered inside. Striated light filtered between the base boards. Space between the rows of stumps had been used as a repository for some broken deckchairs, an oval tin bathtub and a Miller table lamp missing its chimney and glass shade. To the right were stacked several piles of roof tiles, against which was leaning a ladder. An Aladdin's cave. For the second time that day, the stars had aligned.

Though it would mean yet again running a bath, he dragged the ladder out and set it up on the flattest piece of ground at the lowest part of the roof, at the opposite side of the house near the kitchen chimney. He subliminally registered that some time in the recent past, it too had been crudely repaired. He clambered up and stood exposed to the wind on a brittle footing. Arms out, he felt he was walking a tightrope. At the highest extremity the reward was the spectacular sweep of the bay, the dunes and, could it be, a lake nestled behind distant patches of scrub and tea tree? Checking where to place his feet, it was as he suspected – a number of cracked and broken tiles lay awry. Between them he could see rafters and the ceiling below.

Taking his cue from Anita, who would not relinquish any task until it was completed, he set about replacing the most obviously damaged areas until the descending dark obliged him to retire from his labours.

"So, what did you achieve?" asked Anita. She dried her hands and indicated the piles of freshly washed plates and cutlery to be returned to the cleaned out cupboards.

"You've been busy too. There were broken tiles, so I replaced some of them. The rest can be done before it rains again."

"But how can they break? Nothing can fall on them. They don't just break by themselves."

"The wind. Even today when it's relatively still, it's windy up there. In a storm, who knows? I suspect they lift and move. As they rattle about, they crack and break. Maybe the salt air has something to do with it."

With the world explained and therefore secure in its orbit, they ate and talked until the moon rose. Then, arm in arm, they set out to walk the road to where they could look out at the sea below, shimmering in the pale light, the sand laced with shifting gossamer. A long- fallen telegraph pole among the tussocks provided an unexpected and fortuitous resting place. They sat in silence, letting the penguins and the sea play out the voices in their heads. Above, the Southern Cross reached out silently. Finally, drawing deep from a distant past, Frank recited, "How sweet the moonlight sleeps upon this bank. Here will we sit and let the sounds of music creep in our ears. Look how the floor of heaven is thick inlaid with patines of bright gold. There's not the smallest orb which thou behold'st but, which in its motion, like an angel sings."

Anita smiled and looked at him, this dear, wonderful, sad and lovely man. She leaned against him, his arm around her. The moon rose gently and the stars were aligned once more.

∽

"What do you think Johannes? Should we go into Cowes? We could see what they have; maybe buy some fresh food. I can finish the windows in the dining room when we get back. You will need the ladder for the outside."

Relieved to delay further escapades teetering up a ladder, Frank happily agreed.

"If we are going to the city, we need to be properly dressed. You will have to put on your jacket and tie; I will wear a blouse and skirt with a blazer and scarf. Or maybe hat and gloves. That should be fine. What do you think?"

Frank thought nothing could be better and so, twenty minutes later and perched in the Whippet, they motored through the countryside with Anita pointing out the sea to left and right, the farms hidden behind their cypress windbreaks, remarking on the bewildering structure of the chicory kilns, till at last they parked on Thompson Avenue.

There were people about: day trippers either returning from the Nobbies and the Shell House or preparing to visit the penguin parade; farmers coming in to pick up bags of grain or a pipe fitting, and locals catching up on the week's gossip in shops or on the street. Arm in arm, Frank and Anita joined the utterly unfamiliar human tide, conscious that, even among the visitors, they were strangers here. Ahead, on the footpath, were two ladies earnestly engaged in conversation. The looked up, falling silent, as the newcomers approached. Frank nodded an acknowledgement as they drew near, adding, "Good day, ladies." If his dress hadn't already given him away, his accent did. Anita smiled and then, spying a horse and farmer's cart on the other side of the road, pointed her gloved finger and exclaimed, "Look Johannes. Over there!" They paused a moment to take in the sight before moving on to peer into a shop window. Behind them, the two ladies resumed their conversation.

"Who are they?" She sounded astonished.

"I think," her companion replied in hushed tones, "he's an escaped Polish count." She reduced the rest to a whisper, "And that's his mistress."

"Really? Why do you say that?"

"Didn't you hear? She called him 'Your Highness'!"

"Where did he escape from?"

"Don't know; must have been the Revolution."

"Too young. Might have been the War. But how do you know she's the mistress?"

"Ah – he wasn't wearing a ring on his left hand, was he? And she, well she was wearing gloves. Imagine, in this weather, here in Cowes."

"Probably hiding all her rings and jewels. Do you know where they're staying?"

"Must be up at Summerland. They arrived in the guesthouse car."

"Privileged. See, I told you. Could even be spies."

Although they had moved away, Frank and Anita couldn't help but overhear the beginning of their conjectured history and tried not to burst out laughing. Occasionally they would stop, shaking their heads while convulsed with hushed admiration for the Australian imagination.

Shopping proved a challenge. 'Thruppence ha'penny' and 'that'll be a coupla bob' offered a new form of currency, as did 'I can give you change of a quid'. It was easier to simply put the coins on the counter and let the shopkeeper take what he needed. They learned that a florin meant two shillings and the face on the obverse was George the Sixth. But wasn't he the English king? The necessary transactions were all carried out with patience and a good deal of humour, reassuring for a couple of imagined royalty hiding by the antipodean seaside.

The motor carriage being returned, they were about to launch into the rest of the day's tasks when there was knock at the door. Frank answered it and a moment later returned with a nuggetty gentleman wearing dress shoes, long trousers, shirt and tie and a cardigan.

"Thought it best to come over and introduce myself: Alf Nane. I live in the house over the way."

Ensconced in the big club lounge in the sitting room, further introductions revealed he hailed from England, had worked in Melbourne, was now retired and, since his wife's untimely death, had found the peace and solitude he needed in the island's wild desolation. Pity about the tourists. There was another house up the road, a sister to Summerland House. It was called Sea Shanty. Owners hardly visited any more – falling to wrack and ruin. You could do something with it you know. Quite a few Melbourne families come down regularly; Edwards, Thorns, Beveridges. You'll get to meet them in time. He chatted away amiably before he decided it was time to make himself something for tea.

"Rabbit tonight. Plenty of them about. Got a gun, have you? Don't mind a bit of rabbit. When you get a minute, you might like to pop over for a drink – I've got quite a nice drop of port that I'm happy to share."

The thought of a gun in the house shocked Anita. So too the idea of killing a rabbit; killing anything. Still, people had to eat and she recalled Bibo's butcher shop in Bad Schwalbach all those years ago. Pork sausages didn't arrive without the killing of a pig. Given the lateness of the day and the big stove not yet lit, it would be a simple dinner of Heinz canned soup and a sandwich. Rabbit would have to wait.

Later, in the light of a kerosene lamp in front of the embers of the living room fire, they fell asleep on the couch in each other's arms, the Count and Countess of Summerland.

Something happened when Elaine lifted Michael from the car and set him on his feet. Anita watched from the verandah and saw him pause, surprised, as the sea air filled his lungs and the wind ruffled his hair. He turned to listen to the strange soughing in the telephone wires, the distant boom of the surf; saw the wide expanse of sky and stood amazed, transfixed. So wildly strange; filled with un-nameable and mysterious promise that would claim and bind him. In that moment, both she and Frank understood that, if they had left Europe for his sake, then this was where he was meant to be.

His mother's voice broke the trance and he turned and looked up. A week is both an eternity and a passing moment. He was swept up by his father before being handed to Anita, at last reassured in knowing that this was now the time to be together again.

"Let me help you unpack." Frank was by the car as Elaine handed him the boxes: food, additional linen, cookbooks.

"Here, these are Michael's." She called him over. "You take these." She handed him his stuffed koala and Bambi, already threadbare. Together, they made their way inside.

"Goodness, gracious!" Elaine was impressed. "You've transformed the place." It was true: floors mopped, tables set, brass polished, glass cleaned, fresh candles. Even the shabby curtains had been washed in the concrete troughs, ironed and rehung. "Visitors won't know themselves. And see here, I've brought a pile of cookery books we can go through later."

In the afternoon, Limonis and Skydrita arrived with their young son Andrew and his grandmother who would look after him down at the farm while his parents were busy. With the first guests scheduled to arrive within the week, Elaine had prepared lists of tasks for everyone and the next two days were spent explaining the workings of the house, water and electricity and the expectations of the visitors.

By her bed, from the stack on the floor, Anita was introduced to Mrs. McClurcan and her cookery book, together with the ladies of the Country Women's Association, the Presbyterian Women's Missionary Union of Victoria, the New South Wales Public School Cookery Teachers Association and the Australian Women's Weekly. It seemed a lot of ladies were doing a dreadful amount of cooking. *Australian Home Cookery* was supplemented by *Good Housekeeping's Party Cakes and Pastries and the Commonsense Cookery Book* – which made little sense with its unfamiliar weights and measures – featuring such specialities as boiled rice and cabbage. There were *Sweets for Summer,* with chocolate rice mould; summer drinks of lemon and ginger; home-made biscuits and cream crackers; raisin bread pudding; chutney and shepherd's pie. Not to mention the ubiquitous roast lamb, roast beef and chicken. Oh, and baked fish. By the time she had searched for the meals she imagined Australians might like, and Frank had covered his eyes with a folded cloth while imploring, "Weli, enough; come lie in my arm now," her sleep would be fractured by fitful dreams of rare culinary concoctions as she hallucinated over a fire-mouthed iron monster in the cauldron of her kitchen.

The morning came with some reassurance as Elaine returned from where she was staying at Sea Shanty. She proposed they should head into Cowes to personally meet the suppliers and business people. For such an important event, Frank dressed in a silk shirt, elegant fine wool trousers and pigskin gloves, to be accompanied by his equally elegant wife dressed in her European best. Elaine, unable to suppress a smile, said nothing. After all, she was a well-travelled woman who understood the background from which her protégées had come. It might take some time, but Australia would loosen the tie a little and perhaps even allow a bathing costume. Maybe. In the car, Anita felt it important to make the point that during the war, there was little to eat in Germany. "We were starving there for much of the time. The rations were next to nothing. And before that, I had not to cook; we had always a maid and I had not to learn. All I have is the cookbook my sister gave me and, from what I have seen so far, that will not be much help. And for forty people!"

"You will find it much easier than you think, Anita. Besides, I've organised a cook for you - Steve and his wife Lil. You'll like them and they're terrific. Now, here we are at Thompsons. They supply us with the fuel for the engines at the pump and generator."

They stepped out of the car and stood in front of a huge tin shed.

"Come on. He'll be inside messing about with a tractor or something." Elaine led the way and they found William rummaging among boxes of spare parts and drums of oil and kerosene. He looked up with some surprise as the party entered and brushed his hands on his overalls to say hello with a handshake. He hesitated, thought better of it and then, wearing a smile, genially asked, "Going somewhere special, are we?" The situation was explained and the first meeting of the day became the template for a succession of encounters filled with good humour and promise: Jack Phillip's grocery store and Wagner's Butchery on the corner of Thompson Avenue and Chapel Street. And, as is always the case with new faces in a small town, a host of curious friends and well-wishers along the way. As they returned to the car, Anita hooked her arm through Frank's. "I think we could get used to this."

Christmas came, and with it a slew of very exclusive guests; well spoken, educated, successful. Expensive cars, elegant casual clothes and the self-assurance that comes with money and the freedom to be on holiday. At first, their hosts were surprised. Why, with the whole world at one's convenience, choose this remote wilderness? But then, why not? The weather was beautiful, the beach a vast and glittering playground for the children; rock pools to explore and shells to collect, along with driftwood and happy memories. But, when one is up at six in the morning and working all day till midnight and beyond, it's harder to enjoy the summery breezes, the surf and the lapping waves, relaxed on a towel in the sun.

As she lay exhausted in their bed, Anita announced to the ceiling, "We worked like tigers again today," before turning to lie in her husband's arm and letting the day's stripes fade into dreamless sleep. Frank, meanwhile, lay awake, musing on whether his beloved had meant they would now have to ride the tiger for ever or, that he had avoided the door of bloody slaughter and fortuitously chosen the door from which had emerged the lady of his dreams.[11]

Michael had a great time. The guests loved him, took him down to the beach, brought him playthings and indulged him with treats. Until he was given a pop gun, a tin toy with a cork in the barrel. Pull the trigger and it popped out on a string. He trotted off to Mr. Nane and announced he would bring back a rabbit. Later, when the rabbit hadn't arrived, Mr. Nane came over to the guest house to ask why his dinner

---

[11] Stockton, F. *The Lady or The Tiger,* The Century 1882

hadn't been delivered. The mystery unravelled, Mr. Nane huffed off with the stern advice that one shouldn't make promises one couldn't keep – and the dangerous weapon, an all too potent reminder of the past, was confiscated.

The past caught up with them in a letter. Frank had written to the family in Germany and Anita had added her stories of their life in the southern wilds of Australia, living in an old guesthouse and cooking for forty people in the summer heat. It was hardly a tale of misery and hardship, rather and explanation of how they were building a new life they could never have imagined. As she wrote, Anita herself was amazed at how her life had unfolded in this remarkable place so removed from the world she once knew. And so the news was sealed and stamped and sent 'Par Avion, mit Luftpost' in its envelope with the red and blue striped border to the eagerly waiting family in the Apotheke in Tuttlingen.

The reply, when it came, was a cry of despair from Anita's parents. What have you done? How on earth could you end up in such a forsaken place? Think of where you have come from? How you were educated? The life you had. And all this sacrificed to be a servant to wealth and privilege. This is a disaster and your life will be forever ruined. Have you forgotten already the life we prepared you for? How could you? It's too terrible to imagine. Such a tirade of distress and accusation struck deep. Looking at her situation with European eyes, Anita could see it was impossible for them to understand, but this was cruel. She stained the letter with her tears, put it aside and sat on her bed weeping doubt and regret, sensing her mother's grief for a lost life and her father's indignation that she had chosen such a lowly path. Life was hard, but not impossible. How could she explain this new and surprising freedom to people who would never understand it, not even the ones she loved? She read the letter again, hearing in the language she had barely used in the last months, the familiar voices. Homesickness suddenly overwhelmed her and she sobbed for an irretrievable past.

When she emerged, her eyes red, her body wrung with distress, John Edwards had arrived. He was a man of genteel bohemian sensibilities with considerable artistic talent. He found painting en plein air an enjoyably contemplative pursuit, one that also provided some respite from the social proclivities of his alluring wife. Together with their children, they occupied a holiday house among the tea-tree some half mile away on the other side of the road. Learning of the new migrant family, he had thought to bring some Christmas cheer, to be delivered via a selection of recorded German carols which he would play on his portable gramophone. Little could he know the impact this infinitely familiar music would have in such an unfamiliar place.

With the player set up on the living room table, the family gathered, he wound the handle and lowered the needle. It scratched away the first few turns and then arose a choir of children's voices as they sang *Es ist ein Ros' entsprungen*[12]. Suddenly the world in which they stood dissolved and all the flooding innocence and beauty of the past reached out and drowned them, tearing at their hearts. Anita put her hands to her face and sobbed great gouts of anguish and loss, for Christmases past and family forfeited. Frank's eyes filled with tears as he was drawn back to his childhood, his mother's face, her voice, all the love that was understood and the quiet happiness of his home when the world seemed so simple, so kind and uncomplicated. Then came *Alle Jahre Wieder*[13] and Anita saw again the concert hall with the choir and orchestra, the restrained voices of the brass, the hushed audience, her girlhood flooding back and a Christmas tree with its baubles reflecting the lit candles, snow falling on the garden and a world filled with peace and goodwill. *Stille nacht, heilige Nacht*[14] reached into the hearts of even those who knew only the melody and the whole house was filled with tears, if not for themselves, then for those who they saw so overcome. While war had torn lives apart, bombed and obliterated people's homes and blasted the world in fire and smoke, this music existed still and spoke across the years and across the world.

From below, the sound of breakers reached up, together with the voices of the guests returning from a day of sunshine at the beach. And they would be hungry.

Exhausted, Anita sat alone by the window, looking out across the dunes and seeing nothing. Presently, a woman approached, drew up a chair and sat next to her. She waited quietly before gently asking, "Are you all right? Is there anything you need? I'm a doctor, Doctor Osbourne from Collins Street."

Anita looked at her, saw the concern in her eyes and was grateful for the kindness. She took a deep breath and unpacked her sadness

---

[12]A Rose has Sprung; English song title: "Lo, how a rose e'er blooming"

[13]All the years again

[14] Silent night, Holy night

and her parents' despair. When finally there was no more left to say, Dr. Osbourne took her hand and said, "You know, here in Australia we don't look at what a person does, we look at who they are. It makes no difference whether you cook here, or whether you clean a room or whether you're a guest, you are looked at the same way, as the person you are."

There was a long silence. "Thank you," Anita looked up and tried a smile.

"If there's anything you need, you know where to find me."

As she left, Anita turned back to the window. Across the dunes, the beach was already in shadow. Soon, the penguins would return, calling to their families in their burrows as they had for thousands of years.

CHAPTER TWELVE

Adventure Island

The lure of an adventure into a remote wilderness with muttonbirds and penguins was heightened by the possibility of a train trip and a sea voyage. While some could afford the luxury of motoring from Melbourne all around Westernport Bay to the Island, many were happy to pack their suitcases and travel to Frankston and then to Stony Point station with its white picket fence, a cluster of buildings and a background of gum trees. From there, a short walk to the ferry terminal, together with a payment of ten shillings and sixpence, allowed one to board the steamer and head across the waters to Cowes. Some would disembark for the Isle of Wight Hotel, rebuilt after the 1925 fire, or the Phillip Island Hotel, while others would venture the extra leg to Summerland's jetty by Cat Bay. While the waters of Westernport were far more sheltered than the rolling ocean of Bass Strait, the combination of tides and wild weather occasionally provided a level of excitement more enjoyed by the children than their parents who feared catastrophe as the vessel pitched and rolled on the turbulent sea.

The jetty was a magnificent affair set on timber pylons and reaching far out into the deep water. Steep sand dunes had inspired a path through a tunnel of tea-tree that opened to a broad landscape and St. Helen's Road up to the guesthouse. With the wind in their faces and expectation riding the air, the travellers checked they had packed their torches along with the Brownie Box camera that would capture the stories for them to recount to friends in the weeks to come. Sometimes there would be a special request and Frank would take the Whippet to the corner to help those unwilling or unable to schlep their luggage the few hundred yards to their accommodation.

When the last guests of Easter had finally shared their thanks and waved goodbye, the Whippet remained parked alongside the house, left in gear and with the handbrake secure. Michael would often sit in it and, like many a youngster, pretend to be driving it. One morning, probably a washing day Monday, Anita emerged to hang out the sheets and towels and, seeing Michael in the car, warned him not to touch anything but just sit there and be good. That being the least interesting option, he decided to load the back seat with the short wooden surf boards that were hired out to guests for sixpence a day.

Being just five years old, he thought it was a good idea to have them packed and ready to take to the beach. The task completed, he returned to the driver's seat and set about going for a drive. First, he carefully put his foot on the right pedal and pushed. Nothing happened – a good sign. Then he tried the middle pedal. Again, nothing happened. He wondered about the big stick lever in the middle but decided against pushing that and instead pressed down on the foot pedal to the left. With a shock, he realised the car was starting to move.

From where it had been parked, the rough driveway headed towards the cliff before veering to the left and then up past the house and onto the road. If one could get to the road it was possible to turn left again and re-enter the property back to the start. In a panic – and imagining that somehow this miracle would transpire - he heaved left on the steering wheel. By then he had reached the post and rickety gate that led to the crude steps cut into the side of the cliff where the small generator shed housed the Ronaldson and Tippet engine.

The two front wheels knocked over the post and headed over the precipice. The boobialla bush snared the underneath and the chassis hit the ground. Everything stopped, including it seemed to the newly minted driver, his heart. When it finally restarted, he very gingerly opened the door and slipped out onto the running board, found his footing on the grass and made his way inside. Looking back, he saw that he had managed to steer the car fractionally to one side and thereby avoid the direct trajectory that would have had both him and the car plunge into the abyss and the creek below.

Anita instantly recognised that something was wrong.

"What happened?"

"The car went by itself."

The subsequent investigation revealed that he was lucky to be alive. The surf boards packed high in the back had shifted forward nearly knocking his brains out from behind. Besides, the car was balancing precariously over the edge. And though it was explained to him that there was a reason for leaving the car in gear – and he had pressed the clutch thereby disengaging the wheels from the stationary engine – how was he to know that the handbrake was not safe on a slope, or that a car could be so treacherous a plaything?

In the end, the little grey Ferguson tractor was called into service and the vehicle rescued. There would come a time however when, in a moment of folly, an even more spectacular adventure would be played out.

⤿

The telephone rang. Frank picked it up.

"Hello? Mr. Metzger?"

"Speaking."

"Oh, it's Mrs. Spencer, you might remember. We stayed with you over Easter. I was wondering whether you were home. We'd like to come by and have a chat. We're in Cowes at the moment and could be with you in half an hour. Would that be all right?"

Of course it would be fine, and though curious, Frank refrained from any immediate questions. He remembered the family, well-to-do, and with a daughter in her teens. Something had happened during their stay; the husband had become agitated and angry and had driven off for the day. When he returned, he had appeared tense and withdrawn. Even though they had stayed till the Tuesday, the earlier casual light-heartedness had evaporated.

Only mother and daughter arrived. There being no-one else about, they sat in the living room at the table by the window. In the silence as Mrs. Spencer summoned the words for the difficult request she was about to make, the outside wind rubbed the shrubs against the walls, scratching at the awkwardness. Finally, indicating the girl, she spoke.

"You remember Penny, don't you? And I'm Margaret. Bruce couldn't be here; important work in Melbourne, executive meetings. You know how it is." She paused, unsure where to go. "You seem nice people, understanding. We're in a difficult position… Penny… she has an issue with her health. We need to find a place where she can stay for a while. Somewhere quiet, remote. Away from her normal life."

"Is it something serious?" Anita was immediately concerned.

"Not really, no." She corrected herself, "actually, yes it is."

Penny had been looking out of the window, focused on the receding headlands under the overcast sky. Suddenly defiant, she stood up.

"Look, I'm pregnant." She ran her hand over her belly. "It's awkward." She sat down again, leaving her mother to manage the news. Margaret flushed, shrugged her shoulders to ask 'what can I say?'

Frank looked at the girl and saw – beneath the flare of defiance – that she was frightened, hurt and trapped. And young, so young. He spoke.

"This is not a question of health. To have a child is normal and nothing for which you have to be afraid or ashamed. You're still at school, aren't you?"

She looked at him. He had not been unkind.

"Yes, I'm doing my Leaving Certificate."

"She's just sixteen and going to a very good school, a private school, in Brighton. She was going so well." Margaret fumbled in her handbag and drew out a handkerchief. "The thing is, she can't go back like this. Apart from what she has done to her family, the school wouldn't have her back."

Anita asked, "What does your husband say?"

Penny wanted to say 'it's not what I've done to the family, but what the family has done to me', but she corralled her anger for the moment. Now was not the time to destroy the past or compromise the future.

"He wants nothing to do with her. He's angry. He wants to be left out of it. He's angry with me; he's had a frightful argument with his brother. I'm worried he wants nothing to do with any of us, but it would look bad for a man in his position. He can't afford to have a scandal like this derail his career and our security." She dabbed at her eyes. "I don't know where on earth this will end."

Anita understood only too well where such an argument might lead. She asked, "So what would you like us to do? How did you think we might help?"

"Penny and I have talked about it. If she could stay here till she's had the baby, we could simply tell the school the story she's gone to stay with friends overseas – I know that's a bit of a stretch, but sort of true – and the child could be put up for adoption. There are places in Melbourne like the St. Joseph's Foundling Hospital, or an orphanage. I can arrange that."

Frank turned to the girl. "When is the baby due?"

"End of September I think."

"What do you imagine you would do here until then?"

"I've no idea. Maybe I could help out. I should probably do schoolwork.

Mum could arrange some books and ask teachers about some work. I don't know; I just need to be out of sight." The cruel reality of where she now found herself crumpled her face. She looked at the floor.

"Of course we'll pay you for her board and food and anything else you need. That's not a problem. It's really a question of whether you're prepared to have her here."

"What do you think, Johannes?"

"For as long as she is prepared to live under our roof and help occasionally – there's always plenty to do – I don't have a problem. She just needs to take responsibility and talk honestly with us if anything troubles her. I think she's capable of that, don't you?" He looked at Penny.

"Does that mean you'll have me?"

"I think it does." Anita got up and sat on the arm of the chair next to her. "It will be all right. You wait and see."

A week later, Penny Spencer found herself ensconced in a verandah room that opened onto a small sitting room. She had a table and chair, a place to sit and read, a sanctuary for herself and the life that grew within her.

$$\backsim$$

Michael meanwhile had developed a passion for climbing. A step ladder that had been left standing outside the tea-room flats proved a temptation beyond his capacity to comprehend danger. First one step, then the next. The world appeared more vast, the people working along the fence even further away. He tried another step and was taller than everyone. More steps and he could see the sea and the sky. And sea gulls. At last, in the clouds it seemed, he stood on the top step. "Look. Look at me," he called. "I can fly." He spread his wings and launched onto the wind. Horrified cries of "No-o-o!" accompanied his fall. Stunned and winded, he lay on the unyielding earth, unable to move.

How his neck was not broken, his ribs splintered or his brain addled, no-one could explain. The good doctor, Alec Reith, dropped his shovel and raced over, carefully checked for vital signs and declared a most miraculous escape. Michael was carried back to the house where Anita sat by his bed till she was reassured he might survive without more damage than the realisation he was not a bird of the air, but a child of the earth. The lessons of childhood are hard on parents.

At the back of the guesthouse, nearest the road, grew two golden cypress trees. They had been planted some twenty years earlier, one presumed more for their ornament and shade than as a windbreak, given that tempests swept the landscape from the ocean. For a child, cypress trees offer an ideal scaffolding, their branches horizontal and spaced for climbing. A couple of potato boxes stacked below provide the step up to the first limbs and from there it all seems to make sense.

It was a spring morning, with a clear and cloudless sky, when Michael emerged and quite spontaneously decided the weather was perfect for exploring the possibilities of climbing. It seemed the most natural and easy thing to do; each new limb offered a new opportunity above until, sooner than he expected, he was at the very top. With nowhere further to go, he found the two top branches had formed a chair wherein he might sit and survey the landscape. It was amazing. From his secure eyrie there was the roof of his home, the car below, then the dunes and the vast arc of the beach.

Anita appeared far below with a basket of washing on her hip. The lines were stretched between two posts, each with a cross piece. A prop stick held up one side while the lower was being pegged out, and then swapped to the other line. Soon there were sheets and towels, billowing in the breeze.

"Micha? Where are you? Are you here?" She looked around, waiting for an answer. Michael decided he was hiding. Anita called again. The pleasure of witnessing the earth from this high was too great and he called back. "I'm here. At the top of the tree."

"Where are you?" His mother was incredulous. "At the top of the tree?"

"Ye-es. I climbed it by myself."

"What can you see?"

He looked out. The beach ran all the way to the rocks and the bluff. Beyond that, headland after headland, clear in the morning light. And there was the sea, stretching away and away to a line at the horizon. There was nothing beyond it, just sea and then sky. He was struck by a sudden and marvellous realisation.

"I can see the edge of the world!"

Anita heard his piping voice, full of wonder and her love reached out to him over the horizon of her heart.

"Be careful, Micha," she called. "The world is very big." Taking up her basket, she returned inside, her smile as warm as the wind in the washing.

Overland and Sea

The holiday season came to an end, the days grew ever hotter through February until, almost suddenly it seemed, autumn took its appointed place. The tides swelled and banks of breakers crashed incessantly onto the glistening arc of sand or hurled themselves in rolling green against the basalt ramparts at either end of the beach. Afternoons were filled with sunlight and gentle breezes, idyllic times for strolling together arm in arm with little Micha trotting beside or, suddenly arrested by some new marvel delivered by the sea, suspended to drink in the air, the cry of gulls, the open sky. Inevitably the return journey was encumbered by armfuls of driftwood. In the evening, fire sprites would spin crackling stars and coloured flames into the chimney's gaping mouth.

It was on one such afternoon that Frank hit upon the fabulous notion of driving the old 1928 Whippet Tourer down to the beach. Anita thought it preposterous, far too dangerous. Limonis had to go home to the farm to milk the cow and check his old mother-in-law was all right, but Skydrita believed it a wonderful idea and volunteered to come along for the ride.

It being low tide, the pair duly departed, taking the track behind the house that led along the creek till it became a rocky ford leading onto the beach. The thin rubber tyres on narrow wooden wheels were not ideally suited to the environment, despite the word "Overland" impressed on the hubs. After much erratic lurching, punctuated by Skydrita's squeals, they reached the silt made barely navigable by the trickle from the creek.

Once onto the shoreline, it was a different story. The Whippet, true to its name, fairly loped along on the firm sand. The sky was blue, the wind in their faces, the hum of the engine stitching a canvas of pure delight. At the eastern end, Frank turned the car around and began the homeward run. This time, Skydrita was on the seaward side. The beach was a highway, smooth, flat and firm along the water's edge. They sped faster and faster, exhilarated by the narrow escapes as waves ran up the sand to within inches of the wheels.

To play this game, a watery version of Daedalus and Icarus on waxen wings, one needs to observe the larger canvas. The shoreline breakers were a distraction from the heaving ocean, surf that welled and broke, tier upon tier until, with an inevitability long sensed, the breaking wave spilled its contents. Water rushed up the beach, through the wheels and further still. It hung there, suspended in an amazed silence, before swirling away to rejoin the next gentle lap. The car had stopped. So too had the motor.

Frank leapt out and saw that the wheels had sunk about six inches. Frantically he rushed to the front, rammed in the crank handle and tried to turn it. Immovable. The car was still in gear, stalled. He disengaged the gear stick, checked the ignition and tried again. On the fourth turn, the motor fired. He sprang back in, closing the door, finding first gear and gunning the engine. The rear wheels turned, sinking further into the sand.

"We have to dig!"

They both scrambled out and began tearing away handfuls of sand from the front of the wheels. The ocean looked on, breaking waves yards away. It was still low tide. There was plenty of time. With the sand clear, Frank tried again. The car moved about a foot to the end of their digging before struggling to get clear.

"We have to dig more!"

Again they scooped handfuls of sand clear of the wheels. Struck by sudden inspiration, Frank raced up the beach, grabbed armfuls of seaweed and laid a track over the digging.

"Quick! In, get in!"

He ground the gears, slowly let out the clutch, felt the wheels slip, but gradually they inched forward. The sea, impassive, restrained, watched their progress.

Up at the house, Anita was getting anxious. It was getting late and cold. Already they had been gone over an hour. Such unnecessary foolishness. It was time to prepare tea, feed Michael, get him to bed and have peace at the end of the day.

"Where's daddy?"

"Gone to the beach. He's taken the car."

"Why? It's not very far."

"I know pet. It's just an idea – to drive along the sand. Maybe they'll bring back some wood - I don't know."

"When is he coming back?"

"Soon, I hope."

The success of the seaweed road had prompted the impulse to make assurance double sure by gathering more - sufficient to lay a track long enough to guarantee a smooth passage to firm sand. Finally, the adventurers clambered back and gingerly began their perilous escape.

No-one's prayers were answered. After all the subdued lapping of the ocean, it released another cascade that drowned the vehicle and all hope with it. Crushed, Frank and Skydrita stepped down, their feet in the swirling water and knew that their efforts had been in vain. This time, as the water receded, they saw the wheels were hopelessly buried.

"We have to get back. I'll get the tractor and a chain and for sure we can pull it out. As long as the tide stays out. Come on, run!"

Already exhausted, both from fear and her exertions, Skydrita fell behind.

"You go ahead Frank, I'll go up to the house and tell Anita."

Out of breath, her hair in disarray and, flushed from the climb up the cliff, Skydrita burst in the back door.

"Anita? Anita! Anita, are you there? Where are you?"

Anita appeared. Instantly she recognised that something was seriously amiss. The questions tumbled over one another, like water through wheels.

"What is it? Are you all right? Where's Frank? What happened? Why are you here?"

Struggling for air, Skydrita gasped out the catastrophe.

"At the beach ... wave came ...wheels sank in the sand. Car stuck. Frank getting the tractor with Limonis."

Anita sank onto the kitchen chair.

"The foolish man. What will we do now? Can we rescue the car before the tide comes back?" Suddenly, she was resolved. She got to her feet. "You will have to stay here and look after Micha. I am going to the beach to meet them when they return."

Before he even reached the door to the farmhouse, Frank called to Limonis. He appeared at the door in his slippers.

"Quickly! Get the tractor. The Whippet is bogged in the sand. We will need chains."

Limonis stared in amazement, struggling to decipher what had happened. Gradually it dawned. He shed the slippers, pulled on his gumboots and headed for the barn. The key to the grey Ferguson had been left in the ignition, a chain wound around the 3-point linkage. Limonis drove while Frank sat side-saddle on the mudguard.

"Go Limonis, go! As fast as you can. We have to beat the tide."

By the time they crossed the outlet from the creek, the swell was noticeably higher. The tractor travelled well on the sand but they didn't risk going any nearer to the water's edge than they could help. When they reached the car, Anita was already there, her hands pressed to her head, staring as the water swirled around the axles.

"What have you done?"

There was neither time for explanations, nor was there an explanation to give. As Limonis backed the tractor up to the front of the car, Frank dropped to his knees in the water and tried to tie one end of the chain around the front axle.

"Wire!" he shouted. Limonis fumbled in the toolbox under the seat and handed him a short length, enough to fasten the end link after the knot. The other end he inserted into the drawbar and slipped in the pin. He jumped back onto the seat.

"Ready?"

"Yes. Gently. Take up the slack slowly, gently."

The chain rose out of the water and drew taut. It wouldn't do to break anything. Cautiously, Limonis took his foot further off the clutch and gave more throttle. He felt the unyielding hold of the car in the sand.

"Nothing. It's not moving."

"Let me try."

They swapped places and Frank tried the same manoeuvre, sensing the strain. The back wheels of the tractor began to churn water and sand. They also churned his mind.

"It's no good. The water's too deep and the tractor isn't strong enough. There has to be another way."

He surveyed the sky. There was maybe half an hour of daylight left. High tide was still hours away, but every minute the waves were doing more damage. He struggled to think. Maybe it was the shape of the clouds, perhaps the white horses on the waves, but suddenly he exclaimed,

"Mr. Gardiner! Mr. Gardiner!"

The others looked at him in astonishment.

"The horses. The Clydesdales. He has a pair of horses. Horses cannot get bogged. They are strong. The tractor is useless, we need the horses."

This call for the cavalry was accompanied by a string of commands. Anita was to return to the house with Limonis, make a telephone call to Mr. Gardiner requesting his most urgent assistance. And make sure Micha and Skydrita were all right. Limonis was to return with kerosene hurricane lamps and dry matches. He would meanwhile take the tractor back to the house and return to stand watch over the vehicle until the arrival of the lone horseman of this apocalypse.

Mr. Gardiner was in the middle of his dinner when the phone rang. He listened in silence, occasionally peering out of his kitchen window to assess the deepening sky. It was about two miles to Summerland beach. These migrants seemed good people, but were they crazy? By the time he fetched the horses from the paddock, got collar and harness, and made his way there, it would be dark.

An hour later he rounded the dune and saw two figures sitting on the sand with two pale orbs of light between them. Further down, the upper half of the Whippet rose in silhouette from the waves.

The last groups of penguins were still spilling from the breakers and making their way to the rookery. The air was filled with their cries and the thump of water behind them. The three men were grimly silent.

Had anybody observed the tableau that ensued, a Caravaggio of the surrealist school, they may have imagined themselves in the miasma of some opium-induced trance, an hallucinogenic comic opera. In an eerily lit moonscape under a vast and lonely sky, three human figures and two mighty Clydesdales struggled to haul a ton of metal welded to the sand by the sea, while squawking penguins performed a Hallelujah chorus to the orchestra of the waves. It was a true marriage of the sublime and the ridiculous.

In the end, the elements triumphed and, disconsolate, men and beasts waded from the sea.

"What will you do now?" asked Mr. Gardiner as they picked their way over the rocks to the creek.

"I have no idea. Tonight we can do nothing. Tomorrow I will come back to see what can be saved."

At the top of the path, they parted ways, Frank's gratitude as profound as his self-reproach. Anita, anxious, met him at the door.

"Well? What happened? Look at you – wet and exhausted. Dear man."

She held him close, sensing his despair, his drowning in foolishness and failure. She kissed his wet face, hugged him again.

"Sit. Tell me what happened."

Now that he was safe, she was strong again. When it was over, she was smiling.

"You must have looked a proper sight down there in the dark. I wonder what the penguins thought!"

By the time they went to bed, part of the day had resumed its normal proportion. Throughout the night however, Frank lay listening to the sea, hearing the pounding of the waves, fearing the worst, hoping for the best, knowing that against the ocean, a tin car with a canvas roof and wooden wheels would never survive.

At first light he climbed down the cliff path to the beach. The morning sun cast long shadows on the wide littoral now liberated by the ebb tide. Rising from its sandy grave, the skeleton of the Whippet stood stiff and black. The canvas roof had been torn away and disappeared. The tilting windscreen hung awry. There were no doors and no seats. The folding bonnet covers had also vanished. Four wheels, an engine block, a chassis and a steering wheel. That was it.

Despite himself, Frank smiled at the metamorphosis. A cabriolet, a convertible. A Roadster with the top down, sans seats. On a hunch, he headed up the beach to the dunes and scrambled up the collapsing sand to the grass. Presently he came across what he was looking for – one of the seats flung on its side. Nearby he found another, tossed high by the previous night's water. From where it lay, he looked back to the ocean to estimate how high it must have come. Twenty feet? Thirty feet? It seemed impossible, but all along the shore he could see where the sea had eaten away at the dunes. Of all nights, he had chosen the last one. He returned to the house, forming a plan on the way.

Later, with Anita, Limonis and Skydrita, all armed with shovels and riding the little grey Ferguson, he returned and they began the daunting task of digging the wreck from the sand. Without the invasion of water, it progressed rapidly till, an hour later, Frank sat on one of the reclaimed seats and steered the remains behind Limonis on the tractor all the way back to the house. While a curiously novel experience this time, it was the merest foretaste of something more terrifying to come.

"It wasn't insured you know." Elaine's voice was edged with frost. "What on earth did you think you were doing?"

The tirade crackled along the telephone line, the only response a rueful, "I'm sorry, terribly sorry."

The following morning, the Reith's hulking new Ford drove into the yard and parked beside the remains of the Whippet.

Displeasure at the loss of the Whippet was mildly ameliorated by gratitude for the success of the revitalised holiday season. The migrants had worked assiduously to achieve a surprising outcome that, while not catapulting the business to a height greater than ground level, at least justified the replacement of the courtesy car. The price would include the perilous return of the much diminished Tourer to Melbourne by towing it behind the Reith's new Ford. With no more than the mechanical handbrake to slow its trajectory, and without the protection of a windscreen or roof, the exercise was more akin to riding a billy cart over a cliff. Nevertheless, with the seats wired in place, the steering checked for functionality and silent prayers to an invisible deity, Elaine set off with Frank riding the chariot behind. Mercifully, the weather was clear and the wind no more unsettling than the fifty miles per hour at which the flimsy chassis was hauled through the landscape. If there had been times in his short life that Frank had feared for his survival, few were as harrowing as the situation in which he now found himself, one hand on the steering wheel, the other on the brake. Though he couldn't think it at the time, he later mused how it was something of a metaphor for survival in an unpredictable world.

Foolishness is seldom rewarded by anything other than pain and suffering. It is also true that man must suffer to become wise. Whether Frank had already endured enough without having to assume responsibility for it, or whether the inverted world chose to smile on his labours, he could not tell – but the week in Melbourne enabled him to return to Summerland in triumph.

How the deal was brokered remains a mystery. The outcome was not a car, but a motorbike – a BSA 650 A10 Golden Flash with a sidecar. While it might not ferry guests to and from the house, it would most adequately serve the needs of the small family on the Island. Bewilderment and gratitude were seasoned with a tantalising thrill as he straddled the machine, kicked the starter and sensed the throb and growl of its power.

But first, it being September, the Royal Melbourne Agricultural Show was taking place at Flemington. A country fair with a hundred years of history, it celebrated rural industry, livestock and produce all the way from machinery to preserves and scones and cream. Now that he was part of the bucolic rural landscape, Elaine thought it only fitting that Frank should be absorbed in the milling throng that came to cheer the fine specimens of skilled axemen, chips flying, at the wood chopping competition, or marvel at the grand parade with its horses and carriages, and bulls of such stature as would make farmers proud, butchers swoon and cows blush, their swollen udders offering a land of milk and honey-coloured dames. With polished harness, plaited manes and flowing tails, horses pranced or plodded: palomino, Clydesdale, Arabs, Thoroughbred, Australian stock horses and tiny Shetland ponies. Further afield, lambs lay on their beds of straw; rams, heavy with wool, raised their heads and coiled horns and looked at him with their slotted eyes. Hens and pigeons, ducks and geese, fowl in all their infinite variety. And then the dogs – kennel after kennel, from mastiffs to poodles, Labradors and beagles, dachshund and husky, Border Collie and Great Dane. A cacophony of bark and yap, or the yodel of the barkless Basenji.

Something stirred deep within the man. Whether it was a reminder of loss and yearning, or the unspoken loyalty of a creature whose uncritical companionship was the antidote to the vexations of the world, he didn't know. The rationalised urge was 'since we live in the countryside, we must have a dog'. He walked the rows of enclosures. What should it be? Would the dog choose him? Isn't there a moment when one just knows? He paused, reading the names of breeders, the certificates of prize winners, the ribbons denoting the best of the pedigrees. He moved on; it was a fantasy. There was work to be done, a family waiting and the long ride home. He squeezed past the press of people, children excitedly pointing to the puppies, their voices full of longing and imploring, couples debating the respective merits of different breeds while owners explained their history and provenance. Blocking his way was a man perched on his folding chair beside his stand. A gentleman with a sharp eye and the sort of pleasant face that makes one feel as if one has been friends for years. He wore a tweed jacket, a matching cap and a name tag: Alf Michelson. He looked up.

"Sorry. I'm in your way. Just a moment." He stood up. "Are you looking for something? Can I help?"

"Thank you. I thought for a moment I might find a dog, but maybe it's not the right time."

"Is there ever not a right time?" Alf looked at him, the smile asking the question.

"Maybe you're right. What do you have?"

"Gun dogs: setters and retrievers."

Gun dogs. Immediately he saw the pistol, the uniformed soldier, his Alsatian on a leash, teeth bared. But no; these were dogs that would not scare at the report of a rifle; intelligent dogs that could be trained; dogs known for their boundless vitality, their loyalty to their master. A friend, a protector. A companion. A dog that would understand him. Alf saw him hesitate while he resolved the thought.

"Where are you? Your situation is important. These dogs need room to roam." He looked at the young man before him. Instinct prompted him to add, "And you to roam with whomever you choose." Frank understood that a part of him was recognised.

The curly haired retrievers were both fine specimens – a dog and a bitch – their closely coiled curls tight and brown; their heads alert for whatever game was to be played. But Frank had noticed something else in the next pen, black and tan.

"Gordon setter." Alf said. "Three types. Irish – that's the red setter. A bit too skittish for me. Then there's the English, gorgeous dog, black and white and tan variations. Didn't bring them down this time. And then the Gordon, the Scottish version, more stable, intelligent, true to his master. Great temperament."

Frank said nothing.

"That's the mother. Two pups, ten weeks old – a male and a female." He waited. "You'll be wanting to look at the male." He opened the gate and knelt beside the mother, talking to her and running his hand over her head, stroking her long ears. Her brown eyes looked back, full of quiet trust. He picked up the dog and brought him over. He was all head and legs, massive paws and a square face. Frank held him up, felt his weight, the quality of his coat. The pup was surprisingly calm, as if he knew this was his moment. Holding this living creature, sensing its promise, Frank knew it was also his moment.

Arrangements were made, the papers verified and money exchanged, together with names and addresses. As he walked away, Frank's moment of doubt was assuaged by the additional life he was bringing home to his family. There would be consternation, but it would be followed by delight.

New life also invited death. A gun dog invites a gun. Not that Frank could ever conceive of bringing down birds from the sky, fluttering maimed to splash uncomprehending into the dawn waters of a lake, but perhaps Alf Nane was right – there were rabbits aplenty. They would provide food for the dog and there would be fewer wreaking havoc on the fragile environment. How he would manage to take the life and skin the creature were questions he was not ready to contemplate. Maybe necessity would provide the answers. The lessons from past hunger might yet prove useful.

He broke the return to the Island with a visit to Elaine. She shook her head and smiled an indulgent smile. You're a good man, but what on earth are you thinking? Still, he's a lovely dog and Summerland will be the right environment.

"You'll make sure he's kept under control, won't you? Wouldn't do to have him harassing the penguins or the shearwaters."

"Of course. The rabbits will keep him well occupied. Besides, there is nothing worse than an undisciplined dog."

"Good. I'm glad to hear it." She paused a moment. "You don't have a gun do you?"

"Not yet."

"It so happens that Alec has a spare rifle here – no use for it in the city – beside the one at the Island. I can let you have this one. I'm sure he won't mind."

She excused herself and returned a few moments later with the gun in its case.

"A .22 I think. Do you know how to use it?"

"I think I can work it out. More used to having a gun at my head than using one. We'll see how it goes."

"There's something else. That dog of yours is going to need a carry basket and a blanket. It'll be terrified in the bottom of the sidecar. You'll need water. And when you get to Cowes, drop in at Wagner's, the butcher, and get some offcuts to cook for him."

Properly instructed, but grateful for the help, Frank headed south again. At first, the bike felt odd. He couldn't lean into the corners as he had on the Zündapp and he was constantly aware of the shape shadowing him on his left. Turning right felt even more strange – perhaps it would be safer with a passenger lending the extra weight. A puppy was barely sufficient.

Anita was in the kitchen when she heard the bike. Strange, she thought. Someone arriving at the back door. Usually people pulled up at the front and one heard them on the verandah before they knocked. And a motorbike? Who had one of those? She stopped her preparations for dinner and went to the door.

"Johannes!" She was surprised. "Back again, dear man." She was about to embrace her welcome, when she saw he was carrying a bundle wrapped in a blanket. "What have you got?"

He unwrapped the squirming mass and held up his prize. "What do you think?"

"What on earth? What have you done?"

"Don't you think he's beautiful?"

"Yes, but… look at him. All bones and wagging tail. All out of proportion. What dog is that?"

It was as expected. Frank explained how exceptional the mother, the prizes won at the show, the quality of the breed, the shape of his head, the size of his paws. He would grow into his skin and be more wonderful than could be imagined.

"How much did you have to pay for him?"

Frank paused. For a moment he looked sheepish. "Ten guineas."

"Ten guineas!" Anita shook her head, dumbstruck. She took a deep breath. "How could you pay ten guineas? That's a fortune! Do we even have ten guineas?"

"Weli, believe me. Just wait and see. Here, hold him and you will understand."

She took the dog, holding it at arm's length, the better to take in the oddity of the creature. Then, for an instant, she glimpsed it – how he could become something special. She drew him to her and cradled the wriggling bundle as it tried to lick her face. "No, no. Here, on the floor. You can explore your new home." She turned to Frank. "How will we feed him?"

"It will be fine. When there are guests he will have more than enough. They leave more on their plates than they eat. In the meantime, there are rabbits and, in an emergency, we can get meat from the butcher."

"Rabbits? How will he catch rabbits?"

Frank explained his visit to Elaine, the acquisition of the motorbike and the gun. In any other context, he could have been describing preparations for becoming an outlaw. Even so, Anita was doubtful. Was she expected to ride in that shoe of a sidecar? What about Michael and the dog? How would they travel together as a family?

"And all of this," Anita said, "because you decided to take the Whippet for a drive along the sand when the tide was coming in."

While he made conciliatory noises, affecting deep humility and remorse, Frank nevertheless felt immensely pleased with the way things had turned out.

"Not long now." The doctor's voice was kind. "Probably a good time to ring your mother."

Penny ran her hands over her belly and cradled her swollen abdomen. For weeks she had felt the baby's movements, alternately reassured and startled. A deeper unease was eating away at her, a fear she had withheld from even her hosts' reassurances. She had come close when Anita asked about the child's father.

"You have told your boyfriend?"

"There is no boyfriend. That's not how it happened." Her voice was angry, resentful. "I didn't have a choice."

Anita tried to digest her meaning. The girl's mother and father not talking, the anger towards the uncle, the fracturing of the family, a once innocent girl now marooned in this island hideaway. She dreaded the conclusion.

"Is there anything you want to tell me?"

"I can't. It's already too terrible. I'm frightened." She looked away. "And I'm confused. Now that I'm having a baby, I feel I want to keep it, but I know I can't, I won't be allowed. If anybody else knew, they'd think I was easy, had no morals, no standards. They'd never know what happened." She took a handkerchief from her sleeve, dabbed her eyes, then blew her nose. She sat there with the cloth scrunched in her hand and let the creaking of the house swallow her confusion, her sadness.

The months had passed pleasantly enough. As the winter eased, Penny had increasingly spent time at the farm when she wasn't helping at the guesthouse. She found solace talking to the horse, feeding the chooks or harvesting vegetables from Skydrita's garden. She had even tried milking the cows, surprised at the naturalness, the easy rhythm and spurt of warm milk in the pail. Spring had somehow coincided with the emergence of her own new life, one so astonishingly removed from all she had previously known. The reality of her condition was reinforced by the doctor sitting opposite.

"Did you hear me? Your mother."

"Sorry. Yes. I'm scared."

"Of the birth?"

"No, the baby. I ... will the baby be all right, I mean normal?"

"Is there a reason it shouldn't be?

"I don't know. What if the father...?"

"I see." He paused, waited. "For a start, I can't tell at this time. Secondly, who else knows? Is this a matter for the police?"

"Impossible. Nobody would believe me even if I told my story. I can't. I don't want to lose my child, but I know I can't keep it. I have no idea what's going to happen."

"Let's call your mum and then we'll try to sort this out as best we can."

The following day Margaret Spencer arrived, helped her daughter pack her things and said goodbye to the Metzgers.

"You'll let us know what happens, won't you?" Anita was concerned. "She's been a good girl, no trouble at all, helpful and kind. The Rasas will miss her as well and they've been good to her. We hope everything works out."

Two weeks later, a letter arrived.

Dear Frank and Anita,

You will be pleased to learn that Penny was safely delivered of a healthy girl who has been accepted by the St. Joseph's Foundling Hospital and is available for adoption.

As a result of what has happened, the family is moving to Queensland, although my husband will remain in Melbourne for some time. Once Penny recovers, she will hopefully resume her schooling. We wish to make a new start and leave the troubling events of the past behind. I'm sure you will understand.

I thank you for all your kindness and enclose two cheques – one for the board and lodging you provided and another for your personal use. I trust it will make things a little easier.
Kind regards,
Margaret Spencer.

Anita nodded her head. "A sad story, but I'm relieved that things have more or less worked out for young Penny. It doesn't matter who you are, how wealthy your family, how important your position, life catches up anyway, when you least expect it. What will you do with the extra money?"

"It will be banked together with the takings for the house. We did no more than offer normal human decency and a roof over the girl's head, food and shelter. I'm not able to take advantage of someone else's misfortune."

"I thought that's what you would say. I'm glad. A walk along the beach will do us good. What do you think?"

"A fine idea."

Once again they climbed the dune and set out along the sand, the wind catching at their clothes, dispelling the concerns of the house, breathing fresh life into the fading day.

CHAPTER THIRTEEN

Grief and Joy

It was mid-January and the house was full. Days were warm. Guests were up early and went to bed late. Between, there was a constant barrage of requests, of small talk, of questions, clusters of conversations and bursts of laughter. The screen door from the verandah to the passage banged constantly as people rushed to their room to get extra towels, or a hat, or change their shoes before rushing out again to join the latest group making its excursion to the beach. By lunchtime, they would all be back, scraping their chairs in the dining room as they re-formed in shifting friendship groups.

Lunch was served.

By three o'clock Frank had finally withdrawn to the alcove that served as an office off the dining room. He began to make notes about what still had to be done when Anita joined him. A few strands of hair had fallen to her neck; beads of perspiration stood on her brow. She fluttered the blouse at her throat.

"This heat. Unbelievable."

"You have worked too hard. You shouldn't have to do this. You work harder than Elaine, Limonis and Skydrita together. Come and sit."

He motioned to the only other chair in the space.

"It has to be done. People need to be fed. And you, poor man, running with plates of food from table to table. You haven't stopped till now."

"What can I do? They pick at their food, more gravy please, another glass of water. 'Why does it taste so strange? Can we have tea instead?' They know it comes from the tank or the bore. But it's all right – I just smile politely, yes madam, thank you sir. More lamb? More beef?"

Limonis appeared at the open door.

"Frank." He nodded towards Anita, "Mrs. Metzger. Guests to see you, if you're free."

"Do you know who they are? What they want?"

"Couple from number seven. The ones with the imported Jaguar, the black one." He rubbed his thumb and forefinger together and raised his eyebrows with a knowing smile. He went to fetch them.

Mr. and Mrs. Mitchell made an elegant couple – he with a shock of dark hair swept back, obviously handsome, sporting a jacket, despite the heat, and leather dress shoes. Her pale blue eyes, which matched the summery frock, were somehow immensely sad. She also wore a gold bracelet watch and two gold rings. She appeared anxious.

Mr. Mitchell thrust out a manicured hand, unnecessarily formal. His voice was pleasant.

"Sorry to disturb you. Is it all right if we have a chat?"

"That's fine. Come out here where we can all sit." Frank arranged four chairs around one of the tables and, rather self-consciously, they found their places.

"That Jaguar of yours is a very impressive machine."

"Thank you, yes. We're very happy with it. Had it brought back after our trip to England last year. "Finest car of its class in the world,' they say. Makes the trip down a lot easier. Leather seats, very comfortable – whisper quiet."

Mrs. Mitchell added her soft counterpoint.

"You see," he paused, "we used to come here often, every year. There was a group of us, Melbourne people. We would book the entire house you know – so we didn't have to put up with the other holiday makers. It was very lovely, just to be among friends."

There was a silence as the information settled. Mr. Mitchell tilted his head as if questioning whether he had been understood.

"What happened?" asked Anita. "Did something change?"

Mrs. Mitchell took up the story. "No. Well, yes. When we all came here together, we would bring our children too, of course. We had such happy times. The kids would play together, the older ones looking after the littlies. We girls would sit together and chat about anything and everything, the men would have a drink and smoke a cigar or a pipe, talking about everything from golf to their businesses, or the stock market, or their clients. We thought it all so marvellous – and then it happened."

She paused and fumbled for a handkerchief. Her husband offered her one and she squeezed it in her fist.

"It was an accident," he said gently. "An accident. A tragedy."

"You see, we have," she corrected herself, "had a little boy, Stephen. A darling boy. Such a beautiful child, so happy. A group had gone down to the beach after breakfast. They took Stephen with them. He was just four years old."

She blinked, dabbed her eyes and her husband continued.

"Apparently they got distracted down there. The tide was coming in and a wave just washed him off his feet. By the time the others noticed, he had been bowled over several times and he was face down in the water. He must have swallowed a dreadful amount because, by the time they got him out, he'd stopped breathing. They rushed back up here to the house and Bill – a friend, he's a doctor – took a look at him, but it was too late." He stopped before clarifying. "He'd passed away."

"How terrible, how absolutely terrible for you." Anita held her hands together to her lips, an involuntary prayer.

"I'm sorry, very sorry to hear it. Please accept our most sincere condolences."

"Thank you, thank you. That's very kind."

"It must be impossibly hard for you to come back to this place," said Anita. "The memories would be devastating."

"It was. Dreadfully hard, that's why we stayed away, went to England. Our friends were just as horrified. They didn't know what to say, or what to do. What could they do? And then, this year we returned and here you are with your darling little boy. Seeing him just made it so hard."

"Little Michael. Of course, that would be such a reminder. Your Stephen would now have been about the same age."

"That's right. And Michael is so like him – happy smile, full of life, big dark eyes. He's such a beautiful boy."

Mr. Mitchell stepped in.

"That's why we've come to see you. We've been thinking. Here you are, newly arrived migrants to this country and, from what we can tell, you're doing it pretty hard. Not easy to get on your feet – especially in a remote, out-of-the-way place like this. A child can be a drain on one's resources – food and clothes, then giving them a decent education. An expensive business, children. And they deserve the best we can give, a good environment, mixing with the right people, getting a good start in life."

He stopped, awkward for a moment before gathering his resolve.

"To cut to the chase, what we're offering is to adopt your little fella and look after him properly. You could come to see him from time to time, like during the holidays - and for his birthday. We would obviously pay for all his expenses and ..." he paused, "we could make a substantial deposit to your personal bank account, if you understand what I mean."

Frank and Anita did not understand, could never understand what was being offered.

"Do you mean you want to take Michael away? Did you imagine you could buy somebody else's child? We have left one country because of what was done there, for what? To come to this? Such an idea is inhuman, impossible. How can you even think something like this?"

Anita tried to stand. She was shaking. Her heart thumped in her chest, choking her.

"Where is Michael now?"

"He's playing outside with the others. He's fine. He's safe. You know, we meant no harm, no offence. We were only trying to help. You can see our point, can't you?"

Frank stood next to his wife, his arm around her.

"In a strange way, I can see your point, but it is one we reject. Utterly. Such an idea could never work. First, we came to this country to give Michael a chance in life, a new start. He is as much a reason for our coming here as the reasons we had to leave. Second, no child, not yours or anyone else's can replace your Stephen who drowned here at Summerland. And third, no money in the world can buy the peace of heart you have to find."

Half an hour later, the black Jaguar receded in a swirl of dust, turned onto the Ventnor road and disappeared.

Michael was a little confused by his mother's tears when she found him playing on the front verandah. His father too seemed reassured to see him.

And although she didn't know it at the time, Anita was already carrying their second child.

Rabbiters

The season drew to a close. Easter had provided only a temporary resurrection and after the last guests had departed, winter entombed the house once more. The generator was turned off and the lighting reverted to kerosene lamps and candles. Despite the evening gloom, the pulse of the sea and the buffeting wind were as reassuring as the nightly calls of the penguins returning to their burrows. Occasionally the windows would rattle and startle the dog from his slumbers in front of the living room fire. Frank would reassure him, "It's all right Toby, only the wind," and he would lie his head on his paw again, close to his master.

Sometimes, out of the mists, visitors stopped by. Entranced by the wild beauty of the place, they would stay for a weekend to explore the Nobbies and peer through the telescope towards Seal Rocks or clamber the treacherous path to the blowhole. Huge seas drew back from the channel, building a tidal wash that climbed, heaving into the rocky cave till, with a resounding boom, the trapped air detonated a torrent of spray back into the churning water. Rivulets streamed through the crevices of glistening basalt while, further out to sea, a new set of breakers rose, all caps and spindrift, gathering for the next onslaught. Sightseers clung to the slippery steps, awed by the ocean's majesty or thrilled by the dangers it threatened.

A clutch of Melbourne families had cemented their friendships through their long associations on the Island. Curiously, many of them lived relatively close to one another in Hampton and Sandringham and had resolved their retirement would eventually be in a holiday home at Summerland by the sea. Roger and Joan Beveridge, together with their daughters Helen and Sue, were frequent guests and now the time had come to build on their block, just a few hundred yards higher along the cliff than the guest house. In comparison with some of the other shanties hidden away among the tea-tree, it was a substantial dwelling with spectacular views across the curving bay and the diminishing promontories beyond Pyramid Rock all the way to Woolamai. At each stage of the build, they would visit and discover a growing admiration for both the architectural progress and the migrant couple trying to rescue the dilapidating pile that had become their new home. Michael was included in their conversations to the extent he was allowed to call the adults Uncle Roger and Aunt Joan. It seemed he had adopted a complete family in the most uncomplicated way.

Roger's father, who he called his 'old man', became affectionately known as Old Man Beveridge. Maybe it was a carryover from the French, where a title such as 'Père' or 'Veuve' denoted one's familial status. Le Père Beveridge had founded a flour milling enterprise, replete with grain silos and its own railway line bringing in wheat and oats from around the country. It was called Creamoata and situated just to Melbourne's west in Footscray. Roger also held an executive position there, contributing to both the success of the enterprise and his family. He had a fine head for business and quietly wondered how sustainable an operation like the guest house could become. He also wondered how two people so intelligent and industrious could imagine they might ever earn a living from so precarious a project. Nevertheless, the families enjoyed a warm companionship sharing their stories of music, travel, art, architecture and literature. Frank's early years immersed in a world of books, his sharp and enquiring mind – together with his artist's eye for photography – found a new and intriguing dimension in the company of educated and curious people happy to explore mutual interests. They could only ever guess at the submerged past, despite some of their English ancestors having lived through the darkest days of the Blitz.

Once again, the water ran out. Frank decided to try the tank by the servants' quarters. He opened the valve and heard the reassuring gurgle of water in the pipe. In the kitchen he turned the tap and waited and presently a trickle emerged. He filled a glass and tentatively tasted it. Strange. He knew tank water, expected this to be saltier than usual, but it even smelled wrong. He called Anita to try. "No, one can't drink this. You better check the tank."

Frank hauled out the ladder and clambered up to the cover in the lid. Peering in, he could see nothing. The aperture was narrow and it was dark under the cloudy sky. He returned with a torch, sending its beam down through the clear water. There, lying on the bottom, he discovered the problem: the hapless but complete body of a possum. How could it have got there? The inlet pipe from the roof had been filled with a ball of chicken wire. The lid was firmly fixed. He knew there were possums; he had seen them running along the catenary wire from the generator to the house. And now this. He thought aloud, "There are many ways to die. Misadventure doesn't distinguish between man or beast." He would have to remove the creature, drain the tank, wash it out and start again. The season's rainwater would be lost. Yet another trial to test his stamina. He found a rake and climbed the ladder again. If he could lower the implement, slide the tines under the body and lift it out, that would be a start. One thing at a time. With one hand he held the torch, while with the other he immersed the rake, slipping it under the carcase. As he lifted gently, the possum disintegrated in a cloud of dissolving fur and flesh, the bones dangling from the metal.

He disconnected the pipe to the house and opened the valve. It would have to drain. He could do nothing until the water supply from the bore was restored and he could then wash out the tank and flush the plumbing. Then they would have to wait for rain.

He took the bike, Toby riding in the sidecar, and headed for the farm. He guessed that vandals would have again blown holes in the tanks and he would have to repeat his repairs of the past. He also checked there would be fuel in case the pump needed to be started again. It was as he had feared. Two holes in the middle of the tank that was now half full. He swapped over the feeds and was relieved to see there were no leaks. For the moment, there would be water at the house. He checked the pump and the fuel, heaved on the flywheel and heard the steady clattering clap as it ran its 900 revolutions per minute. Then, a new sound; the flicking of a frayed drive belt. One of the two belts than ran from the engine to the pump was coming apart. It would mean a trip to Cowes to get a replacement, but in the meantime the machinery could run till it fell off or broke.

He whistled for the dog, three short and one long, and Toby appeared, weaving between the tussocks. Frank pointed to the sidecar. "Up." With the dog safe, his nose to the wind, he set off for home, the last of the daylight settling over the landscape and the evening chill biting through his clothes.

The day had been hard and long. They lay in the dark, listening to the soughing wind and the muffled boom from below. The penguins under the floor had fallen silent.

"You have fixed the pump?"

"Yes. But the belt is worn and we will have to get another. Hopefully, it will last till the end of the week when I go into Cowes."

"We have no more meat. Just some eggs and potato."

"Tomorrow, early, I shall go out to shoot a rabbit or two – one for Toby, one for us."

Frank turned and kissed his wife gently on the lips, then her forehead, before pulling the blanket over his shoulder and settling to sleep. Anita lay awake in the dark, marvelling at the preparedness of the man to undertake no matter what task for her sake and that of their child. She ran her hand over her belly, feeling for the heart she knew lay beating within. Soon, conceived under the constellations of a new hemisphere, a new life would be brought into the world. Silently she counted the weeks to come. Finally, she too surrendered to the fatigue of the day.

With Toby loping beside, Frank turned the motorbike and sidecar off the road onto a dirt track through the tussocks. He stopped, switched off the engine and retrieved the .22 rifle from the sidecar. The dog meanwhile was zigzagging his way through a confusion of trails, occasionally leaping above the grass to better locate the elusive smudge of brown fur. The air cracked. The rabbit flipped and the dog bounded to retrieve it. Seconds later he returned, dropping the still twitching animal at his master's feet. Blood began to clot the smashed neck and presently a glaucous shroud dulled the eye. Two more lives were sacrificed on the altar of necessity, extinguished with a matter-of-factness that belied the sensitivity of the man. Whatever god looked on did so with the same indifference to suffering as ever.

On the desolate, windswept plateau with its low and spiny vegetation, Frank leaned against the sidecar and surveyed the landscape. At his heel sat Toby, head raised, nose reading the breeze. It seemed as if all was air and light, a chimera of shadows and scudding clouds lofted further than the floor of heaven. Beyond the sweep of dun grass and tea-tree, a palette impossible elsewhere, was the sea – a wrinkled sheet shimmering under the morning sun. From deep within the man, rose a surge that might burst his chest. In this isolation, into this vast emptiness, he began for the first time to surrender the grief of all his losses, father, mother, friends and homeland, all the dreams of youth, childhood laughter and security. In their place poured a flood of relief and wordless gratitude.

When, some time later he returned to the house, Anita remarked that he appeared transfigured.

"What is it, dear man?" her voice gentle as she kissed his cheek. She stood back to look at him.

"It's fine – everything is fine."

He swallowed, then turned to look at her and smiled. In his eyes she saw both the tears and the immense depth of his love. He held her to him, so close she could drown.

"You are my all. You are everything in this world."

The following morning, Frank knew that a letter he had carried for a week could be submerged no more. In a quiet moment in the sitting room, he tried to forearm her.

"I'm sorry Weli, but there has been difficult news from Tuttlingen. I have no idea how to tell you, but here is a letter I wish I had not to deliver."

She hesitated, unsure, trying to imagine what it was that could not be spoken. As she drew out the pages and unfolded them, the card that fell from the letter was edged in black. The news it announced was the untimely death of Anna Gallo, née Hilge, aged just sixty-three. A wave of giddiness washed over her. She said nothing, but lifted her head and gazed, unseeing, into the void. Then, with her hand over her mouth, the tears began to run down her cheeks. Frank watched, apart, knowing that this was her grief, a loss that expected no intrusion. The time for words, for consolation, was yet some interval away.

When she returned, after some hours by herself and having walked the road along the cliff, it was to spill her regret, her blind presumption that there would be time to share the pregnant news she carried. Remorse that she had not more often and more clearly written the reassurances that would have comforted her mother's heart. And even if she knew, all those years before that she would never see her mother again, never hear her voice, never embrace again the woman who had been her consolation and support, even that impossibility was now forever denied.

She sat with her arm cradling her belly and spoke silently to the life within. "And you, my child, will never know your grandmother, her kindness, her love - and she, while she lived in this world, could only ever imagine your existence. Forgive me little one."

The playmate

"Micha?" His mother's voice contained the question, 'Are you paying attention?' He looked up from the blocks he was arranging by colour in the wooden trolley. "Micha, you will soon have a playmate."

Michael had no idea what she was talking about. What was a playmate? Why did he need one? What was he expected to do? He asked the question. "What is a playmate?"

"Someone you can play with."

"Why?"

"So you don't have to play alone."

It still made no sense. He was happy just as he was. He could play with the dog; he could explore the rock pools when the tide was out. There was plenty to occupy him climbing the cypress trees or reading a book in his room. Besides, when the guests came and wanted to take him to the beach, it was already more than he needed; he didn't know what to do with other people. Except for Barrie. Barrie was unusual. Somehow, he made you feel as if you were the centre of his world. And while he was already twelve years old, he was still just a big kid, full of laughter and imagination. He talked like a waterfall and was excited by whatever you were doing, turning it into an adventure full of possibility. But Barrie wasn't there all the time. He lived with his parents, Anne and Leslie Thorn, in Sandringham. He was their only child but made friends with everybody. At least he tried to. Not everybody could accommodate the vast inner life that cascaded through him and spilled out with his exuberance. Michael was intrigued by what he knew and the stories he told of floating up to the ceiling or playing music in the moonlit garden, inhabiting places where spirits roamed and objects moved by themselves and people knew things that could not be known.

Still, from time to time, his mother would announce that it wasn't long now before the arrival of the mysterious playmate. Michael had no idea how it would arrive, or when – after all, it seemed to be taking its time – so he dismissed it as insignificant and something that would resolve itself eventually. Nevertheless, he retained the sense that it was important for his mother and that perhaps she was preparing him for something that could impact his life. By the end of June, he had not thought to make any observation on his mother's changing shape. One evening, as she sat by his bed, she took his hand and gently placed it on her belly. "Micha, can you feel anything?" He wasn't sure; didn't know what he was supposed to feel. "I'm going to have a baby. It's inside me now, growing." Michael tried to understand, but was left only with unformed questions, an embryonic idea to which he was unable to give birth. "You're going to have a brother or a sister. We don't know yet. Imagine – another little person in our family."

Michael said nothing. Whether he sensed a threat to the exclusive attention he had enjoyed for four and a half years, or whether the mystery of how a child had arrived in his mother's womb would for the moment remain unanswered, he didn't know. The answers, however, came soon enough.

It was a tight squeeze fitting everything into the sidecar. A carefully packed bag was pushed down to the front; then Anita carefully positioned so that she would be comfortable, before Michael was slipped in alongside, despite his protestations to ride on the tank and hold the handlebars. Toby had been left in the care of the Rasas at the farm and the guesthouse locked up with a 'No Vacancy' sign. Despite the fastidious preparations, it seemed to Michael that everything was happening faster than necessary as Frank turned onto the Back Beach Road. Though it was the shortest route to the mainland, it was regrettably the most uncomfortable, with potholes and washaways, loose gravel, dips, crests and hollows.

"Johannes!" Anita called from the sidecar. "Johannes." She reached out and tapped him on the leg. He looked over and slowed down the better to hear her. "Johannes, you mustn't go so fast. I'll have the baby by the side of the road."

"The faster I go, the less you feel it," he called back. He straightened up and gave the beast its head.

Arrangements had already been made. The Edwards had a house on Bluff Road where it was possible to stay for a few weeks; Anita would be taken to the Royal Women's Hospital for her confinement and stay there until all was well enough to revisit for a convalescence before returning to the Island, this time by car while Frank rode the bike home.

It rained for the first few days, but Sunday the nineteenth of August dawned bright and clear. There was considerable commotion even before sunrise as Anita was sped away, leaving Michael in the care of Cath Edwards who let him out into the back yard where he could amuse himself down by the chook pen or giddy himself on the swing suspended from the branch of a tree. As she clung to the walls of the sidecar, Anita recalled Professor Keller's words, "Now you have a son, you will need to have a daughter." "Never," she cried. "After this, I think I have had enough!" And yet, here she was in transformed circumstances. Apprehensive, yes, but somehow reassured that this would be different.

At 3.15 in the afternoon, just as her own mother had done forty years earlier, she gave birth to a daughter. Quietly she thanked God for the perfection of the child and her safe deliverance. Here, on the other side of the world, her family was now complete. The infant would be called Vivien, from the French 'to be alive', and her second name Anne, in keeping with her maternal line. Eventually, according to the rules of decorum, Frank was admitted to his wife's room. He found her tired but flushed with relief and happiness. He took her hand and let his heart speak for the love and gratitude that could find no words sufficient. His augmented fatherhood brought a heightened sense of responsibility, together with the unanswerable question of how father and daughter would weave their relationship.

On the following day, Michael was introduced to his sister. He had no idea whatever to make of the newborn face asleep in its swaddling, the skin smooth, eyes closed, a soft fuzz of hair tufted to take a ribbon. He didn't understand how they would play together or what they would share. Instead, he asked, "Will she grow?"

"Of course. In a few years she will be as big as you are now. And once upon a time, you were just as tiny as she is now."

Michael looked at her again and then lost interest. Anita pulled the blanket away from the baby's face, showing it to her father. "Don't you think she is just lovely?"

The beauty of an infant is probably confined to the eye of the beholder. It may even have something to do with the capacity to establish an articulate relationship. Maybe a mother has a limitless capacity to know beauty from the womb and beyond. Either Frank had none of those advantages, or his sense of humour landed on uncomprehending ears. His unfortunate response was, "She will have to improve if she wants to be attractive." Anita bristled and was not amused. All her protective instincts were aroused and from that instant her defence of the fruit of her womb would be unwavering.

Into the awkwardness of the altered mood, Frank offered the news he had heard from his telephone call to Limonis. "Toby has cut his paw. Apparently there was a lot of blood, but the foot has been bound up and they think it will heal quite well." The response was muted and Frank realised it was probably best to simply sit quietly and keep his musings to himself.

Two weeks later, John and Cath Edwards returned mother and daughter safely to the guesthouse while Frank rode the bike with Michael in the sidecar.

The winter months had been quiet, but as spring arrived, so too did the regular visitors. Responsibilities shifted. Skydrita had also delivered a daughter, Antje, to her family, so her work at the guesthouse was abbreviated. It was fortunate her mother was there to help look after the child and the farmhouse. Limonis found himself milking two cows instead of the one, feeding the hens and managing the vegetable garden for two families as well as the visitors. Anita's time was now divided between two children and her husband and Frank wondered how they would manage once the summer weather and the Christmas holidays invited a new congregation of pilgrims to the penguin parade. On top of that, building was taking place to create a supplementary venture: the tea rooms with picture windows over the bay, and four additional flats. The kitchen was certainly going to be busy - and throughout the day. Stevo and Lil would have their work cut out. And no-one knew what was going to happen next.

CHAPTER FOURTEEN

An Aussie Education

The egg-beater was clattering before 6am on New Year's Eve. Stevo the Little-O, chef's hat higher than ever, was already in the kitchen with Lil preparing for the celebrations. Doyen of the desserts, she didn't rely on the fictional Betty King, but made her own creations: lamington cake with strawberry jam, vanilla slice with honeycomb, and chocolate and caramel slice. These and a host of other delights would be laid out on a trolley in the sitting room.

Lil loved a party - after all, she had made all the party food and surely she was entitled to enjoy some of it. Besides, the Metzgers were all very nice people, but a bit serious for her audacious spirit. The same with the other Europeans, different customs, different traditions. You needed to let your hair down. Steve understood that. He was funny, could turn a trick on the dance floor, loved a bit of popular music from the radio, especially Freddy Martin and Sammy Kaye's *I've got a lovely bunch of coconuts*. He would jig about the kitchen and affect lascivious glances at Lil while singing the words. As the mood changed, he would hum along to The Weavers and *Goodnight Irene*, or Patti Page's *Tennessee Waltz*. But these were not the tunes for the staid guests at Summerland – it would be *Auld Lang Syne* with everybody crossing their arms, holding hands and rocking from side to side. It could be sung just as appropriately at funerals as people remembered the days long gone. Better to drink to the days gone by. She liked a drink, did Lil, and normally she knew her place - and it wasn't to be drunk while at work. But tonight was different, she was feeling sociable. Having already surreptitiously slugged the last of a bottle from the dining room, she felt it only appropriate she should say Happy New Year to the guests.

Stevo tried his best to restrain her, but she was adamant. One didn't argue with Lil. She disappeared into the chattering throng and emerged a little time later with one of the guests brandishing a bottle of wine for the kitchen staff. Stevo put up both hands in protest. "No. Sorry, we don't drink." It was true. The reason they had come to the Island, was to get away from the drink. Lil had been – and probably was still – an alcoholic. With temptation removed, she had managed to abstain for weeks at a time, until tonight. Alarmed at the way the evening was progressing, Stevo called for reinforcements.

Frank and Anita saw Lil behaving badly and knew there was little they could do without further inflaming the situation. "Try to keep the stuff away from her Steve. You understand her better than we do. You sort it out; what you do is your business." With that, they excused themselves to the remaining guests and headed for bed. "She's off her rocker," said Anita, her accent strong and having no idea where that expression came from, but it sounded perfect.

The next morning the night revealed itself. Lil had gone over to the servants' quarters, tyrannising and threatening them with the most terrible stories of how she had a sister who was queen of the underworld in Sydney. Stevo surrendered and disappeared under the house, sitting against the stumps in the dark with the moonlight gleaming between the base-boards. He emerged with the daylight, tousle-headed, to confront his employers in the kitchen. Lil was already there, stumbling about and collecting the tools they had brought, knives and steels, skewers and cleavers which she piled onto the table. Blinking and confused, she turned to Anita. "I'm leaving." Then with a sigh, "Oh, Mrs. Metzger..." and she slumped over the assembled implements.

"No, no, you'll cut your throat!" Anita tried to pull her away, fearing any moment she would be dead in a pool of blood. But no, she roused herself, put out her arms to steady herself and said, "There's a plum pudding cooking on the stove," her final words slurred as she stumbled to the door and disappeared into the new year.

Frank was pragmatic. "If she's gone, then she's gone. Probably for the best. We've still got Stevo." While Steve could resist the demon drink, he couldn't resist the demon woman. He didn't know what to do without her; it would be too hard to stay on by himself; they worked well together. His uncertainty was resolved when the telephone rang. It was Lil, in Cowes, needing to speak with Steve. When finally he replaced the receiver, he turned to Frank, "I'm sorry, but I have to go." Refusing to listen to all exhortations to the contrary, he packed his things, slung his swag over his shoulder and headed down to the Ventnor Road. It wasn't long before he hitched a ride into Cowes to never be seen again.

Frank furrowed his brow and tried to assemble the unfamiliar pieces. The day before, Lil had asked whether they could have their money in advance for a critical purchase. He had naively written a cheque for their wages, including the coming four weeks. Suddenly hearing the rattle of dropping pennies, he cranked the phone handle. "Guesthouse. Frank Metzger. Put me through to the bank please, it's urgent." Under the circumstances, there was no way they would withdraw the cash. He explained the situation to the manager.

"Look, Mr. Metzger, I'm sorry to have to tell you, they've just been. They said it was terribly urgent; they had to go to Tasmania. A dying relative. They needed the money for the fares. What could I do?"

Frank, resigned, accepted there was nothing he could do. A country bank manager trying to be helpful. A phone call and he could have checked, but... it was all too late now. A harsh lesson, but one that probably had to be learned. He would work harder and try not to carry his anger, as much towards himself for being so blind. After all, there was a house full of guests, no help and a plum pudding on the stove. Happy New Year!

⁓

Since Michael had recently watched his fifth birthday pass with little ceremony other than some of the guests giving him a Christmas chocolate and a plastic toy tractor, it was time to go to school. He wore a shirt and shorts, shoes and long socks, and a leather satchel strapped on his back. State School No. 1282 was a single room weatherboard building stuck in a paddock. Attached to the side was an entrance porch and on the other, a water tank collected the rain from the corrugated iron roof. A smattering of scrubby trees dotted the landscape and to the rear of the property was a corral for the horses children rode to school from the outlying farms. Inside featured a blackboard along one wall above a platform so the teacher might better supervise the pupils. The board was divided into six by strips of red tape, each section representing the work for each of the six grades, each with their row of desks. Michael was told to sit in the first row behind two other new students. In front of him was a wooden framed slate and a piece of chalk. He looked around. Four or five students in the next row, then another two or three and, in the farthest row, one boy sitting at the back. They all had exercise books and pencils. There was writing on the blackboard in front of the grade six boy, together with some numbers. Michael concluded he must be a genius.

Words were spoken and most of the children seemed to know what to do. Michael had no idea. The teacher told him to copy the words from the blackboard onto his slate. He scratched away but it was cramped and messy. He left his seat and approached the desk.

"Please may I have a book and pencils?" He still carried an accent and the request sounded formal.

"Later," came the impatient reply.

He returned to his seat, erased what he had done and started again. The same unsatisfactory mess. He waited a few moments and then approached the desk again.

"May I have them now?"

"I said later."

"But it is later."

"Next year. Now sit down."

The first day of the first year had not started well. Over the next term, it seemed nothing much improved. He was isolated and alone, a stranger. The only redeeming moments came when he could climb the trees at playtime. He understood trees. He didn't understand the arithmetic on the blackboard, a drawing of a simple house with sums in the wall, the door, the windows, the chimney and roof. Complete the sums and you built the house. The idea was good, but it came without plans or an explanation and so the roof fell in. So, instead, he hung by his knees from the branch of an apple tree in the front yard. Suddenly, all the other children running about decided to race off to the horses at the bottom of the paddock. Michael was urged to follow them but descending by climbing back up and down again would take time. He let go.

Beneath the tree, hidden in the long grass, lay a rusting wheelbarrow, its sharp edges embedding themselves in his forehead. A couple of children who witnessed the fall rushed in to find the teacher.

"The new boy. He fell out of the tree. He might be dead."

Newton may have discovered the laws of gravity by sitting under a tree and having an apple land on his head; Michael would discover the laws of gravity by falling out of an apple tree and landing on his head. When he finally came to, he was in a strange house with a towel around his skull and his father's face swimming in front of him, his lips moving soundlessly as he tried to talk. The telephone call from the house next to the school had prompted an instantaneous flight on the motorbike, because surely he could not arrive so quickly by the road. His boy alive, Frank carried him to the sidecar, lowered him gently and headed for the doctor in Cowes. Four stitches later, Michael was pronounced well enough to return home where his mother's ministrations provided additional comfort as he was put to bed.

Surviving a near death experience seemed to add both credibility and social status among the juniors at school. In addition, each morning at nine o'clock, the youngsters were squeezed into the entrance porch to listen to Kindergarten of the Air on the ABC. The presenter was a young lady called Jan and, quite miraculously it seemed to Michael, had been to Summerland. She visited again and introduced herself to the family, thereafter writing amazingly illustrated letters to her little protégé – pictures of him in the sidecar with his father on the bike; Toby bounding after rabbits through the tussocks and muttonbirds flying across the moon.

Once the Easter guests had left, it became clear there was neither the money nor any further need to pay domestic staff; the quarters could be put to better use. With the hen population at the farm now diminished, it was resolved to attempt a breeding program. Raising poultry seemed the ideal project to challenge amateurs in the pursuit of farming and fortune. It was really a simple equation of multiplication. Take six hens by one rooster, collect the eggs every day and incubate them. Six eggs by one week equals 42 eggs; by two weeks equals 84 eggs. Eighty-four eggs become 84 chicks which, by 3 weeks have become hens or roosters – to lay more eggs or become someone's dinner.

If there's a difficulty, it's getting six broody hens to sit on 84 eggs. But to every problem there's a solution. In 1952 that solution came in the form of a kerosene heated brooder with no need of a sitting hen at all. The apparatus was as simple as it was ingenious. Imagine a galvanised cake tin, but about five feet in diameter with sides about a foot high. In the middle sits a kerosene lamp base, but larger – about fifteen inches in diameter and with a metal flue instead of the glass chimney. Above that, supported by either a wire frame or suspended from the ceiling above, is a large metal Chinaman's hat that can be raised or lowered to control the temperature – critical at 99 degrees Fahrenheit. In the big tin base is a layer of straw on which the eggs are placed; the heater is filled with kerosene, the wick lit and the canopy adjusted. A thermometer makes sure the temperature is just right for the eggs to incubate. Surrounding the whole affair are bowls of water to ensure humidity at around 40-50%. Every day, the eggs need to be turned – it's not easy being a mother.

During the first attempt, Michael accompanied his mother to watch the progress, intrigued by the glow of the orange light under the canopy, the eggs comfortable on their bed of straw and the promise of new life. And then, miraculously, it happened. An egg cracked and from it emerged the damp and straggly creature that, over the next few days became a dry and fluffy chick. No sooner had one emerged, than several more followed and before long there were dozens of little chicks. Anita's excitement was infectious and the whole cheeping enterprise brought a good deal of happiness and extra work.

The second attempt proved just as exciting and successful. Wondrous hatchings took place, the chickens grew and had to be relocated and fed. But joy is short-lived and not all effort is rewarded. There came a day when smoke could be seen rising from beneath the roof of the breeding bungalow. And where there's smoke, there's fire. Straw in the base of the brooder had been flicked up into the heater, had caught alight and set the whole contraption ablaze.

Water knapsack sprays and buckets quelled the flames, but most of the young lives had been snuffed out by heat and smoke. The few chicks that survived joined the previous generations down at the farm with Skydrita and Limonis who either sold them, or brought them back to be executed at the chopping block.

Multiplication had become division and subtraction and the end result a zero. Farming animals can be a vexed pursuit – taking life to feed a life – and it sat uncomfortably with the family for some time, despite the deliciousness of pork and veal, and even the occasional rabbit.

Winter forced everyone indoors again. It seemed to rain continuously, long soaking downpours that turned the road to slush and made the ground squelch underfoot. The beach could barely be seen through a veil of mist that even the wind couldn't dispel. Wood for the stove and the open fire was wet and smoked sullenly, needing the encouragement of a dash of kerosene to get it started. Nevertheless, the little family battled on with Michael getting a drenching as he rode to school in the sidecar and Vivien finding her way around the house on all fours together with the dog. Toby was let out for a run, only to come back sopping wet and shake himself in a flurry of additional precipitation before being allowed in to be dried with a towel.

It was midmorning in the kitchen on a blustery day, the biting wind buffeting the house with such noise Anita thought the chimney might be blown down again. Vivien was sitting in her little chair with its fold down tray when, for no apparent reason other than trying to stand up, she tipped forward and fell onto her face.

"Gott in Himmel!" Anita rushed to pick her up, quench the crying and inspect the damage. A cut, small but significant, had started to bleed on her lower lip. "Johannes, we need to get the doctor. He has to come. You can't take her out in this weather on the bike."

Frank ground the handle on the phone and listened. Nothing. He tried again. Still nothing. The line was dead. "I don't believe it. There is no telephone. The line must have come down somewhere."

"So what will you do?"

"I have to try to see if I can find where and fix it."

"You can't go out in this weather. You'll catch your death of cold."

"We can't be without the telephone. What else can I do?"

He collected pliers, grabbed his raincoat and a cap, and opened the door. Gusts of rain pushed past him as he slipped out and rounded the house to the bike. Not knowing if the line had come down, or where it might be, he chose to ride, hoping to see what he suspected through the murky weather. Just a couple of miles past the turn onto the Ventnor Road, he spied what he was looking for. Sure enough, one of the two wires had been snapped off where it wound round the insulator on the pole. He knew it carried sixty volts at low amperage but was unsure whether that was only when one cranked the generator. Anyway, it wouldn't kill him and it wouldn't matter. He knew he couldn't pull it tight enough to tie back to the broken piece, so he would need an extra length. The fence nearby provided what he needed. He cut a couple of yards from where it mattered least and formed a loop to which he tied the end that had fallen to the ground. He looked up. From the road, the poles didn't look that tall. Standing next to one, slippery in the rain, it seemed impossible. If the break had occurred between the poles, it would have been easy;

but no, this was the challenge he was expected to meet.

He embraced the pole, cold, wet and slippery. He tried to get a grip, wrap his legs around it. The wind cut at his face; his fingers felt numb. He backed away, looped the end of the fence wire through his belt and tried again. He had watched koalas climb, but even a koala would struggle with this, and besides, he didn't have the claws to grip. He struggled with his upward clinch, clinging to desperate hope and each inch gained. Eventually he managed a hand hold at the top. With the pole in his armpit he succeeded in having both hands free enough to tie the end around the insulator, making contact with the end of the broken wire. For a moment, elated, he hung at the top of a pole in the wintry blast above the landscape, a lone figure silhouetted against the pewter sky.

Carefully, he lowered himself and stepped through the wet grass to the road. He brushed himself down, kicked the bike into life and surveyed his handiwork. The line sagged, fearfully close to the ground, but the connection had been made. He rode home.

Anita met him at the door. "Johannes, look at you! You poor man." She took his coat. "Wait, I get you a towel." She returned a moment later. "What did you find?"

Frank explained his adventure. "Now comes the moment. Let us try the telephone." He lifted the receiver and cranked the handle. It rang through to the exchange.

Later, after the doctor had been, the children put to bed, the dog fed and asleep by the fire, Anita lay in her husband's arm. "You know, Weli," he said, "today is the day I think I became an Australian."

⌒

Showtime

The Gordon setter is a single person hunting dog. Toby and Frank both understood that from their first intuitive encounter two years earlier. As Frank had predicted, the dog had grown into a fine specimen, well-muscled, strong and lean from his freedom to roam the beach, working up into the sand hills and high on the bluff, weaving between the tussocks to run down his quarry. Whistle or call him and he instantly and willingly obeyed, looking up with his deep brown eyes, alert, waiting for what was next.

It was a bold move, but as September rolled around again, Frank decided to put his judgement to the test. He would enter Toby in the Royal Melbourne Agricultural Show All Breeds Championship competition. Anita was sceptical.

"He's certainly a lovely dog, but do you know what to do? The others will have been showing their dogs for years."

"I have no idea. But I know he is a fine specimen; just look at him. I will watch the others, talk to the handlers. It can't be too hard. And whatever I don't know, Toby will work his magic without me."

Meanwhile, at the Ventnor School, it was also show week; an opportunity to celebrate the best that country life could offer. Everybody was invited to bring something – a pet sheep, or a canary in a cage. Many of the children rode horses, so that became their natural choice. Others had pigeons – fantails and tumblers. There was a pet rat, a goldfish in a bowl and a clutch of guinea pigs in a box of straw with a chicken wire top. And while it was considered perhaps too ambitious to bring a cow, a white Saanen goat was included in the menagerie. It wasn't only an opportunity to bring livestock to school, but every child had to look after their pet, feed it, make sure it had water, was well-groomed and comfortable. They also had to give a talk about the animal for the edification of others. Some mothers, anxious to display their home preserved wares and cakes, added to the extravagance by having their youngsters set out the home-made goodness on trestles until the end of the week when it could be shared among the hungry and the tempted. Michael had no idea what he should bring and dumped his confusion and disappointment in front of his parents. After some deliberation, they made a suggestion.

"You could take a duck."

It was true, there were ducks at the farm. A cage could be made and the duck given a lead by which it might be led around the parade ground. It seemed a novel idea, and after some practice taking the duck for a walk, it was loaded into the sidecar and duly delivered. There being no parade ground with stands of cheering spectators, a parade nevertheless took place around the schoolhouse, after which the livestock was delivered to various quarters – the horse yards, the shelter shed and, for the smaller creatures, the classroom itself. It was an auspicious beginning to the week.

Meanwhile, with Toby washed and brushed, the feathers on his legs and tail combed out and his head held high, he was a sight to behold.

The judges surely would be impressed. With more grooming tools than he would ever need for himself, Frank took the highway back to Melbourne, the dog riding the sidecar, his head to the wind. Arriving at Flemington, Alf Michelson was impressed. "I'm glad I stood in your way," he said. "That fine animal couldn't have gone to a better home. You've done my kennels proud." Almost as if he'd known there was little point in bringing his setters, Alf had brought the best of his curly-haired retrievers, fine dogs, with good coats and bright personalities. He resolved to provide all the assistance he could to Frank and Toby.

The list of criteria was long – sturdy, well-muscled, upstanding and stylish, showing strength and stamina. What distinguished Toby was his frame, classically square, as long in the body as high to the shoulder. He moved fluidly, well-balanced, impeccably obedient and his tail the barometer of his willing temperament. It was a faultless performance from dog and master and the first of what would become a galaxy of blue ribbons thereafter. As Frank prepared to leave, Alf approached.

"We really must keep in contact, Frank. These are my details in Bendigo. You can call me any time. And if you like, I'm happy to send the best of my dogs to you to train. You've obviously got the perfect environment and a great relationship with the animal." He paused, smiling, and put out his hand. "Congratulations! If you ever want to make any money from him, I'm happy to take him off your hands and put him to stud. Just a thought."

With the headiness of success, it was not a thought Frank could entertain. He understood where Alf was coming from but putting the dog to work for money was far beyond the compass of his consideration. As for parting with him, that was simply impossible. He was stitched into the fabric of the family, part of the order of things, integral, necessary.

More troublesome however was the viability of the enterprise. Christmas had been hard work without the kitchen staff. Elaine had always insisted that the hours worked should not exceed the wages, but such an arrangement was impossible given everything that needed to be achieved. Frank and Anita understood that their hours would be long and worked them willingly. In the interests of fairness however, a new contract was arranged – they could work whatever hours they needed to hold the enterprise together, pay a percentage of the takings, and keep the rest. While at first that sounded reasonable, the season was effectively eight weeks and that meant forty-four weeks without an income besides the stragglers and occasional visitors. Roger Beveridge was concerned.

"I've said it before, and I'm only saying it to you, but it should be obvious there's no way to make a living out of this. Look at your expenses – running the pump and generator, the repairs, the wood for the stove and fireplace. On top of that there's food and petrol. And in the season, you've got wages. And you've got a couple of kids to look after."

It was true. Even without the generator and relying on lamps and candles, times were difficult. "What do you think we should do?"

He leaned forward and lowered his voice. "The best they could do would be to set a match to the place and collect the insurance."

Such a prospect was, of course, impossible, outrageous. Fortunately, Frank understood the real message. "You are really suggesting we should leave and try something else, no?"

"I've been thinking. I've had a chat to the old man; Joan and I have talked about it. You're wasting your years here; the place will never pay. You can see that. If you want a job, I'm prepared to offer you one. You can come to work with us at Creamoata. You can take the position of despatch manager, an office job dealing with all stock into and out of the factory. Regular salary. You'll work with Jack Watkins, rough diamond, but a good man."

It was a lot to take in, the world suddenly upended again. This wild, wonderful, demanding isolation had removed them from the past. Its windswept beauty, the call of its birds, the rhythm of the ocean had bound them to each other and to their new land. What would it mean to forsake all this, to live in a city, ride a train to the office? And what of the dog?

"We know you'll need to think about it. But you've got kids now who are going to need a proper education. What are your options? Michael finishes school here and then it's off to Wonthaggi. Is that what you want? Schooling opportunities in Melbourne and then university. That's not going to happen here. And Vivien, you'll be wanting an environment that gives her opportunities more available in Melbourne, maybe a private girls' school." He stopped, letting the seed germinate. "We can help you, set you up, get you on your feet."

There had been a time in Germany when everything was lost. Starting again as far from grief and pain as possible seemed not only promising, but necessary. Now, here they were, safe, happy – and they should surrender what they had come to know for the unknown? Was happiness here sustainable? What would be lost by leaving? In leaving Europe they had bargained on a better life for Michael and here, on the Island, he had at last thrived. For the sake of the children, might they not thrive further with even greater opportunity?

As summer subsided into autumn and the earth yielded the last of its harvest, the inevitability of having to relinquish both the burden and the freedom of life at Summerland became plain. With the passing of Easter, they would pack their things and begin a new chapter in Melbourne. Frank accepted the Beveridge's work placement. John and Cath Edwards offered their house on Bluff Road as the first staging post with a large bed-sitter, kitchen and bathroom. Thereafter, they would move to the Beveridge's house in Park Street while they travelled abroad for six months. Michael would go to Sandringham East primary school. Toby would be surrendered to Alf Michelson and the BSA650 would remain with the guest house.

No matter the preparations that are made, no matter the support of friends, no matter how clear and rational the objectives, the moment of departure came too soon. Michael had not understood his mother's words, could not comprehend that there was to be a change to his life. He had already been uprooted once; now he was to be transplanted again. The life he knew was this life, here, the call of the penguins, running with the dog through the tussocks on the bluff, down at the farm with Limonis, the cows and the chooks, picking up driftwood on the windswept beach under a sky of scudding cloud; sitting at the top of the cypress tree and looking out to the edge of the world.

The day dawned bright, a blue sky, feathers of high cloud and a gentle breeze. Four cars were lined up in front of the verandah. Alf Michelson had come down in his green Morris Minor 1000 Traveller station wagon with its timber trim, and stayed, allowing the dog to become re-acquainted before his return to Bendigo. Elaine and Alec would take boxes and suitcases; Anita and Vivien would go with John and Cath Edwards and Michael and Frank with Roger and Joan. The tin bath had been re-purposed with a bed of straw for Michael's duck.

"You don't mind if we just go down to say goodbye to the beach?" Frank tried to smother the choke in his voice. He pressed his lips together and looked up to contain the stinging in his eyes. Anita took his arm and, carrying Vivien on her hip, they walked together to the road that led down to the beach. Michael paused, uncomprehending, before catching up and taking his father's hand. Once again they crossed the creek and waded up the sandy path to the top of the dune. The familiar arc of the beach swept away to the left and before them the sea heaved and rolled, a high tide, the breakers forming from far out, rising to crests trailing their long veils, cascading over themselves to thump and spill in long, flat sheets that ran up the beach and disappeared into the sand and kelp.

It was this that had set them free, that had breathed its new life into them each day, the timeless, constant pulse that affirmed one's place in the universe. They faced the wind, Anita's hair fluttering against her cheek. Michael marvelled silently at the enormity of the waves, the immensity of their plumes, the all-consuming roar of the ocean. It was as if he had never seen such a sea before. Then it was over. They turned and stumbled back across the shifting sand and climbed the hill to the waiting cars. Seven sentinels and a dog were waiting for them, a silent guard of honour. There was no room for words. Frank knelt down beside Toby, put his arm around his neck and wept into the coat of black and tan. When he could weep no more, he staggered to his feet, turned and walked to the car as the others took their places.

One by one, the vehicles filed onto St. Helen's road. As the cortège turned towards Ventnor, Frank and Anita each looked back at the house, stark, imposing and empty on the bluff, with the wind sighing in the wires.

～

Suburbia

For all their promise, the first weeks in Melbourne proved a rude shock. On a day when Frank had caught the train to his new posting, Michael was released into the back yard to play. There being no dog, a tree whose branches were so far from the ground it couldn't be climbed, and therefore with nothing to do, he wandered down to the chook pen. He might at least talk to the duck. He arrived to find the wire door had been torn open in the bottom corner, the flimsy wooden frame cracked and broken. While the hens were there, too cautious to emerge, the duck was nowhere to be seen. Bewildered, he started looking, behind the garden tool shed, between the fence and the abandoned vegetable patch and along the side of the house. It was then that he saw it, walking slowly and lop-sided on the narrow path. Something was wrong; the insides of the duck were trailing on the ground, outside its body. There was blood on its chest. Michael was confused; all these parts needed to be put back. He didn't know what he should do. He called inside. "There's something wrong with the duck. Come and look."

Anita emerged and immediately realised what had happened. A few yards away on the path, the neighbour's fox terrier was dancing about and barking, not prepared to approach, but spoiling for a kill. As it backed away, snapping and yapping, Anita gently picked up the wounded bird. "Open the door Micha." She brought it inside and knelt beside it on the floor. There was nothing to be done; already the creature was dying on its feet, its eyes unable to stay open, blood dripping from the breast, ruby on the white feathers.

"You stay here Micha and just hold her gently so she doesn't try to walk. I don't think she will make it. I'm going next door."

Michael knelt down. It was hard to look at the distended and protruding entrails, the bird turned inside out. Lightly, he stroked her back, the body smooth and strong, the wing dropping. He waited, struggling to understand this slow departure from the living world, this extinction. Presently, he heard voices. His mother was angry. He didn't understand the words but he knew their feeling. A man's voice, whining and defensive, tried to interrupt. "No, it is your dog and you will take responsibility. You will do as I ask and you will not argue with me." The man must have upset her because he had not heard such defiance from his mother before. She opened the door and the man was silent. "This is what you have done. Look."

He was a small man, a wheedling man, a man who didn't know how to apologise. A man who took his stature from a small and snarling dog, one that would attack and run away; a cowardly dog.

"You will dig a hole, deep enough to bury this bird and my son's grief. And you will chain your dog, or I will see that it is put down. When you are finished, we will clean up the mess you have caused."

An hour later, he reappeared. "I've done as you asked. I found the hole under the fence where he dug his way in. I've filled it in and added a couple of bricks." He shuffled off, his dog barking from inside his house.

The duck was laid to rest, covered with a hessian sack and the hole filled in. The door to the chook pen was pushed back into place and secured with a sheet of tin held in place by some garden rocks. That evening when Frank returned, he could only shake his head as Anita conveyed the news. He said nothing before getting up and heading next door. He was not gone long and seemed to have unburdened himself. Anita asked, "What did he say?"

"He said it's what dogs do and offered to pay for the duck."

"And you said?"

"I told him that a dog worth keeping is a dog that can be properly trained. And I told him he could keep his money. Money can't buy one a clear conscience – nor intelligence or a backbone it seems."

Michael went to his room, curled up on his bed and pulled the covers over his head. The last of Summerland lay deep in a hole in a stranger's yard.

The house on Bluff Road was relinquished and, as had been planned, there followed a short migration to Park Avenue, the house distinguished by its curved corner windows and the name 'Minorca' over the front door. A small porthole window has the etched glass of a sailing ship. In the back garden is a doll's house, large enough for children to play in, a world of fantasy and home-making for the two Beveridge girls. They are not here for the next six months, instead on the other side of the world with Roger and Joan and an extended family of real aunts and uncles. From here, it's just a short walk to Sandringham East Primary School and, at the beginning of term, Anita walks Michael to the gate from where he must make his own way in the world.

It appears vast, an asphalt playground and a surging sea of children, more than he has ever seen in one place before. The air rings with youngsters' voices and he is marooned as they swirl past, intent on their chase and their laughter. Suddenly there is a clanging and the murmuration shifts and re-forms into ordered lines, subsiding into silence. Out of nowhere comes a garbled voice, blurred and meaningless and loud; it seems it will never stop. But there is a brief pause, only to be followed by a thumping beat joined in turn by a raucous blaring, a huge overwhelming cacophony, harsh and strident, insistent. He puts his hands over his ears, he is drowning in noise and cannot see from where it assails him. Overwhelmed, he begins to cry. Around him, the children begin to walk, stiffly, some of them in time to the beat, swinging their arms. Then they are gone and he stands alone in the empty square. The noise is cancelled.

He wipes his face on his sleeve and looks around. There is a woman approaching him, her face concerned. She crouches in front of him. "Are you all right? Can you tell me your name?"

"Michael." It comes out high and tear-stained.

"You must be the new boy. My name is Mrs. Ebbs. You come with me." She held out her hand. Michael took it and was led away. "Did something frighten you?" she asked.

"That noise, a big noise."

Anna Ebbs thought for a moment, untangling the child's fear, and then understood. It was a band playing marching music through the loudspeakers pointing over the quadrangle. She took him to the office and sat him down while the necessary arrangements were made. "Now you can come with me, Master Metzger, and I'll introduce you to your new friends."

Those who were to be his friends were either shy or looked doubtful about the intrusion into grade 2B. The one person who did become his friend was Mrs. Ebbs, kind, warm, understanding like his mother. Most of all, she read aloud, not pointless stories that were just words for their own sake, but tales of mystery and adventure in faraway places where magical things happened; places where he could be lost and happy, instead of lost and alone.

—

Frank and Anita resolved that they would use the six months to find a place of their own. The generosity of the Beveridges was welcome and genuine, but it felt wrong to depend on their kindness, to create a debt of obligation, an implication they could not stand on their own two feet. Frank scoured the newspapers, frustrated by not knowing which suburb was which, whether there was a railway station nearby. He pored over *The Age*. Where was Clifton Hill – was there a hill? Or Moonee Ponds – did it have lakes? Bentleigh, Coburg, Eastern suburbs? He looked at the prices: 'Charming new timber home, triple-fronted in Blackburn, £500 deposit.' Impossible. 'Essendon, lovely area E.H.W.S.' – what did that mean? Again, £500 deposit. 'Sorrento, timber villa, £1000 deposit'. He turned to The Argus on the last day of August. 'Highlight of the week' – a 3-room brick cottage in North Melbourne for £2525. He shook his head and ran his finger down the page. 'Glenroy – made road; £320.' The agent was Wilmore and Randal. At least it was a number that made sense, but what did it buy?

He made enquiries and heard there were advertisements in German for land sales at Broadmeadows and Fawkner, but the buildings were defective and exploitation was rife. Broadmeadows sounded bucolic, expanses of fields nodding with wildflowers, while in reality they were mostly paddocks of rock and dry grass infested with thistles. Those wanting to escape the migrant camps in the hope of new beginnings were often naïve and unsuspecting, easy targets for the unscrupulous and opportunistic. He waded through the real estate sections, caught the train, wrote directions and drew maps. It became clear that anything close to the city would be well beyond their means or in places where reputation bred risk. He caught the train to Glenroy, just ten miles from the city centre. As it clattered its way north, the dwellings thinned out till there were long stretches with nothing but paddocks occasionally studded with a house or shed and clumps of nondescript trees.

Unlike the origins of its name, Glenroy was nothing like the Valley of the Kings. In fact the rising gradient of the Glenroy bank is one in fifty for nearly two miles, one of the steepest inclines on the metropolitan rail system. Opposite the station was an imposing flour mill, its concrete silos towering above the landscape. Though he didn't know it at the time, Otto Müller – not a relative – was a German flour miller whose son Rudi bought the Hartington Street land in 1930 and within six years was running a one ton per hour mill. By 1949, Robert Hutchinson had paid £10,000 for the enterprise and added laboratories and amenities. Given that Frank himself now held a job at *Creamoata*, he felt a surge of kinship.

The street he was looking for was a ten-minute walk back along Waterloo Road, finally arriving at Kalang Road, an unmade stretch with just five houses scattered on the south side and a paddock opposite. It was bordered by box thorn that had grown over a sagging wire fence and studded with three large cypress trees. In one corner was a small dam with a few straggly sugar gums and a peppercorn. Horses grazed quietly. Opposite the middle cypress was Lot 8, with a small wooden bungalow and an outhouse. Some haphazard stumps of 4x4 redgum stuck out of the ground to one side. No garden, no trees, just a paling fence on three sides of a quarter acre block. As he contemplated a future from these sparse beginnings, a train rattled down the hill on its way to the city. In the silence that ensued, he resolved to talk to the owners, but not before he had returned to the station and telephoned Anita.

"Weli, I think I have found a place. It's not the wilderness of the Island, but it's in the countryside, just paddocks, walking tracks, no traffic on the unmade roads. Simple; you might even call it beautiful."

She was to catch the train to Glenroy and they would decide together.

For the next hour, he wandered the streets, found the shopping centre, the general store, a butcher shop and a produce store that sold hardware. State School Number 3118, a fine brick structure, was only a five-minute walk away. It was still a month to summer, so the paddocks were green, some with stands of scotch thistles, their purple heads bright against the green. Anita met him, wearing her elegant coat, a hat, and a smile of happy anticipation.

"You really think this will be it?"

"Wait and see. The station is nearby, and even if the land is small, there is room for the children to play and grow. Perhaps we can make something of the place, build a house in a few years and plant a garden." He sounded optimistic.

Presently they stood in front of the block. Anita looked sceptical. After the expanse of Summerland, the huge house, the surge of the ocean and the boom of the breakers, this was just a doll's house in a naked field. She tried to see it differently, as something they could own, without responsibility for scores of guests or struggling to make ends meet. Cooking for four instead of forty. Maybe she could coax and nurture a garden. Micha might be happy again and Vivien could play safely outside. She would sew clothes for her and she could attend school nearby. As they stood, trying to imagine a life in these new surroundings, a young couple emerged from the bungalow.

"Can we help you? Are you looking for someone?"

Frank was direct. "Hello, yes. We understand that this property is for sale. If that is correct, then yes, perhaps you can help us."

Will and Stella Lauder were enthusiastic. "Yes. Yes, you must come in." They led the way. Attached to the side of the dwelling was a lean-to porch. Instead of glass, the top of the frame was covered in a plasticised flywire. Inside, a tin meat safe was fixed to the wall. The threshold to the entrance was adorned with a sheet of tarnished brass nailed over it. The interior was a crude construction – basically a 12 x 24-foot shack with some linoleum on the floor, Masonite on some of the walls and ceiling, a pink plastic sink with a brass tap and an old, green IXL woodstove. A fold out table, also covered in Lino, was propped from the wall under a louvre window. On the other side of the wall that divided the kitchen was a bedroom, containing just a bed, a plywood wardrobe and an old roll top bath.

"We know it's pretty simple," said Will, "but we intended to build when we had the money. This was going to be the garage, or a shed;

that's why the front wall has got provision for a pair of doors. It's got electricity and water – just cold though. There's a tap over the bath and the sink and one outside. We haven't planted a garden yet." While that was obvious, there were other questions, including what to do about a laundry and a toilet.

"There's a wood fired copper in the yard behind the house and there's an outhouse down the back. The night man comes every Monday to empty the can." More explanation was needed.

Stella and Will had only recently married and believed that they would have the time and the energy to establish themselves, but love being as urgent as it is, they were now going to have a child. It was no longer possible to raise a family in such a small space and they would move in with Will's family and sell the block; £150 would enable them to put aside the deposit for something larger in time to come. Anita understood only too well the urge for nesting, and Stella's warm enthusiasm for the infant yet to be born and for the happiness it would bring was infectious. The kettle had been put on the stove and a cup of tea provided to lubricate the last of the conversation before Frank and Anita took their leave and headed back to the station and their accommodation on the other side of the Yarra River.

"We have come a long way from the elegant home in Dortmund, or nights at the opera in Wiesbaden, or Aachen," remarked Frank as the train rattled south.

"Yes, but Germany has been flattened. The way of life we enjoyed there was taken from us. Our lives were very nearly taken from us as well. It doesn't help me to think of what was lost."

"No, you're right. We have been lucky. Merzhausen was a struggle, but we had a roof over our head, even if it wasn't ours. The Island gave us a new start, but one that led nowhere, even if we could ever have afforded to buy it."

"We have, somehow, managed to survive. I don't think this will be easy. It will certainly be different; but it will be ours."

They settled into silence, rocked by the swaying carriage, the roller-coaster of memory and wavering hope. In the end, they silently agreed that, for all its primitive modesty, especially in comparison with the grand and sumptuous European homes bombed by the Allies or claimed by the Nazis, this little weatherboard and tile-roofed hovel with its louvre windows was really a mansion in the countryside; they would own it and be free.

On a Sunday afternoon with the lunchtime dishes cleared and the radio playing quietly in the living room, Vivien had gone outside to play in the garden and the dolls' house while Michael had settled into a lounge chair with another book from Mrs. Ebbs. Pigeons were cooing in the street, insistent, unrelenting, hypnotic. There was quiet conversation in the kitchen. As Anita came in to put a vase of fresh flowers on the side table, the music on the radio changed, classical, but with a different rhythm underpinning the melody. Frank entered, paused to listen and, with a smile, turned up the volume. As Michael watched from the anonymity of his chair, he saw his parents meet in the middle of the room, pause for the music, and then swirl away together across the floor, moving together, their feet stepping in unison, his mother's skirt flowing as she turned, his father tall, his arm around her waist and gliding, swirling, turning, lilting and laughing, lost in each other, lost in something so far and so profound he could not comprehend. Turn after turn, abandoned in another world, once lost and now, in this moment, regained, floating on a floral carpet in a borrowed room in a foreign land.

Just before Christmas, the Beveridges returned, glad to be home but full of stories from abroad. Anita had made sure everything was in order, the house immaculate and their few possessions packed up ready to move.

"You didn't need to be gone so soon. More than happy to have you stay for as long as you need. How did you go looking for a house?"

They told their story with a deal more enthusiasm than it received. For a start, it was on the wrong side of the river, a completely different social demographic. Where were the private schools, the libraries, the social amenities? What about doctors? And so remote from the beach. They would be removed from their friends at the opposite end of the Sandringham line. What was the hurry? All the support they ever needed was right here – even financial if the kids were to go to a decent school. The only answer Frank could provide was they didn't want to be a burden, could not impose themselves on a family needing to live its own life or rely on others to set them up financially.

"You're a proud pair, aren't you?" While he might be offended, Roger nevertheless understood their position.

"It's not pride, Roger. It's respect for you and your family, and a friendship we don't ever want to compromise. It's also about retaining our self-respect and integrity, our need to make it on our own."

"Okay, I accept that. What are you going to do about paying for the place?"

"Perhaps we can make an arrangement whereby the sum is repaid from my salary. We should talk about that."

While Anita thought it a pity that their choice was so poorly met and that the disappointment of their friends was so palpable, she also hoped that this fragile seed of opportunity might take root and grow, might in time yield a harvest that would sustain them. And if Frank believed it possible, then it would come to pass and she would be by his side, whatever the days might bring.

CHAPTER FIFTEEN

Home

Summer shrivelled the green promise of rural life. Dusty roads, dry grass and tumbleweeds enveloped the ramshackle bungalow on its barren allotment. The shimmering heat of a still day was exchanged for the dry north wind and high, empty clouds that drifted past. The cramped space became oppressive; the wood stove only adding to the discomfort. The fire was necessary – to cook and heat water for doing dishes or the children's bath. There was, however, much to do in securing a wooden bed for Michael, a wicker cot for Vivien and a mattress and base for Frank and Anita, all to be manoeuvred into place beside the bathtub and a space for some wooden storage shelves. An old plywood dresser with a sliding leadlight door, a sewing machine, three chairs and a highchair furnished the kitchen. The gleaming jewels were the brass tap and threshold, polished as never before. Hope needs to be active.

In the first weeks, each time Anita stepped outside she would hesitate, flinching, and look up to the sky, listening. Aeroplanes - their heavy passing drone awakening a submerged memory, but one not so deep as to easily dismiss the devastation it brought. Frank's reassurances that these were merely passenger planes flying in and out of Essendon airport provided little comfort. In fitful dreams he sometimes saw the belly of the plane open and passengers fall out, transforming themselves into jackbooted soldiers of the SS or parachuting across the landscape. Some would fall to earth and explode in sheets of flame and sulphur stars, silently as if he heard them underwater. He woke, staring into the darkness of the four walls that closed him in and breathed to quell the sudden beating of his heart.

"It's just that we're under the flight path. Eventually, it will become so normal you won't even hear them."

"Let us hope so," was all she could reply.

A covered horse-drawn cart comes twice a week to deliver bread, the baker taking a basket which he fills with the varieties he imagines will tempt the householder – a pipe loaf, or a white Vienna, even the occasional French stick. Anita refuses the one she has seen fall to the ground, or the one he placed on the horse's rump while he rearranged his assortment. She is adamant, and he is offended by the migrant woman with the German accent, but peace is restored and he pockets the money after offering her a fresh loaf.

Before first light, the milk is delivered in bottles with their silver foil top. The horse knows its way as the 'milko' trots from house to house replacing the empties that have been left out to tell him how much to leave. Each week he comes to the door to be paid. Mostly the amount is correct, but there are times when the delivery is contested.

"I left a note in the bottle for Wednesday, only two pints, and you have charged me for three. And on Monday, there was only one."

"Look, you'll have to sort it out at the office." Anita would trudge to the suppliers behind the flour mill where the cashiers would know that she was always right.

"You will not be-diddle me," she would say. "I have been be-diddled enough."

The slender, silvery trunk of the Lemon-scented gum rises to a small canopy of tapered leaves; a fine sapling that inspires Frank's admiration. Whether it is emblematic of his new Australian home, its elegant stature or the stark purity of its bark, he cannot tell. He runs his hand over the silky smoothness of the stem and is struck by a sudden thought. Stepping back, he surveys the tree, resolving his idea and then heads inside to the trunk in the corner of the bedroom. Michael is there, reading.

"What are you doing?" he asks.

"Come and see."

From the bottom of the trunk Frank takes out a carefully wrapped parcel and heads outside again. Michael follows in silence. At the base of the gumtree, his father kneels down and carefully undoes the string, folds out the newspaper to reveal an old towel in which are several handfuls of reddish-brown soil. Curious, Michael asks what it is.

"This is the earth I collected from my father's grave in Brussels. It's all that's left, everything else has gone, everything we ever had, all he ever owned. This is what remains." He lets out a grim sigh. "Earth to earth."

So saying, he carefully spread the soil around the base of the tree. Michael was struck by his gravity and the significance of these handfuls of dirt, this talisman of his past and the grief that came with it. After some moments, he rose from his knees and said, "Now, as I look at this tree, I can think of him, even though he is so far removed from this place and the life he envisaged for us."

Though Michael could not understand so specific a loss, so profound a grief, there was a sadness in his father's voice that betokened deep solemnity, a reverence for things that only time would reveal. Thereafter, every time there was a strong wind, or a storm that threatened to break the slender fragility of the tree, Michael feared for the broken memory and the man broken by war and loss.

⟿

It was a Sunday afternoon, in that soporific hour after lunch on a warm day, when a Morris Minor station wagon, green with varnished wooden trim, pulled up outside.

"Alf Michelson! What a surprise!"

"Happy to find you at home. Just dropped by on my way past."

"Come in; come in. You must tell us how you are and all about Toby."

"A bit different from Summerland," remarked Alf as they entered the bungalow. "Still, you've got it all neat and tidy. Shiny tap." He pointed to the sink.

In all the excitement about the family, the happiness of wife and children, the success of the kennel, Anita somehow managed to cobble a bite to eat and a cup of tea in the humble space they called home. They learned Toby had been exhibited at countless country fairs and had won a swag of fifty-two ribbons. Alf had brought them with him and would be able to show just how many were first prizes. At last it was time to say thank you and goodbye and everybody walked Alf back to the car. He opened up, reached in and brought out a satchel which he opened on the bonnet. Inside were ribbons and certificates, Alf pointing out what was most important and how Toby had contributed to establishing the best of the breed in Australia.

"I hope you don't mind, but I'd like to keep these if it's all right with you," he said.

"Of course. You've invested a lot of time and energy making it possible. We're just glad that you could build on the first one from the Melbourne Show. Glad that Toby turned out so well."

Alf packed the treasures back in the satchel and put it back on the passenger seat.

"Well, that seems to be it. Thanks for your hospitality; it's been a lovely afternoon." He put out his hand to say good-bye. Then he remembered something.

"Just a moment, there's something else I have to show you." He walked round to the back and carefully unlocked the doors.

"Come and see."

Everybody crowded around – and there was Toby. He looked up – and as is true with most dogs – recognised first his master, and then the family. There followed a deluge of tears, patting the dog, marvelling at his condition. In the midst of the joy and the consternation Alf spoke quietly.

"He's yours. He knows you. He's come home. Take him."

Alf unclipped the leash and stepped aside. The dog looked at him, looked at Frank and jumped down. Frank turned and walked away, the dog following at his heel without command.

"He knows where he belongs," said Alf.

Anita recognised the loss in his voice as he turned brusquely away and got in the car. It was some time before he pulled away from the kerb and could not wave back.

Inside the bungalow, Frank had taken his father's old greatcoat from the trunk and laid it under the fold-out table affixed to the wall. Once again, Toby lay hundeplatz and would not move. He heard the car leave, raised his head momentarily, and then rested it again on his paw. He had earned his place and, like each of the family, had at last come home.

Two Deaths

Thirty-seven years have passed. Nurtured by a new landscape, the surge of sea under open skies, the stillness of the night and the howling of the storm, Frank and Anita, together with their first-born son – a stranger in a strange land – become naturalised citizens of Australia on the second of May 1956. They are each given a certificate and a bible, King James Version, tokens of their entitlement.

Life has tried them and blessed them, the past ever-present in its shallow grave. Frank retired from a distinguished career, Michael embarked on his own perilous journey and Vivien, after an illustrious beginning, was about to embark on one of her own.

The guests had gathered, crowding the narrow passage to the sitting room and beyond. Extra chairs were brought out and the babble of conversation rose higher as the introductions and recognitions multiplied. Happy engagement Vivien, congratulations and best wishes. Hello friends, double kisses of greeting, warm encouragements to assuage the apprehension of newcomers to this partnership of new acquaintances and joint allegiances.

When Michael arrived, the embarrassment of effusive greetings in the face of occasional and distant recognition propelled him haltingly to the couple most distinguished. His father, oddly it seemed, sat on a chair pressed against a side table, with Anita standing next to him. Salutations dispensed, the question was answered before it was asked.

"Your father's back has been giving him trouble again. He finds it hard to stand for any time. He must go to see a doctor this week. It can't go on like this."

Soreness and twinges, sporadic crippling had, for years past, evaporated after ministrations of massage, manipulation, and even more cautious management and drugs. Behind Frank's eyes, Michael detected an altered awareness of the inner condition that no amount of considerate good will and concern for others could disguise.

"Let me know what happens."

That was Saturday afternoon, August 19, 1989.

The news, when it came, was simply a progress report whose steps led blindly to a conclusion utterly removed from possible consequences. Perhaps, in the wakeful dark of sleeplessness, Frank's thoughts turned heavenward to a god in whom he might hope, while Anita lay in his arm, her quiet breath against his skin.

Finally, presumptuously, came the advice that required the packing of pyjamas, a toothbrush, a comb and such personal items as might be needed into an overnight bag that would accompany him to the Alfred hospital. He made the journey from home on All Souls Day, the first of November 1989.

Hope alone, no matter how great, how urgent, is not enough to stay the inexorable decline as bone capitulates to cancer, and awareness shifts from this world to whatever is the next. Frank wrote to his children.

> *"When I ceased to be a child, I lost the faith of my childhood. I never stopped searching. The God with whom one enters into a covenant is not the God of philosophers, but the God of Abraham and Isaac and Jacob revealing himself in the events of history. Too often do we perceive history as something which just happens to us and we overlook the responsibility we have in shaping it or responding to it. And thus the meaning of our life eludes us.*
>
> *I give thanks to God who has showered us with blessings. I give thanks for my parents whose hands have continued to guide me to this day. I give thanks for the gifts passed down to me by those who went before my mother and father. I do not know how to give thanks for your mother and still less do I know how to thank her. Your mother's love, her courage, her caring, her sacrifice, is beyond my capacity for thanks."*

The doctor, professor of oncology, swept into the ward trailing an entourage of students who, ordered by a sweep of the arm, gathered around the bed of the dying man. The shrunken frame, drawn face, thinned hair and pallor of mortality lay like a shroud across the sleeper. Drawing himself to his full height, the better to impose his condescension on the underlings who would benefit by his pronouncement, the eminent doctor surveyed his charges, indicated with his manicured hand the bed and proclaimed, "Here you see a patient whose condition has clearly overtaken him."

He paused a moment so that his grandiose observation might sink in and was about to turn for his exeunt when a voice beside the bed quietly interrupted.

"Excuse me. I don't know who you are, but that is my husband whom you have so callously dismissed. I am Anita and you would do well to remember who you are and why we are here." She looked at him steadily.

The students, suddenly embarrassed and a little shocked that the great doctor could be challenged so, shifted uneasily. Unsure how to respond, the professor hesitated and then brusquely strode from the room. He did not see Anita take again her husband's hand and sink her face to the pillow beside him, the slow howl of anguish smothered in her heart.

Before dawn of the 27th of February 1990, Frank surrendered his life to the God that awaited him. His earthly remains were farewelled by a Carmelite congregation in Melbourne's Middle Park and laid to rest under a tree by a stream at the Fawkner cemetery. And while he was neither Elijah[15] , nor the brook Cherith, the ravens that fed there, and those who looked back on his life, knew that it was good.

---

[15] 1 Kings 17:1-7 King James Version

17 And Elijah the Tishbite, who was of the inhabitants of Gilead, said unto Ahab, As the Lord God of Israel liveth, before whom I stand, there shall not be dew nor rain these years, but according to my word.

2 And the word of the Lord came unto him, saying,

3 Get thee hence, and turn thee eastward, and hide thyself by the brook Cherith, that is before Jordan.

4 And it shall be, that thou shalt drink of the brook; and I have commanded the ravens to feed thee there.

5 So he went and did according unto the word of the Lord: for he went and dwelt by the brook Cherith, that is before Jordan.

6 And the ravens brought him bread and flesh in the morning, and bread and flesh in the evening; and he drank of the brook.

It is evening. Lamp light fills the corners of the room. From the galaxy of framed photographs on side tables, walls and the top of the television, the frozen smiles of family stare self-consciously through the years into the room. Moments and memories behind glass, reminders of what was, what could have been. On the dresser stand the few remaining treasures that miraculously survived war and loss, caressed halfway around the world to a whole world away, keepsakes of generations already turned to dust. Two cut crystal wine glasses, pieces of fine porcelain hand painted with flowers.

In her corner of the settee, Anita dozes, head bowed, engulfed by tiredness. She is blind in her right eye, deaf in her right ear, her hands folded over her swollen abdomen and the ileostomy that has exhausted her for years. Wisps of grey hair that have escaped the chignon fall on her neck. In the soft light, her skin is almost translucent, thin as the finest parchment, veined with infinite care. She is ninety-eight years old.

While the rest of her body inexorably relinquishes its hold on life, her heart beats as strongly as ever it did, willed by the same indomitable spirit that has brought her defiantly through fire and loss, joy and heartbreak, memory and yearning. And though the faces who surround her are those of her children, her grand-children and her great-grandchildren, a collage of reverence and awe, she sleeps alone, her solitariness amplified by absence. Ever since Frank's death more than nineteen years past, the ecstasy of her longing has only been magnified by his overwhelming absence. Having lived her life through him, with him and in him, there is no other desire than to be reunited with him in whatever heavenly kingdom her faith may bring her to. Even in her sleep, there is no more devout consummation to be wished.

Now she sleeps. Later, she will rouse herself and re-establish her bearings. With a huge effort of will, she will move to the edge of the couch, arms outstretched for her wheeled walker and get to her feet, struggling to stay steady. At last, composed again, she will slowly make her way through the tasks of evening – a glass of water, the bathroom ablutions, and finally, fold back the covers on the marriage bed in which she sleeps alone, the space beside her reserved still for the greatest love she has ever known.

⌐

Anita Helen Metzger (née Gallo) died on 12 April 2012 at Cabrini Aged Care in Melbourne. She was laid to rest in the grave at Fawkner cemetery where Frank had been buried twenty-two years before. Their headstone, hewn from the pink granite of Phillip Island's Woolamai, avows that, where there is courage and sacrifice, "Love is Everlasting".